"Why are you here." Shay fought to keep her voice steady.

"Maybe I had the urge for dessert." Tyler grinned.

"Then you'll find more of a selection at SugarPie's."

"Could be. But maybe what I want's right here."

Once, she would have fallen for that line and hoped he wanted *her*. She was so over that now. So over him.

She slid open the freezer case and reached for an empty ice cream tub. It gave her an excuse to avoid his blue-eyed stare.

But Tyler stepped up beside her. "I'll get that."

"Thanks, but I'm pregnant, not incapacitated."

"I didn't think you were." He closed the freezer door. "Let's just say I'll scratch your back, you scratch mine."

He looked away, as if he'd only now realized what he had said. He cleared his throat and looked back at her. "I'll take care of this, then you can take care of a few things for me."

Unfortunately, his attempt to make his point clearer only filled her mind with more images and memories of their night together.

Suddenly, Shay didn't feel quite so over Tyler Buckham.

Three for the Cowboy

BARBARA WHITE DAILLE

NEW YORK TIMES BESTSELLING AUTHOR
TINA LEONARD

**Previously published as *The Cowboy's Triple Surprise*
and *Callahan Cowboy Triplets***

Recycling programs
for this product may
not exist in your area.

ISBN-13: 978-1-335-01615-7

Three for the Cowboy
Copyright © 2019 by Harlequin Books S.A.

The Cowboy's Triple Surprise
First published in 2017. This edition published in 2019.
Copyright © 2017 by Barbara White-Rayczek

Callahan Cowboy Triplets
First published in 2013. This edition published in 2019.
Copyright © 2013 by Tina Leonard

Printed in U.S.A.

HARLEQUIN®
www.Harlequin.com

CONTENTS

Barbara White Daille and her husband inhabit their own special corner of the wild Southwest, where the summers are long and the lizards and scorpions roam.

Barbara loves looking back at the stories she wrote in grade school and realizing that she's doing exactly what she planned. She has now hit double digits with published novels and still has a file drawer full of stories to be written.

Barbara hopes you will enjoy reading her books! Visit her website at barbarawhitedaille.com.

Books by Barbara White Daille

Harlequin Western Romance

The Hitching Post Hotel

The Cowboy's Little Surprise
A Rancher of Her Own
The Lawman's Christmas Proposal
Cowboy in Charge
The Cowboy's Triple Surprise

Harlequin American Romance

The Sheriff's Son
Court Me, Cowboy
Family Matters
A Rancher's Pride
The Rodeo Man's Daughter
Honorable Rancher
Rancher at Risk

Visit the Author Profile page at Harlequin.com for more titles.

The Cowboy's Triple Surprise

BARBARA WHITE DAILLE

To Marlene and Vinnie
for the years of friendship, fun, love and laughter...
and to Rich for all the same and more.

Chapter 1

Tyler Buckham's life in Texas—though he wasn't sure you could call it a life lately—had become as dry as the Sonoran Desert. He liked the ranch he'd been working for some time now, and yet boredom and restlessness had both begun cropping up with increasing frequency. When he'd first noticed the signs setting in again, it never crossed his mind to turn to what he'd normally do: head out to another rodeo. Try for another prize. Find another buckle bunny to help fill a few empty hours.

That failure to go for what had always worked in the past proved just how stale his life had become.

As a last resort, he had given his notice and hit the road. Everybody needed a change of scenery once in a while. Running *to* something didn't have to mean you were running *from* something else. Or so he told himself.

With an effort, he brought his focus back to the den

where he now sat, and looked at the older man across the desk from him. He had met Jed Garland, the owner of the Hitching Post Hotel, last summer, when he'd come to Garland Ranch to stand up as best man when Jed's granddaughter Tina married Tyler's friend Cole.

Jed laced his hands across his middle. "Nice to have you back."

"It's nice to be back," Tyler returned, though he felt uncomfortable saying it. He should have visited Cowboy Creek again long before this. Cole had invited him for Christmas, but he'd turned down the offer. Instead, he'd spent the holidays with his folks. Three months later, he was still kicking himself over that mistake.

"Cole will be pleased to see you when he gets home," Jed told him. "I'll need to have a talk with that boy, though—he didn't so much as hint about you coming for a visit."

"He didn't know I was headed this way. Stopping by was a spur-of-the-moment idea."

It was worse than that.

What would Cole and Jed and the rest of the Garlands think if they knew just how close he'd come to passing right by? Though he'd headed to New Mexico deliberately to put Texas behind him, he'd been on the fence about whether or not to visit Garland Ranch.

Fate had taken a hand, pushing him off the highway at the Cowboy Creek town limits. The gas gauge on the pickup had nose-dived, and he'd had to top up the tank. If he could have made it through to the next town, he might have left the hotel and dude ranch behind him in a cloud of road dust.

Instead, he'd given the truck its head the way he did his stallion. Like Freedom, the truck seemed to know exactly where it wanted to go. By the time he'd pulled into the parking area behind the Hitching Post, he had begun to wonder if fate had had this trip in store for him all along.

"Well," Jed said, "when an idea spurs you on, that's usually a good sign you should get moving on it."

"Yeah. And here I am." He glanced over at the Stetson he had tossed onto one of the small couches in the office. "But speaking of moving, I guess I'll hit the road again since Cole's not around."

"What's your hurry? He'll be back in a couple of days."

Tyler looked at Jed. The man was past seventy, but those clear blue eyes, topped by pure white eyebrows, wouldn't miss much. At Jed's scrutiny, he broke eye contact, using the excuse of grabbing his Stetson.

"It's almost time for lunch," Jed went on. "Why not stay to eat with us? Then you might as well stick around here till Cole gets home. We've got plenty of room in the hotel for you, and a stall out in the barn just standing empty waiting for your mount."

"I don't—"

"You know Tina and I will be glad for the visit with you," Jed went on, as if he hadn't heard Tyler. "And I know you're not planning on running off without seeing Paz."

The mention of Tina's grandmother, the hotel's cook, brought back some great memories. He smiled. "She sure took good care of me when I was here for Cole and Tina's wedding."

Jed smiled broadly. "Feeding people is what she does best. We don't like seeing anyone going hungry here. And we're not fond of empty spaces at the table. We'll be happy to have you sitting in for Cole and staying with us for a while."

"I don't—"

"You won't be the only guest at the table today," Jed broke in again. "Shay's joining us for lunch, too."

"Shay?" Tyler's pulse revved up a notch.

"Yeah, Shay O'Neill. You met her at the wedding last summer, remember?"

How could he forget? "Yeah, I remember Shay." Understatement of the century. The mention of her name brought to mind a handful of other good memories.

"So, that's decided." Jed rose from his chair. "C'mon out to the front desk and we'll find you a room. You haven't got much time to settle in before we eat. Just a word of advice, though. I'd do my best to show up in the dining room as soon as possible, or you might get done out of something special."

Yeah, something special like sitting next to Shay O'Neill.

As he followed Jed down the hall to the hotel lobby, his thoughts stayed with Shay. Shay, who was as sweet as the ice cream she sold at the Big Dipper in town. And who was way hotter than any other woman he'd ever seen.

Shay was another reason he should have come back to Cowboy Creek before now. They had had a good time in the few days he had stayed there last summer. No reason they couldn't have just as good a time while he was here now. Lucky for him, that brief visit had included a night in her bed. He looked forward to having that pleasure again.

Above all, Shay was guaranteed to make him forget his troubles for a while. He needed that kind of forgetting more than he'd realized until this very moment.

* * *

Once he'd settled Freedom in his stall, Tyler made quick work of hauling his duffel bag from the back of the pickup truck to the room Jed had assigned him. Minutes after tossing the bag onto the king-size bed, he was downstairs again and on his way to the dining room.

From up ahead, he could hear more than one conversation going, a child's shriek and, in a sudden beat of silence, a woman's familiar laugh. That last sound made him both hard and hungry, but not for anything the Hitching Post might serve for lunch.

The dining room was crowded with Garland family members and hotel guests, yet the instant he paused in the doorway, he spotted Shay. She sat on the far side of the long center table reserved for the Garlands, half turned away from him as she talked with one of Jed's granddaughters. He recognized the straight, wheat-blond hair that fell below her shoulders and felt like silk against his fingers. He knew when she looked his way he would see eyes one shade lighter than her green sweater. Her cheeks held a natural pink tint. Her lips curved in a soft smile.

Just looking at her from a distance made his pulse speed up and his jeans tighten.

She reached for a cloth napkin and unfolded it. As if she'd given a signal, the folks around him began heading toward the tables. The movement spurred him toward the vacant seat at her side before anyone else could grab it.

As he slid onto the chair, she turned his way.

The smile stayed, but the light pink color drained from her cheeks. He saw her fingers clutch the napkin she had draped across her lap. And then he saw the rounded expanse of belly straining the knitted weave of her sweater.

She was extremely pregnant.

Thoughts of anticipated pleasure flew from his head. Words did, too, leaving him struggling for something to say.

Jed Garland had no such problem. "Shay, you remember Tyler, don't you?"

She nodded.

"I thought you might."

Tyler couldn't tear his eyes away from her. He also couldn't miss hearing the satisfaction in the older man's voice. What had brought that on? And why had Jed mentioned Shay's invitation to lunch but said nothing about her condition? Of course, Jed—and everyone else at the Hitching Post—probably thought he and Shay were just passing acquaintances.

He tried for a casual smile. The one she gave him looked about as sincere as his felt.

"Tyler," Tina said, "Abuelo says you're staying with us for a while."

Shay's sweater rose, telling him she had sucked in a startled breath. She covered it with a small cough and a grab for her water glass.

The reaction made sense. Obviously, she'd met someone else since they were together last summer. Or she'd already been involved with the man when they'd had their fling. Either way, she wouldn't want him hanging around, maybe bringing up their brief relationship in some conversation. As if he would. The boys at the ranch back in Texas always said he needed to have "Love 'em and leave 'em" tattooed across his chest. That didn't mean he'd make a public announcement about a one-night stand. Shay couldn't know that, but you would think she'd at least give him the benefit of the doubt.

Finally dragging his gaze away, he turned to Tina.

He gave her his killer grin—to kill time, to try to pull himself together and recall what she had said… *Staying with us for a while.* Yeah. He sure regretted that right now. "I'll be here at least till Cole gets back. I wouldn't want to miss seeing him."

"He definitely wouldn't want to miss the opportunity, either. Meanwhile, we'll all have the pleasure of your company."

Not such a pleasure for Shay, considering the way she had reacted to finding him beside her and hearing he planned to stay. But that was nothing compared to the way he'd felt at seeing *her*.

Well…at seeing her *pregnant*.

While he liked a roll in the hay as well as any man, he had two rules for those occasions. First, always make sure your companion's unattached. Two, keep the relationship no strings. Obviously, he had let the first rule go by the wayside when he met Shay, but he sure intended to hold fast to the second.

Shay's condition now made him cross her name permanently off his interest list.

A waitress passed around several bowls filled with dinner rolls, then began serving the food. He managed to keep up his end of the conversation with Jed and Tina.

Shay apparently was making a deliberate effort to remain turned away from him as she talked to Jed's granddaughter Jane. Fine by him. The less they had to see of each other, the better. This lunch would soon be over, and considering the short time he planned to stay on the ranch, chances were good he wouldn't run into her again.

He passed the basket of rolls her way. As she took it from him, he glanced at her left hand. No chunky flashing diamonds, no gold band. And no surprise there.

The boys he'd worked with had also filled him in about pregnant women. Namely, that toward the end of a pregnancy, they often gained too much weight to wear their wedding rings.

"Tyler?"

Abruptly, he became aware of Jed waving from the head of the table, attempting to get his attention. The man's tone made it apparent he'd said his name more than once. Flushing and hoping no one had noticed, he nodded at Jed in acknowledgment.

"If you haven't got any plans for the afternoon, the girls could use some help."

The girls meant Jed's adult granddaughters. "Sure. I've got nothing on my agenda." Besides avoiding Shay. "Need a hand with some heavy lifting?"

Jed nodded. "We're setting up for a wedding reception, and with Cole away, we're shorthanded around here. If you wouldn't mind going along to the banquet hall after lunch, maybe you can lend some assistance."

"No problem."

Jed beamed. "Thank you kindly. I appreciate it, and I know the girls and Shay all do, too."

"Shay?" he blurted, nearly dropping his fork.

To his relief, no one seemed to notice. Jed turned to talk to one of the hotel guests at an adjacent table. Tyler gripped his fork and tried not to look at the woman beside him.

He didn't feel comfortable being here with her. Judging by her white-knuckled grip on her water glass, she felt the same.

Things had definitely changed between them since the night they had spent together.

Chapter 2

After lunch, Shay hurried out of the dining room as quickly as she could, wanting to put distance between herself and Tyler. She gave a shuddering sigh and rested her hands on the small folding table she had set up near the entrance to the banquet room. The short walk here had left her unsteady on her feet, but for once she couldn't blame her shaky balance on the extra weight from her pregnancy.

She had never expected to see Tyler Buckham again, not after he'd left so many months before.

Eight months before. But who was counting?

In the short time he had been in Cowboy Creek last summer, she had fallen hard and fast for him. She had let just a few conversations over just a handful of days lead her to fall into his arms. And then she had made the awful mistake of taking him to bed.

The shame she felt about that now ranked right up there with the worst moments of her life, which included the day she finally acknowledged she wasn't going to hear from him again.

Now she had another item to add to the list—finding Tyler beside her an hour ago in the Hitching Post's dining room. Well, he wouldn't hear anything from her, either, about the fact he had gotten her pregnant before he'd left town.

"And he's not worth worrying about now, babies," she said under her breath. "Mommy needs to focus on the reason we're here at the Hitching Post."

The next wedding reception being held at the hotel was only a day away. And yet with all they still had left to do in the room, she had been demoted to assembling table decorations.

She had spread her supplies across the small table. On the far side of the room, Jane and a couple of the hotel's waitresses were taking care of the seating arrangements.

Truthfully, setting up chairs would almost be easier on her now than bending over the display cases at the Big Dipper to scoop up mounds of rock-solid ice cream. But she couldn't argue about being given light duty here, not when she knew the Garlands were only looking out for her.

Which was exactly what she needed to be doing right now for them.

She walked over to the corner of the room to get more of the wedding favors. Before she could lift the carton of vases from the stack, a man stepped up beside her. She nearly jumped a foot in the air.

Then she froze, knowing it was Tyler and refusing

to look at him. Yet, without even a glance in his direction, she picked up so many of the same details she had tried not to notice at the dining room table. So many memories from their brief time together.

From the corner of her eye, she caught the scuffed and creased cowboy boots. The well-worn jeans. The snapped cuff of a long-sleeved Western shirt. With one breath, she took in the scent of musky aftershave and of the man himself. Standing so close to him, she couldn't miss the heat of his body. She forced herself to remember that warmth was only on the surface and didn't touch his heart.

"So," he said, "you're helping out the Garlands this afternoon, too?"

"I work here," she corrected.

"You gave up the job at the Big Dipper?"

She shook her head and finally glanced at him. "No, I'm doubling up. I'm working my way up to banquet manager for the hotel." She hoped for that, anyhow. With the babies on the way, she needed more money than she made now.

"Nice." He sounded impressed.

Good. Let him see she didn't need anything from him.

"Hey, I'll give you a hand." He grabbed the carton. Glass clinked.

"Careful," she snapped, half out of annoyance at herself for taking so much of him in, the other half out of irritation at his thinking she needed help—or anything else—from him. "Those are fragile."

Eyebrows raised, he eyed her middle as if to say the same applied to her.

She crossed her arms, intending to stand her ground

and stare him down, but the large baby bump made the stance awkward. She lowered her hands to her sides.

"Don't worry," he said, "I don't make a habit of dropping things."

"Oh, really? I'd have said you were an expert at it." She could have bitten her tongue at the instinctive response, but even that pain wouldn't have come close to the way he had hurt her.

"What does that mean?"

It was too much to hope he would have just let her statement slide. But why should she let *him* slide when he had treated her so badly? "Sorry. I suppose I shouldn't have said that." She kept her voice down, but still, nerves and anger made her pitch high and her tone arch. "I really don't know how you are about dropping *things*. But I sure know how you are about dropping *women*, since you did such a great job of that with me."

Abruptly, he shifted the carton. Glass clinked again, and this time she was too annoyed to care. How could he sound so offhand after what he had done?

"I didn't drop you," he said. "You knew I was only in town a few days for the wedding. While I was here, we had a good time together, and that was it. I didn't make any promises." He looked at her stomach. "Besides, you obviously didn't waste any time moving on to someone else."

She swallowed a gasp. He couldn't possibly think she had slept with him one night and then gone on to someone else the next. Then again, considering how quickly she had wound up in bed with him, why wouldn't he think that?

As for not wasting time... If he only knew how many sleepless nights she had spent since he had left, especially once she found out she was pregnant. But he wouldn't know, and she had to stop thinking about that. He had already stolen too much time from her, had already hurt her enough.

"Don't worry," he said in a lower tone, "I'm not planning to say anything about what happened last summer. Your secret's safe with me."

"My—" The sound of footsteps made her cut herself off. This time she turned. One sneak attack was enough—although no one could have startled her more than Tyler had.

Tina was coming toward them from across the room.

Shay glanced in Tyler's direction and gestured to the table she had set up. "You can put the carton over there. Thanks." She forced a smile.

He locked gazes with her. She refused to be the first to look away, which left her staring into his midnight-blue eyes. To her dismay, her stomach did that funny little flip it had taken such a short time to learn months ago.

"Tyler," Tina said, "thanks so much for agreeing to help us all out. I think Jane's trying to flag you down. Would you mind giving her and the waitresses a hand with the banquet tables?"

"Sure." He glanced toward the other side of the room. Then he nodded to them both and ambled away.

Shay tried not to stare after him. She didn't care where he was going or what he was doing, as long as it wasn't near her. Let him think what he wanted about her pregnancy, too. She didn't have to correct his assumption.

"Shay?"

Startled, she turned to stare at Tina. "I'm sorry. What?"

"I said, why don't you sit and take it easy? It's hard to be up on your feet, especially when you can't even *see* your feet."

"You should talk," Shay said, glancing pointedly at the other woman's middle, then blinking as she recalled Tyler doing the same to her. "You're not that far behind me."

"But I'm experienced. And I'm not carrying three babies."

Shay tried not to wince, not to react at all to what Tina had said. She shot another look across the banquet hall. To her relief, Tyler had reached the opposite side of the room. Even with the acoustics in the high-ceilinged ballroom, he couldn't possibly have overheard.

"Actually," Tina said, "I'll give you a hand, since I have some free time this afternoon." She took a seat at the table.

Shay followed and returned to her own chair. Again, she couldn't argue. Tina was only looking out for her. And as one of the Garland family, the other woman was more or less her employer.

She didn't know what Tyler was doing back here in Cowboy Creek, but for all she knew, Jed might have hired him, too. She might have to face him every time she came to the hotel to work.

The thought was too much for her to consider.

She reached for the ribbon dispenser. Right now, she needed to push aside her reluctance to be near him for even part of this afternoon. She had to focus on the job that was going to help her pay her bills.

And still, she stared across the room.

Tyler had gone down on one knee to inspect something under a table. His broad shoulders strained against his flannel shirt the way her stomach strained against her maternity top. His belt encircled a waist as rock hard as his abs and now slimmer than she was around the middle.

"Shay," Tina said, "do you mind if I borrow that dispenser before you run out of ribbon?"

Shay looked down at the table in front of her. Her face flamed. While trying to distract her thoughts from Tyler, she had coiled a length of ribbon into a tangled mass around her fingers. She grabbed the scissors and snipped the ribbon free.

Without another word, Tina took the dispenser, then reached for an undecorated vase. Shay sent her an apologetic glance, but the other woman didn't look her way.

For a while, she managed to focus on the vases and the ribbons and a casual conversation with Tina. Then, all too soon, she found herself tuning in to the thump of Tyler's boots from the other side of the room, the rumble of his voice as he spoke to one of the women, the sound of his deep laugh as he responded to something one of them said.

A spurt of jealousy hit, an unwanted, unwelcome emotion that twined itself—like the ribbon twisted in her fingers—around her heart.

She should have expected it and been prepared. And she couldn't let it worry her, because she knew what caused the sudden upswing of emotion.

From the day Tyler had left to the day she finally acknowledged he didn't plan to contact her again, her up-and-down feelings had run out of control. Late-night anxiety triggered her bouts of insomnia. Stiff-necked tension left her no comfortable position even if sleep had wanted to come. Anger and depression had made her days as uncomfortable as her nights.

There had been no way she would have run after Tyler, no way she wanted an unreliable cowboy in her life. Anger at herself, at how far she had let herself fall, had triggered every one of those reactions. She had simply waited them out, knowing they would pass, and they had. Eventually.

After she had discovered she was pregnant, she had again fought—and won—a battle to get her emotions in check, but there were times, like today, when her hormones won out. Green-eyed jealousy was trying to entice her. She wouldn't let it succeed. Tyler didn't mean anything to her anymore. She couldn't care less who he flirted with now. Though he had fathered her babies, he was a free man.

She didn't plan to do or say anything to change that.

When his youngest granddaughter, Tina, entered the kitchen, Jed Garland took notice. Her grin made him sit back in his chair and nod in satisfaction.

Paz, standing near the refrigerator, stopped and turned their way.

"Tyler went for the bait, did he?" Jed asked.

"I don't know about that." Tina laughed. "But as you would put it, let's just say Jane had him well and truly hooked by the time I left the banquet hall. He's helping with the table setups, though his attention keeps wandering, and so does Shay's. I'm now beginning to think you were right all along. You're some matchmaker, Abuelo."

"I try," he said modestly.

Both she and Paz laughed out loud.

"I'm curious," Tina said. "Tyler seemed so reluctant to help after you told him Shay would be working with us. I'm surprised he's cooperating now. What did you say to him after the rest of us left the dining room?"

"I simply mentioned that no able-bodied man would let a woman in Shay's condition get overworked."

"Mentioned?" Paz repeated.

Chuckling, he looked over at the hotel cook. She had worked for him for more than twenty years now, since before they had this granddaughter in common and long before those gray streaks had started threading through her hair. "Well, maybe a bit stronger than mentioned. What do *you* think of his reaction?"

She crossed the room to take the chair beside Tina's. After a glance toward the kitchen door, she smiled at them both. "I think it has proved your point. If we didn't already believe that Tyler is the daddy of Shay's babies, I would surely think so now."

He nodded. "We'd have had to be imbeciles not to have caught on months ago. The boy's reactions today only confirm he and Shay had something going on."

"True," Tina said. "I was watching, and the look on his face when he stood in the doorway and saw her was priceless. So was Shay's when she found him sitting beside her. But I'm feeling a little guilty you didn't tell either of them ahead of time that they would see each other at lunch."

He shook his head. "There's a lot to be said for shock value. And there's even more to be said about keeping those two on their toes. Jane and the other girls are still with them in the banquet hall, aren't they?"

Tina nodded.

"Good. Nothing like holding something a man wants within his sight but just out of reach. I'm betting the longer he has time to question things, the more eager he'll be to stick around to get answers. And in the long run, the more Shay will benefit."

"Yes." Paz nodded. "We have to think of Shay."

"We do," he agreed. "It's best we all pretend ignorance for as long as we can. Then they'll never suspect we're trying to get them together."

"You think this plan is a good one, Jed?" Paz asked.

"Of course, I do. And it's not just me and the girls who believe in it."

Tina gasped. "You talked to Mo?"

"I did, just before lunch. And she's in complete agreement. Shay puts on a good act when she's with any of us, but her grandma said she's been moping for months now at home. And that's not good for her."

"Especially in her condition," Paz said in alarm.

"Exactly. Well, don't worry. We'll be keeping her much too busy to worry about anything…except Tyler."

"You are a devious, scheming man," she said, shaking her head.

"Thank you," he said with a grin.

Chapter 3

"We need that table over here," Jane called across the banquet room.

"No problem." Tyler turned in midstride, rolling the round table on its edge across the hardwood floor toward the space she indicated. "You ladies sure do know how to put a man to work around here."

"Are you complaining?"

"Heck, no. Hard labor is my middle name." Though Jane laughed, he couldn't keep from wincing. Head down, he busied himself with pulling out the legs of the table and tightening the supports. Then he crossed back to the wheeled cart and took down the next table.

The phrase he'd jokingly tossed out—*hard labor*—had made him think of Shay and her pregnancy. Where was the man who had gotten her into that state? There had to be someone in the vicinity. A husband. A boyfriend. Someone. Despite her lack of a wedding ring, for all he knew, she had married that someone a week after he had left town.

It looked to him as though she might be ready to have her baby at any minute. But what did he know about that, either? After lunch, she had stood from her seat beside his and lumbered away. Except for the rolling gait of a saddle-sore greenhorn, from the back she seemed just the way she had when he'd met her months ago. Quite a few months ago.

For a moment, his thoughts got hung up on the time frame. But only for a moment. He couldn't have been the one to get her pregnant. After all, when he had said something about her moving on to someone else as soon as he'd left town, she hadn't denied it.

"Hold up, Tyler," Jane called. "The reception's in this room, not on the patio."

To his chagrin, he saw he'd overshot his mark and was almost to a pair of doors leading outside. "Got it," he said, forcing a laugh. Abruptly, he turned back and took the table to the appropriate spot.

As he continued to work, Shay remained absorbed in her vases and ribbons. Every time he attempted to set up a table closer to her, Jane sent him to another area of the room.

Maybe that was for the best. He and Shay didn't have anything left to say to each other. And they couldn't have talked much, anyway, with Tina or Jane constantly by her side. It was as if they were standing guard over her. Every time Jed stopped by the room, even he seemed to take up a protective stance. Because...

Because she *was* due to have that baby at any minute?

Despite his own reassurances to himself, he did some

quick mental math. The results caused him to pull his bandanna from his back pocket. It took him two tries to wipe the cold sweat from his face.

"You okay, cowboy?" Jane called teasingly.

Across the room, Shay looked up from her work.

"Ma'am," he said to Jane, "I've had a change of heart. You're about working me to death here." He grinned. "Even the hired hands ought to be entitled to a cold drink now and then, don't you think?"

He saw her fighting to hide a smile. She made a show of glancing at her watch. "Well, I suppose we can spare you for a minute."

"Good." He ambled across the room, deliberately avoiding Shay and Tina and aiming straight for the corner table a few yards from them. Earlier, one of the waitresses had brought in a jug of sweet tea. He filled a glass.

After a mouthful of the drink, he turned to look at the two women. Both were pregnant. Was there something in the water around here? He eyed his tea glass and swallowed a laugh. Then he looked at Shay's belly again, and his sense of humor deserted him.

He needed to act normally around her, as though he didn't have a care in the world. Which he didn't. Hoping for a casual approach, he headed toward their table. From across the room he saw Jane start their way, too.

He came to a stop beside Shay, not too near, but close enough to see the long sweep of her lashes as she kept her eyes down, her gaze focused on her work. Close enough to smell the same flowery perfume she had worn last summer when he'd danced with her at the wedding and, a few nights later, when he had slept with her in her bed.

He gulped another mouthful of sweet tea and nearly choked on it.

Shay never looked his way. The chances she would even throw a glance at him seemed less likely by the second. That only made him more determined to get her attention. He gestured toward the vases lined up on the table. "Looks like this is going to be one big wedding."

He stood facing Shay, but Tina answered instead. "The biggest we've had here yet," she said emphatically.

He knew she was the financial genius in the family. "The thought of all that income must make your accountant's heart beat faster."

She laughed. "You must have heard that phrase from Cole."

"I did." He looked at Shay. Another, more intimate memory of them together flashed into his mind. "What makes *your* heart speed up?" he blurted.

"Heartburn," she said flatly.

He blinked. Maybe that was a symptom of pregnancy. Or maybe she was just pulling his leg.

"*This* worker is due for a break, too," she said, bracing her hands on the table. She seemed to have trouble pushing herself to her feet. Afraid she might overbalance and fall over the chair, he held it steady for her just as he'd done in the dining room after lunch. And just like then, she gave him a curt, dismissive nod. "Tina, I'm going for a walk. I'll be back in a few minutes."

"Good idea," he said. "I feel the need to stretch my legs, too."

Her eyes narrowed. "You're not—"

"—thinking of leaving us, are you?" Tina finished. "Tyler, I'm surprised at you. We've still got so many tables to set up."

"We certainly do," Jane said. "And we've run into a little problem over there." She pointed to the far side of the room. She raised her brows.

Tina smiled.

Shay turned and left the room.

Shrugging, he followed Jane across the banquet hall. He'd been roped into helping again, and danged if he could think of a single good excuse that would cut him loose.

Somehow, he managed to carry on a conversation with Jane and the rest of the women while his brain focused on the topic of Shay's baby. The first chance he had to find her alone, he wanted an answer to the question that continued to nag at him:

Just how far along is she?

For the rest of the afternoon, Jane kept him hopping. The closest Tyler got to Shay was when he set up chairs at the tables in the area near where she was working.

He had just come within yards of her when she pulled a cell phone from the bag she had hooked over the back of her chair. After checking the display, she turned to Tina. "I need another break. And I missed a call from my grandmother."

"Give Mo our regards," Tina said.

Shay nodded. This time she appeared to have less trouble getting up. She also seemed to be in a hurry, as if she wanted to get out of her seat before he could lend his help.

He watched her walk off.

A few minutes later, Tina left the ballroom, too.

Time ticked away, and neither of the women returned.

Eventually, Jed and Paz stopped in the doorway and surveyed the setup. Tyler tucked the final two chairs beneath a table, then sauntered in their direction.

"Looking good," Jed said.

Tyler eyed the room and tried to see it from the older man's perspective. All the tables had been covered with long white cloths and shorter pale blue ones, but only half the sets of silverware wrapped in white napkins had been put in place. And there were no decorations around the room yet.

He gestured to the folding table at which Shay and Tina had been sitting. "Looks like two of your helpers have deserted you."

"Tina had to go back to work in her office," Paz said.

"And Shay left," Jed put in, answering Tyler's unspoken question.

"Left?" he asked, startled. Then he backpedaled, trying to downplay his interest. "I mean, I thought she was in charge of table decorations."

"She is. But she got a call from her grandma and said she had to go home."

Jed made the statement so calmly, Tyler couldn't jump to the conclusion that anything was wrong. He also couldn't keep from wondering whether Shay had wanted to avoid him. At that thought, the hairs on the back of his neck stood at attention. She had no reason to stay away from him now. He'd assured her he wouldn't bring up their past.

He thought back to Cole and Tina's wedding and what had happened a couple of days after, and couldn't help rechecking his math. But even if the dates tallied, that didn't have to mean a thing. They'd seen each other less than a handful of times. They'd slept together once.

What were the chances she'd gotten pregnant from what amounted to a one-night stand? A heck of a lot slimmer than her waist right now, that was sure.

He focused on his surroundings again and found Paz looking his way. If he didn't know better, he'd swear he saw sympathy in her gaze.

"Shay told me to tell Jed she was sorry," she explained. "Her grandmother is fine. I think it was Shay who wasn't feeling well. Tina will call her in a little while to make sure she arrived home."

"Good idea." Jed nodded.

"If she felt that sick," Tyler said, "you'd think she'd have called her husband to pick her up."

"Doesn't have a husband," Jed returned.

"No *novio*—boyfriend—either," Paz added.

Exactly the question Tyler's mental mathematics had caused him to consider all afternoon. But asking Jed or Paz about Shay's pregnancy would only bring more unwanted attention to his interest in a woman he should only barely know.

Shay stretched out on her friend's couch, putting her tired feet up in hopes of easing the swelling. She pulled the afghan from the back of the couch and spread it over her, but even the weight of the knitted wool couldn't banish the chill she felt.

Layne came from the apartment's small kitchen carrying a tray with a couple of mugs and a plate of cookies. When she held out one of the steaming mugs, Shay took it gratefully.

Though she hadn't eaten much of her lunch at the Hitching Post, she couldn't even look at the cookies. When she got home, she would have to have something.

Not now. The way her stomach felt at the moment, she almost didn't want to risk a sip of tea, either. But she needed the warmth. Needed the mug to hold on to.

She sighed again and glanced at Layne, the only person who knew the truth about her pregnancy. "Tyler's going to figure out the timing, if he hasn't already. Even if he's not the type to keep track of dates—" *or to keep track of his conquests* "—he'll remember the month of the wedding. So many brides get married in June."

As if to challenge that tradition, Layne and her ex-husband had remarried at the Hitching Post just this past weekend.

Shortly before that, Jed's widowed granddaughter, Andi, had gotten married, too. Those newlyweds were still away on their honeymoon.

Like Tina, Shay had always dreamed of a June wedding and lots of children. Her dreams never included having those children first or raising a family on her own.

But she wouldn't be alone. She had Grandma and Layne and the Garlands, and the rest of her friends. They were all she needed. All her babies needed, too.

"He'll figure it out," she said again. "Or maybe someone at the Hitching Post already told him my due date."

"Is that so bad?" Layne asked quietly. "You're going to tell him, anyway, aren't you?"

"No, I'm not." A flash of anger left her breathless. But it was fury at her own actions that caused tears to rise beneath her hurt. What a fool she had been to fall for Tyler's dark good looks, his great pickup lines and his pretense of genuine interest. Well, he *had* truly been interested in something, anyhow. In getting her into bed. And she had made it all too easy for him. She tightened her fingers around the mug. "He slept with me—once—and never looked back. Why would I chase after him to tell him the news?"

"Because he's the father."

"No, he's not."

Layne's eyes opened so wide, Shay couldn't help but laugh. Then, sobering, she slumped against the couch cushion. "Of course he's the father. I don't…"

I don't sleep around. But she had. One single time.

She glanced across the living room to where Layne's little girl lay sleeping in her playpen. Layne's new husband had left a few minutes ago, taking their son into the kids' room to read him a story.

"Don't worry," Layne said, "they'll be good for an hour or more."

Shay nodded. Still, she lowered her voice, as much out of reluctance to confess the truth as from the worry she would be overheard. "I only meant that Tyler wouldn't be a real father. How could he be? And why would I *want* him to be, when he didn't care enough about me to come back again, or even to call or send me a text?"

"You don't know what happened after he left."

"I don't want to know," she said flatly. "I don't want to know anything more than I do already—that he was so hot and such a sweet-talker. And I was such easy pickings."

"Don't say that."

"Why not? You know it. I know it. And worst of all, he knows it, too."

"I know *you*, Shay. You wouldn't have slept with him if you didn't care about him."

"I can't believe this." She stared down at her tea. "At the wedding, the two of us just clicked."

"I know you did."

As the groom's sister, Layne had attended the wedding last summer, too. At the reception, she had witnessed Shay's first meeting with Tyler. So had almost everyone else in Cowboy Creek. "The day after the wedding," Shay said slowly, "he came to the Big Dipper with Jane and Pete and the kids. He came back *every* day. He borrowed a truck from Jed."

She had already told Layne all that, but not the rest. "The night before he planned to leave, he showed up again. It was so beautiful out, and after I closed up the shop we went for a walk. We wound up at my house and...and Grandma was out at her bridge club. And I guess you can figure out the rest." She blinked. "I didn't plan it."

"But you wanted it to happen," Layne said softly.

Shay nodded.

"Because you cared. And because you thought he cared about you."

"Yes." She shrugged. "What difference does it make what I thought? Obviously, I was wrong." At least, on one of those counts. "And how can I ever face him again?"

"He's not just passing through?"

She shook her head. "Oh, I'm sure he'll be leaving soon enough. But..."

"But he came to see Cole," Layne guessed. "And Cole's gone to Denver to check out that new stallion for Jed."

"Right. Tyler's staying until he gets back. And I've got to go to work at the Hitching Post again. We've got the wedding tomorrow night." She winced, filled with

guilt about the way she had sent along an apology with
Paz earlier, and then escaped from the hotel.

Still, she couldn't regret leaving. The Hitching Post
was *not* the place for a reunion with Tyler. She'd needed
to get away. Needed to get some space while she figured out how to do what she knew she had to do. Tell
him the truth about her pregnancy.

She had to tell him about the children she would soon
be having. Not one child. Not two. But three small, un-
expected babies, already growing and thriving inside
her. Already very much loved.

Not his babies.

Hers.

"How did you get away from the hotel today without
having to talk to Tyler?" Layne asked.

Shay explained about the missed phone call, which she
had noticed on her cell phone at the best possible time.
"Grandma just wanted to remind me not to hurry home,
since she had plans to be out for supper at SugarPie's."
The sandwich shop in town was one of Mo's favorite
hangouts, and Sugar Conway, the owner, was one of her
best friends. "It gave me a reason to leave the banquet
room. Once I was away from everyone," she confessed,
"I used the call as an excuse to run. Which is going to
make going back tomorrow even more awkward."

"Couldn't you just call in sick?" Layne asked.

She almost choked on a laugh. "I wish. But I can't let
Jed and everyone else down. Besides, I need the money.
Neither of my part-time jobs comes with insurance."

"I thought you told me you had money from your
parents."

"I do. From their life insurance policies. So at least
I won't have to worry about the hospital bills."

She didn't want to think about those policies and what they represented—the mom and dad she had lost years ago. Money couldn't take their place in her life. But in reality, she had lost them both long before the accident that had taken them away. Her dad had chased the rodeo and her mom had chased her dad, and as a result, she had never really had them in her life to begin with. All the more reason for staying away from Tyler.

How could she have let herself...

How could she have *slept* with a rodeo cowboy?

"Grandma practically raised me," she said in a low voice. "I know how much she loves me, and I know she'll help me out. But I'm trying to save up as much as I can for everything else the babies will need. I *have* to report to the Hitching Post tomorrow."

She looked at Layne. "But I'm just dreading having to walk back into that hotel and see Tyler again. Or having to face any of the Garlands. Everyone else in Cowboy Creek must know the situation, too. What did I think?" she added, rolling her eyes. "That I could hide my head in the sand like an ostrich, and they wouldn't figure out the timing as soon as they saw my stomach getting bigger?"

Layne smothered a laugh. "Sorry. That's some visual. But if hiding the truth was your goal, I'm afraid you can forget it. Take it from a mom twice over. Nobody around here messes up the math on a pregnancy." Sobering, she added, "I know you don't want to tell Tyler the news, Shay. But you should think about it. Before someone else does."

"People ought to respect my right to privacy," she snapped.

"In *this* town? No. Someone, sometime, is bound to

tell him—out of the goodness of their heart, though. You know that."

"Oh, I do know. They'll have the best of motives, thinking they're making things easier and doing me a favor."

"Exactly. The longer you wait, the more you run that risk. And worse, the more gossip and speculation will fly."

"I know that, too," she mumbled. Her eyes blurring, she stroked her stomach and sighed.

Chapter 4

Tyler patted the stallion's flank, then left the stall.

In the corral outside the barn, a few of the hotel guests were saddled up, looking stiff and serious as they took instruction from some of the cowhands.

He headed across the yard to the Hitching Post.

The wind had picked up a bit, but the midafternoon sun had gotten stronger. Together, they kept the temperature at a comfortable level. Too bad they couldn't do anything about *his* temperature. Since yesterday, he had jumped from hot to cold and back again every time he thought of Shay.

As he reached the hotel, the back door opened. Pete, Jed's ranch manager and Jane's husband, came out of the hotel and down the porch steps. "In for the day?" he asked.

Tyler nodded.

"Whenever you're needing another ride, you're welcome to any of the mounts here."

"Needing?" Tyler echoed.

Pete shrugged. "The way you tore out of here after lunch, I'd have said you were looking for more than just time in the saddle."

"Yeah." All morning, he had helped Tina and Jane in the ballroom again. Shay hadn't been around, and no one had mentioned her name.

They had released him from duty just before lunch, and afterward he and Freedom had done some hard riding on Garland Ranch. The long trek had been designed to help him outrun his thoughts. Instead, it had only given him more time alone, ample time to envision what he'd seen yesterday.

Shay, with her belly so big she looked like she might give birth at any moment. Not that he was an expert on pregnancy. But he could count. And he still didn't like the numbers he'd come up with.

"The ride doesn't seem to have done you much good," Pete said. "Or else that expression of yours is saying you hit a cactus patch somewhere out on the ranch."

"I hit something thorny," he agreed, wondering just how much the other man could help him. Pete had two kids of his own. He certainly ought to know something about the stages of pregnancy. He might also know when Shay was due to have her baby.

But he didn't intend to stand there gossiping about her with Jed's ranch manager. Or even to discuss her with Jed. He had to talk to Shay. All day, he'd replayed their conversation in his mind. Her lack of reaction when he had said he would keep her secret told him he couldn't be the daddy. But he needed her to tell him herself.

"See you later." Tyler made his way into the Hitching Post. A short walk down the hall took him to the wide doorway of the hotel's kitchen.

Paz stood near a counter, where light glinted off a knife resting on a cutting board filled with raw vegetables. She broke off from what she was saying to gesture toward a large coffeemaker on one counter. "Coffee is brewed there."

"Thanks."

At the large table, Jed sat with a mug in front of him. "Take a load off," he invited, waving at an empty chair.

Tyler filled a mug and took his seat at the table.

"As I was saying," Paz said to Jed, "Tina talked with Shay and told her we won't need her for the reception tonight. Shay's planning to work at the shop instead, but she said she'll be here tomorrow afternoon."

"Good."

Not so good for him. Tomorrow afternoon seemed a long time away. And if the Garlands herded her like a stray mare again, chances were good he probably wouldn't get to talk to her alone. He couldn't let this opportunity pass him by. "Shay seems to be pretty far along."

"She is," Paz confirmed. "She has just a few weeks left."

"We're trying to keep her from overdoing it," Jed put in. "That's why we appreciated your help yesterday and this morning. You deserved the break after lunch. Enjoy your ride?"

"Yeah," he said, not satisfied with changing the subject but unwilling to push the issue. "It felt good to get out."

"Of the hotel?"

"Just out. On horseback." What had those all-knowing blue eyes seen to make Jed ask that question? He couldn't tell the man the truth.

Last night, he had spent the evening with the Garlands and their hotel guests. And yeah, between that and today's stint in the ballroom, then at the crowded lunch table, he *had* felt the need to get out of the hotel, to get away on his own. To put some space between him and the Garland family. Along with Jed and Paz, and not counting the absent newlyweds, that included two granddaughters, one of their husbands and a handful of kids. A lot of Garlands to go around. He'd needed some breathing room.

Maybe it was having all the other hotel guests there, too, that left him feeling boxed in. Maybe it was just the fact he'd grown up without brothers or sisters and had gotten used to the quiet.

But mostly, he suspected it had to do with needing to escape his thoughts of Shay. Like that had worked.

"Cole ought to be back tomorrow," Jed said.

"Good. I'm looking forward to seeing him." Heck, he needed the diversion. "He's flying in from Denver?"

"Driving. He was making a couple of stops along the way." Jed took another sip of coffee. "Paz and I were just talking about you before you walked in."

"Me? What's up?"

"With this reception going on, we're all going to be tied up most of the evening. I'm afraid you'll be on your own."

"No problem. I'm sure I can find something—" *or someone* "—to keep me occupied."

Shay slid the decorated cake into the large freezer in the Big Dipper's workroom. Their ice cream cakes were always in demand for birthdays and other celebrations. And though SugarPie's bakery supplied the wedding and party cakes for the Hitching Post, the Dipper always took care of the hotel's ice cream orders.

She didn't want to think about the hotel or about the man she had last seen there yesterday. She touched her stomach. "I probably should have stayed to talk to him," she murmured to her babies, "but the two of us were never alone." She laughed softly. "And I don't mean because *you* three were there with me." She sobered again. The thought of having her conversation with Tyler in front of any of the Garlands had done her in, making her run at the first opportunity.

With a sigh, she closed the freezer door securely, then returned to the empty front room of the shop.

They did a booming business in the warmer months, good enough for her boss to pay her a decent wage all year round. Unfortunately, the job was only part-time. As she had told Layne, she needed her income from the Hitching Post, where they paid her an even better part-time rate.

As if the thought of Layne had summoned her, the door to the shop opened and she stepped inside.

"What brings you here?" Shay asked in surprise.

"A pint of chocolate-marshmallow swirl, for one thing."

"You're not pregnant again, are you?"

Layne laughed. "That's what Jason asked. No, I'm not. But the craving was a good reason to get me over here." She went to the small freezer off to one side of the room.

"Like you need a reason for ice cream." Shay leaned against the counter instead of taking the high stool out from beneath it. She didn't trust herself on the stool. After growing so much in the past few weeks, she was finding it harder to keep her balance even with her feet flat on the floor.

Layne set her container on the counter. After looking around the still-empty shop, she said, "I stopped in at the L-G to pick up a few groceries this afternoon and ran into Mo. We had quite a chat."

The look of excitement on Layne's face made Shay blink in surprise. "A chat about what?"

"Your hours."

Again, Shay blinked. Her hours wouldn't have given anyone reason to feel excited...unless Grandma had heard something from Jed about giving her more work time.

"Mo told me you were here tonight and not helping out at the Hitching Post."

"Oh. That." Usually, she waitressed at the receptions and parties.

"Yes, that. What did you think we talked about? What happened?"

"I don't know for sure. Tina called earlier today and told me they wouldn't need me for the reception. They're probably worried I'll go into labor in the middle of the dance floor."

Layne laughed. "You know that's not it."

"Well, maybe not." She shrugged. "She did say Jed wants me to come out to the Hitching Post tomorrow afternoon. I hope he's planning to give me more hours." Or a raise.

"I hope so, too, at least until it's time for you to stay off your feet. Which is getting close, isn't it?"

"Don't you start, too. I saw Dr. Grayden Thursday

morning. The babies are doing fine, and he said I'm still good to go with the date we've scheduled for my C-section. And he and my specialist in Santa Fe gave me their okay to continue working."

"With no restrictions?"

"I just have to take things easy," she admitted.

"We all realize that. So remember, if Jed doesn't offer you as many extra hours as you'd like, it's because everybody out at the ranch is concerned about you."

"You could have fooled me," Shay said as she rang up the purchase. "Jed might be, but Tina and Jane spent more time falling all over Tyler than they did watching out for me. I was glad they kept him occupied—and away from me." They had kept him busy on the other side of the room, except for that short time he had stood next to her. She had continued working, had forced herself not to look up, yet she had been as aware of him as if he'd plopped himself down in the center of all the vases on the table in front of her.

"Have you decided what you're going to do about talking to him?" Layne asked.

"Not yet." Sighing, she scooped up the pile of pennies in the cash register drawer and let them trickle through her fingers. "I know you're right. If I don't tell him, someone else will. But I want to do it my way. In my own time."

"Which still means not at all," Layne said wryly. "Otherwise, you would have managed to talk to him at the ranch yesterday."

Shay reached for the twenty-dollar bill Layne held out. "I couldn't have, with everyone around."

"That makes sense. With news like yours to share, you're going to need some time alone with him."

Her insides turned as cold as a tub of ice cream. It had nothing to do with the freezer case beside her and everything to do with the picture Layne's words had formed in her mind. "At the rate things are going, it doesn't seem likely that's going to happen."

But even as she said the words, she knew she was going to have to *make* it likely. No matter how she felt about Tyler, he was going to have to learn the truth. And *she* wanted to be the one to break the news to him.

The one to tell him he had gotten her pregnant, and she didn't want him anywhere near her or her kids.

As she handed Layne the change, she saw, beyond her, a customer standing outside the glass-paned front door. She curled her fingers against her empty palm and swallowed a groan of frustration.

Tyler swung the door open. When he stepped into the shop, the temperature suddenly seemed to rise by a hundred degrees.

He nodded at her and removed his Stetson.

Layne looked toward the door. "Well, hi there. It's been a while."

"Yeah, it has."

Layne said something else; Tyler replied. Shay saw their mouths moving, but panic seemed to have closed her ears.

"Well." Layne turned and sent Shay a sympathetic glance as she reached for the sack with her ice cream. "I'd better get home before this melts," she said brightly. In a lower voice, she said, "Good luck with your private chat."

Not here. Not now. "You don't have to go," she protested just as Tyler opened the door again. For a moment, she held on to the hope he planned to leave. But he was only being polite for Layne.

Too bad he hadn't been a gentleman for her.

She flushed, knowing she was at least half to blame for winding up...*together* with him. At least half to blame, if not much more, for believing in something that wasn't meant to be.

He closed the door behind Layne and turned Shay's way.

The room seemed to spin—not a symptom of pregnancy she had experienced before. She put her hands on the counter in front of her. "Don't tell me they've sent you here from the Hitching Post for ice cream." She fought to keep her voice steady. "I happen to know what's on the menu for the reception tonight, and everything's covered."

"Nobody sent me here. But everyone's all tied up, and I had time on my hands."

"Really? You didn't have Jed to talk to?"

"He said he'd be busy all night at the reception."

She frowned. "That's strange. He always makes an appearance, but he's never stayed the entire time, except at his granddaughters' weddings. Well, then, what about Pete?" Jane and her husband lived in the manager's house on Garland Ranch. "And if he's busy, you've got plenty of cowhands to hang out with."

"Maybe I had the urge for dessert."

"Then you'll find more of a selection at SugarPie's."

"Could be. But maybe what I want's right here."

Once she would have fallen for that line and hoped he wanted *her.* She was so over that now. So over him.

She slid open the freezer case and pulled out an empty ice cream tub. It gave her the excuse to walk away, to go into the workroom and avoid his blue-eyed stare. Shaking her head in disgust at herself, she crossed to the big freezer.

She had been all too good at analyzing his expression these past couple of days. She had seen the surprise on his face after he noticed the size of her stomach, had witnessed his frustration as she stood to leave the banquet hall. And just a minute ago, she had clearly read the determination in his eyes.

As she pulled open the freezer door, cold air blasted her. With luck, it would shock some sense into her. Hands shaking, she reached up to the top shelf for another tub of butter-pecan ice cream.

Just as he had yesterday, Tyler stepped up beside her. Again, she nearly jumped out of her shoes.

"I'll get it." He grabbed the tub she intended to take off the shelf.

"Thanks, but I'm pregnant, not incapacitated."

"I didn't think you were." He slammed the freezer door shut. "Let's just say I'll scratch your back, you scratch mine."

The image that followed his words stole her breath.

He looked away, as if he'd only now realized what he had said. He cleared his throat and looked back at her. "I'll take care of this, then you can take care of a few things for me."

Unfortunately, his attempt to make his point clearer only filled her mind with bittersweet images and memories. Tyler flirting with her at Cole and Tina's reception... Tyler's hand brushing hers as they walked the streets of Cowboy Creek on a moonlit night... Tyler kissing her thoroughly as he ran his fingers through her hair...

She had to get her thoughts and this conversation back on track. "Take care of a few things?" she repeated.

"Questions."

This close, he seemed to tower over her. It wasn't a menacing stance, just a result of the difference in their heights. She had grown up as one of the tallest girls in school, and after meeting Tyler at the wedding, she had liked that he made her feel petite. She still liked it. His towering didn't bother her.

It was his nearness that left her feeling shaky. This close and at this stage in her pregnancy, her rounded stomach nearly brushed his flat abs. This close, she could see every darker fleck in his dark blue eyes, making her wonder if any of her babies would have eyes the same shade.

She didn't move. He didn't, either. After a moment she realized she stood leaning back against the freezer door. The cool metal sent another shiver through her. The cold tub he held in one arm, so close to her, added to her chill.

And still, they stood as frozen as two ice cream sandwiches.

Finally, she tore her gaze away, breaking whatever spell had captured her, and pushed past him. It took effort for her not to run. "If you intend to help me, you can put that tub in the freezer case up front."

As he followed, she heard his boots on the tile floor behind her. She should have heard him in the ballroom yesterday and here in the workroom a few minutes ago. But, no, both times she had been so wrapped up in thoughts of him, she hadn't noticed his approach. Not good at all when she needed to stay in control any time she was near him.

She had lost control with him once, and look what had happened.

At the freezer case, he slid the tub into the empty space. To her relief, he then walked back around to the front of the counter.

Through the plate glass of the front window, she saw a family walking up to the shop. Her heart tripped a beat, whether from anxiety or elation, she wasn't sure.

"You can't stay here," she hissed.

"Why not? It's a store."

"But we can't talk here. Or now." Behind him, the door opened. She waved to the Walcotts and their two kids. The family went to their favorite table near the front of the store, and she glanced up at Tyler again. "Please go," she murmured.

"You'll talk to me when you get off work."

He hadn't made it a question. "Yes," she said between clenched teeth.

"What time do you finish up?"

She could tell him a lie. Give him a later time. Or, if the shop stayed as quiet as it was at the moment, she could tell him the truth, then rush through closing and leave before he returned.

Anything to avoid the conversation she didn't want to have.

He must feel as uneasy as she did about their impending talk, or why wouldn't he just have blurted out the crucial question and been done with it?

As wonderful as all her options for evading him sounded, she knew she couldn't be that devious. She sighed and admitted, "I'll be done in a couple of hours." At least that would give her time to collect her thoughts and plan exactly what she would say.

"All right, then," he agreed.

Relieved, she sagged against the counter.

"I'll just stick around," he added.

"But… I'm working."

"We covered that. And I've got nowhere to go except back to the Hitching Post. No sense in my driving all the way out there just to turn around and come back. Give me a triple dip of that butter pecan."

When she hesitated, he shot a glance toward the front table, where the Walcotts were still deciding on their own order.

He faced her again and leaned across the counter, bending down so close she could feel his breath against her cheek as he spoke quietly into her ear. "The Garlands corralled you at the Hitching Post yesterday. Then you ran off from the banquet room and never came back. And now, thanks to your customers, you've been saved by the bell. In case you weren't counting, that's three strikes for me. Do you seriously think I'm going to walk off and let you make yet another escape?"

Chapter 5

Three scoops of ice cream might have been more than he'd needed, but after witnessing Shay's obvious desire to see him gone, Tyler had been doubly determined to find an excuse to stick around.

He'd given her his exact reasons for his plan to stay. The question he'd thrown at her about her potential for an escape hadn't been idle talk, either. If he'd left the Big Dipper and come back again, he wouldn't have been a bit surprised to find the door locked and Shay long gone.

From the booth he'd taken in one corner of the room, he could watch her as she worked behind the counter. He could also listen as she chatted with one customer after another while filling their orders. Now, she had gone to the back room for something, and it was all he could do not to get to his feet and follow her.

The shop had stayed busy for the better part of an

hour. It was as if everyone in Cowboy Creek was scheming to keep him from having things out with her.

Of course, that was paranoia talking.

Even as he had the thought, danged if the bell over the door didn't ring yet again. This time, he recognized the customer who entered. The man took one look at him, grinned, and headed in his direction.

Cole Slater slid into the seat opposite, and Tyler's heart slid down to the vicinity of his knees. Was he never going to get to talk to Shay alone?

Happy as he was to see his buddy, this wasn't the time or place he'd have chosen for them to get together.

Cole had no inkling of that, though. Still grinning, he reached for Tyler's hand. They shook, and the other man said, "Tina told me you were here."

"How did she know?" Tyler frowned in confusion.

"No, not *here* at the Dipper. I meant, in Cowboy Creek. We talked earlier today, but she was tied up getting ready for the wedding reception at the Hitching Post, and we didn't have time to get into much detail."

"Then what brings you to the Big Dipper?"

"Ice cream, what else? Hey, Shay!"

She had returned from the back room and looked over at their booth. Reluctantly, it seemed to Tyler, she headed their way. "A pint of the usual?" she asked Cole.

"You've got it. I'm surprising Tina. She gets cravings," he said to Tyler, then turned back to Shay. "How about you? Working right here in an ice cream shop, you ought to be able to get your fill of any flavor you like."

She shook her head. "No, I see it so much every day, ice cream's not on my list."

Tyler wondered what she *did* crave, but she didn't say.

"Let me know when you're ready and I'll get your

order together." She walked away to greet an elderly pair who had come in and taken seats near the counter. As she stood beside their table, chatting, her hand went to her lower back.

Tyler frowned. With the weight she was carrying up front, she probably ought to be sitting once in a while, taking a break. Taking it easy.

"She's due even before Tina," Cole said, as if he'd watched Tyler watching Shay.

He nodded, but didn't comment. Right now, he didn't want to talk about due dates with anyone but Shay.

He sure couldn't escape the irony of this situation. All his life, his parents had nagged him about making something of himself. About acting like a responsible adult. Maybe they'd been right. Because, even unconfirmed, his suspicions regarding Shay had sent him on the run out at the ranch this afternoon.

Only the knowledge that he had to find out the truth had kept him from leaving Cowboy Creek altogether and brought him here tonight.

Deliberately, he changed the subject. "How's it feel to be on the verge of becoming a daddy again?" he asked Cole.

"Great. I highly recommend it. You ought to give it a try sometime."

He blinked. Could there be a chance he had jumped to the wrong conclusion about Shay's pregnancy? Was he going to make a fool of himself with his question to her?

"Are you planning to stick around for a while?" Cole asked. "Tina didn't say."

"That's because I haven't decided yet."

"Well, we'll have to make sure you stay longer than you did last time. I barely got to see you."

Last summer after meeting Shay, Tyler had spent most of his free time during the short visit hanging around the Big Dipper. Guilt made him cringe—until he recalled the circumstances. His buddy couldn't have had a clue about anything he'd gotten up to. "Not my fault, man. You took off on your honeymoon, remember?"

"That's not something I'll ever forget. But that's exactly my point."

"I don't plan to stay very long," he said truthfully.

Cole nodded. Normally, he could talk the ears off a donkey. But to Tyler's surprise, the other man stood abruptly, ready to depart. "We'll catch up when you get out to the ranch. Time for me to go home to my family."

He said those last two words with unmistakable pride. Pride and family—a combination Tyler didn't know much about.

Cole went to the counter to get his order, then waved farewell as he left the shop. Most of the other customers soon followed him, except the older couple near the counter.

When they finally made their slow way across the room, Tyler was about at the end of his patience. Shay seemed to miss that fact completely. After walking the pair to the door and waving goodbye, she turned the open sign to closed. She wiped down the couple's table and tucked their chairs neatly beneath it. She closed out the register and straightened up the counter. Then she disappeared into the back room and didn't return.

It felt too much like yesterday afternoon when she'd run off from the Hitching Post. He wouldn't put it past her to have slipped out a back door.

Frowning, he tossed his ice cream dish into a nearby trash container and stalked across the tile floor to the doorway behind the counter.

In the workroom, Shay stood with her back to him, leaning over an industrial-size dishwasher while she loaded ice cream scoops and metal milk shake containers into the compartment inside. As he watched, she paused to rest her hand against the washer's door. With her free hand, she rubbed her lower back. He felt another momentary pang of concern.

"Come take a load off." At the sound of his voice, she shied like a startled rabbit. "Sorry. Didn't mean to scare you."

"But insults don't require an apology?"

"Who insulted you?"

"You did. Is that what you think about pregnant women—they're just carrying a load?"

He ground his teeth together. So much for his show of concern. "It was a turn of phrase."

"One that turned in the wrong direction."

"Jed said the same thing to me this afternoon, and I didn't take offense. Maybe you're being overly sensitive." Or maybe that sensitivity came along with pregnancy. Suddenly, he felt as if he were walking on eggshells in the middle of a henhouse—a helluva place to be. "Let me rephrase it, then. Come and take a seat. We might as well both be comfortable, because there's no way I'm leaving until we're done talking."

"What if I have nothing to say?"

He laughed without humor. "You've said plenty already, even if you haven't run off at the mouth. Leaving the Hitching Post yesterday was only the first of a long list of clues."

She raised her chin belligerently, but he stared her down, waiting her out. He'd stay here all night, if necessary.

As if she could read that thought in his expression, she finally sighed and closed the dishwasher door. She crossed the workroom warily, the way a horse accustomed to mistreatment approached someone she feared would deliver more of it. A pang of regret flowed through him. Only his need to hear the truth from her kept him standing there.

When she came nearer, the light scent of her perfume surrounded him, unsettled him, bringing back a time he didn't want to think about.

"Have a seat," he said as pleasantly as he could. He gestured to the booth where he'd been sitting. "I've kept it waiting for you."

She slipped onto the bench and tried to slide behind the tabletop. Her belly, nearly pressed against the table's edge, made her movements awkward. The sight made him swallow hard. He took the seat across from her and knocked back the cup of water she'd given him along with his triple dip of ice cream.

She folded her hands on the tabletop in front of her.

Suddenly, his palms began to sweat. He wiped them on his jeans, rested his hands on his thighs and waited. Let her make the first move.

"Well, obviously," she said at last, "you're not here just because you had a sudden desire for my company. Or for ice cream."

"And obviously, you've got something you don't want to tell me."

She looked away. The pale green shirt she wore rose and fell with her deep breath. Her reaction didn't come as a shock. He knew what it meant. No matter what he'd tried to tell himself, or what that brief uncertainty he'd felt a few minutes ago tried to tell him, he had known the truth the moment she'd turned pale in the Hitching Post's dining room.

She turned back to him, her green eyes glittering. "I'm sure you've already guessed. I got pregnant the night we slept together."

"And you didn't think to tell me?"

"Why would I?"

He stared at her, not trusting himself to speak.

After a moment, she lifted her chin again as if it bolstered her courage to attack. "How exactly was I supposed to tell you? You didn't leave a forwarding address. And you never got in touch with me. What was I supposed to do, tell the Garlands I needed to contact you about a little something you left behind?"

"There's nobody else?" Again her face drained of color, and he realized how she had taken what he'd said—because he'd phrased it like a fool. "I mean, is there anybody else in the picture now?"

"Why is that important?"

"It's not, I guess." Or was it? He needed to get his head together and focus on what *did* matter. "When are you due?"

"In about three weeks."

He eyed what he could see of her over the tabletop. "Are you sure? You look as though you're...ready right now."

"I feel ready right now. But my doctors say otherwise. At least, at the moment. But they also say anything could happen."

The words acted like a kick to his gut. "Is something wrong?"

"No. But first babies can come early—"

He rubbed his palms against his jeans again.

"—especially when there's more than one of them."

"More than—? Are you telling me you're having twins?"

"No. Triplets."

His jaw dropped. He clamped his teeth together and stared at her until he could find his voice again. "You're saying you're having *three* babies?"

"That's usually what triplets means."

His ears rang, the way they had that time he'd been tossed from the back of a bull and jarred his skull against the hard-packed dirt. *Three babies...?*

Just as he had that day, he shook his head, as if he could throw off the noise and the blurred vision and bring himself back to normal. But he doubted he'd ever return to normal again.

She had tightened her jaw and crossed her arms high over her belly. He didn't appreciate the defensive position or her suddenly narrowed eyes. He sure didn't like the panic running though his entire system. This time, when he tried to speak, he could only gulp a mouthful of air. Cold sweat dotted his forehead. His fingers trembled so badly, he had to mimic her body language and tuck his hands under his arms.

How in hell was he going to deal with this?

Shay took one look at the terror in Tyler's eyes and, despite her anger at him, couldn't keep from feeling a rush of sympathy.

Seeing the results of the home pregnancy test had

shocked her, too, but as she had already missed her period, she had suspected the indicator would turn blue. Dr. Grayden's announcement of the multiple babies had stunned her, but at least by then she had known for certain she was expecting.

For Tyler, all this had come…well…out of the blue.

Still, considering both how he had treated her and what she planned to say to him, she couldn't let sympathy get in the way. She tightened her arms across her chest and forced herself to keep her expression neutral. "Don't worry," she said evenly, "you're off the hook."

He looked even more shell-shocked. "Off the hook for what?"

Did he look relieved? She said nothing, letting a beat of silence go by.

"Are you telling me I'm not the dad, after all?"

The hope in his expression crushed her. In the two days she had agonized over informing him about her pregnancy, she had envisioned him happy at hearing she wasn't holding him responsible, ecstatic once he'd realized he wouldn't owe her anything. Somehow she hadn't realized she had still held on to the tiniest hope, too, that he would be glad to hear he was becoming a daddy.

"No," she said flatly. "I'm not telling you that. I'm just saying, as far as I'm concerned, that night with you never happened."

To her surprise, he gave a strangled laugh. "Kind of hard to get away with that story, isn't it, when no one can miss the obvious?"

"It's not so obvious. At least, not that you…were the one who got me pregnant. People will speculate all they want, and I can't stop them. But unless I make an announcement, nobody can know for sure who fathered my babies. *I* certainly don't intend to breathe a word. And I don't want you stepping up and acknowledging the fact it was you."

"Wait a minute…let me get this straight. You're saying you don't want anything from me?"

"Exactly."

His forehead creased in a frown. The skin around his eyes tightened. His mouth settled into a hard line. These were all responses she had never in a million years expected to see.

"And you're not planning to tell people?" he asked.

"No." It wasn't a lie. Other than Layne, who already knew, she didn't plan to discuss Tyler with anyone.

"That's not right."

In the pit of her stomach, she felt a butterfly flicker of fear. "It's not up to you who I tell and who I don't."

"Fine. Do what you want with that. But I'm not walking away without taking some responsibility for the situation."

Eight months of anger and resentment at him bubbled up inside her and overflowed. "We're not talking about a *situation*. They're three lives, three babies. They might not have been conceived in love—" Her voice cracked. She stopped, swallowed hard, went on. "But they're loved now. They'll come into this world knowing they're loved by me, and that's enough. They'll have me and my grandmother and our friends and each other, and none of us—especially me—needs you tagging along for the ride."

He reared back against his seat as if she'd slapped him. Sympathy flared inside her again but was quickly doused by another wave of the anger she had been forced to hide for so long. Getting carried away by these feelings couldn't be good for the babies. She took another deep breath, willing her temper and blood pressure to subside.

"You can forget trying to cut me out," he snapped. "I don't walk away from my obligations, no matter what anyone thinks."

"I don't think anything. I'm just telling you how it's going to be—"

"And I'm telling you I won't—"

"Shay!"

At the sound of a woman shouting her name, Shay froze. So did Tyler. They had both leaned forward across the tabletop to stare each other down. Now they turned abruptly in the direction of the shout.

The clerk from the convenience store adjacent to the Big Dipper stood by the door in the far corner of the room, her hands fisted by her sides. "Are you all right? What's going on? Do you need me to call the sheriff?"

"No, no—everything's all right. Sorry, Beth. We were just…arguing a point. And with no one else in the shop, I guess we got a little carried away."

The other woman looked unconvinced.

Quickly, Shay made introductions, being careful to add, "Tyler is friends with Cole Slater and the Garlands."

"Uh-huh." *And not a friend of yours,* Beth's tone seemed to say. "Are we still planning to head out together?"

"Of course." Hiding her sigh of relief at this chance to escape, Shay edged out of the booth. "I'm almost ready to leave. You, too?"

"Yes."

"And Tyler was just about to go." She glanced his

way, daring him to disagree. He had returned to leaning back against the booth, but he slid from his seat, then rose to tower over her.

"I'll leave through the store with Beth," she told him. "You can go out the front door." She crossed the room ahead of him, attempting to seem relaxed but feeling acutely conscious of her awkward gait, Beth's wary expression, and the lingering anger she had seen in Tyler's dark blue eyes.

She held open the door. Without uttering a word, he resettled his Stetson.

"I'll say good-night here, then," she told him brightly, hoping her tone would convince Beth this was simply the end of a casual chat.

After a long moment of silence, he muttered, "I'll say this conversation is to be continued."

Chapter 6

A short while later, in the small house she shared with her grandmother, Shay collapsed onto the couch. Her confrontation with Tyler had left her body trembling with rage and her head swirling with emotions she didn't want to name. It was only when she was halfway home that she had finally stopped shaking.

She struggled to raise one tired leg and then the other, stretching them out on the couch cushion.

"Relax while you can, lass. The time will soon be here when you won't have a moment to yourself."

Shay smiled. Grandma Mo, as almost everyone in Cowboy Creek called her, had never lost the Irish lilt she'd picked up from her own parents and grandparents. The added flavor to her voice somehow made everything she said sound special to Shay.

"Can I get you something to eat?" Grandma asked now.

"No, thanks. I had some of the leftovers I took along with me tonight."

"That's good." As far back as Shay could remember, Grandma had had the full head of snow-white hair that somehow fit with her unlined peaches-and-cream complexion. She had the same green eyes she had passed down to her son and then to Shay. Those eyes twinkled as she glanced at Shay's stomach. "You don't want to go hungry. You're eating for a family now."

Though she had never named her babies' father, from the moment Shay had revealed she was pregnant, Grandma had stood by her, no questions asked. She had sat by her, too, in her rocking chair just a few feet from the couch. Over the winter months, while Shay's need to rest her feet grew at about the same rate as her middle, Grandma had knitted sweater after sweater, bootie after bootie, blanket after blanket, all meant for the impending arrival of her great-grandbabies. Shay's heart swelled every time she looked at the neat stacks already filling a shelf in her bedroom closet.

"Was the shop busy tonight?" Mo asked.

"Yes, especially in the first few hours. The Walcotts were in with both kids. And the Shaeffers stopped by, too."

"Del surely wasn't eating ice cream, with his sugar levels?"

There was no hiding anything in this town. "Sugar-free frozen yogurt," Shay reported.

"Good. I hope you didn't overdo it tonight. You look worn out."

"I'm tired," she admitted.

"That must be so. You're home early. Wasn't Layne in?"

When she and Layne worked the same nights, Shay

would stop by SugarPie's to see her friend and stay for a cup of tea and a snack. Sometimes Beth came along and, afterward, Shay would often drop Beth at her apartment before heading home herself.

Tonight, the atmosphere in Shay's old car had felt heavy with questions Beth wasn't asking and Shay didn't want to answer. When the other woman had yawned and said she was ready for an early night, Shay had nearly sighed in relief.

"Layne was in," she said. "But Beth and I decided to skip SugarPie's tonight."

"Sugar mentioned you hadn't been by."

Shay shot her grandmother a look. Grandma sat focusing on the bootie she was currently knitting—which was a dead giveaway that she was attempting to appear innocent. Mo could knit an entire wardrobe almost without looking at her needles.

Shay laughed. "I guess the gossip mill wasn't a bit tired this evening, was it?"

Along with Jed Garland, Grandma and Sugar were the biggest storehouses of gossip in Cowboy Creek. And Shay didn't doubt there was plenty of that floating around concerning her pregnancy. But really, with Tyler gone from town so soon after she had met him, folks couldn't have any definite knowledge that he was her babies' father. As she had told him, they might wonder, but they couldn't *know*.

Suddenly she sobered. Word about Tyler's return could easily have made it into town by now. But neither Grandma nor Sugar could have learned about his visit to the Big Dipper tonight…could they?

The memory of his statement about continuing their conversation made her shudder. She pulled the afghan from the arm of the couch and wrapped it around her. If either of the women had any inkling she and Tyler had talked about her pregnancy, that she had told him he was the father of her children...

Another shiver ran through her.

Sugar and Grandma would gang up on her—out of concern for her and her babies, of course. Sugar had never had children and Grandma had lost her only son when he had gotten hooked on following the rodeo. Yet they both strongly believed a family should stay together. They would try to help fix things between her and Tyler.

But she and Tyler never would be a family. And what was wrong between them could never be fixed.

After being thrown out of the Big Dipper, Tyler had tossed and turned for most of the night, wasting valuable sleep time in his comfortable bed at the Hitching Post. He had risen early, dressed and gone straight to saddle up Freedom. It being Sunday and too early for the hotel guests even to have had breakfast, the corral was deserted.

From a distance, he saw Jed's ranch manager headed toward the barn, but he simply waved at the man and turned Freedom toward the trail beyond the corral.

The morning air was cool enough for him to want a jacket, but not cold enough to help clear his head.

As it turned out, his path and Cole's had never crossed again last night, and by the time he returned to the barn, he was glad to find his buddy inside. Cole stood at a workbench where he was cleaning tack, a job that could never be set aside on a working ranch.

When Freedom was back in his stall, Tyler grabbed a bucket of water and joined Cole.

"You looking for work?" Cole asked. Unlike at their meeting at the Big Dipper, this morning he seemed more than ready to talk. "If you're job hunting, I hate to tell you, but Pete's gone back to his house already, and Jed hasn't been out yet to make his morning rounds. Don't bother trying to impress me. I'm just one of the hired hands."

"And Jed's first new grandson-in-law."

Cole snorted. "First in a line, which also doesn't impress anybody. And if he comes after you, don't say I didn't warn you. Don't get me wrong, Jed's happy for the additions to the family and more than pleased about the baby Tina and I have on the way. He's all about adding to his list of great-grandkids. But I really might've won a special place in his heart if I'd managed to get his granddaughter pregnant with a few of those kids at once."

Down on one knee, Tyler froze with his hand clenched around the sponge. Cole knew. How could he not, considering the crack he'd just made?

So much for believing what Shay had said last night.

I certainly don't intend to breathe a word.

His stomach churned in a slow boil. His face grew hot from discomfort and anger. Did she really think she could get away with her lie? That no one would say anything to him before he left town?

He stood and met Cole's eyes. "Who told you?"

"Tina."

"You could have said something, man."

"I didn't hear about it until I got home last night. I don't think anybody knew for sure until they saw you and Shay together again. And even I'm not supposed to know everything."

"What's that mean? Shay swore the whole damned town to secrecy so I wouldn't find out?"

"Whoa." Cole dropped his sponge into the bucket beside him. Arms crossed, he stared. "You're saying this is a surprise to you?"

"Damn right it is. All of it. Including the fact Shay's carrying more than one baby."

Cole gave a long, low whistle. "That's what you get for not returning my calls for the past few months. I'd hassle you more about that, except it looks like you've got enough to deal with at the moment. Anyhow, my point is, if you had replied to my messages—or come by for Christmas, like I asked—you and I might have figured it out sooner. I had my suspicions about you two once Shay started showing, but Tina finally confirmed my thoughts last night."

"You didn't know before then?"

"Nope. Scout's honor. I wasn't about to bring up your name around here until we talked. I imagine Jed and Paz and the rest of the women suspected the truth from the beginning, but they didn't let me in on the news. The Garland family can play their hands close to the vest when they want to." He shook his head and whistled again. "I'm getting nervy over one baby on the way, and you're having three at once."

"Don't remind me."

"Somebody has to. Those kids are going to be here before you can turn around."

"What did you mean, that you're not supposed to know everything?"

For the first time, Cole hesitated. Then he shrugged. "What the heck. Friends have to stick together—even if they don't always return phone calls. The thing is, you already know Jed decided to try a little matchmaking when he brought me and Tina together. He hasn't let up since, not with any of his granddaughters or even my sister, Layne. Nobody's said anything definite to me, but I'm betting you're next on the list."

When he could catch his breath again, Tyler gave a hollow laugh. "Considering the way Shay and I left things last night, Jed won't have any chance of playing matchmaker. I doubt I'll be seeing her again."

"I wouldn't count on that one, buddy."

Tyler narrowed his eyes and said flatly, "What."

"She's coming out to the hotel this afternoon."

He'd forgotten Paz had said that yesterday. Maybe it was for the best. What had sounded then like a long time away now seemed much too soon. But like it or not, he would have to see Shay. He would have to get a few things straightened out with her. Finish their conversation, the way he'd promised her last night.

A heavy lump dragged him down, the same weight he'd felt since the moment she had made her announcement about the babies—the weight of responsibilities he hadn't expected or intended to have.

Life with his folks had cured him of the idea of ever getting married or raising a family. With his parents as role models, he wouldn't know the first thing about raising a kid. But now he was facing becoming the father of not one, not two, but three babies—in only a few weeks!

He could imagine his father's scorn at hearing he'd been irresponsible enough to sleep with Shay without using protection. That was the least of his worries now. He had to do the right thing for these kids, financially, at least, both to prove to his parents he was a responsible man and for his own peace of mind.

Of course, the *real* right thing was to be a *real* daddy. He wasn't going there. He wasn't cut out for the role. And, as Shay had made sure to stress last night, he wasn't the man she'd choose for the job.

By midafternoon Sunday, Shay had changed her mind a half dozen times about whether or not to keep her appointment with Jed. At the moment, she wasn't up to talking to her boss or any of the Garlands—and most especially not to Tyler. If she hadn't so badly needed the extra income from her job at the Hitching Post, she would have canceled the meeting without a second thought.

Of course, the minute she drove into the parking area behind the hotel, the first person she saw was the one she didn't want to see. Tyler stood in the barn doorway with a couple of the ranch's cowhands. When he spied her car, he appeared to break off his conversation and strode in her direction.

She clutched the steering wheel for a moment, took a deep breath and let it out again. "Brace yourselves, babies," she said, looking down at her stomach. "This could get ugly."

As he approached, she considered simply rolling down the window and waiting. Let him bend down from his great height to talk with her. She could rest her back and legs. On the other hand, she would also be caught without a way to make her escape.

That thought had her out of the car and slamming the door shut before he could reach her.

He came to a halt in front of her. "I told you our conversation would be continued."

"Not for very long. Jed's waiting for me. But we

might as well finish what we have to say right here and be done with it."

She exhaled heavily. She had practiced her part in this talk over and over in her mind all morning. She could say what she had to say now. For the sake of her babies. Yes, they needed a daddy, but not one who claimed that relationship simply by right of their birth. They needed someone who would love them and care about them as much as she already did.

"I let my temper get away from me when we talked last night," she admitted. "But I meant what I told you about being off the hook."

"What if I don't choose to be? Don't I have a say?"

"Why would you?"

"Because those kids you're carrying are mine, too."

His eyes glittered in the sunshine, more from repressed anger than concern, she was sure. Again, she had to remind herself of the responses she had rehearsed. "And are you planning to be their daddy? Planning to…to be a family with us?"

"Whoa." He raised his hands and backed up a step, as if she were a horse that had suddenly gone wild. "I never said either of those things. Neither one of them was ever in my plans."

"I thought not." Clearly, he had also never considered the word that wouldn't leave her lips, either. The *M* word. "Well, it doesn't matter. When it comes down to it, we barely know each other, do we? And we obviously seem to care about each other even less."

She waited a beat, but he said nothing, which only reinforced what she had feared all along. He had never cared about her. How could she believe he would feel anything for her babies?

Unable to look at him, she began walking toward the hotel.

She *had* cared about him, at least in those days he'd spent in Cowboy Creek. She had just lied about that.

When he fell into step beside her, she swallowed a bitter laugh, admitting she had also failed dismally at fooling herself. She knew many things about him. How he held a woman when he slow danced. How he liked to flirt. How he liked to kiss. How he went after what he wanted.

Right down to her bones, she had known he would follow her now, that he wouldn't give up. As if he planned to prevent her from getting away, he walked close beside her, close enough that she picked up the scents of his aftershave and his freshly washed cotton shirt. His boots were free of dust and scuff marks, as if he'd worn his Sunday best. For her?

The thought left her swallowing another laugh. Even she couldn't fool herself about that.

A quick glance around the stable yard and ahead toward the Hitching Post showed her they were alone. Once they went inside the hotel, they would lose any chance of a conversation without witnesses.

She stopped abruptly, then waited until he turned to face her. "They're not your children, Tyler. Not the way that's supposed to mean. I don't understand why you believe you even have the right to a say."

"They're my responsibility, that's why. At least until they're of legal age."

Her breath caught in her chest. Even knowing how little he cared, that dry, flat statement hit like a slap to her face. To her senses. "Just how do you think this parenting thing works? You support your children all through childhood, then dump them when they become adults?"

"By that age, they need to learn to accept responsibility for themselves."

"You brought up that word last night. You said they were your responsibility. Your *obligation*." She shook her head. "To you, they're a temporary investment, but to me, they're the children I'll love for the rest of my life. Don't you see the difference?"

Chapter 7

Even as Shay asked the question, she knew in her heart Tyler wouldn't understand. How could he? He had already admitted to her he had never wanted to be a daddy or to have a family. And as much as it hurt to acknowledge it to herself, she had been right. All those months ago, he had only been looking for a good time, not a relationship that could lead to a lifetime commitment.

A few yards away from them, the door of the Hitching Post opened. Her boss stepped out onto the back porch, his face creased in a familiar smile, and her spirits lifted. Immediately, she lost her reluctance to meet with Jed. Now, she wanted only to thank him for the rescue.

"Looking for me?" she asked as cheerfully as she could. "Here I am." Carefully holding the wooden railing, she climbed the steps and, at Jed's sweeping gesture, let him usher her into the hotel.

She walked beside him down the long hallway to

the Hitching Post's banquet room, her ears tuned to the sound of boots on the hardwood floor behind her. A sound that never came.

"What's your hurry, girl?" he asked. "Take it slow, or else you'll be giving those babies a bumpy ride."

Smiling for his benefit, she stroked her stomach and slowed her pace. She *had* been hurrying, for once not caring who noticed her ungainly stride. She had been trying to put more distance between herself and Tyler. And yet she couldn't help wondering why he hadn't followed them into the hotel.

"Bet you're curious about why I wanted to see you today," Jed said.

"I am, actually. Very curious." She envisioned crossing her fingers on both hands, hoping he had found some additional hours for her. From the ballroom up ahead, she heard a burst of laugher, which helped to reinforce her wish. "I guess Tina and the rest of the girls are working overtime this afternoon, too."

"You might say that." His blue eyes twinkling, he grinned at her and stopped short of the wide doorway. Again, he gallantly ushered her in ahead of him.

Immediately, the air was filled with the sounds of women clapping and yelling, *"Surprise!"*

Through a sudden blur, Shay looked around the crowded ballroom to see the face of almost every adult woman she knew in Cowboy Creek.

Jed gave her a hug. "I'll leave you and the ladies to it. Have fun!"

"Thanks." Quickly, she kissed his cheek.

Tina stood at the head of the room, waving to Shay from beside a comfortably padded lounge chair draped with ribbons. "It's all yours," she called.

"It's even got a footrest," Tina's best friend, Ally, added.

Shay laughed. "That sounds perfect." She stopped at a table to hug her grandmother and Sugar. "Grandma, I can't believe you didn't breathe a word of this to me last night."

"And where would the surprise have been in that?" Grandma asked archly.

"Don't worry," Sugar said, "I kept her busy on the phone so she wouldn't have too much time to chat."

"And so I could fall asleep," Shay guessed.

"So the *babies* could fall asleep," Grandma said with a smile.

Shay continued to the front of the banquet hall. The room had been decorated with pale blue streamers and pink balloons. Pastel paper umbrellas dangled from the chandeliers. A long table off to one side of the room held a row of metal chafing dishes and a large pink-and-blue-frosted sheet cake. Another table was piled high with packages tied with pastel ribbons and adorned with baby rattles, booties and other small gifts.

"How did you manage all this so quickly after the reception in here?" she asked Tina as she settled herself in the lounger. Maybe today's surprise explained why Jed had told her she wasn't needed to work last night. They didn't want to risk her finding out about the shower.

Jed was very good at arranging people's lives. She recalled what Tyler had said about Jed's claim he would be busy at the reception. At the time, she had found that odd. Now she wondered if her boss had had a reason for deliberately leaving Tyler on his own last night. But he couldn't have suspected Tyler would track her down at the Big Dipper…could he?

"We had no trouble getting everything ready," Tina

said. "Abuelo rounded up some willing helpers to give us a hand."

She couldn't keep from wondering if Tyler had been one of those helpers and what he was up to at the moment. Then she pushed the thoughts aside. She wasn't going to let anything upset this special celebration for her babies.

Ally, her dark eyes wide and sparkling, came up to Shay and gestured toward her stomach. "*Chica*, you've gotten so big since the last time I saw you."

"I know," she said happily. "Stick around. My doctors have me counting kicks, and the babies have been active."

"We're not going to have to cut this party short, are we?" Tina asked, smiling.

Shay shook her head. "No, I think we're good. And one day, Ally, we'll be having a party like this for you."

"Oh, no, not me," the other woman said in pretend horror. She fluffed her long dark hair and added, "Thanks, anyway. But between you and Tina, we'll have enough babies around to last us for quite a while. That lets me off the hook."

At the echo of her own words to Tyler, Shay had to force herself to continue smiling.

Think about the babies.

Don't think about the man who fathered them or what he might be up to right now.

Sunday was a day of rest for the hands on Garland Ranch, except for those whose turn it was to work with the hotel guests.

For lack of anything else to keep him busy, Tyler had volunteered to help out this afternoon. With those guests now all saddled up and paired with a cowhand, he'd run out of things to do.

He fought the urge to run. Restlessly, he paced the corral fence line.

A dozen yards away, Jed stood with one elbow propped on the fence's top rail and his Stetson tilted back, and somehow Tyler knew the older man was waiting for him. He walked in that direction, feeling like a kid being called on the carpet once again—though only grass and bare earth lay underfoot, and Jed wasn't like his father.

Shaking off the crazy thoughts, he walked up to the ranch owner.

"You have a nice way with the guests," Jed said.

Not at all like his father. "Thanks," he said, smiling.

"'Specially the young ones."

The smile slid away.

"Cole said you and he talked earlier this afternoon."

"We did."

"Good. Then there's no need for me to beat around the bush about Shay and the babies, is there? What I want to know is, what do you intend to do?"

He might have felt taken aback by what seemed like outright hostility on Jed's part, except the man's gruffness couldn't hide the kindness in his face. Cole had long ago told him Jed had a heart of gold. He also knew Jed made a point of looking out for everyone in town. And then, of course, there was the man's sideline in matchmaking. If Cole had been right, Jed planned to turn his attention to *him*.

"I appreciate your interest," he said sincerely, "but first of all, you need to know that where I'm concerned, there's no sense wasting your time planning another wedding."

To his surprise, Jed nodded. "I agree. Son, the last thing I'd want to do is ruin my winning streak. But that doesn't mean I want to see you shirking your responsibility."

There was that word again, the one Shay hadn't hesitated to throw back in his face. "Yeah, well, at least you and I are in agreement there." He leaned back against the fence and glared at the Hitching Post.

"Then what's the problem?"

"Try putting that idea across to the other party."

Now Jed chuckled. "That Shay's a stubborn one, just like her grandma Mo. But don't go telling anyone I said that."

"I won't, if you won't repeat any of this conversation."

"You've got my word on that." After a while, Jed added, "Mo and Shay have been on their own for quite some time. Along with the stubbornness they share, Mo gave that girl a big helping of independence."

"That's a good thing. But from now on, it's going to be more than just the two of them—with the babies coming along," he added in a hurry.

"And isn't that something," Jed said wonderingly. "First time Cowboy Creek has had a family with triplets. It's an amazing thought. It was a bit of a shock for you, I'd imagine."

"That's an understatement. And as you said, it's a responsibility. One I don't intend to walk away from."

"Good." Jed clapped him on the shoulder. "I have to say, I'm proud of you for wanting to man up and do the right thing."

For a moment, he couldn't respond. After knowing him less than a year, Jed had given him a compliment his own father never had. "Thanks," he said, now sounding gruff himself. For a minute, he watched the horses in the corral patiently carrying the weight of people on their backs and walking in circles. He could relate. "Guess I'll head over to my room to clean up."

"And after that," Jed said, "here's what I'd recommend. You need to track Shay down and see if you can't come to some kind of understanding. After all, it's for the good of those babies. For their sakes, there has to be a way you two can set aside your differences."

Don't you see the difference? Shay had asked.

Maybe he couldn't, not the way she had put things. But that couldn't keep him from fulfilling his obligations.

The cake had been cut and devoured by the attendees at the shower. One by one, the women had given Shay hugs and goodbyes before leaving the ballroom. Layne had gone into town for her shift at SugarPie's, and Ally had left, too.

Grandma and Sugar had stood at the doorway seeing everyone off. Now they, along with Jane, had disappeared. They had probably gone to the kitchen to help Paz and the waitresses with the leftovers—not that there were many of those. She wondered whether the men in the Garland family would get their share. Jed's grandsons-in-law...and Tyler.

With so many people constantly around her this afternoon, she had hoped she could stop thinking about him. Instead, with every package she opened, she was reminded of the dreams she had so briefly built around him in the few days after they had met. Dreams she no longer believed in.

She and Tina sat alone at the head table, both of them with their feet up on chairs.

The gifts had all been opened, and every time she

looked across to the table at one side of the ballroom, her eyes filled with tears.

"You've got a lot of presents to take with you," Tina said with a smile.

"I sure do." Each gift she'd received had been matched twice over. "Three playpens. A trio of car seats. And every outfit and accessory a baby could need, in triplicate. I don't know how I'll ever thank everyone for being so generous."

"Your reaction today was thanks enough. They're all thrilled to know they're helping to make you and the babies happy."

"They've done that, all right." She felt tears welling again. "And thanks to Grandma, I've already got three cribs at home. But I don't know how I'm going to fit all this into the babies' bedroom."

"That's the good thing about infants. Everything they own is in miniature. Of course, they don't stay that way for long."

"Please, let's not go there. I don't want to look that far ahead. The thought of taking care of three infants, let alone dealing with three toddlers, is already enough to overwhelm me."

"Don't worry. You'll be surprised at how quickly you adapt."

"I hope so."

Grandma and Sugar reappeared in the ballroom and approached their table.

"How's the cake?" Sugar asked.

Shay took another tiny forkful from the plate in front of her, swallowed it and rolled her eyes. "Phenomenal, as usual. But I'm afraid to dig in or I'll break the scale at my doctor's appointment tomorrow." Now that she was so close to her delivery date, she was seeing either Dr. Grayden or the specialist in Santa Fe twice weekly. "I've decided I'll have one good-size mouthful of cake for each baby."

"And one for yourself, as well," Grandma said.

Shay rolled her eyes again. "If you don't stop," she pretended to scold, "you'll have me as big as a house by the time your great-grands come along."

"As long as they're healthy, lass, that's all that matters."

"We've just talked to Jed," Sugar said. "He's going to get some of the boys to help you load your car."

"That's great." Shay put her feet on the floor and prepared to stand.

The sound of boot steps in the hall and then the appearance of a handful of men in the doorway made her settle back into her seat.

Jed led the way into the room.

Behind him followed both Tina's and Jane's husbands...and Tyler. Even seeing him from this distance made her heart skip a beat. He was the tallest of the three younger men and, no doubt about it in her opinion, the hottest looking. He had changed into a pale green shirt that contrasted with his dark hair. Up close, it would make his eyes look an even deeper blue. Deep enough to drown in, as the saying went.

But now, at least, she had more sense than that.

"Looks like you could use a trailer for all your loot," Jed said.

"I'm sure we can manage to fit it into my car," she told him.

"Not of all it. You'll need another vehicle."

She had a sinking feeling she knew where this conversation was going. Tyler was the only unattached male in the room, aside from Jed. And Jed would never pass up a chance to fulfill his role as Cowboy Creek's head matchmaker. "That's fine," she said hurriedly. "Grandma can—"

"I left my car in town," Grandma broke in. "Sugar drove, and she has to get back to the shop. We're just leaving."

"Oh. Well." She tried again. "Jed, please don't have anyone go to any trouble. I can take some of the gifts home today and then pick up the rest tomorrow."

"Why do that when I've got an able-bodied assistant right here?" He clapped Tyler on the shoulder. "Son, you wouldn't mind helping Shay get all her gifts to her house, would you?"

"No, not at all."

She swallowed a groan of pure frustration.

Tina led the younger men over to the side table.

Jed remained standing beside Mo and Sugar.

After one glance at their smiling faces, she knew there was no point in arguing. They were determined to have this happen. They had probably conspired to *make* this happen.

Like it or not—and she didn't—she would have to accept Tyler's help.

Chapter 8

As Shay entered through the front door, it was impossible for her not to know Tyler had come into the house directly behind her. The sound of his heels rapping against the oak flooring nearly drowned out her lighter steps.

She switched on a table lamp near the doorway. The soft light accentuated the wooden accents of the couch and chairs and burnished the maple of Grandma's rocker. The light played up the jewel tones of the afghan she had left in a heap on the cushions that afternoon. To her the lived-in room had always represented an equal measure of security and love. She hoped it would mean the same to all three of her babies.

Tyler carried two armloads of packages while she, at his insistence, held only the handles of a shopping bag filled with boxes of baby clothes. Truthfully, she admitted to herself that even adding that small amount of weight on one side left her more unsteady than ever. So did being near Tyler again.

For such a brief time, she had had so many dreams about him, so many hopes. Now she had only the need to keep him from ever knowing how hard she had fallen.

"I could have carried another bag," she said. "It would have evened out my load. Besides, I told you it was just a short walk to the front door."

"You didn't need to tell me. I've been here before."

"I haven't forgotten," she snapped. Too late, she realized it was probably the wrong thing to say. He didn't need to know that night still lingered in her memory. Grimly, she held on to her anger and irritation, knowing they would keep her safe from so many other emotions she couldn't afford to feel. "Well, it was easier for me to agree to carry a lighter load than to stand there arguing with you."

"And the faster we unload the car, the sooner I can leave, right?"

He wasn't asking. He had mocked her tone, telling her he knew what she was thinking. She pretended to misunderstand. "You know," she said as pleasantly as she could manage, "no one's forcing you to do this. You can leave everything down here in the living room. There's nowhere to put the gifts in the bedroom, anyhow, except in piles on the floor."

"That's good enough. They'll be near at hand for when you need them."

Swallowing a groan, she crossed the room but came to a stop at the foot of the stairs. She might as well have stood looking up at a mountain soaring above her. Already short of breath after the brief walk from the car to the house, she would have no chance of quickly leading the way up to the second floor.

"You go ahead. I'll only slow you down. I switched rooms a few months ago, so the babies could have my bigger bedroom." Her face flamed from a mixture of awkwardness at the reference to their past and her irritation now. She gestured to the staircase. "Second door on the left. You probably remember the way."

"Yeah."

He moved swiftly up the stairs. She followed much more slowly. Her head filled with images of what had happened between them the last time—the one and only time—he had been here, images she didn't want to remember but couldn't make herself forget.

Suddenly, she felt overwhelmed at having him in the house with her again. Physically, he took up too much space, upsetting the comfort she normally felt here. His presence brought back too many memories, too many emotions, and she was hit with the realization of why she had brought him home with her in the first place. She hadn't made the decision based on just how well they got along, how easily he made her laugh, how close she felt to him after only a few days.

She had brought him home because she had fallen in love with him the night she met him.

And he had fallen far short of the man she'd thought he was.

Before she reached the landing, he returned and started down again. While she wouldn't change her current physical state for anything in the world, she wished she could recall the last time she'd had that much energy.

Keep it light. Keep him from knowing how much you care.

"Show-off," she muttered.

With a laugh, he stopped beside her. "I'd be slow, too, if I were carrying that much weight."

"Gee, thanks. You're really good with an insult."

"You know what I mean." He touched her arm. "Hey, you okay? You look all in."

"I'm all right." Or she *would* be, if only he would never again touch her or look at her the way he was looking at her now.

He stood a couple of steps below her, which put them on a level. On this side of the living room where the lamplight couldn't penetrate the shadows, his eyes appeared darker than ever, blue-black and gleaming and filled with something she didn't want to think of as concern.

"I'm fine," she said firmly. "It's just been a long day." A longer weekend. An even longer eight months.

"Why don't you sit and let me take care of everything."

Oh, no. She wouldn't fall for that line, no matter how good it sounded. He would be gone soon, and good riddance, and she would be on her own again. "You're letting Jed's compliments go to your head. You might be able-bodied, especially compared to me right now, but that doesn't mean I'm helpless."

"I never thought you were. And I wouldn't let Jed's words concern you. He was only being nice so I'd go along with him."

"Now, why does that seem familiar, cowboy?"

He frowned. "That's hitting below my champion belt buckle, Shay."

She couldn't keep from glancing at that buckle.

"Impressive, huh?"

She snapped her gaze up and found him grinning at her. "Not at all. It's just a reminder you're only a rodeo cowboy, which still doesn't impress me. And I don't make things up, I just call them as I see them."

"So do I. That night at Cole's wedding, I saw a woman who was as ready to flirt with me as I was to flirt with her." She refused to react or even to look at him, but he touched her chin, bringing her gaze to his again. He leaned closer and said quietly, "I saw a woman who wanted me as much I wanted her. How do you call that one, Shay? Are you planning to deny it?"

She couldn't speak, let alone deny his words. Arguing would only make her a liar. For the first time in her life, she had let herself get close to a cowboy. And she *had* wanted him, almost from the minute she had met him. Only she had been thinking about forever and he had wanted a one-night stand.

Even now, she longed to lean closer—an irrational thought but one she struggled to control. His hand on her chin and his face so close to hers revived the most special memories she had ever known.

As if he'd read her mind, he said, "We had a good time, Shay. And when it comes to what happened as a result, I'm willing to take some of the blame. But not all of it." He dropped his hand. "For the record, when I said you should sit and let me take care of things, I wasn't attempting to get anything out of you, just giving you a chance to rest. Don't judge me by what happened in the past. We're in the here and now, and I'm trying to do what's right." He moved past her and continued down the stairs.

As the front door closed behind him, she patted her stomach with an unsteady hand. "Don't worry, babies,

I'm not falling for any of that. He's just trying to make himself look good. Your da—"

Oh, no. She also wasn't falling into that trap.

"Your *mommy's* the one in charge around here, and she's perfectly capable of taking care of you all by herself."

She didn't need the help of a rodeo cowboy.

Thanks to her father, she knew all about the lies they told, the promises they broke, the important events they didn't attend, the holidays they missed. She would be doing her babies a favor by keeping Tyler out of their lives.

Three days later, Tyler sat in his truck outside Shay's house. He tried not to think about what had happened inside that small two-story building on his last visit, and especially not what had happened when he'd gone upstairs with her the previous summer.

After bringing her home with the bounty from her baby shower, he had spent the next couple of days seething over her insults—which, unlike his unfortunate turns of phrase, were very much intended. First, her hint that he'd said things to her just to get what he wanted, and then her odd emphasis when she'd called him *only* a rodeo cowboy. Both had been designed to hit him right where it hurt.

He glanced down the empty street. Jed had assured him Shay would be there within the hour. Tyler had no doubt the old man was up to something.

These past few days, Jed had gotten him to spend plenty of time helping his granddaughters around the hotel. Their grandpa also had taken every opportunity to make sure his new assistant wasn't far from Shay whenever she came to work at the Hitching Post.

He could see right through the older man's scheme. Jed had accepted his statement about not being interested in matchmaking services. In fact, he had seemed relieved at not having to risk his perfect record. Still, he appeared to want to help pave the way to a truce.

Tyler didn't have the heart to tell the man again he was wasting his time and talents.

From the other end of the block, a car approached. He recognized the sedan's outlines, then the dust covering every inch of the vehicle and, finally, the silhouette of the woman inside. He braced himself for the unhappy reception he expected. He didn't have long to wait.

Before she'd even put the car into Park, he could see Shay's frown. She had been brief and formal when she'd thanked him for his help the other day. At the Hitching Post in the presence of others, she had been civil enough. Now, evidently, it was a case of her rodeo, her rules. He slammed the door of his truck and went to meet her at the walkway to the house.

Her face looked drawn and tired. Her gaze seemed unfocused with fatigue. He clenched his fist by his side to keep from reaching up and smoothing away the lines in her forehead. It was almost a welcome relief to see a fire suddenly light her eyes.

"What are you doing here?" she demanded.

"I've come to help you set up the baby's room."

"Jed told me he would have Cole do that, which is why I hurried home from the shop. What happened to him?"

"He's still out riding the ranch."

"And Pete?"

"Waiting for the vet to take a look at one of the foals."

"And Mitch?"

He held back a growl. Barely. "I imagine the deputy sheriff's busy keeping your fair town safe from evildoers. And before you ask, the rest of the cowhands are taking care of their chores and the stable boy's mucking out the stalls and Jed's too old to be moving furniture—but don't tell him I said that. So the deal is, you're stuck with me."

"Thanks, but I'll pass."

"And not have the room put to rights before the kids come along?"

Her face settled into the determined scowl of a bull protecting his territory. Likewise, he felt himself stiffening, preparing to dig in his heels. Whether or not Jed had misguidedly instigated this arrangement on his behalf, he had agreed to help, and that's just what he intended to do.

And, unlike last time he'd come here, he also intended to keep his hands off Shay.

"Look," he said patiently, "once I left town last summer, I couldn't have known you'd gotten pregnant, but I know it now. You don't want me to have a role in the kids' lives. I get that, and I told you I don't want to be a daddy, anyway. But I'm leaving in a few days. I want to make sure you're all set up before the babies come. And then after I'm gone, I'll send you money every month to help take care of them. It's the least I can do."

Now her expression changed to disbelief and distrust. The sight hit him harder than the verbal insults she'd thrown at him.

Who would have won the standoff, he didn't know. As it turned out, events didn't have time to come to a head.

The front door of the house opened, and Shay's grandma stepped onto the porch. She was carrying a handbag and a couple of plastic sacks. As she came down the steps, she left the door open behind her. Tyler had met the woman at the Hitching Post, though they hadn't yet had a private conversation. Maureen, her name was. She had told him to call her Mo.

He didn't know if she knew he was the father of Shay's babies, and she'd never given him an indication one way or the other. But she had both a head of white hair and a sharp eye in common with Jed, and the two older folks appeared to have a shared interest in helping Tyler's cause.

"Ah, Tyler," she said with satisfaction. "Jed told me you'd be here shortly. I'm glad you've made it and Shay is home now, too. I have to run, and it wouldn't have been much of a welcome to leave you sitting out on the porch."

He hadn't received much of a welcome, anyhow. "It wouldn't be a hardship to spend some time in that porch swing up there," he countered, a pleasure he and Shay had never shared.

"Well," Mo said with a smile, "maybe you'll have that opportunity after your work is done today."

The look Shay shot him told him he'd have no chance of that. Her expression softened as she turned to Mo. "Don't you want to stay and help us set up the room?"

"I would love to, lass, but I'm on my way to the community center."

"I'm sure they could manage without you for once."

"Not this time." Mo gestured to her sacks. "I've got the rest of the yarn for our current project, and the knitting circle can't make progress without it. No, you two go along and get to work. I'll be up to see the room as soon as I'm back again."

She stepped aside on the walkway, giving them space to pass her, and stood there smiling. And waiting.

He could see Shay struggling, unwilling to give in and accept his help. Maybe what he had said about not having the room ready in time finally swayed her, because after another beat of silence, she nodded. "All right, see you later."

As Shay started up the walkway toward the house, Mo patted his arm encouragingly.

This time when the urge to smile struck him, he didn't fight it. He'd have to save his battle strength for when he and Shay were alone.

After Tyler followed Shay upstairs to the bedroom that used to be hers, she quickly ran down a list of what needed to be done. Of course she wouldn't want him spending any more time here with her than he absolutely had to. As she probably had it figured, the sooner she outlined what he had to take care of, the sooner he could get to it and be on his way.

"The cribs still need to be assembled, and when that's finished, we can set them up with the changing table and bureaus. And then I can fill the drawers." She gestured across the room. "You can see I didn't make much progress with the bags from the shower," she mumbled.

He'd wager she wouldn't confess to what he knew had to be the reason, that she was more worn out than she let on.

As he worked on unboxing the first crib, she moved around the room, unpacking bags and going back and forth to put things in the closet. When he started his assembly, she was at his side, helping to steady the railing as he lined up the head-and footboards and slipped the bolts into place.

He frowned. "Shouldn't you be taking it easier?"

"I'm just holding on to a strip of wood."

"You're on your feet. And you've been on your feet a good part of the day. Don't you want to sit down?"

"Don't you want to get this done?"

He tightened one of the bolts. "I'm not in that much of a hurry."

"Well, I am."

With one hand, she stroked her round belly, a move he'd seen her make many times at the Hitching Post. Now, he saw her belly move in response. He stared as the stripes on her shirt rippled like a windblown wheat field. His heart thumped and his throat tightened and for the first time the truth of what she had said to him the other day hit home. These were three babies she was carrying, three lives she would soon bring into the world.

"The babies are active today," she said, looking down, a soft smile curving her lips.

Once, she had shared those smiles with him. Those days were gone. The thought left him feeling hollow.

"Guess the kids are getting ready to come take up residence in these cribs." Suddenly, he felt less irritated about her need to hurry him along. Maybe it wasn't directed solely at her desire to get him out of her house. Maybe she knew more than she was telling him. His hand slipped. The tool that had come with the kit nicked a tiny scratch into the wood of the headboard. "You've still got a couple more weeks left, at least, right?"

She laughed without humor. "Are you worried I might go into labor as we speak?"

"Heck, no," he fibbed. "Just thinking about how long it might take me to set up three cribs. It's not as easy as just one." He paused, then said, "Raising three babies at once can't be as easy as just one, either."

"I don't know about that. You just batch tasks and get everything over with at once." The twitch at one corner of her mouth told him she was teasing and trying to hide a smile.

Suddenly he felt a little less hollow.

"That's providing all the babies cooperate." Again, he hesitated, but her reaction had seemed to lower the wall she'd erected between them by a few inches. "How did you take hearing the news you were having the triplets?"

"About as well as you did."

"It was that obvious, huh?"

"Oh, yeah." Her gaze met his then lowered again to her belly. "It's a lot to deal with at once. Overwhelming. But exciting."

"And scary."

"And scary," she echoed.

And she would have to face every overwhelming, exciting, scary step all on her own.

On her own except for her grandma and all their friends, as she had been sure to tell him when she had said she didn't need him along for the ride. That was okay with him. He hadn't signed on for a ride like this one. He only wanted her to agree to take help from him, and then he'd be out of here, his obligation fulfilled and Cowboy Creek in his rearview mirror.

His hand slipped again. No scratch this time, but it was a close call. He wiped his palm on his jeans. "I need to get out. To the truck. For another screwdriver.

The tools they give you with an assembly kit don't always do the best job."

"All right." One hand on her back, she made her way to the doorway ahead of him. "I think I'm going to go and put my feet up for just a minute."

He watched as she moved down the hallway, her pace so slow and steady no one could have noticed anything awkward or ungainly about her progress. Probably no one would even realize she was pregnant and carrying three babies.

He knew. And that hand at the small of her back bothered him more than he could say.

He went down the stairs to the first floor at about Shay's speed, his thoughts still upstairs with her. She was independent, not a bad trait to have and one he hoped she passed along to the kids. But as for that danged stubbornness—

He hadn't yet made it to the front door when she called his name, her voice shrill.

Frowning, he about-faced and went up the stairs again at a run. The hallway was empty. He didn't know where she had gone. As he passed the babies' bedroom, she called him again.

Third door on the left, into a smaller bedroom. She sat on the edge of the bed with her arm cradling her belly. After one look, he went down on his knee beside her and took her free hand. It was shaking. Or maybe that was his. "What's wrong?"

"I don't know," she said, her voice still high. "I'm having pains."

"Hey, hey, calm down," he said soothingly, he hoped. "It's not too soon for the babies to come, is it?"

"No. We were hoping they would hold out a bit longer, but my doctors told me I could go into labor at any time. It's just…" She swallowed hard. "I'm scheduled to deliver in Santa Fe."

"And maybe you still will. Everything will be all right." How would he know? But when she nodded, seeming calmer, he was glad he had given her the reassurance. "Why don't you call your doctor and let him know what's going on."

She nodded. "My cell phone. It's in my bag. I think I left it on the couch when we came in."

"I remember. Be right back." He strode along the hall and took the stairs three at a time. He'd told her to calm down, but who was there to say that to him? As he grabbed the bag, he stole the time to take one steadying breath before going back up the stairs. It wouldn't help Shay if he fell all to pieces.

She must have had the doctor on speed dial, because in seconds she was talking to someone on the other end of the line, explaining about the pains. Even as she described them, another one seemed to hit her. She gasped but kept her attention on the conversation. He paced the room, wondering how he would handle it if she had the babies right now.

A few moments later, midsentence, she grabbed at her stomach and slammed the phone on the bed.

He took the cell from her and spoke into it. "My name's Tyler. I'm…here visiting with Shay. What should we do?"

A reassuringly steady voice said, "This is Dr. Grayden. Have Shay lie down with her feet up. We're sending an ambulance to her address. It's already on the way."

"Are the *babies* on the way?"

"I won't know that until I see Shay."

He must have mumbled something, because the doctor said kindly, "Don't worry, young man. Once the ambulance arrives, she'll be in good hands with the EMTs and then with the staff at the hospital. Until that time, you're to tell her she's in equally good hands. Yours. Keep her calm and relaxed and remind her to practice her deep breathing. Understood?"

"Understood."

"Good. I'll be waiting when you arrive."

He disconnected the call. Shay stared at him, wide-eyed. He took her hand. "It's okay," he said firmly. "They've got an ambulance on the way. You're supposed to lie down and practice breathing."

Nodding, she lay back against the bed. He lifted her feet so she could stretch out comfortably.

"Want a blanket?"

"No, I'm fine. But I'm supposed to be having the babies in Santa Fe," she said again. "That's where the specialist is. That's where they have the high-risk NICU."

High risk? No wonder she was in such a panic. He took another deep breath. "Dr. Grayden says you'll be in good hands at the hospital here." He didn't tell her what the doc had said about *his* capabilities in the meantime. With luck, the man was right about that, too.

"I know," she agreed, "but this isn't what we expected to happen. One of the babies is turned. I can't deliver. I'm supposed to have a C-section."

"And you will," he said as soothingly as he could. "They can deliver the babies here in Cowboy Creek, can't they?"

She shrugged. "The specialist said they have a special care unit at our hospital. And a nurse on staff trained to handle multiple births."

"Then the hospital's on alert and ready, right? And remember, you told me the doctor said anything can happen as far as the timing. Maybe the babies are just tired of waiting and eager to get here."

She gave a half laugh that made his heart flip. "Not as eager as I am."

"Well, then, that's what we'll keep thinking." He squeezed her hand slightly.

As another pain hit, she moaned and gripped his fingers.

Chapter 9

Chasing an ambulance to Cowboy Creek General Hospital was another ride Tyler hadn't signed on for. Driving white-knuckled and leaning over the steering wheel hadn't helped to make the trip any shorter.

The ambulance had seemed to take forever to arrive at the house. In reality, the clock on Shay's cell phone when he dropped it into her bag showed only eleven minutes had passed since she'd called her doctor. One of the benefits of living in a small town.

One of the drawbacks was now staring him in the face, her expression stern and forbidding above her nurse's uniform. She was half his size and judging by her gray curls probably three times his age, and still she held the power to stop him in his tracks. "I'm sorry, but as I've told you twice already, no one but the designated support person is allowed beyond this point."

"But I followed Shay here in the ambulance," he protested.

"I'm sorry."

"I have her bag." He held it up as if it were a talisman that would magically grant him entrance through the doors just yards away.

"I'll see the family is notified when they get here."

"When will that be?" His voice had risen a few notches in frustration. The nurse frowned at him. He glared back. He wanted to throttle the woman. He wanted to push past her and go down the hallway and through the automatic doors into the bowels of the hospital, to wherever he would find Shay.

In the minutes they had waited for the ambulance to arrive at the house, then for the medical techs to transfer her onto a stretcher and downstairs and into the emergency vehicle, she'd had a few more pains or contractions or whatever they might have been. The anguish on her face just before they'd closed the ambulance doors had torn at his heart.

That was the last he'd seen of her, and now this dragon of a hospital employee was keeping him from seeing Shay again, turning down his requests to talk to her doctor, refusing to let him know her status.

But these are my kids *she's having,* he wanted to snap at her.

The knowledge finally hit, a solid blow that almost sent him staggering.

Yes, Shay was bringing these lives into the world. But no matter what she said, they were his as much as hers. Not just his responsibility. His *family.*

The nurse took him by the arm, urging him away from the admittance desk. His heart lightened at the knowledge she was finally going to take pity on him. Instead, she led him aside and nearly backed him up against a wall, most likely, he belatedly realized, to get him as far away as possible from the curious stares of everyone else in the room.

"You're not listed on our paperwork as the father of record or even a close family member." She gave him a small, malicious smile. "Therefore, I'm not allowed to divulge any further information to you."

Of course not. Why should she be allowed to do that when she wouldn't do anything else?

Then the implications of what she had said sank in. She wasn't allowed to divulge any further information to him. He wasn't listed in Shay's records. Did that mean she had named someone *else* as the father?

The dragon turned and walked away.

He glanced around him. Everyone in the place sat staring at him as if *he* were the dragon. One with six heads.

Suddenly he felt grateful for the wall behind his back. He sagged against it and ran his hand over his face. The evil nurse might have control at the moment, but somehow he needed to get information from her. Acting like a real jackass wasn't going to get him anywhere. Desperately, he searched for a single sane thought to hold on to—and couldn't find one. Every thought he had was jumbled, erratic and fleeting.

He'd never planned to become a daddy. Never wanted to be a daddy. And yet, here he was, in a panic because that's exactly what was going to happen, and that dragon nurse was telling him *he had no rights to his own children*.

Now she stood with her back to him calmly flipping

through a few charts on the desk in front of her. He was tempted to vault over the front counter and tear across the space behind her and through the double doors.

That idea was put to rest when the automatic doors from the street swished open and Grandma Mo entered the emergency room with Jed Garland at her side.

Tyler had lost track of time.

He and Jed had taken seats while Mo stopped at the counter, evidently to provide the staff with all kinds of information he wouldn't have known. He leaned forward, face tilted down, elbows on his knees, in an attempt both to avoid the continuing stares of those around him and to get his head together again.

Eventually, Mo returned to lead them both down the hall to a family waiting room. Lightly padded plastic chairs made a corral around a low table holding some magazines and a few books.

He tried to get comfortable in this awkward situation. Jed knew the truth. But did Mo know who had fathered her granddaughter's babies?

He told them what had happened back at the house, describing Shay's pains, the phone call, the arrival of the ambulance.

The nurse, whose name turned out to be Annabel, entered the room with a tray of paper cups filled with water. "Cafeteria's closed for the night, but I thought y'all might like something to drink."

Sitting had put him at about eye level with her. He couldn't avoid meeting her gaze. As she handed him a cup, she gave him the same small smile she'd given him earlier, which he now could see didn't have a trace of malice in it. Instead, it was a sympathetic smile. She wasn't a dragon nurse after all.

Panic could make a man think crazy things.

"Sorry about before," he muttered, taking the cup.

She patted his shoulder. "Most men aren't at their best when they show up here with a woman in labor."

Yeah, but how many of those men were daddies with three babies arriving at once? And could the fact he would soon face just that event excuse some of his behavior?

As for the staring faces in the waiting room, he didn't know whether it helped or hurt that, very likely, those were all folks who knew Shay—and Mo and Jed. Just as likely, they were all thrilled to finally have a look at a potential candidate for the father of Shay's babies.

Jed and Mo sat watching him. Grandma Mo hadn't said a word about his panic. More importantly, she hadn't reacted to Annabel's reassurances, which answered his question about whether or not she knew the truth about him. Either she'd known all along, or the surprisingly kindly nurse had clued Mo in when they were filling out hospital forms together.

As Annabel left them, he took a gulp of water, then looked at Mo.

Green eyes almost the shade of Shay's stared back at him.

"You know?" he asked.

She nodded.

"Shay told you?"

She shook her head. "No, it was more a case of putting two and two together."

"Or two and three, as it's turned out."

She gave a soft laugh. "That it has. Never did I think

I'd be having my great-grandchildren by the handful. I'm happy for it. But I'll be happier once I know they're all here and healthy."

"That makes a few of us." He hesitated, then admitted, "I kind of went off the deep end when the nurse wouldn't let me know what was going on with Shay."

Jed settled back in his chair and stretched his legs out in front of him. "I was in that position when my Mary and I had our first boy. Sometimes, with all the hustle and bustle and everybody knowing their jobs and doing them, it feels like the daddy's the last to learn the details."

"My husband felt the same when I delivered Shay's father," Mo said. "It's no shame that you felt a bit frustrated, Tyler, when Annabel wouldn't answer your questions. If it's any consolation, she said you were almost persuasive enough to make her bend the rules."

"Obnoxious enough, she means."

"Well," Mo said, her eyes twinkling, "that *may* have been one of the words she used."

He sent her a rueful grin.

The doors to the waiting room opened again. A silver-haired man wearing a white coat and a wide smile came directly to Mo.

"Everything's fine," he said promptly, to Tyler's immediate relief. That feeling disappeared just as quickly when the man, his expression now solemn, took a seat beside Mo and rested his hand on her shoulder. "We're not going to be able to transfer Shay and the babies up to Santa Fe as planned."

"But you're prepared for the births here, Jim?" she asked. Tension ratcheted up the accent he'd noticed in her voice.

"You already know we are, Mo. Now, don't worry about that."

"What about her pain?" Tyler demanded.

The doctor glanced at him, then back to Mo again. She nodded as if confirming she wanted the information, too.

"We don't have a definitive answer for that yet," the doctor told him. He returned his attention to Mo. "All four of them are being monitored closely while we run some tests. The babies' lung development has already been checked, and everything is just as it should be. The tests will tell us if there's anything more. From everything we've seen so far, in my and my colleague's opinions, the babies are getting restless."

He smiled, and Tyler liked the man for trying to ease Mo's worry.

"When we have any news," he continued, "you'll be the first to know. Once the testing is done, you may be allowed in to see her. You alone, but it may be a while."

She nodded. "I'll be right here."

"Good." The doctor nodded to Tyler and Jed, then left.

"Well, son," Jed said, "looks like it might be time for us to go home."

Stalling, Tyler pretended to take a drink from his already empty cup.

Shay wouldn't acknowledge his rights. The nurse wasn't allowed to accept his word. The doctor addressed all his comments to Shay's grandma. And it looked like Jed wanted him to walk away.

That left Mo, who sat quietly watching him.

"I'll stay for a bit," he told Jed. "You've got a way to get back to the ranch?"

"Got my truck. Don't worry about that."

The echo of the doctor's words to Mo made Tyler think again of Shay. And her pain. And their conversation at the Big Dipper when he found he was going to become the father of three.

It's not up to you who I tell and who I don't.

He winced, sure he knew how she would feel about him discussing her with her grandma. But there was nothing he could do about that now. And it was the least of his worries.

Mo sat with her head tilted, studying him thoughtfully. He'd bet her next words wouldn't make him feel any better.

"Since we can't tell how long I'll be sitting here," she started, "and as Dr. Grayden said I'm to be the only one allowed in to see Shay…"

The only one Shay wanted to see.

The cup he held seemed to vibrate in his hand. Slowly, he curled his fingers around it, crumpling it in his fist. He tossed it into a trash basket near the end of the couch.

Mo continued gently, "In view of the circumstances, Tyler, I think it might be best for you to go with Jed. I'll be in touch when I know something."

Jed clapped him on the shoulder as if to second her request.

Looked like no one thought he had the right to be here.

Chapter 10

"Your babies are beautiful."

At Layne's enthusiastic assessment, Shay couldn't hold back a grin. In the two days since she had given birth, she hadn't been able to stop smiling. Other than informing her the babies had a case of jaundice, Dr. Grayden had pronounced them perfect.

Even the exhaustion from two days and nights of sleep broken by multiple feedings couldn't dim her happiness. Her babies were safe and sound, healthy, and finally *here*.

She looked at the small cribs lined up against one wall of the hospital's neonatal care room. "Thanks. I think they're beautiful, too, but it's good to hear it confirmed by an expert mommy."

Layne laughed. "I'm no expert. And according to Mo, you're doing fine yourself."

"So are the babies. We should be able to move into a room together soon. Right now they're here under a special light to help with their jaundice. Dr. Grayden says they may need to stay an extra day in the hospital because of that, but their color is improving. And they all have great appetites."

"I thought they looked bigger already," Layne teased. She had seen the triplets for the first time the day before.

"They *are* bigger. Timothy met the minimum birth weight to go home. Jamie was just under the wire, but he's above it now, too. And Bree has only a few ounces to go before she catches up with her big brothers. I'm having to supplement with bottle feedings. It wasn't my first choice, but…"

"Nothing wrong with that. You wouldn't have enough milk to nurse three babies," Layne said matter-of-factly.

"That's true. They do seem to eat a lot. And when they're not eating, they pretty much spend their time sleeping."

"Be grateful for that," Layne advised. "In just a few days, you'll be wishing for more nap times."

"For them or for me?"

"Both."

They laughed.

"I know Mo's been here," Layne said. "Sugar and Beth told me they stopped in, too."

"I'm glad to have the company." Dr. Grayden and the staff were all business when it came to watching over her babies, and she couldn't have asked for better care even from the neonatal unit in Santa Fe. There, visitors might not yet have been allowed, but in a small-town hospital like Cowboy Creek's, the rules were more flexible.

"Has anyone from the ranch been to see you?" Layne asked.

"Yes, Jed and Paz were here yesterday after you left, and Tina and Jane were in this morning." Layne continued to look at her expectantly. Shay frowned. "I know what you're thinking, and the answer's no."

Layne gave a small gasp of surprise. "But now Tyler knows he's the daddy. He didn't even make an attempt to get here?"

"Not as far as I know. Witnessing my panic at the house the other day must have given him a big dose of reality. And watching me being taken away in the ambulance probably made him think about the craziness of life with three babies. No wonder he hasn't come to the hospital." She shrugged. "That's fine with me. I don't want to see him. And the babies are too little even to notice who visits them."

But were they? In just these two days, all three of her babies had bonded with her. They appeared comfortable when Grandma and Paz and Jed held them. They seemed quick to respond to anyone who came into their very small world. But of course, they couldn't miss someone they'd never known.

Layne said nothing.

"I know what you're thinking again, but he doesn't have any right to be here. He doesn't plan to be…anything to my babies." She looked away from Layne and focused on the cribs. "Grandma and Jed are stopping by this afternoon. They'll be here soon. Please promise me you won't bring up Tyler's name in front of them."

"Tyler who?" Layne asked airily.

Shay laughed, but somehow, she didn't trust that tone. No matter what excuses she had just made, she had been surprised that Tyler hadn't shown up at some point during visiting hours. He had been with her when she'd gone into labor. He had held her hand and tried to calm her while they waited for the EMTs. Even in the hustle of her transfer to the ambulance, she recalled him in the background, lending her silent support. She had thought for sure he would want to see their babies.

But that was just wishful thinking. She needed to stop those crazy thoughts. As she had told Layne, he didn't intend to have anything to do with the triplets.

She felt the same about him. And to her relief, it looked like he had walked out of her life again for good.

In the hospital parking lot, Jed held the door of his truck open until Mo settled herself inside. Then he went around to the driver's door and climbed in to sit beside her. Even if he hadn't volunteered to pick her up from her house and take her home again, he'd have come to see Shay and her little ones, just like he had with Tina when his first great-grandson had been born in this very hospital, too. For him, new life was a sight that never got old.

"Your girl seemed more restless this afternoon than she did yesterday," he said. "What did you think?"

"I agree. She'll be wanting to get those babies home."

"And something else?"

Mo tilted her head, considering. "I've not quite figured her out yet, Jed. She hasn't said a word to me about Tyler. Has she mentioned him to you?"

"Nope. Nor to Paz. More than likely she doesn't want to make a fuss. She doesn't ask about Cole or Pete or Mitch, except in general. If she singled Tyler out, how would she explain her interest in him, since she doesn't know *we* know why she's interested?"

Mo frowned. "It's a good thing I know how your mind works after all these years, Jed Garland, or I'd never have understood a word you just said."

He laughed. "You know darned well your mind's working just the same as mine. Now…once Shay gets home with those babies, we need to make sure she and Tyler have plenty of time alone with them."

"I don't see how that can happen. Our schedule's already full with women who have volunteered to come in to help."

"Schedules often change, Mo."

She smiled. "That's true enough, isn't it. And until then? I haven't a clue in my head as to what to do next."

"That's just it."

"What is?"

"We don't do anything next. We let nature take its course." He gestured toward the hospital. "Shay's been in here for a couple of days now, and I've got everybody at the Hitching Post staying quiet about how she's doing. I figure the less we say to Tyler, the easier it'll be to flush him out."

"Meaning…?"

"Meaning he can't show his hand by asking too much about Shay, either. But I don't think he'll be able to hold out much longer. Eventually, he's going to talk to me outright about her."

"And what are you going to tell him?"

Grinning, he started the pickup. "Haven't got a clue in my head."

Tyler parked his truck in the hospital lot between two cars only half its size. He hadn't wanted to come. Shay wouldn't want to see him. She wouldn't even admit to anyone he had fathered her babies. And still, here he was.

He had lasted three days. Three long days of hearing the Garlands talk about Shay and the kids without revealing much of anything new. Three frustrating days of learning next to nothing after Paz and Jed's visits to the hospital. Three anxious days without knowing how Shay was doing, other than Jed's uncharacteristically brief reports of "fine."

"Fine" didn't tell him anything.

The rest of the Garlands had to know he was the babies' dad, but it was as if they were deliberately shutting him out. He couldn't ask questions, couldn't show too much interest. Not after he'd made a point of telling Jed he had no plans of marrying Shay.

But what if they all were trying to hide something from him? Maybe that ride in the ambulance hadn't been good for her or the babies. Maybe something he'd said or done had upset her enough to make her go into labor early.

He needed to satisfy himself she really was okay, to obliterate the memory of his last sight of her—of her agonized face as the medics loaded her into the ambulance. Somehow, the fact he had witnessed her panic in that ambulance made him feel responsible for it. The fact he couldn't do anything for her had left him feeling helpless.

She'd had plenty of visitors since she had been checked into the hospital. The Garlands had said that much, and they'd mentioned that the staff was taking excellent care of her. She and the babies were in good hands. Still, he needed to see that for himself. Just once.

Inside the hospital, he made his way to the reception desk.

"Shay O'Neill," he said.

From memory, the teenage volunteer recited the room number and gave him directions for finding it. He considered himself lucky Shay hadn't left his name and description at the front desk along with a caution to the staff to keep him from visiting her.

After he'd pushed the call button for the elevator, he stared down at his hands. They were trembling. Worse, maybe, they were empty.

On the other side of the lobby he spotted the sign for the hospitality shop. Flowers, candy, stuffed animals and balloons filled the shelves inside. He could take his pick.

A stuffed tiger and a lion, both sporting blue bows, seemed to call to him to take them from the shelf. He also chose a plush gray elephant wearing a big pink-and-white-striped neck ruffle. At the last moment, he grabbed a large ceramic mug with a couple of balloons tied to the handle and "Mom" stenciled in both pink and blue multiple times around the outside.

"This looks just right for the new mother of a few kids, doesn't it," he said to the clerk at the register.

"Shay will love it."

Stunned, he stared at her. Maybe his description *had* been circulated throughout the hospital. After all, the day Shay had been brought here, no one had wanted him hanging around. Not Annabel. Not Mo or Jed. And especially not Shay.

Then he realized…small town, small hospital, three babies. It couldn't have been a stretch for the clerk to figure out his reference to a mother with multiple kids.

He left the shop with his arms full, refusing to admit

even to himself that he needed all this as an excuse for his visit.

When he reached the room, he felt immensely thankful to have something to hold on to. He spotted Shay first, sitting in a padded chair with wooden arms and legs. Her wheat-blond hair was ruffled, as if she'd rested her head against the chair for a nap. He wanted to reach out and smooth the strands into place. Instead, he clutched his peace offerings.

She seemed sleepy, her attention unfocused—until she registered him standing in the doorway. She said nothing, which made him doubly glad to have something to do with his unsteady hands.

She glanced past him to the doorway, maybe hoping someone would come along to kick him out. Then she stared across the room, as if searching for an answer from the babies. Finally, she looked back at him.

"Hey," he said, raising his purchases slightly. "I'm in charge of the new-baby welcome wagon." Stupidest remark he'd ever made. And yet his heart lightened when her lips curled slightly in a reluctant one-sided smile. "How are you doing?"

"Okay."

That didn't tell him much more than "fine."

"Are you sleeping all right?"

"Sleep? What's that?"

At least she still had a sense of humor. "Eating okay?"

She nodded. "I have to, since I'm feeding three."

"So." He cleared his throat. "Mind if I come in?"

"You already have."

It wasn't the warmest reply he might have gotten, but it would have to do. A look around him proved, sure enough, he had edged a step into the room. He couldn't back out now.

"Thought you might like this." He gestured with the mug and crossed the space between them to set it on the small table beside her. The balloons scuttled sideways above them like clouds in a driving wind.

"Thanks."

Smiling, he shrugged and held up the animals. "Didn't want anybody feeling left out."

She nodded, her eyes suddenly glistening.

Just as suddenly, he couldn't think of another thing to say.

Over against one wall, three cribs stood in a row.

"Want to take a peek?" she asked.

His throat tightened, and now he couldn't have spoken even if he'd come up with something else to discuss. Jed and Paz had said the babies were in a special room of their own. He hadn't thought about seeing them here. He didn't intend to walk over to them. But when a new mom sat looking at you the way Shay looked at him, you really didn't have a choice.

He clutched the stuffed animals, took a deep breath and nodded. As he took his first steps across the room, his legs threatened to give way. He attempted to tread lightly, not wanting the sound of his boots clomping on the tile floor to startle the occupants of the cribs.

He needn't have worried. They all looked sound asleep.

His throat tightened another notch. The babies were tinier than he'd expected and wrapped in blankets, blue for the boys and a pink one for the girl. He had heard Paz tell Tina and Jane their names and the order of their births. The same as the order of their cribs, with each name posted on a plastic card at the headboard.

Timothy. Jamie. Bree.

Gripping the stuffed animals, he looked down at the babies again.

Jamie and Bree lay curled up, completely covered and apparently comfortable in their blankets. Big brother Timothy had worked one hand free. On the edge of the blanket he had rested his fist, no bigger than a walnut and just about as wrinkled.

The sight of that fist, of the babies themselves, suddenly made it hard for him to catch his breath.

"They…uh…they've had jaundice," Shay said softly.

He hadn't heard her come up beside him. "They're—" His voice cracked. He tried again. "They're okay, though? They'll get over that?"

She nodded. "They're better now."

"When do you get to take them home?"

"Dr. Grayden says if all goes well with their checkups tomorrow morning, he'll release them then."

"That's good."

"Yes." She paused. "I appreciate all you did…the other day."

He nodded.

They stood beside each other, staring down at the cribs.

Finally, she sighed. "Well…thank you for the gifts," she said stiffly. Formally. In a tone meant to tell him his visit had ended.

He gestured with the toys in his arms. "What should I do with these? Put them in the cribs?"

She shook her head. "No, I don't think the nurses would go for that." A moment later, she said, "Maybe you should leave them at the Hitching Post. I can pick them up from there."

After you've gone.

That's what she meant. This time, both her tone and her expression got her message across. "You don't want me here, do you?"

She didn't answer. Her silence bothered him. He hadn't intended to stay once he'd seen her. He had only wanted to satisfy himself she was all right. He had done that now, hadn't he? And yet he didn't move. This stand-off reminded him of the day he had first come to the hospital.

"When they brought you in, I followed you," he blurted. "Followed the ambulance, I mean. They wouldn't let me ride with you. Downstairs, they wouldn't tell me what was going on. Not a word about how you were doing. Nothing about the babies' conditions. They shut me out, as if I had no rights at all."

For a moment, her expression froze. Her eyes seem to dull. She took a deep breath and sighed again. "I don't understand," she said finally, pacing her words. "You've already told me you don't want to be a father. You don't want a family. So why would it matter to you? Why do you even care about rights?"

Chapter 11

Tyler must not have realized how upset he had sounded. For a long moment Shay teetered on the brink of believing he cared about her and the babies more than he wanted her to know. After all, there he stood holding an armful of gifts for the triplets. Then she weighed her belief against what he had said that night at the Big Dipper.

Evidently her reminder about his not wanting kids or a family had hit home. Now, he said nothing. Her slim hope he had changed his mind disappeared as rapidly as the light left his eyes.

"You've got a point," he said.

"I thought so."

"But that doesn't do away with my obligations."

From the hallway, the rattle of a hospital cart on the tile flooring alerted her that Patsy, the day nurse, was on her way into the room. "You should go," she said quickly. "Morning visiting hours will be ending soon."

"I didn't hear an announcement."

"They don't broadcast that over the speakers in this wing. It's intensive care. But visits here are limited."

Patsy entered the room, pushing the cart ahead of her. "Lunchtime," she announced. "Ah, I see we have someone new to help today. Won't that be nice?"

Shay forced a smile. "He's just leaving."

From pure contrariness, she was sure, Tyler smiled at the nurse. Or maybe he had the reaction so practiced, he never had to think about it twice. The grandmotherly nurse responded to his playboy smile the way *she* had done at first sight, too—like a teenager in danger of breaking out in giggles at the attention of a cute boy.

"No, I'm not leaving yet." He set the animals on the edge of her bed. "Happy to lend a hand. What can I do? Clear off the table for Mom's lunch tray?"

And yes, Patsy giggled. "It's not Mom who's eating now, it's the babies."

The look of alarm on Tyler's face almost made up for his insistence on sticking around. Almost. He had been right a few minutes ago—she didn't want him here.

For their maternity patients, the hospital allowed a spouse more visiting time. If she had listed him as the father on her admittance forms, he could have been with her and the babies most of the day. As she had a private room, he could have stayed overnight. Her heart hurt at the loss of too many could-haves.

"Since I don't see any other visitors," Patsy went on, "I'm sure Mom will appreciate your help. So will I. Three babies are too much for one person to handle alone, and I've got to go check on a new patient we've just admitted. So let's get this assembly line going. Shall we start with Timothy, Shay, since he's always the one most interested in his bottle?"

"Yes," she said, trying to sound cheerful. Trying for the babies' sakes not to get upset.

As much as she longed to toss Tyler out of her room, she didn't dare. He had agreed with her point about his not caring about her babies. But he had pushed the issue about his obligations. If she spoke up, she wouldn't put it past him to claim his parental rights here and now.

Patsy wheeled the cart close to the bedside table and transferred the babies' bottles. Then she turned her attention back to him. "Your name is…"

"Tyler."

"All right, then, Tyler. Follow my lead. All you'll be required to do is carry the babies back and forth from their beds. Mom does all the rest."

She went to Timothy's crib. "Now, just in case you've never been told, what's most important with the little ones, infants especially, is that you support their heads. Both with lifting and while holding the babies. Like this." After her demonstration, she reached up to hand the baby to Tyler.

He took the infant hesitantly, then seemed at a loss.

Patsy laughed. "It's all right. Most people are a bit nervous the first few times they handle a newborn."

With her assistance, he held the baby in one arm. Tyler's height and the breadth of his shoulders made the blue-wrapped bundle appear even tinier against the black T-shirt snugly fitting his chest. The look of concentration on his face, his slight frown as he adjusted his hold, the careful way he crossed the room as if afraid he might drop her son, all made Shay's vision blur.

Blinking her eyes rapidly, she kept her head down and her gaze focused on Timothy as Tyler transferred him to her arms. Tyler's hands looked so big and sturdy as they cradled the baby, felt so warm as they brushed hers. He seemed so in control.

She couldn't believe that, though, considering he'd held her son for less than a minute. Just as she couldn't believe in him. This was all a playboy pose for the nurse's benefit.

"Have you had a good day, lass?" Grandma asked when she arrived for the afternoon visiting hour.

"A *very* good day," Shay said. "Dr. Grayden stopped in to see the babies. He said chances are still good we'll go home after the checkups tomorrow."

"Good. The house is quiet without you."

She laughed. "Enjoy it while you can, Grandma. I don't think it will ever be quiet again."

"And that's not such a bad thing, is it?"

"Not at all."

"You've had other visitors?"

Automatically, Shay's gaze went to the Mom mug with its colorful balloons and, beside it, the three stuffed animals. The toys sat in a row on the windowsill, a reminder of her babies lined up in their cribs. She had spent too much time this afternoon staring at those gifts. Resolutely, she looked away.

"Layne stopped in on her way to work, at the beginning of this afternoon's visiting hours." Feeling guilty, she slid past a mention of the visitor who'd arrived after Grandma had left this morning. But the fewer people who knew about him, the better.

Tyler had stayed longer than she had expected, long

enough for her to feed all three babies and for him to tuck them back into their cribs. She had planned to tell him she could handle Bree, who would be the last to eat, so that he could be on his way. But at that point, Patsy had bustled back into the room to check on her tiny patients.

He had made a big show of his expertise in carrying Jamie back to his crib and resettling him, then bringing Bree to Shay, all under Patsy's smiling approval.

She held back a sigh. The day he had insisted on helping to set up the babies' room, he had claimed that, after he left Cowboy Creek again, he would send her money for the babies. Seeing him here this morning had only made her wish he wanted to do much more. Yet, she knew better than to expect anything from him.

She looked up to see Grandma watching her and realized her thoughts had distracted her for too long. "You just missed Layne by a few minutes," she said quickly.

"I'll see her at SugarPie's later. Now, I hope you won't be too upset, but I've made arrangements to meet a few of the girls for supper. I may not make it back in time to visit with you tonight."

"That's fine. I'm going to try to nap as much as I can between feedings today. It won't be as easy for me to sleep once I'm home again."

"I'll be there to help, of course."

"Oh, I know you will. But I can't take up all your time. You've got so much going on."

"And what could be more important than taking care of my own great-grandbabies?"

"What about the knitting circle, and the bridge club, and everything else?"

"They rank far down the list after babies one, two

and three." Mo smiled. "Don't worry, lass, we'll work things out. And we've got all the ladies coming in to help us."

For the first few weeks, they would have daily hands-on assistance and the delivery of home-cooked meals from friends. After that, they had made plans to alternate their time with the babies so Shay could get back to work. Despite Grandma's telling her not to worry… she worried. Not that Grandma couldn't handle a baby on her own. But they were talking *three* babies.

Even as their mom, she wasn't sure how she would manage, but saying so might add to Grandma's unspoken concerns.

Luckily, she had other outlets for sharing her worries. Between Layne and Tina and Tina's cousin Andi, she would have plenty of people to go to when she needed to ask advice…at least, when it came to babies.

One of Shay's biggest worries showed up again for the evening visiting hours. When she heard a familiar tread in the hallway approaching her room, she closed her eyes in dismay, somehow hoping that not being able to see Tyler would mean he had disappeared.

When she opened her eyes again, he stood in the doorway, nearly filling it. Instantly, she thought of the first moment she had seen him, the day of Tina and Cole's wedding, dressed in a tux with a deep blue tie and cummerbund that made his eyes even bluer. He had walked through the doorway into the Hitching Post's small chapel looking so tall, so dark-haired and handsome. So *hot*. Now, she felt that same larger-than-life sensation and a powerful fluttering in her stomach.

"Did I wake you?" he asked.

She blinked, trying to chase the images and feelings away. "No. I was just…resting my eyes."

"Babies awake?"

"They have been, off and on."

He hung his Stetson on the corner of the extra visitor's chair. Then he took the other, quietly pulling it too close to her bed for comfort. So close she could see things she didn't want to see. This late in the day, his jaw sported a five-o'clock shadow, a dark growth she knew would feel prickly-soft against her fingertips.

He had changed into a long-sleeved white Western shirt that made his eyes look as blue as sapphires. The shirt brought back more memories she didn't want. She had once opened a shirt just like that one, snap by snap, planning to take it off him. But he'd turned the tables, reaching for the buttons on her blouse.

"You sure you're not sleeping?"

Starting, she blinked hard, then cleared her throat. "I'm awake. Wh-what are you doing here?"

"Jed was missing from the table at the Hitching Post tonight. Tina said he'd made plans with Mo for supper at SugarPie's."

She frowned. "Grandma's supposed to be meeting some of her friends. Female friends."

He shrugged. "Well, I guess Jed got himself invited along."

"That wouldn't take much," she agreed.

"Since they're tied up, I thought you might need an extra pair of hands. Have I missed the rounds tonight?"

"No. I expect at least one of the babies to wake up and be ready to eat soon."

"Good. Having three kids to practice with has made

me feel like I've passed a crash course. In fact, I think I'm due for some kind of merit badge."

She lost the fight not to smile. "I have to admit, I think I need one, too. *And* a medal for stamina. Between feeding and diapering, I've been putting one baby down only to pick up the next one."

"Like a merry-go-round that doesn't stop."

"Just like that," she said, surprised at how accurately he'd described what she had been feeling.

She should tell him to go. Patsy would soon be here with the bottles for the evening feeding, and the babies would awaken, and again she would have to see Tyler hold them close and carry them to her. Watching him this morning had been heart wrenching. She didn't want to have to face that again. She didn't want her babies to get used to having him around.

"Time for a bed check?" He tilted his head toward the cribs.

She hesitated, then gave in, only because she would never turn down a chance to look at her babies. "Let's go and see." Dr. Grayden had given his okay for her to get up and moving. In fact, her good progress was a deciding factor for her upcoming release from the hospital. She pushed aside the sheet covering her and stood.

Her eagerness had nothing to do with walking beside Tyler, with standing beside him in front of the cribs and looking down at the babies they had brought into the world. It had nothing to do with wanting to lean into his warmth and let him wrap his arms around her. Nothing to do with wishing, just for a few minutes, that being with their babies would somehow instantly make them a family.

After a moment, he reached down to touch Timothy's hand. "There's that fist again. Looks like this one's going to be a fighter."

"He'll need to be when he has to stick up for his little brother and sister."

"They ought to learn to do that for themselves."

"Well, yes. But it will be good for Jamie and Bree to have a protector if the schoolyard bullies start pushing them around. I didn't have any brothers or sisters to do that for me."

"Me, either. I didn't have anybody sticking up for me when I was a kid."

"Except your parents, you mean. The way Grandma did for me."

He laughed shortly. "My parents were the last ones to have my back. My father would tell me to fight my own battles, then push me outside again to 'face down my fears.' And my mom went right along with that."

"When you were still in school?"

"Yeah. High school. Grade school. Kindergarten."

"That's awful."

"That's my old man for you."

No wonder Tyler had talked about children becoming independent the minute they became adults. He had never known what it was like to receive a parent's unconditional love, the way she did from Grandma. Then again, he might be viewing his father from the perspective of a grade schooler or kindergartner.

"Maybe," she said, "in his eyes, he was helping you. Maybe trying to—"

"Trying to make a man out of me? Yeah, so he said. I hope that's not the way you plan to go about it with the kids." As if he felt uncomfortable, he looked back at the babies. "Anyway, these three were only born a few minutes apart from each other. Who's to say Bree won't be the leader of the pack? Equal rights from nursery school on."

She laughed. "I like that idea."

A smile played on his lips, softening the hard lines of his shadowed jaw. She liked that, too.

Sobering, she looked down at the babies again. She didn't want to like anything about Tyler. She didn't want to see anything else that would bring back memories they had shared. But that was an impossible wish.

With a sigh, she stroked the small patch of hair atop Bree's head. The color wasn't as dark as Tyler's. But like her brothers', Bree's brown fluff was already much darker than Shay's blond hair. Chances were, all the babies would eventually have a shade much closer to Tyler's rich, dark brown.

She would always have visual reminders of him, whether or not she wanted them—and she didn't. A few minutes of feeling closer to him couldn't make up for the fact he chose not to stay.

Chapter 12

After an early breakfast at the Hitching Post, Tyler left the hotel. The sun was already bright, promising a warm day. Long, empty hours stretched ahead of him, and he planned a ride to fill up some of that time. He couldn't have described his surroundings, could never have found his way back to the hotel later on, if not for Freedom. He trusted the stallion to be his eyes and ears.

More than once, he had acknowledged he'd long passed the point he should have headed back to Texas. That wasn't going to happen while he had unfinished business here.

He returned from his ride midmorning, and had just settled Freedom in his stall again when Cole came into the barn.

"Tyler, we meet at last. You're making a real habit of disappearing. I went to the dining room for breakfast, and Jed said you had eaten already. And when I finished reading Robbie a story after supper last night, I couldn't find you anywhere."

"Keeping tabs on me?"

"No. But it looks like I might have to start, just to make sure you stay out of trouble. Where'd you run off to last night?"

"The hospital." During the evening visiting hours, his conversation with Shay about the babies had given him the feeling he had made a degree of progress at winning her over, that he had taken one step down the road to making her understand he was serious about helping her…financially.

"How are Shay and the kids? Tina went into town to see them the other day and said those babies are really something. Then again, she says that about every kid."

"They *are* something, all three of them. Cutest babies I've ever seen." Not that he'd seen many of them that up close and personal. "Smart, too."

"Sounds like you've got a big helping of fatherly pride there."

He shrugged. "Just stating the truth. When I went back last night—"

"Back? You mean you went there before?"

"Yesterday morning. What's the matter, doesn't the Cowboy Creek gossip make it out here to the ranch?"

Cole snorted. "Sometimes I think it all gets reported in here. Jed always knows what's going on—though I'm not knocking him. I told you before, he's got a good heart. Now, what makes these kids of yours so smart?"

"When I picked them up out of their cribs again last night, they recognized me."

"How could you tell?"

"They smiled at me."

Cole snickered. "Man, newborns don't smile. They were only making faces at you because they were passing gas."

"No, they weren't."

Now the other man laughed out loud. "You think you have this new-daddy role figured out, don't you?" When Tyler frowned, Cole raised both hands. "Calm down. I'm just pulling your leg, not picking on your kids."

The comment made him think of what he'd said to Shay about his father not supporting him. He hadn't intended to tell her that, but her easy assumption about his parents being as caring as Mo pushed him into it.

"There won't be anybody picking on Timothy once he gets bigger." He went on to tell Cole about the little boy's strength, Bree's patience, Jamie's playfulness... and a handful of other things. He hadn't realized he'd noted so much in just a couple of visits with the babies. After a while, he had to force himself to come to a stop. "Guess I'm boring you with all these stories."

"What are you talking about? I'll be trying to one-up you with stories of my own as soon as Tina has the baby. Speaking of which, you ought to think about staying around till then."

Suspicion made Tyler snap his response. "What for?"

"I already let the boss know I'll be taking time off once the baby arrives. We'll be shorthanded. That might be a good opportunity for you to slide right into a permanent spot here on the ranch. If you and Shay get a few things settled and you decide to stay, you'll need the work."

"Not going to happen, so don't go trying to play matchmaker." He'd already warned Jed about that, too.

"You ought to know." Cole shrugged. "Well, whatever happens, I'm taking the break. I might already be a daddy, but this is the first time I'll be around to see my son or daughter as a newborn. And this time, I'm not missing out on a thing."

When Cole walked away, Tyler stood deep in thought. Once he was gone from Cowboy Creek, there would be lots of new things happening with the babies, plenty of progress he'd never know about.

What did that matter? As Shay had reminded him, he didn't plan to get attached to the kids. He didn't intend to stick around. But while he was here, he had to stay close to her. It was plain from their truce last night that helping her with the babies was the key to earning her trust.

Tyler drove along Canyon Road, the center of Cowboy Creek, feeling in a better frame of mind than he had in quite some time. After leaving the barn, he had run into Jed in the hotel hallway. The man claimed he'd been trying to hunt him down.

Between Jed and Cole, he didn't lack for people keeping an eye on him. But any irritation he might have felt fled once he'd finished talking with Jed.

Now, in the hospital parking lot, he tapped the hood of the car for good luck.

According to Jed, Shay had been given the okay from her doctor to bring the babies home. Upstairs, he found her in her room. Today her hair was smooth and flowing down her back. She wore a loose yellow top, jeans and a pair of running shoes. A small overnight bag sat on the floor beside the chair.

She looked at him in surprise. "What are you doing here?"

That seemed to be her standard question every time she saw him. Maybe his luck wasn't going to hold out, after all. "I'm taking you and the kids home."

"Grandma said she was picking us up."

"Jed told me Mo asked for help. Something about her women's circle and a big project they have to wrap up. She needed a stand-in, and Jed volunteered me. Are you ready to go?"

He could see the indecision in her face, the reluctance to accept his help at odds with the excitement at taking the kids home. So much for the truce he thought had been struck between them.

His luck held—her excitement won out.

"Yes, we're ready. Annabel's on her way with the wheelchair."

His mind flashed to the image of her being carried by stretcher to the ambulance. "Wheelchair? Is something wrong?"

"No. It's just a hospital rule."

"Oh." He forced a laugh. "Yeah, they have a lot of those around here."

She went to the cribs. He followed. The triplets were out of hospital wear today, too. They wore knitted caps and were wrapped in knitted baby blankets—blue for Timothy, green for Jamie and yellow for Bree.

"Three colors this time," he said.

"Yes. I didn't want to go with traditional pink and blue, anyway, and the reason for all the colors is, I didn't know how many of each we'd need."

"You didn't find out the sex of the babies beforehand?"

"No." She smiled. "I wanted to be surprised."

At least there had been *some* news she hadn't held back from him.

He glanced down again. "Well, you've got a pair, any-how," he said, lifting Bree from the crib. He didn't care what Cole had told him—the baby's smile proved she recognized him. "She's all dressed up to match her mom."

"I didn't think of that," Shay said softly. "These were the first caps and blankets Grandma made, so I wanted them to be the first the babies used."

"Good idea. And since there are two of you dressed in yellow, obviously that color wins."

"I didn't think about that, either. But it's not a contest. We're all in this together."

Her words hung in the air for a long moment, and he wondered if she'd said them deliberately. *We* meant her and the babies. It didn't include him.

The silence stretched on as they stood there together, staring down at both boys in their cribs. Watching the babies sleep seemed to cast a spell over him, helping to push away some of his tension.

Annabel's cheerful arrival broke that spell. She had brought a couple of nurses with her to help carry the babies. A teenager wearing a volunteer badge said she had come along to assist with everything Shay had collected over the days she'd spent here. He noted she—or maybe a nurse—had put the three stuffed animals and the mug with the balloons on the windowsill.

He was still holding Bree. "I'm the official driver. I can carry Bree downstairs and take a bag of those gifts, too."

"I'm afraid not," Annabel said.

"Let me guess. You're not allowed to let me do that."

"You've got it." She gave him her small, sympathetic smile. "But as you're the chauffeur, you *can* go downstairs and bring your vehicle to the rear entrance of the building. You do have car seats for all three of the babies, don't you?"

"Of course."

To his satisfaction, this earned him a full smile from every female in the room—except Bree, who had fallen asleep snuggled against his chest.

Their release from the hospital turned out to hold more surprises than Shay had expected.

The first had been seeing Tyler walk into her room and announce why he was there. She still wondered about Grandma's sudden absence. Yet, to her secret shame, she couldn't manage to suppress her little rush of happiness at knowing Tyler would help take the babies home.

She also couldn't keep from eyeing him when he wasn't looking. The sight of him standing in the bright sunshine streaming through the window beside her bed was enough to dazzle her. But it was the details that held her gaze. His dark hair gleamed, his belt buckle sparkled and his boots shone, as if he'd made a special effort to dress up this morning.

He had definitely made an impression with all three nurses and the teenage volunteer.

After he had left the room, the staff escorted her to the elevator for the trip downstairs.

"Was that your boyfriend?" the volunteer asked.

Keeping her gaze focused on her babies, she simply shook her head.

"He's a friend of Jed Garland's," Annabel announced. "Just came to give Shay and the triplets a ride home."

"Well," one of the other nurses said with a laugh, "any friend of Jed's is a friend of mine."

"Mine, too," the teenager said eagerly.

Listening to the women's conversation as they waited for the elevator, she fully expected them all to request Tyler's autograph when they saw him again downstairs. Or, in the case of the volunteer, to ask him for a date.

The little rush running through her now was a surge of pure jealousy, something she had no right or desire to feel. Resolutely, she pushed it down and determined to forget it. She didn't care who went after that cowboy.

The second surprise arrived when they reached the lobby, where a reporter from the local newspaper greeted them.

"Smile for the camera," she called.

Shay didn't need the encouragement. From the moment she had woken up that morning, she had been smiling from sheer happiness at the thought of taking her babies home.

Worry over how she would get rid of Tyler once they got there didn't make her quite as happy.

When he walked into the lobby, the reporter immediately latched on to him.

"No pictures," he said quickly. "I'm only the designated driver."

"Just one shot," she said, pretending to pout.

Shay frowned. He wouldn't believe in that act, would he? And what was wrong with the reporter, anyway? They had gone through school together, and in all those years she had never once seen the woman act this way.

Then again, the teenager and the two younger nurses were fawning over Tyler now, too, trying to convince him to take advantage of the photo opportunity. And yesterday, Patsy had giggled like a teenager.

Maybe his playboy charm was irresistible to any woman.

Maybe she shouldn't beat herself up for having fallen so hard and so fast. But she certainly wouldn't let herself fall again. She cared for him now as much as he had *ever* cared about her—which meant not one bit.

Her two attendant nurses put her sons into her arms, and she forgot about Tyler altogether...until he spoke again.

"I'm happy to hold a baby for the photo," he told the reporter, "as long as Shay agrees."

All five women swung their heads in her direction. Tyler stared at her, too. She stiffened, then forced herself to relax. With him acting so accommodating, she couldn't afford to look like the bad mom in this situation. Besides, after only a minute, the photo shoot would be over and they could be on their way.

All that mattered was her babies were going home.

The thought made her smile again.

Evidently taking that as an agreement, the reporter set them up for the photo. Shay sat in the wheelchair holding Timothy and Jamie. Tyler stood behind them with Bree in his arms.

After the reporter had gotten a number of shots, Annabel urged their group to the doors. "I know this is a big day for Cowboy Creek, but these babies need to get home for their next feeding."

"True," Tyler said. "Let's get them all strapped in."

And then came the final surprise of Shay's morning. When Annabel wheeled her out of the building, she saw the vehicle standing at the curb.

"You brought my car? And you had it washed?" she asked him in disbelief.

"Cleaned it myself," he said smugly. "Detailed it inside and out, too. I didn't think Annabel would approve of newborn babies in a dust-covered vehicle." The nurse laughed. "And after you've just had three babies, I sure don't want you having to climb up to get inside my pickup."

His concern about her children's health and her comfort touched her more than she could say. "Thanks," she murmured. But the word was drowned out by the awws and exclamations from all the women.

Tyler Buckham, playboy, strikes again.

They were halfway home before she remembered she didn't care.

His plan was working.

Shay had been grateful he'd cleaned up her car for the ride home with the babies. Once they'd gotten to the house and upstairs to the babies' bedroom, she had seen the fully assembled cribs and turned away just a second too late to hide her suddenly teary eyes. Both reactions had to mean he'd taken at least one more step forward.

He looked around the room. "Mo said to wait for you to decide how you wanted everything set up."

"It's fine the way it is," she said faintly.

"What about this…whatever you'd call it? You surely don't want it here in the middle of the room."

"It's a changing table. Over there along the wall by the closet will work, please."

She had already prepared the bottles and was feeding Bree, sitting with her in a small pine rocker in one corner of the room.

Finished moving the table, he looked across at her and the baby. "Ladies first for a change, huh? That's a surprise."

"There have been a lot of surprises this morning." She paused, then continued, "When I went to get Timothy, Bree was already fussing."

"Is she done eating now? Let me put her in the crib." He took the baby from her. "Who do you want next?"

She hesitated, then said, "Timothy. He's been kicking at his blanket."

"He's not used to being second. And that's not like Bree to want to eat first. The other times I've been around, she's been willing to wait."

"I think she wanted to get ahead of the boys. I guess she's learning to assert her rights."

She put a slight emphasis on her final word. Again, an awkward silence fell, the way it had in her hospital room just before the nurses had shown up. What had she said then? *We're all in this together.* She and the babies.

Now he knew she'd deliberately aimed that comment at him. She had wanted to get the point across he was the odd man out. He handed Timothy to her and took a step back. "You might as well say outright what you're thinking."

Another silence fell. For a minute, he thought she was going to deny anything was bothering her. Then she took a deep breath and said flatly, "I don't like that you just showed up this morning without letting me know first."

"I told you, Jed asked me."

"But I didn't. I didn't know anything about it."

"I had no control over that."

"Even so, I don't like you thinking you can walk right into my hospital room and take over."

"I was trying to help out."

"The nurses were there."

"Forget that," he snapped. "This is all misunderstandings and things easily explained. Surface stuff. Why don't you go deep and tell me what's really bothering you?"

She cuddled Timothy close to her as if to shield the baby.

His heart thudded. She couldn't possibly feel she had to protect her kids from their own dad.

He blinked. When had he started thinking of himself in that role?

The deep breath he took didn't do much to steady his heart and his nerves.

No matter what he thought or what he did, he wouldn't win with Shay. She was determined to reject his good intentions. Clamping his jaws together, trying to hold back a response that wouldn't help matters at all, he simply stared at her.

She said nothing.

Despite his irritation, the steady creaking of the rockers on the wooden floor and the sight of her feeding Timothy began to calm him. Even Shay had seemed to relax a bit, her expression looking more serene.

He had a feeling this happy state wouldn't last long.

Before either of them could speak again, he heard the sound of the front door closing downstairs, then Mo's greeting. "Where are those great-grandbabies of mine?"

"In their bedroom," he called back.

Instantly, an expression of annoyance crossed Shay's face.

"What?" he demanded. "You think I'm taking over again, just because I answered Mo? Better that than have you yelling in Timothy's ear."

"It's not that," she said swiftly. "I don't think you should be here, around the babies. They'll just start getting used to you, and then you'll be gone."

"They're already used to me."

"No, they're not." She looked stricken but kept her voice hushed, probably because she heard Mo's footsteps in the hallway. "I want you to go."

He said nothing.

A few moments later, Mo entered the room and Shay said brightly, "Grandma's here now. She can help me."

"That I can't, I'm afraid," Mo said. "We've had an emergency call from the women's club, and they need me at the community center right away. I just stopped in for a moment to welcome you all home." She cupped her hand on Timothy's head and smoothed his hair. "There's my little love. *And* his brother and sister." She moved over to the cribs. "Tyler, you should unwrap Jamie's blanket a bit before he gets overheated."

He crossed the room.

"Grandma," Shay said almost plaintively, "can't you stay at least for a little while?"

"You'll be fine," Mo said in the same soothing tone she had used with Timothy. Obviously, she thought Shay was requesting assistance with the kids.

Tyler knew she wanted Mo to stay so he would leave.

"Where's Carol?" Shay asked. "I thought she was on the list to be here today."

"She was, but she called me earlier. Her own little one is down with the sniffles, and Carol doesn't want to bring any sickness around the babies. And rightly so." She smiled. "Isn't it fortunate we have Tyler here to help?"

Chapter 13

Shay awoke with a start. She still sat in the rocking chair in one corner of the babies' room. Her first thoughts flew to the triplets, but from her seat she could see they all lay sleeping peacefully in their cribs.

Confused, she stared down at the afghan draped across her. She didn't remember covering herself with it. The last thing she recalled was Tyler taking Bree from her at the end of another round of feedings. She had watched him place the baby in her crib, then stop by each of the boys' cribs to check on them.

She had closed her eyes tightly to block out the sight of him and to stem back a sudden flow of tears.

And now here she was.

The room faced west, and sunlight slanting through the windows told her it was later in the afternoon. Horrified, she realized she had no idea exactly how long she had slept. Part of her day had disappeared. Evidently, so had Tyler.

She also realized she didn't know who was in the house with her.

After a quick check of the baby monitor on the dresser, she made her way downstairs. From the kitchen, the homey sounds of refrigerator and cupboard doors being opened and closed calmed her tension. Grandma was home again.

But it wasn't Grandma who stood at the stove holding a wooden spoon and stirring a small pot on one of the burners.

"Tyler! What are you still doing here?"

Muttering a curse, he started. The spoon fell to the floor. He picked it up and tossed it into the sink before turning to face her. "It would have been nice if you had coughed or something instead of sneaking up on me like that. Suppose I'd been holding one of the babies?"

He had a point. Flushing, she said, "Sorry. I just woke up. I'm not fully functional yet. And I don't know how I could have crashed like that. I didn't miss hearing any of the babies crying, did I?"

"Nope. I stayed upstairs for a while after you all went to sleep. And I haven't heard a peep out of that." With a fresh wooden spoon from the crock near the refrigerator, he gestured to the baby monitor on the counter.

"Thank goodness for that," she breathed. "But why are you still here? Where's Grandma?"

"She called a while ago and said she wouldn't be home again until later this afternoon."

She hadn't even heard the phone ring. "And you are…?" She pointed toward the stove, where steam rose from their biggest stockpot.

"I'm making supper."

"Grandma *asked* you to do that?"

"No. I volunteered. I make a mean baked ziti. I hope you're hungry." At that, her stomach gave a loud growl. He grinned. "Guess that answers my question."

"Of course I'm hungry. I haven't eaten since early this morning at the hospital."

"And the ziti won't be ready till tonight. Well, that won't do. How's tea and toast sound? That's about the only other thing I'm good for. Or eggs, if you'd rather have those."

"Toast sounds great," she admitted, "but you don't have to cook for me."

"I'm waiting for the water to boil, and you know what they say about a watched pot. Have a seat." He took the loaf of wheat bread from the bread box. "You have to eat to help keep up your strength to feed the babies. And you might as well conserve your energy while you have the chance."

Though it hadn't been a long walk from the kitchen to the bedroom, she was still feeling tender from her C-section. Her usual chair seemed to call to her. She took a seat at the table and, while Tyler's back was to her, watched each move he made. Filling the teakettle. Unerringly finding the plates in the cupboard near the sink and taking the butter dish from the top shelf of the refrigerator door. Adding pasta to the stockpot on the stove. He worked as if he were comfortable in the room, but as far as she knew, he'd never been in her kitchen... only in her bedrooms, both old and new.

After a few minutes, he carried her plate and tea mug to the table and set them down in front her. Then he went to the seat at the head of the table as if he had sat there many times before.

She stiffened.

"Don't worry," he said, "it's been washed more than once in hot, soapy water."

Only then did she notice the mug he had given her with the word *Mom* stenciled on it multiple times. Her eyes watered. She bit her lip to hide the smile that came so naturally to her. The smile she didn't want him to see. "How are you managing to find your way around our kitchen so easily?"

"Mo told me where to find the stew pot. The utensil drawer's easy to spot. Everything else is just common sense. Besides, I saw the dish cabinet when she gave me a cup of tea and a piece of cake."

"Today?"

"No, yesterday afternoon. I stopped by after I left the hospital."

Glancing down, she traced the handle of the mug with her finger. "When you finished assembling the cribs."

"Yeah."

Setting up the cribs had been his "least I could do" offer and part of the bargain that, technically, she hadn't yet agreed to when her pains had begun. Visiting her and the kids at the hospital, complete with gifts for them all, had gone beyond that least of his efforts. Bringing her and the babies home from the hospital, staying here with them, making tea and toast and ziti all were so far above *and* beyond what she had expected, she didn't know what to say.

She knew what she wanted to *believe*...but that wasn't somewhere her thoughts should go.

"Thank you for your help with the cribs and the bedroom," she said.

"No problem."

"Also for backing me up this afternoon. I don't know how I could have fallen so soundly asleep with three new babies to watch over." She paused, then added, "And I don't know what would have happened if you weren't here."

"If they had cried, you'd have woken up."

"I hope so."

"You would've. It's one of those mother's instincts you just haven't had to put to the test yet."

"Oh, really? And how would you know about that?" He smiled. His blatant attempt to make her feel better worked better than it should have. The smile did even more, sending a wave of pleasure through her. Again, she hesitated. Finally, she said, "You covered me with the afghan upstairs, too."

"Yeah. I didn't have the heart to wake you to see if you wanted it or not. You looked so tired."

She smiled wryly. "You're always good for a compliment, huh, Tyler?"

"I'm good for a lot of things." He reached out as if planning to touch her cheek. For a moment, he held his hand in the air. Then he pushed the plate a little closer to her. "Eat."

She took a bite from a half slice of toast. When she looked up again, he sat staring back solemnly, his gaze unblinking, his black lashes contrasting with his blue eyes. She drew in a breath and choked on a mouthful of crumbs. Covering her mouth with her arm, she coughed. And coughed.

He reached over and patted her back. "Now, that's

the noise you should've made when you walked in here, instead of scaring me half to death."

She couldn't help but laugh.

His hand on her back stilled. His splayed fingertips grazed the back of her neck above her shirt, spreading warmth across her skin, sending hot shivers along her shoulders. Her mouth dried. She pressed her lips together, wanting to lick the taste of melted butter away but afraid he would take it as a tease. Resting his fingers against her neck might have been a move as innocent as when he cradled one of her babies' heads in his big hand.

Then he leaned closer, his eyes gleamed, and she knew her rationalizing hadn't come close to the truth. His touch was anything but innocent and his intentions even less so.

She wanted to protest. She had so many reasons to protest...

Before she could name one of them, he brushed his mouth against hers. All she could think of was how much time had passed since they had been together like this and just how much she had missed his kiss. Missed *him*.

Their relationship last summer hadn't given them much time with one another, but they hadn't needed time to learn what they each liked in a kiss. As he'd done back then, he started soft and easy and sweet but soon sent the heat level soaring. She could swear she heard a sizzle each time their lips parted and met again. Then she realized the sizzling was more than a feeling against her lips—it was a sound filling the air.

It was the sound of starch-filled water spattering on the stove top.

"I think something's burning," she murmured against his mouth.

"Darned straight," he said enthusiastically.

"No, I think something's burning on the stove."

He sat back, looked across the room and swore under his breath.

She wanted to pull him to her again, to lose herself in another kiss, to forget why she should keep her distance and why he wasn't the man for her. She didn't dare do any of that. Despite how his kisses made her feel, she couldn't give in. He didn't really care for her. He was just a playboy doing what he did best.

She sat back and grabbed her tea mug and stared down at it. The words inscribed on it danced before her eyes, reminding her just why she should protest if Tyler ever came close to her again.

If anyone had ever told Tyler he would be having dinner with this family of five, three of them babies under the age of one week and one of them a woman he'd like under—

Whoa!

He reined in, bringing his thoughts to a bone-jolting halt. How could he think of the babies and…and want their mother, all in the same breath?

Looking down, he stabbed at his plateful of baked ziti, probably the best he'd ever made. It tasted as dry as dust to him. Fortunately, the other two adults in the room didn't think so.

"Tyler, you may cook for us anytime," Mo said, forking up another mouthful of pasta.

He smiled but didn't speak. There wouldn't be an *anytime*. That kiss this afternoon had shown him that.

He needed to settle things with Shay. Tonight. After that, he wouldn't be back.

"This is delicious," Mo went on. "Isn't it, Shay?"

Beside him, she nodded but kept her gaze on her plate.

"It's my specialty. I'm not good at cooking much else," he admitted.

I'm good for a lot of things, he had said to Shay just before he lost the willpower to keep from kissing her.

Her gaze snapped up to meet his, then away. Was she remembering, too?

Both the statement and the kiss had been foolish moves on his part, considering the circumstances and his need to earn her trust. Worse, that foolishness had caused a major setback to his plan.

She had escaped from the kitchen while his back was turned and, for the rest of the afternoon, had stayed upstairs. After he'd gotten the ziti into the oven, he'd ventured up there, too, intending to apologize for his actions. He'd lost his nerve once he saw she sat holding one of the babies.

One of *their* babies...

Then Mo had arrived and he'd lost his chance, as well as his nerve. He had left the women together with the kids and come back downstairs to put the finishing touches on supper. Wanting to keep busy, to keep his mind occupied with something other than babies and kisses and Shay, he scrubbed the pots and utensils he had used to make supper. Then he needed another diversion. He had sat at the kitchen table with a copy of the local paper spread open in front of him.

At the supper table now, he smiled, thinking of the photo shoot at the hospital that morning and wondering when the picture would appear. He glanced across the room to the portable playpen Shay had set up in a quiet corner. He could see Timothy stirring. The kids would soon outgrow that small space, and the boy's strength could create a problem.

Tyler considered. He'd have to…

No, he would have to do nothing except give Shay enough money to buy a bigger playpen.

"I'll make corned beef and cabbage for you one night," Mo said. "It doesn't call for as much work as your dish. Still, it's one of our favorites."

He could envision more nights around this table, with the babies a little bigger and sitting up in high chairs, spreading mashed-up peas on the trays with their fingers. A good thing the adults and kids were evenly matched.

Once he was gone, the adults would be outnumbered.

He couldn't control that. But he could keep Mo—and Shay—from making plans around him. "I doubt I'll be here for too many more nights."

Again, Shay's gaze snapped to his, then moved away.

Mo sent him an unreadable half smile.

Timothy let out a little wail. Shay pushed back her chair and went to the playpen.

He had no clue what Mo's expression meant. He didn't care to know. Not wanting to encourage her and grateful for the excuse to look away, he glanced over at the babies. "Sounds like that boy's lungs are getting stronger by the day. You're going to have yourselves a time when they all start yelling like that at once."

"We are, indeed," Mo agreed.

Shay lifted Timothy from the playpen. "I'll take him upstairs. He likes me to rock him while he eats."

He watched her cross the room and walk through the doorway. He wondered whether she had left just to get some distance from him. The thought shouldn't have bothered him. But it did.

He looked back to find Mo staring at him from across the table. She smiled, a full smile this time. "You've been wonderful these past few days, Tyler, helping with the cribs and then bringing the babies home with Shay. I don't know what we'd have done without you today, too. I'm grateful to have your help again tomorrow."

"Tomorrow? I don't—"

She leaned forward and said in an urgent whisper, "Let's turn off that baby monitor for a moment, shall we? It picks up sound from both directions, and I'd just as soon keep this conversation between us."

Nodding, he rose. What was this about? A prickle of unease made his shoulders stiffen. Once he had turned off the monitor, he went back to his seat.

"You've been very giving of your time," Mo said quickly, "and I would never ask this of you if I weren't in a bind. But that's exactly it, you see. I've run into some trouble. Our helper scheduled for tomorrow has had to cancel, too. And just the hour or so upstairs with Shay and the babies this afternoon wore me out." She sighed. "Though I would never in a million years say this to Shay, I'm forced to admit it to you. Tyler, three babies are just too much for me to handle."

I need your help.

She didn't have to say it. He could see it in her eyes.

Now a hint of mistrust blended with his unease. The woman looked spry enough to him. She sure seemed to have enough get-up-and-go to roam all over town. It sounded like she all but ran the women's club and the knitting circle and a bunch of other groups. But despite her apparent energy and her clear green eyes, as he had already noted, her hair was as snow white as Jed's. No doubt she came somewhere close to the man's seventysomething years.

He also had noticed how much those green eyes were like Shay's.

Unlike her granddaughter lately, Mo held his gaze. He couldn't have looked away if his life depended on it.

And he wouldn't turn her down.

It felt good to finally have *someone* willing to trust and depend on him.

Chapter 14

Finished settling Timothy in his crib, Tyler turned to watch Shay. She stood at the changing table closing the snaps on Jamie's pajamas, just as he had done a minute ago with Timothy. "I'm getting pretty good at this baby-changing business, don't you think?"

She threw him a glance. "*Pajama* changing, you mean. You don't get credit for the full job unless you've changed the diaper, too."

"Well, that's where I have to draw the line. But my tucking skills aren't bad, either. Here, give Jamie to me. I'll put him back in his crib."

He had given in to Mo's request for more help. Since his return this morning, he and Shay had tiptoed around each other—and not solely because they didn't want to wake the kids.

She had been careful to keep out of his reach ever

since he'd kissed her yesterday. Obviously, she regretted that kiss as much as he did. There was nothing he could do about his actions except apologize. The opportunity for that conversation had never arisen, and he felt reluctant to bring it up now.

When he walked up to her, she nearly shied away. Just as obviously, she was still being careful, choosing not to get too close to him again. She had the right idea. They seemed to have reinstated the truce that had been broken after they'd brought the babies home from the hospital. He didn't want to say anything to damage that again.

He lifted Jamie, holding the baby's head the way the nurse had taught him. "Doc Grayden's going to be impressed when he sees this big guy. He's put on weight since we brought him home."

"They all have."

Rooting for the underdog, he had already starting encouraging the smaller of the two boys to be more active. "He's getting to be as strong as Timothy already, too. Watch this." Carefully, he touched his little finger to Jamie's fist. The baby spread his tiny fingers, then latched them around Tyler's pinky. "That's the way, buddy," he murmured. Grinning, he told Shay, "He did that yesterday for the first time. Now whenever I touch his fist, he grabs on. He thinks it's a game."

"Does he?"

"Sure he does." And every time those little fingers wrapped around his, Tyler felt his chest constrict. "I bet he'll be great with a lasso."

"I doubt he'll ever have his hands on one."

"Why not? This is cowboy country. Ropin' needs to be on every kid's list of skills."

"No, it doesn't. Not if he doesn't plan to be a cowboy. And he won't. Neither will Timothy."

Frowning, Tyler returned Jamie to his crib. After a deep breath, he turned to face Shay again. "The babies aren't a week old yet. How can you know what they'll want to be when they grow up?"

"I'm their mom."

"That's a heck of a reason. And a crazy one. You can't plan your kids' entire lives when they're still in the cradle." Too bad nobody had told his parents that. "But I guess some people don't care. You and my folks would get along just fine."

"They don't like having a rodeo cowboy for a son?" she asked coolly.

"I think sometimes they don't like having a son at all. But no, they don't like the fact I'm a cowboy."

"Because they probably want more for you than that."

"Why do I need more?" Her words and expression made something click in his mind. "The afternoon we came back here with your shower gifts, you told me you appreciated the reminder I was *only* a rodeo cowboy. What did that mean?"

"Nothing. That's what you are, isn't it?"

"Yeah. But why did you need the reminder?"

She shrugged. "No reason."

He didn't buy that answer for a minute. She had a reason, all right, and though he was *only* a rodeo cowboy, not a rocket scientist, he had figured it out. "You're not going to let the kids make up their own minds. You're going to keep them from becoming wranglers because *I'm* one, aren't you?"

"Don't flatter yourself."

He clenched his jaw. Clearly, she wasn't any more

impressed than his parents were by his choice of career. Like them, she felt cowboys didn't amount to much.

Shay watched anxiously as Dr. Grayden went to each crib in turn, checking the triplets' eyes and ears and testing their reflexes. When he touched Jamie's hand, she couldn't help but smile as she recalled Tyler grinning with pleasure over Jamie clutching his finger. Over Jamie playing their game.

At the thought of the rest of that conversation, her smile slid away.

Once, her dad's broken promises had broken her heart. Tyler's refusal even to make promises hurt so much more. She would cope—she would always survive, even without him. But *how* could she have fallen for a rodeo cowboy just like her dad?

Dr. Grayden tucked his wire-rimmed glasses into his breast pocket and turned to her. "I'd say they're thriving, Shay. Amazing what a steady diet and a little love can do, isn't it?"

"A lot of love, Doctor," she corrected. "Grandma and I and…well, the two of us just can't get enough of them."

"That's good. Sometimes with multiple births, a new mother is too tired to interact with her babies except during feedings. Physical contact is critical, especially in these early days."

"No problems there." Even Tyler had done his fair share of holding the babies. Connecting to the babies. But not for much longer. She sighed.

"Something worrying you?"

She started, not realizing he had heard her sigh. She shrugged. "I have to admit to being tired."

He patted her arm. "That's almost a given with one

baby. With three it's impossible to avoid. I gather you're having no trouble sleeping when you have the opportunity?"

"Oh, no," she assured him as they left the bedroom. "I nap every chance I get." Guiltily, she thought of waking up in the rocking chair. She had been truthful with Tyler—she didn't know what she would have done if he hadn't been there.

Downstairs, Dr. Grayden repeated the results of the babies' checkup for the benefit of Grandma and Layne. Once he had left, Grandma gestured to the teapot on the coffee table.

"A cup for you, Shay?"

She nodded and reached to take her Mom mug from the tray. Grandma must have noticed that she had started to use it. The mug had already become her favorite… because she *was* a mom now, multiple times over, and not because Tyler had been the one to give it to her.

After Grandma had poured the tea, she said, "I think I'll just go up and check on my great-grands."

Shay and Layne looked at the baby monitor on the end table beside the couch, then exchanged smiles.

As they watched Grandma move out of sight up the stairs, Shay murmured, "She hasn't had as much time as she'd like with the babies. She's been so busy, even more than normal." She frowned. After a moment, she realized Layne hadn't responded. She looked over to find her friend eyeing her.

"And…?" Layne asked.

"And what?"

Layne rolled her eyes. "Mo might be busy, but I hear you're not all on your own with the babies. She tells me

Tyler was here all day yesterday, and today, too, until he left just a while ago. What's up?"

"I don't know. It's very odd. Every person on our list of mother's helpers has let us down."

"That's not what I mean, and you know it."

Shay pulled the afghan from the back of the couch and settled it in her lap as if it could shield her from Layne's question and from thoughts she didn't want to have. The action again made her recall waking up in the rocking chair to find Tyler had draped an afghan over her. He looked after her as well as he did the babies.

When Grandma had arrived home this afternoon, followed a few minutes later by Layne, Tyler had announced he was off to run errands. He hadn't been gone five minutes when she found herself missing him. Since yesterday, she hadn't been able to get through more than ten minutes at a stretch without thinking about their kiss.

Flushing, she settled back against the couch. "I don't know what's up," she admitted. "I'm surprised Tyler didn't stay to find out the results of the checkups. He takes as good care of the babies as I do. Better, even. He's a natural, Layne."

"That's great. So why do you look like you're about to lose your best friend?"

No, she was about to lose something much more than that. "Whether he's got the knack or not, he's still not ready to be a daddy."

"Then make him ready."

She shook her head. "I can't. Besides, I don't want him around the babies."

"Yeah," Layne said drily, "I can see that, all right."

Again, Shay flushed. Layne had hit on the one thing

that had bothered her since Tyler had first come to the hospital. She *did* want him around the babies—permanently. Except…how did that old saying go?

If wishes were horses, beggars would ride.

She wasn't about to beg him to stay. Or to accept handouts he offered only because he felt pressured into giving them. She couldn't let a few tender moments with the kids and a heart-stoppingly hot kiss make her give in. "He's still a cowboy," she said bitterly.

"And he'll probably always be a cowboy," Layne said in a soft tone, "just like nine-tenths of the men in Cowboy Creek. If you're holding out for someone who *doesn't* wear boots and a Stetson to work, you may be waiting a very long time."

"Stop. You know what I mean." She and Layne had long ago shared the stories of their childhoods. "I won't get involved with a cowboy."

Layne laughed. "Too late for that, girlfriend. Once you're sharing children, you're already as involved as you can get." She sobered. "Look, I know it was rough for you, not having your dad around and, most of the time, not your mom, either. But there are worse things than absentee parents."

Yes, like falling for a man she couldn't trust.

"You're right," she said. Layne and Cole had grown up with parents who were there physically but didn't support them in any way. Tyler seemed to think his parents were made from the same mold. She couldn't see his situation from that perspective. To her, what he had said made it clear his mom and dad cared about his future. What more could a child ask of a parent?

Seeing how Tyler cared for her and the babies, what more could she ask of him?

* * *

After his tense conversation with Shay, Tyler had been glad when Mo and Layne showed up at the house within minutes of each other. It gave him the excuse he needed to walk away. He might only be a rodeo cowboy, but he had smarts enough to know where he wasn't wanted.

And when a rodeo cowboy felt his presence wasn't welcome, he…

…went shopping?

Swallowing a laugh, he shoved the paper sack under his arm. The boys at the ranch in Texas had better not hear about this.

He rang Shay's doorbell, feeling eager to get back inside the house. In this short time away from the kids, he had missed them.

Suddenly, he realized his eagerness came from more than just *missing* the babies. Now that he had seen and held them, changed their pajamas and watched them smile, he had grown to care about them. His obligations had become much more personal.

These were his kids. He needed to provide for them.

As for Shay…well, she'd been right all along. Despite the family they'd begun, he wasn't the man for her.

And considering the way she felt about his being a cowboy, she sure wasn't the woman for him.

The door opened. Shay stood looking up at him, one hand gripping the door. The lowering sun made her squint. The light turned her eyes into sparkling emeralds. Her long hair had fallen forward over her shoulders and trailed down the front of her shirt, the blond strands looking like pure gold in the light.

He cleared his throat. "How are the babies doing?"

"They're still sleeping."

"All good, then." Her face was pale with faint shadows below her eyes. Before he could think twice about it, he raised his hand to her face and traced his thumb lightly along her cheekbone. "Did you get any rest?"

She shook her head. Her hair brushed the back of his hand. They weren't meant for each other, and yet he couldn't keep from running his fingers down the long strands of her hair. He settled his hand at her waist. She had filled out since last summer, and the knowledge that her lusher curves and thicker waist had come from carrying his babies filled him with a need he couldn't name or describe or resist.

He slid his hand around to press it against her back and tilted his head closer to hers. For the life of him, he couldn't recall why he'd been irritated when he had left here or why he'd taken so long to come back. For his pride's sake, he only hoped she wanted to kiss him as much as he wanted to kiss her.

To his undying relief, she tilted her chin up, willing, but waiting for him to make his move. A growl rose inside his chest, like the building roar of a lion preparing to defend his jungle.

He didn't want to raise any defenses with Shay—he wanted her against him, willing and warm and his.

When Tyler tightened his arm around her waist, Shay nearly melted into him. As always, his mouth was sure on hers. This time, his kiss was immediately hot and hungry, as if he were too impatient to give her the slow and easy buildup she had learned to love.

She discovered jumping straight to hot and hungry could satisfy her as well.

She curled her fingers in the fabric of his shirt and

pulled him closer. When he raised his hand to the back of her head to hold her steady, to deepen his kiss, she wrapped her arms around him. The crackle of paper and the sudden stab of a hard protrusion into her milk-swollen breast—from well above his waistline—made her grunt in surprise.

He raised his head and stared down at her. "What's wrong?"

"I...uh...think you just poked me...with something." She laughed uncontrollably and covered her mouth with one hand. With the other, she pointed to the sack he held under his arm.

"Oh. Sorry." He smiled. "It's something for the kids. But I didn't plan on giving it to you this way."

Her thought in response to *that* statement made her cheeks burn.

Her feelings for him flared just as hot, her response to his kiss overwhelming. Out-of-whack hormones, that's what she had to blame, along with lack of sleep and tension over trying to take care of three newborns at once. She *couldn't* feel anything for Tyler.

And still, she did.

As hard as she had fought to deny the truth to herself, she had to accept it now. The day they had met, she had done more than fall for him. She had given him her heart.

Now, she couldn't go back into the house and face Grandma, not with her face still flushed and her pulse still pounding. Quickly slipping through the doorway past Tyler, she crossed to the wooden porch swing and sank onto it.

He followed, as she had dreaded but known he would. He couldn't do what he did best from a distance.

After taking a seat beside her, he plopped the sack into her lap.

She looked down. "You already bought gifts for the kids—the stuffed animals."

"And now I bought them something else. I'm entitled." She said nothing, and a beat later, he added quickly, "After all, I've been one of the best babysitters they've ever had."

"The *only* babysitter, you mean."

"Even more reason for me to spoil them." He gestured to the sack. "Go ahead, open it."

She unrolled the top and reached inside the sack. Her fingers touched something soft and padded. She pulled out a stuffed terry-cloth pony with a mane made of woolen strands. Then she pulled out its twin and finally their triplet. Each wore a ribbon around its neck—blue, green or yellow, just like the blankets and caps her babies had worn home from the hospital.

She didn't know whether to laugh or cry. All his gifts were heartfelt and precious. And they weren't enough.

Her heart ached, but looking at the silly smiles on the ponies' faces finally brought a small smile to her lips, too. "Thank you. The babies will love them."

"There's more," he said.

"Oh." She reached into the sack again and pulled out a handful of tiny garments on plastic hangers—the source of the surprising stab that had interrupted their kiss. The hangers held one-piece pajamas patterned with horses. A multipack of bibs sported horseshoes and saddles.

She couldn't miss the message.

One way or another, Tyler was determined to have their babies grow up to be cowboys.

* * *

Shortly after his greeting to Shay on the front porch, Tyler sat sharing yet another meal with her and Mo.

The conversation when he'd come back home…come back *here*…had been all he could have asked for. Shay hadn't rejected him when he had taken her into his arms. Heck, that kiss might have gone on for quite some time if the sack he'd held hadn't gotten in the way.

Mo looked across the table, beaming at him. "Those are lovely gifts you brought for the babies, Tyler."

He laughed, shrugging. Why he'd gone into the department store and wandered to the children's section, he still didn't know. "Kind of a coals to Newcastle gift, bringing new clothes into a house already filled with them. But I saw them on the hangers and that was that."

"Ah, but infants need more clothing than most children."

He frowned, puzzled. "I'd have said they would hardly need anything but diapers and an outfit or two."

"They grow so quickly," Shay explained. It was the first time she had spoken since they'd sat down to supper.

"That they do," Mo agreed. "Sometimes they barely have the chance to wear an outfit before they've outgrown it."

"But not bibs," he said quickly.

"No, not bibs." Mo laughed, and even Shay smiled.

To his satisfaction, she had seemed to like the gifts he'd brought. Of course, a new mom would probably be overjoyed by anything given to her babies. Still, he told himself she especially liked his gifts. *And* his kiss. To his surprise, he found the knowledge of each brought him equal pleasure.

Now, her brow wrinkled in a frown, Shay stared down at her serving of the chicken casserole that had been delivered by a friend. "I don't understand this, Grandma," she said, sounding bewildered. "The women of Cowboy Creek are there for each other, always. And you and I have never hesitated to help anyone out. All our friends who signed up to bring food are delivering as promised. But we had a full roster of assistants, and not one of them has shown up."

He didn't get it, either, but he knew better than to say so. For sure, he realized the wisdom of keeping quiet about his agreement with Mo.

"They've had their reasons, lass."

"Well, yes. Sickness and toothaches, I can understand. But a haircut and a manicure?"

"Those seemed rather flimsy reasons, to be sure," Mo agreed. While her granddaughter's attention was still diverted, she shot Tyler a glance, then quickly looked away again.

Suspicion landed like a punch to his gut. Shay was right. Some of those women were bailing out with poor excuses. Did Mo have a hand in that? Had she arranged to have the women skip their assignments? But with Mo too busy to help, why would she leave a brand-new mom like Shay on her own with three babies?

Because…because Shay hadn't been alone. She'd had him here.

As if Mo had read his mind, she said, "We've been very fortunate that Tyler could help out."

He narrowed his eyes. He sensed strings being pulled here and felt sure she wasn't working alone. Jed Garland had his hands in this, too. He was certain of it.

Was that the matchmakers' plan—to give him and

Shay time alone? If so, their plan had succeeded. And was that why Jed had claimed he would be busy at the wedding reception the other day—the old man had deliberately left him at loose ends, hoping to drive him to the Big Dipper and Shay? That had worked, too.

He'd been played.

He'd also been given time to play.

But much as he liked the idea of another kiss, a cuddle and the hope of something more, getting even closer to Shay wasn't a smart idea. Not when he'd be leaving again…soon.

Judging by her stiff expression, she seemed to be thinking along the same lines. "We…we can't keep relying on Tyler," she told Mo.

I can't rely on Tyler. That's what she meant.

He had walked away from her once and, kisses aside, it seemed she planned to hold that action against him forever.

Chapter 15

From the back booth of SugarPie's, his favorite seat, Jed Garland could watch everything that went on in the sandwich shop. He could even get a peek through a doorway into the adjacent bakery. Both shops were quiet now, though. At this hour of the morning, too early even for the townsfolk to be headed to work, no one had stopped in yet to have breakfast or to pick up some of Sugar's famous sweet rolls.

He reached for the plateful of them she had just set in front of him.

"Is Mo stopping in?" she asked.

He swallowed a smile. Sugar Conway was appropriately named, all right. Her sugar-wouldn't-melt-in-my-mouth Southern accent might deceive those who didn't know her. But he'd watched her eject a rambunctious group of teens from the shop without lifting a finger. No, her sweet tone didn't fool him.

"You know darned well Mo's meeting us here this morning," he said. "I gather that's the reason I'm getting your special attention. You're as eager as I am to find out what's going on with Shay."

Laughing, she wedged herself into the seat across from him. "Jed, *you* know darned well you get the royal treatment every time you walk in. And yes, I want to hear what's going on. Tongues have been wagging in here and all over town."

"That's only natural for folks in Cowboy Creek. But Mo and I between us have managed to keep everyone away from the house." He filled her in on the latest developments with the new mom and her brood…and their daddy. "We're very pleased with the way Tyler's managing to take care of the babies."

"That does sound promising. Besides, he wouldn't hang around if he didn't have an interest."

"In the babies *or* in their mama," he agreed. "We just need to find out which one's the driving force." He glanced past her. "And here's Mo now. Let's hope she's got an answer."

Mo took a seat in the booth beside him. Sugar reached across the table with the carafe and poured her a mug of coffee.

"Thanks, Sugar."

"It'll cost you," the other woman said with a grin. "Let's have the news."

Even he couldn't wait to hear. "Which one has Tyler got his eye on?"

"Both," she said promptly. "That's my best guess. Yesterday afternoon Jim Grayden stopped in to check on his patients. Tyler left for a while, then came home with an armload of gifts for the babies."

"And for Shay?" he asked.

"I'm thinking he gave her something, too." She smiled. "Just after he returned, they spent some time out on the front porch. When they walked into the kitchen, her hair was mussed and she looked apprehensive, as though afraid I would guess what the two of them had been up to."

"Too bad you don't know for sure," Sugar said.

"Who says I don't?" Mo grinned wickedly. "I peeked into the living room and saw them together at the front door. As in, lips locked together."

"So everything's going according to plan," Sugar said complacently.

"Well…" Mo shifted her coffee mug in a circle on the tabletop.

"Out with it, woman," Jed demanded. "The news sounds promising. But what's got you on the fence?"

"I don't quite know. It's hard to put my finger on it, but something's still not right between them."

"Even after their kissing in broad daylight?"

"Yes. And we've had a major upset to our plans this morning, as well. Tyler called just as I was leaving home and said he won't be by today."

"What?" He frowned. "The boy left the hotel bright and early this morning, as usual."

"Well, he didn't come our way."

"Hmm." He brooded for a minute. "I think maybe those two need a break from the babies. Some time on their own to talk, and to get up to whatever they want to get up to."

"Oh, that will never work," Mo protested. "Shay won't leave her little ones, not for a good while."

"She won't have to if you volunteer to bring them

out to the ranch with her this afternoon. Tell her Tina and the other girls want to see the babies. Also, tell her I need to see her about her hours at the Hitching Post. She can hardly say no to either of those, now, can she?"

"But what about Tyler?"

"Don't worry. I'll take care of him."

At first, Shay had balked about taking the babies out to Garland Ranch. On their visit, they could run into Tyler. Or, worse, they might not.

"Isn't it too soon for the babies to be out?"

"They've already been exposed to plenty of hospital staff and visitors," Grandma had said. "And we're only planning to see Jed and the girls while we're out there."

Jed and his granddaughters…and not the babies' daddy?

The question made her determined to turn down the trip to the Hitching Post.

The message Grandma passed along that Jed wanted to see her had made her change her mind. In the dark hours of the night, alone in her bedroom between feedings, she would—and did—allow herself to think about Tyler. At any other time, her thoughts had to focus on taking care of her babies. Extra hours at the Hitching Post would go a long way toward helping with that.

Now, in the sitting room of the hotel, she watched Tina and Jane and Andi ooh and aah over the babies. She couldn't help but smile. At the same time, her spirits sank lower than they had when she and Grandma and the triplets had arrived. As she had feared, Tyler had been nowhere to be found.

Maybe he had left town already. Maybe that was why

he had called to say he wouldn't be at the house—he was on his way out of Cowboy Creek.

He had hung up after delivering his message to Grandma, not even asking to speak with her. She didn't care. So then why, ever since that phone call, did it feel as though her heart had broken?

So much for not thinking about the man.

Tina looked up from cuddling Bree. "Robbie was so disappointed he couldn't be here. Once Grandpa Jed told him the babies were coming for a visit, he didn't want to go to school this morning."

"Neither did Rachel," Jane said. "And I heard about it all the way to the bus stop."

Everyone laughed. Even Shay managed a genuine smile. Pete's young daughter never hesitated to share her thoughts. "Robbie will have a baby brother or sister to keep him company soon."

"That doesn't matter," Tina said. "He still wants to see the triple kids, as he calls them."

Shay laughed. "Then I'll plan to bring the babies out here again soon. Or you all can come visit us at home." At home, where she and the babies and Grandma would get along just fine without...their absent helper.

"I'm not sure where you'll find the time to spend at the house, lass," Grandma said. "Not if Jed's planning to give you more hours."

"And I hope he is," she admitted.

"I'm pretty sure he is," Tina said with a smile. As the bookkeeper, she would probably know. "But don't let him hear I spoiled the surprise."

"I won't." Shay didn't want to spend time away from the babies. She didn't want more hours, but she needed them. As a bonus, staying busy would help keep her mind off her worries. It would help remind her—as if she could forget—that she was now a parent and had obligations...

Which was just the way Tyler felt.

How could she have been so upset with him about that?

The sudden sound of boot heels and deep voices from the hallway made her pulse spike. The sight of Tyler standing beside Jed in the hotel's wide sitting room doorway set off a fluttering in her chest.

His gaze met hers, then jumped to the babies. She couldn't fault him for that at all. She wouldn't have had it any other way.

"Abuelo, look who's here." Tina rose and crossed the room to show off Bree.

"Well, let me get my hands on that little girl." Jed took the baby from her. "She's a cute one, isn't she, Tyler?"

He smiled and nodded. "Gonna be a heartbreaker someday."

Just like her daddy.

Tyler reached over to adjust Bree's knitted cap, then stood smiling down at her. His half smile and rapt expression made Shay's eyes sting with tears. He'd become so good at handling the kids in such a short time. Even more, he cared about them. She could see that plainly, even if no one else could. Even if he wouldn't admit it to her.

He cared for his babies, that's what counted most.

And she cared for him. She loved him and always had. That had to count for something, too. She had to talk to him, to find the courage to tell him how she felt. And most of all, to make sure he would be there for their babies.

* * *

Halfway down the hall to the Hitching Post's kitchen, Shay reached Jed's den, where Tina had told her to meet him.

She stepped into the room and stopped short. No Jed. Instead, Tyler sat on the couch along one wall, his legs stretched out in front of him, boots crossed at the ankles, giving every appearance he had settled in. If only she could convince him to feel that way about Cowboy Creek.

"I'm supposed to meet Jed here," she said.

"So am I. Have a seat." He began to rise.

"Don't get up." When she took one of the visitor's chairs by the desk, he sank back into his seat. She had wanted to speak to him privately, but not here, not now. When Jed walked in, she would need a clear head to discuss her job at the Hitching Post. But if Tyler did plan to leave town at any moment, this might be the only chance she had to talk with him.

She rested her hands on the arms of the chair and shot a glance in his direction.

"The babies look fine this morning," he said stiffly.

"They *are* fine."

"Is Timothy still ruling the roost at mealtime?"

"He is. But Bree beat Jamie to her bottle this morning." At the memory, she couldn't help but smile.

He did, too, a small, almost wistful smile. "Wish I'd been there—"

"You could have been," she said quietly. "You could be there often, if you wanted to." He ran his hand down his arm, smoothing his shirtsleeve. Or was he literally brushing away her words?

Uneasiness ran through her. She took a deep breath

and reminded herself she had found the courage to do this. "Tyler, maybe we went about everything out of order, with me getting pregnant before we had the chance to have a real relationship. But I… You have to know how much I care about you. I care about your relationship with the kids, and I see how much you care about them, too. We can make sure your relationship with *them* goes the right way. If you'll stay in Cowboy Creek."

Now he rose from the couch. Though he stood a few feet away, his height and broad shoulders still managed to give the impression he towered over her. She didn't fear him. Just the opposite. Heat flushed her cheeks and flooded her body, and she knew her appeal to him to stay in town came equally from concern for her babies—*their* babies—and wishes for her own future happiness.

He stood shaking his head. "That's not going to work, Shay. I know it. And you know it. We don't agree on a single thing, especially when it comes to the kids."

"What do you mean? We agree on lots of things—"

"Not the ones that matter."

Now her seated position made her feel she was losing ground. She stood to face him. "I told you, my dad followed the rodeo, too, and—"

"And that's exactly what I'm talking about. We don't agree on the work I do. We don't even agree on the gifts I bring home…bring to the kids. Bibs and pajamas. How could I go wrong with those? But somehow, they're not good enough for you."

"Bibs and pajamas with horses and saddles on them. They were just your way of trying to get your point across." Her eyes stung with angry tears. "Maybe I'm wrong about being able to make your relationship with the babies work. You're not thinking about them at all."

"I am, probably more than you are. You're the one pulling strings already, when they haven't even cut their first teeth."

"How is that any different from what you're doing? The last I heard, you've got your plans for them all mapped out, too."

"No. I was showing you an alternative. I'm trying to give the kids options."

She gasped. "And don't you think that's what I want?"

"I think you're controlling their futures—"

"I'm not." She stopped and took a deep, steadying breath. Arguing like this would only help to prove Tyler's claim that they couldn't agree on anything. "You're just seeing me the way you are because of how your father treated you."

"And you're not holding what I do for a living against me, for the same reason? I'm a cowboy. That doesn't mean I'm just like your dad." He shoved his hands into his back pockets. "It doesn't matter. I'm not staying. That's what I told you from the beginning, and I never said anything otherwise. As it is, I shouldn't have stayed this long. You've made it plain you don't trust me, but I'm telling you something you can take to the bank— literally. Not a promise. Fact. I'll be sending you cash to help support the kids."

The words hit like a knife piercing her heart.

"I don't want your charity," she snapped.

"It's not a handout. It's—"

"I know. It's your *obligation*. Money. Financial help. And you, at a distance." Her frustrated sigh bordered on a sob. "How can you walk away from our babies, especially after all the time you've spent with them? They've bonded with *you* as strongly as they have with me."

He said nothing.

She wanted him here, being a daddy to her children. He wanted to negotiate a deal and then write the babies off as a business expense.

She took another deep breath and let it out slowly. "Nothing I've said—or can say—will change your mind?"

"No."

The unyielding response left her speechless from stunned surprise and a flash of rage. The reaction gave her a beat of time to raise her defenses, to realize she was determined to win this battle...even if she'd already been defeated in the war.

She would not let him see her break. She raised her chin. "It's just as well, then," she said firmly. "If you're not prepared to stay for the long haul, you might as well leave town."

Chapter 16

When a resounding knock thumped against his door, Tyler started. He stared suspiciously across the hotel room. He had left Shay downstairs in Jed's den only a short while ago. She wouldn't have had time to reconsider anything he'd said. And surely, she wouldn't have told Jed about their conversation.

The knock came again.

"It's open," he called.

The door swung wide. Cole stepped into the room and shut the door quietly behind him. "Hey, buddy, what's going on? Tina tells me you're all of a sudden set on leaving."

"Nothing sudden about it. I've been planning to go for days now. I told her I'd be checking out this afternoon. It's about time I got back home."

Home. Where there would be no babies, no Shay. And now, not even a job for him to go back to.

Cole started across the room.

"Don't get comfortable." He knew his buddy well. Give the man a minute and he'd talk for an hour or more. Tyler took his duffel bag from the closet and tossed it onto the bed. "I'm leaving as soon as I've packed."

Ignoring him, Cole dropped into one of the armchairs by the window. "So I hear. Just one question. Have you lost your mind?"

Tyler stiffened. "What does that mean?"

"You know what it means, man. You're a brand-new daddy. And you're walking away from your kids? From your family?"

"Stop right there. We're not a family."

Cole shrugged. "Okay, maybe not at the moment. But you'll never have a chance of becoming one if you're nowhere in sight."

And you, at a distance.

Shay had called that right. He was planning to put miles between him and Cowboy Creek. "What are you, an advice columnist now?" He opened the dresser drawer and scooped up a handful of T-shirts. "You've been hanging around these matchmakers too long."

"Hanging around, heck." The other man grinned. "I'm a walking, talking advertisement for their services."

Tyler dropped the shirts into his bag. "I'm glad it worked out well for you. I'm not in the market."

"You might live to regret that."

"But I'll live."

"What kind of life, though?"

Tyler laughed shortly. "And now you're a shrink,

asking me to contemplate the meaning of existence? Give it up, Cole. Not all of us take to being a dad the way you have."

"That'll come with a little practice. Believe me, I didn't know if I could handle it at first, either. You haven't been with the kids long enough to know what kind of dad you'll make."

"I'm not talking about *learning* the ropes. I meant not all of us *want* to be roped and tied."

That stopped the other man—for about two seconds. "Funny, I used to think exactly that myself. Sorry to hear you saying it, too. And that's your final word?"

Nothing I've said—or can say—will change your mind?

"That's it."

Cole sighed. "So be it. Then here's my final piece of advice, no charge. I know you well enough to realize why you're running. I also know from my experience it's something you need to work through on your own. But don't wait too long, or you might miss out." He crossed the room, and they shook hands. "The Hitching Post will have a room waiting when you change your mind."

"I won't."

"Suit yourself. But in any case, the room will be here. Don't be a stranger. Like it or not, the Garlands consider you family."

They've bonded with you as strongly as they have with me.

Tyler had barely made it to the bed again with a handful of socks when another knock came to the door. This one sounded soft, almost tentative. His heart jumped to his throat.

He crossed the room and opened the door. Shay's grandma stood in the hallway. He swallowed hard and stepped back. "Would you like to come in?"

"That *is* why I'm paying you a visit, love. One of the reasons, at any rate." Like Cole, she claimed a seat by the window.

This time, he followed and took the armchair opposite. He could be as rude and blunt as he liked with Cole, but Grandma Mo was another story.

"Tina told me you were planning to leave," she said.

Cole's wife had a lot to answer for. Keeping his expression neutral, he said, "Yes, ma'am, I am."

"Is Shay aware of this?"

"Yes."

"Are *you* aware you'll be breaking her heart?"

...you have to know I care about you.

What he had seen from Shay was a far cry from a broken heart. But now, he did see something else she had told him, in action right here. Her grandma was sticking up for her just the way she said Mo did, the way his father had never done for him.

Suddenly, he wished Cole hadn't left. His buddy could talk his way through a conversation like this one, while he'd never been good at discussing his feelings. He rested his elbows on his knees and linked his fingers together in front of him. "I'm not—" He stopped, cleared his throat, tried again. "I don't know what Shay told you."

"She hasn't told me anything, Tyler. She doesn't have to. I raised the lass, almost on my own."

The way Shay would raise their babies. He comforted

himself with the thought she did have her grandma to help her.

"She's still in talking with Jed," Mo went on. "Once I see her, I'll only need to look at her to know how she feels. Just as I'm looking at you now and know how you're feeling. You're not happy."

He shrugged. "I've got a long drive ahead of me. I'll be happy when I put it behind me."

And you, at a distance.

That again. He had to stop replaying everything Shay had said. He had to forget Cole's unwanted advice and Mo's gentle insistence that she knew him better than he knew himself.

"Shay and I came to a mutual understanding," he assured her.

"Did you, now? Well, then, I suppose you'll both have to live with that."

What kind of life?

Now those were Cole's words, not Shay's. And not his. Trying to block out the noise in his head, he gripped his linked fingers so hard his knuckles cracked.

"Will you be seeing the babies before you leave?" Mo asked.

He swallowed hard. "No. I think it would be best if I don't."

"Well, perhaps you're right. Better to leave things as they are." She reached over to pat his arm. "This will be hard enough on you *and* them once you all realize the bond between you is broken."

Tyler was almost done packing when a third knock came to the door. This one sounded less tentative than

Mo's but not nearly as thunderous as Cole's. Again, his heart jumped to his throat.

Third time lucky?

He pushed the crazy thought aside and went to the door. His conclusion jumping aside, he had the distinct feeling he wouldn't find the woman he…the woman he could have found outside in the hallway.

Jed Garland stood with his thumbs in his belt loops and a smile on his face.

And now Tyler's heart sank. He let the man into the room, then took a quick look through the doorway. At this rate, he expected to find a line of Garland family members waiting their turn to enter. The hall was deserted. He closed the door and turned to Jed. "I don't think you're going to have to tell me why you're here. Let me guess. You talked to Tina."

"That I did."

"I thought Cole's wife was the quietest of your granddaughters."

Jed chuckled and went to the same seat Mo and Cole had taken.

This conversation wouldn't be as quick as the other two that had been held in the room this afternoon. He shoved his hands into his back pockets and sat on the end of the bed.

"So, you're on the run," Jed said.

Tyler eyed him suspiciously, wondering if the man had just made a judgment call about his decision. Jed rested his hands on the padded arms of the chair and sent him a level gaze. Tyler returned it. "You're here to try and convince me to stay."

"Nope. Haven't got an idea in the world about doing that."

At the older man's denial, he blinked in surprise. Shay's grandma and his own best friend both had made attempts. Maybe Jed wasn't the matchmaker he was cracked up to be. Or more likely, the man had meant what he said the day they had talked about Shay. "I'm glad you're not in any danger of destroying your winning streak."

Jed smiled. "So you remembered that? Yes, I'm grateful for holding on to my record, too. And I'm just as glad not to ruin the reputation I've built."

So much for his earlier suspicions that Jed had been pulling strings to get him and Shay together.

"Some people are made to be matched," Jed continued, "and some aren't, and fortunately, I've got a sixth sense about which is which."

Why did that statement bother him? It wasn't like he had expected Jed to work harder. Or in his case, to work miracles. "Yeah. Well. Your sixth sense must have earned some overtime in the past week or so."

"It did. I guess you and Shay did some extra work these last few days, too. Taking care of one baby is a chore. Three must have really worn you down."

"It wasn't hard at all."

"No? Routine work, then—all those bottles and diapers and such."

"It wasn't routine, either. You'd think with the babies being triplets, they'd all behave the same. But they don't. They react to things in their own way. They don't look exactly alike, either."

"I don't know how you can figure that at their young age, except when it comes to telling Bree from her brothers, of course. I'd imagine those two boys get you all mixed up."

No, their *mother* got him all mixed up. "They're easy to tell apart. Timothy and Jamie look a lot alike, but they're not identical. Jamie's got more hair. Timothy's bigger and more active, although Jamie's catching up in both those departments. Bree—" He thought of her and smiled. "Bree's just a little sweetheart."

"That she is. It'll be amazing to watch how much they'll all change, even from one week to the next."

"Yeah." He wouldn't see that and didn't want to think about what he would miss. He tapped the duffel bag on the bed beside him. Shrugging, he said, "All of the kids look more like real little people every day. I've already seen lots of differences with each of them."

He would have the time he'd spent with the kids to help him remember them after he was gone. The time, and the photos from the local newspaper.

The article had been the talk of the Hitching Post's dining room this morning. As soon as breakfast was done, he had driven into town to get his own copy of the paper. The photos didn't show all the differences he'd learned about the babies, but he *had* learned them, and no one could take those memories away.

"Speaking of differences…"

Tyler looked up from his duffel bag to find Jed eyeing him.

"I gather you and Shay didn't have any luck patching up your differences."

"No." He tried not to frown.

"Just as well that you're leaving, then."

It's just as well, then. If you're not prepared to stay for the long haul, you might as well leave town.

Now, he did frown. He had expected that statement from Shay but hadn't seen the same reaction coming from Jed. The man really must value his reputation. "Yeah. Just as well. But I told you when we talked that I would do the right thing by Shay, and I am."

"That's good to hear."

"I'll be sending her money regularly."

"I'm sure it'll come in handy."

Handy? "She'll need the support. For the kids. For food and clothes and diapers and stuff."

"Well, yes. But I've arranged for her to take on more hours here at the hotel."

"So soon? She just delivered three babies. And they need her at home."

"Yes. But she wants the work."

"I can send her enough cash so that she won't have to add on hours yet."

Jed spread his hands palm up. "That's between the two of you. She'll do all right, though."

She won't need you. That's what Jed meant. He could hear it in the man's words and read it in his so-what gesture.

"Of course, money will get tighter as the triplets get bigger." Jed chuckled ruefully and shook his head. "I remember how it was with my three boys—just one thing after another. They'll constantly outgrow their clothes, quicker than Shay can turn around. And unlike my boys, she'll have three kids the same age. Not much chance of hand-me-downs in that family."

Was it getting hotter in here? He wiped his brow and stared at Jed. "I'll send her more money as the kids get older."

Jed nodded. "I reckon that might not be a bad idea. There will be doctor and dentist bills, a chance of braces and glasses, too. And then will come the day they all want cars and college."

Tyler exhaled heavily. Maybe he'd been wrong about the man. The way Jed was piling all that on, it seemed he was trying to scare him *away* from shouldering his responsibility. "You're right about all those things. But the babies aren't even a week old yet." He had said that to Shay, too. How could so little time have passed when he felt as though he'd gotten to know them all so well? "Aren't you jumping the gun, thinking about those things at this stage of the game?"

"That's just the thing. Raising kids isn't a game. Of course, there are lots of fun moments and rewards along the way, if we take the time to enjoy them."

Yeah, for the folks around *to enjoy them.*

"But that time is going to fly." Jed shook his head. "No, when all is said and done, caring for a family is a serious business. And it should only be done by folks who plan to take it seriously."

"I *will* take it seriously." He'd be responsible for his actions, would send Shay money for the kids. He would do the right thing to prove himself to Jed. To his parents. To himself.

...at a distance.

Chapter 17

Shay set a plate of chocolate-chip cookies on the kitchen table and took her seat across from Layne. "Homemade, from Mrs. Browley." Mrs. Browley was one of Grandma's best friends and a regular at both SugarPie's and the Big Dipper.

"Oh, yum." Layne reached for a cookie. "I love these. And they're Jason's favorites."

"You'll have to take some home to him. We've got more food and desserts here than we can eat, thanks to our volunteers." Not one of them had dropped off a tray of baked ziti, though. The thought of Tyler's specialty made her mouth water. The thought of Tyler's mouth on hers made her press her lips together to keep them from trembling. She forced her gaze to Layne. "I'm glad you found some time to stop by."

"Going a little stir-crazy?"

And now Shay forced a laugh and reached for a cookie. "You don't know the half of it. Not that I mind being home alone with the babies," she added quickly.

"Of course not. But are you still alone?"

"Well, I shouldn't have put it that way. For the past few days, all our volunteers have shown up on schedule. This afternoon's helper left just a little while ago. With Grandma off to her knitting circle, I really am happy for your visit."

She loved her friends and felt grateful for their volunteer time, too, but their attentions to her babies weren't the same as Tyler's. He had been out of their lives for three days now, and she knew the triplets missed him... because she missed him, too.

With a sigh, she pushed around the cookie she had dropped onto her plate.

"Have you heard from him?" Layne asked quietly.

She shook her head.

"You don't think getting in touch is worth a try?"

"You didn't hear him, Layne. He doesn't want to be around, even now that we have the babies." She winced, realizing what she had just unwittingly said. Layne's sad half smile said she had picked up on it, too.

She had to face the truth. Tyler hadn't wanted to stay around even before she had gotten pregnant.

"I don't have a way to get in touch with him, anyhow. We texted a few times when he was here for the wedding last summer, and then I... When I didn't hear from him, I deleted his texts and his number from my phone."

She had been upset then. She'd been more upset— and hurt—three days ago at the Hitching Post, the last time she had seen him.

"You could talk to Cole," Layne said. "For that matter, *I* could talk to Cole."

"No, thanks. Your brother is friends with Tyler. I don't want you—or me—to use him as a go-between."

"All he would be doing is passing along Tyler's phone number."

"No," she snapped. "If Tyler wants to talk to me, let him get in touch." With another sigh, she sank back in her chair. "I'm sorry, Layne, I don't know what's the matter with me."

"Don't apologize. I've been there, too, and not so long ago. And you know exactly what I'm talking about."

She nodded. "Yes, I do know." Layne definitely had suffered the symptoms of a broken heart, too.

"Then do you really need me to spell out your problem for you?"

"No. But you don't know the worst of it. I'm almost too embarrassed to tell you. We were so awful with each other that day." Poking at her cookie, she thought of the verbal jabs she and Tyler had thrown. She pushed the plate aside and stared at Layne. "I was so upset with myself for falling for a cowboy and so angry with him for leaving me last summer. For not wanting to stay now. But *he* was angry on behalf of the babies. He argued with me about them. He *fought* for them. Why would he have done that, why would he have tried so hard, if he didn't already care about them?"

"I think he does. But he's a mixed-up male who doesn't recognize his own feelings and probably wouldn't talk about them even if he did."

"He tried, I think. He started to talk to me, but I cut him off."

"Did he do the same to you?"

"Yes."

"Then you're even. Seriously. Don't try taking all the blame for what happened. You were both in the argument together."

That made sense, and yet it didn't fit—because Layne hadn't been there and didn't know the whole truth.

Tyler *did* care about the babies. He didn't love her, but he loved his children. And she had been so unyielding, had pushed him so hard, he would never come back.

Tyler crossed the barn to dump the bucket of water he'd been using to clean his tack.

Not knowing where else he wanted to go when he had left Cowboy Creek, he had returned to the ranch where he'd been working when he left Texas. With extra hands always needed for the spring roundup, the manager jumped on the chance to take him on again. He had hoped the return would let him settle for a while.

For more than a week, he had stayed almost too busy to think. Almost. He had acquired a steady job, a stall for Freedom, a place to rest his head at night. And still he had the sense of being more aimless than ever.

As he rinsed the sponge and set it on the shelf beside the utility sink, he thought about scrubbing pots in Shay and Mo's kitchen.

He had told Mo he would be happy when he had put his long drive home behind him. He hadn't lied, just hadn't realized the strategy wouldn't work.

Such a short time ago, it seemed wanderlust had sent him on the run, on the road to New Mexico. Maybe it wasn't wanderlust, after all. Maybe he *had* been running from something when he'd left Texas. But the visit to Cowboy Creek hadn't given him answers. In fact, it had only raised too many questions about worries he hadn't known existed for him until he had arrived.

And still, back in Texas again, he continued to feel unsettled.

"Hey, Buckham," one of the cowboys called across the barn. "We're heading to Roy's tonight for some wine, women and song."

"Forget the song," another of the hands called. "I'm just in it for the wine and women."

Somebody else snickered.

"Wanna join us?" the first man asked.

"I'll pass on this one." More proof things weren't right with him. Normally he'd have been the first one out the door headed to Roy's.

"Man, I don't know what happened on your trip to New Mexico. If I ever head that way, remind me not to drink the water."

More snickers.

That first afternoon in Cowboy Creek, he had stood in the ballroom at the Hitching Post with a glass of iced tea in his hand. He had looked at Shay and Tina, both pregnant, and jokingly asked himself if there was something in the water around there. If only he'd known then what he knew now.

Heck, if he'd known then what he'd known just a day or two later...

Most likely, even if he had heard sooner about Shay and the babies, nothing would have changed. He would have done the same things. He would have tried to do the *right* thing...and had it come out all wrong.

"I heard the boys talking about you the other night,"

one of the newer hands said to him. "They're all glad you're back, since you're the pasta expert on this spread."

Tyler forced a laugh. "Not an expert. I've only got one specialty. Baked ziti." Mo had loved it. Despite Shay's grudging nod, he was sure she had liked it, too. The woman wouldn't give an inch sometimes, even when it was in her own best interest.

"Yeah, that's what I'm talking about," the cowhand said. "That ziti. If you're hanging around the bunkhouse tonight, maybe you ought to whip up a tray or two. Isn't it your turn to cook supper tomorrow?"

"Yeah. Sounds good. I'll run into town after I shower."

The idea sounded even better on his walk to the bunkhouse. Cooking would keep him busy. He had nothing else to do.

He thought of what had happened that afternoon he'd made the ziti at Shay's. She had come downstairs to the kitchen, where tea and toast had led to a kiss.

Frowning, he pushed the memory away.

At his bunk, he stripped off his shirt and went to his locker to gather what he needed for a shower. His gaze fell on the envelope on the top shelf. His hands stilled.

For a long moment, he looked at the envelope and fought the urge to take it down. A losing battle, as he had known it would be. He hadn't won the conflict once yet. Why should this time be different?

He sank onto the edge of his bunk and balanced the envelope on his knee. Two choices. Put it back and pretend it didn't exist. Or open it and wallow in self-pity.

He opened the flap. With two fingers, he pulled out

the folded newspaper. He spread the paper wide and laid it across both knees.

"Hey, is that you?"

Tyler jumped. He hadn't heard the younger cowhand come into the bunkhouse. The man stood only a foot away. *Dang.* It was too late for him to hide the paper that had riveted his attention. "Yeah. That's me."

"Who all is that with you?"

He looked down again. "Family," he said.

From the front page of Cowboy Creek's local newspaper, Shay looked up at him. She sat in her wheelchair outside the hospital, cuddling Timothy and Jamie to her, the blue-and green-wrapped bundles looking so small in her arms. He stood behind the trio, holding Bree against him. The baby of all his babies looked—and was—even smaller than her brothers.

"Is that your sister?" the cowhand asked. "No wonder you had to take some time off, if she needed help. Families have to stick together, right?"

"Right." He didn't bother to correct the man's assumption. He didn't flinch as he agreed to something he hadn't done.

"Looks like she's got her hands full. And so do you."

"Yeah, we do."

The cowhand grabbed something from his locker and left the room.

Just as he'd done every night in this bunkhouse since his return, Tyler stared down at Shay's image. The photographer had caught her with her eyes crinkling at the corners and her smile wide as she laughed. She looked beautiful, happy, content. She looked like she was meant to be a mom.

He slid the newspaper back into the envelope and

returned the envelope to his locker. He would rather
have the photo out where he could see it, but it wasn't
like he could frame it to hang on the wall or display on
the shelf at the end of his bunk.

He'd gotten off easy with the new cowhand's faulty
assumption. Some of the boys he'd worked with for a
while here wouldn't have let the conversation go at that.

And what could he tell them? It was a picture of the
woman and the kids he'd left behind?

Already, he missed the sight of the photo. He missed
the babies. He missed their mom.

That restless feeling hit again.

He was back home, earning a living, still trying to
do the right thing, but going at it all wrong. He had too
many questions. And he wouldn't find his answers here.

After making sure the baby monitor was working,
Shay turned off the overhead light. She clicked the
switch on the small lamp on the dresser. In the dimmed
light, she stood and watched her babies sleeping.

Tyler had been gone just over a week. In that time,
the triplets had grown and changed so much—in her
eyes, at least. She noted each new fraction of an inch
of fingernail, every additional ounce the babies drank
at feeding time, all the extra minutes they now slept
between feedings at night.

While she was grateful to have them sleeping more
soundly, the minutes added up to more time alone for
her. She spent too much of that time in her bedroom
thinking of Tyler.

Sighing, she went downstairs.

Grandma sat in her rocker in the living room, working her knitting needles in her hands. "Are they all asleep now?"

"Yes." Shay took a seat on the couch and poured herself a cup of tea from the carafe on the table. The *Mom*s on her mug made her smile. The memory of Tyler coming into her hospital room with the mug and the stuffed animals was bittersweet.

"Good to see you looking happy, lass. What's on your mind?"

"I was just thinking about the days when the babies won't be babies anymore. When they'll be toddlers running around the house and calling out 'Mommy' and 'Grandma.'"

"Let's not rush things, shall we? We have so many precious stages to experience before that happens."

"Oh, I'm not rushing anything." The slower time passed, the less Tyler would miss.

What would Grandma have said if she had shared the rest of her thoughts over this past week? She had envisioned the babies crawling, toddling, walking, going off to nursery school, to kindergarten and then to Cowboy Creek Elementary. Whether she rushed her thoughts or not, the triplets would grow so quickly. Soon, they would realize they were growing up without a daddy.

"You've stopped smiling," Grandma said. "You're not still with the babies. Now what's in your thoughts?"

She cradled the mug in her hands. "Nothing much."

"I taught you better than to give me a flip answer, Shay," Grandma said mildly. Shay flushed. "Should I have said *who's* in your thoughts?"

She shot a glance across the space, but Grandma's gaze focused on her knitting. There it was. The dead giveaway, the studied innocence that told her the question was anything but harmless. "And I know you better than that, Grandma. You could knit in your sleep."

Grandma laughed. "I think I have, at times." She set her project on the coffee table. "All right, let's stop talking circles around one another and go right to the point. You haven't been yourself this past week."

Shay opened her mouth, but Grandma held up a hand.

"Now, don't be citing chapter and verse to me about being a new mother, adjusting to new responsibilities, and losing out on sleep. Those are all true and valid points, but we both know they're not what's causing your distress. It's Tyler, isn't it?"

She wanted to deny it but couldn't. Silently, she nodded.

"I imagine you wanted Tyler to spend more time here."

She tried to bite her tongue to keep from responding but couldn't manage that, either. "No. I want him to *be* here. To *stay* here. For the babies' sakes."

"I'm sure you do. But you can't convince a person who doesn't want to change his mind."

"I know." Shay repeated what she had said to Layne. "He doesn't want to be around."

"Then you have to let him go."

"I did. I told him to leave, and he went."

"You're doing the right thing, love," Grandma said gently, "putting your babies first. But putting your feelings into words with Tyler is not what I meant. You have to let him go from your heart."

Chapter 18

Last night, Tyler had cooked the requested trays of baked ziti. Tonight, he had left the cowhands at the ranch to enjoy it without him while he made the trek into Houston. He was forced to park his truck several blocks away from the towering building he planned to enter.

The streets were congested with cars and people. The air felt thick and heavy, weighing him down, and even the late-afternoon sunlight didn't seem as bright as it did out on the ranch.

The building's lobby doors automatically swished closed behind him, cutting him off from civilization. As the elevator slammed shut, it seemed to swallow him up. Nothing had changed. He had hated everything about this place when he lived here and didn't like it any better now.

Once off the elevator, he strode down the hall to a shiny-clean white door with a gleaming brass bell plate. He rang the bell and waited. Part of him hoped no one was home.

He didn't belong here. He never had. The road had taken him to a life spent doing what he did best. Rodeo, wrangling, and everything else a cowboy did. Everything Shay didn't like.

After a few minutes, the door swung open.

The look of surprise on his mother's face didn't fool him. She would have checked the security peephole in the door. And she must have recognized him. After all, he'd just been there a few months ago for Christmas.

"Mom."

"Tyler." She wore one of the long, floaty dresses she always changed into for supper—*dinner*—every evening. Her hair looked perfect, her makeup immaculate. She tilted her head to accept the kiss he left somewhere in the air near her cheek. Stepping back, she swung the door wide. "Do come in. Your father's not here. He should be home shortly. Can I get you something to drink?"

He blinked. An excited smile or a spontaneous hug would have been too much to expect. Still, he had thought his appearance would warrant more than the standard cocktail-party greeting. "No, I'm good." He didn't care for cocktails, anyway. And they wouldn't have beer in the house.

"You'll excuse me if I make myself one."

It wasn't a question, but he nodded. She headed in the direction of the kitchen. He looked around him, taking in the room he had been happy to escape years ago. Glass and chrome, lacquer and acrylic. The furnishings and decorations were the same throughout the condo, even in his bedroom.

As a kid, he couldn't breathe with so much fake glare and glitter around him. One weekend, he had pasted nature and rodeo posters all over his bedroom, including the mirrored doors of the wall-to-wall closet. When his mother discovered it and told his father what he had done, he'd been grounded for a month. He had spent every evening after supper alone in his room with a bucket of water and a paint scraper. The fee the condo management charged to refurbish the room had come from his allowance. His father had wanted him to learn a lesson.

He *had* learned one—that a condo in Houston wasn't where he wanted to be. As soon as he had finished high school, he had moved out, found a job wrangling and spent weekends and whatever free time he could get following the rodeo.

His mother returned from the kitchen, her slippers tapping on the tile floor. She carried a tray with a bucket filled with ice and a bottle. Alongside the bucket sat two crystal tumblers. Ice tinkled as she set the tray down on the glass-topped coffee table. They took seats on opposite sides of the table, and she poured herself a drink.

"It's been a while since we've seen you," she said, skipping over the part about their uncomfortable holiday reunion. He and his father had never gotten along well, and he had always hated his parents' fake merriment of the season, too. They couldn't even get a real tree. "What have you been up to?"

He swallowed a laugh. Where would he start? Might as well go straight to the highlights. "I've got some news for you and Dad. I'm… I'm a daddy myself now."

She blinked. He had inherited the same shade of blue eyes. "What? Why…? Why didn't you tell us this when you were here for Christmas?"

"I didn't know then."

The condo door opened. Tyler John Buckham Sr.—called John his whole life—stepped into the living room.

His eyebrows went up at the sight of his son sitting on the couch. "Tyler."

Tyler rose and they shook hands. He had gotten his dark hair from his father and would someday get the silver streaks, too. Probably sooner than he anticipated, considering what had happened lately.

"We weren't expecting you."

"Sorry. Should I have called in advance?"

His father's eyes narrowed. He leaned down to pick up the extra tumbler from the tray. Tyler took his seat again.

As his mother poured a drink, she said, "John, Tyler has news for us. He's become a father."

Still standing and now blank faced, Tyler's dad looked at him. "Is that so? Why is this the first we've heard of it?"

"As I told Mom, I didn't know it myself. I just found out a few weeks ago." He took the folded-up newspaper from his back pocket and handed it across the table.

His mother took it and looked down at the front-page photo. She let out a gasp. "Tyler! Are these *all* yours?"

"All?" His father took the newspaper from her and glanced at it, then at Tyler again. "*Three* children? So that's why you're here."

For a moment, Tyler was taken aback. He should have expected the reaction. Playing daddy had made him forget what his own father was like. Had also made him forget why he wasn't cut out to be a dad himself. "Yes. That's partly why I'm here. I wanted you and Mom to know."

"And the other part? You want help taking care of these kids, I suppose."

I don't want your charity. Shay had told him that. Suddenly, he knew how she felt.

"Why else would you be here?" his father went on. "You can't possibly raise three kids on what you make."

"I'll manage."

"Does your wife work?"

"We're not married. We're not together."

His father stared at him. "Then what was this, a one-night stand? And now you've got three children to support, all at once. What were you thinking, Tyler?"

"I wasn't expecting three kids, that's for sure."

"Watch that backtalk."

"Dad." He forced his jaw to unclench. "I couldn't have controlled how many babies came along."

"You could have controlled yourself. At the very least, you could have been responsible enough to use protection."

He had him there. He'd nailed it all. It *had* been a one-night stand, a good time that wasn't supposed to turn into anything else. Instead, it had led to more than Tyler could believe. "Protection doesn't always work. But no, I didn't use it. The point is, the babies are here now."

"And you're expecting us to help you out."

"No, I'm not. I told you, I wanted you and Mom to hear the news. I thought you would be happy to have grandkids, that you might want to see them." He rose from his seat and grabbed the newspaper from his father's hand. "I should have known better. You're not even happy to have a son, let alone grandkids."

"Tyler—"

"Forget it. We all know I'll never be good enough to measure up to your standards. I've just figured out my kids never will, either—because you won't give them a chance. But they won't ever know that. I'll make sure to keep them away from here."

He was careful not to slam the condo door as he left.

He was more careful not to run.

Hadn't he done that enough times already? He had taken off from his parents' home at seventeen, run from Texas just a couple of weeks ago. Worst of all, he had left Shay again, just as he had soon after they had met. This time, she had told him to go. But he hadn't argued.

The elevator doors slammed shut. He stared at his reflection in the stainless-steel doors. He didn't like what he saw, and he liked even less the way he felt inside.

This visit home proved what he had known all his life. He couldn't be the son his parents wanted him to be.

He wasn't the man Shay wanted for herself or their kids.

Out on the street again, the heavy air made it hard for him to take a deep breath. Or maybe the struggle came from the tightness like a band across his chest.

He couldn't exist the way he had been living, couldn't keep feeling so aimless and unsettled, couldn't keep running. It was time to figure out who he was and what *he* wanted.

Shay sat on the bed in the hotel suite she and Jed's granddaughters used to prepare for weddings held at the Hitching Post. She leaned back against the head-board and shifted a couple of the sample books she had spread out around her.

At the sound of heavy footsteps in the hallway, she looked up expectantly. It sounded like Jed. It was her first day back to work since he had given her extra hours and, knowing him, he wanted to make sure she wasn't overdoing it.

It was also three weeks since Tyler had left...but she didn't want to think about that.

Sure enough, the minute Jed walked into the room, he gave her his usual smile and said, "How are you doing, girl?"

She spread her arms wide, her palms up, gesturing at the suite. "Living a life of ease, thanks to you, boss."

He chuckled as he took the chair at the desk adjacent to the bed. "That's what I like to hear. And the babies?"

"They're wonderful. They're nearly a month old already, and they just had another checkup yesterday. Dr. Grayden says they're doing fine. They've grown so much. They've gotten so strong." She thought of Tyler's excitement over Jamie's grip...and pushed the vision aside. "Grandma and I have been exercising the babies. She says moving their legs—as if they were riding a bicycle—will help strengthen the triplets' muscles for when they're ready to crawl and then to walk."

"You're going to have your hands full when that day comes." He smiled. "I'm planning to stop by to see them again soon."

"I wish you would."

He nodded. "In the meantime, don't you wear your-self out. Mo and Paz both would have my hide if they thought I was running you into the ground."

"No chance of that. This is easy work compared to mommying three infants."

"And I'm sure you would much rather be home doing that than working here."

She would, but she could never say that to Jed. His generosity was going to help her take care of those infants. Instead she laughed. "It's a moot point, since I didn't have a chance of staying home, anyway. You should have seen Grandma shooing me out the door. And our volunteer for the day hadn't even arrived yet."

"Mo wanted some time with her great-grandbabies, I'll bet."

"Yes, I think you're correct—Grandma did want the babies to herself."

"That's only right. Grandparents need that alone time."

So did daddies.

"I didn't like it at all," he went on, "when my three boys left Cowboy Creek, especially when two of them got married and then Jane and Andi came along. I was glad whenever they came to visit."

"I'm sure you were. It must have been so nice for you to have Tina grow up right here."

"It was. I learned more about her quicker than I did with the other girls. But that doesn't mean I didn't get to learn about them, too. Every time they arrived, though, it came as a shock to see how much they had changed."

If Tyler never visited, he wouldn't face those shocks. He wouldn't see any of the changes or the stages their babies went through. "They do grow fast," she murmured.

"They do," he agreed. "And they're all so different, just like your three little ones. But of course I love all my girls, just the way you love your babies." He smiled. "Tina always was the one with her nose in a book, yet she also had a good head for numbers. Jane was the artist in the family, always drawing or painting—sometimes on the other girls' books."

They both laughed.

"I'll probably have to face some of that, too," she said.

"I reckon you will. Most likely, you'll also have one of the three who's a peacemaker, like Andi. Tina never was one to get riled, except those times Jane drew all over her books. Andi could always get in between the other two girls and calm them down."

"That will be Bree, I'm sure. She's more relaxed about everything. Tyler says—" She stopped short.

As if he hadn't noticed, Jed spoke again. "That's the thing about babies. Triplets or not, they can all pretty much seem alike when they're so tiny. It's only after they grow a bit that you get to see they have their own ways. And of course, the older they get, the more evident that becomes. With Tina and Jane and Andi, I never could have predicted exactly how they would turn out or what they would eventually do with their lives."

"That's not completely true." She grinned. "You more than predicted who they would marry."

He laughed. "So I did. Well, after all, those couples needed a few nudges along the way. But I'd never have gotten involved if I didn't think the matches were meant to be."

She froze in the process of shifting one of the sample books aside.

Was that why Jed hadn't helped her? Did he believe she and Tyler wouldn't make a good pair?

"The point is," he continued, "you have to respect those differences. You have to stand back and let your grandkids—and your kids—manage on their own."

It seemed almost as if Jed had overheard her argument with Tyler.

I think you're controlling their futures—

When Tyler had begun to speak, she had cut him off. Now she would never know what else he might have added. She would never know if he might have been right.

She looked at Jed. "You have to help guide your kids as they grow up, though."

"Of course you do. But, within reason, you've also got to let them make their own choices and their own mistakes. Aside from that, all you can do is love them and be there when they need you."

Her babies would need a daddy, too, but they wouldn't have one. They would have her to blame for that. "I'll always be here for my kids."

"I have no doubts about that." He smiled at her, his clear blue eyes holding her gaze.

"And I think I've got your message, boss," she said softly. "I should have expected you to try a little reverse psychology. You did everything you could to bring us together, didn't you? Including leaving Tyler on his own the night of the wedding?"

He chuckled but said nothing else.

Jed was helping, after all. He was teaching her about love and acceptance…and learning from mistakes.

Suddenly, she realized Grandma had used the same tactics on her.

You have to let him go from your heart.

She couldn't let Tyler go. He was in her heart and always would be.

She stared back at Jed. "You and Grandma know exactly how I feel about Tyler, don't you?"

"I think we do."

She sighed. "I've messed things up, Jed. Tyler left because I told him to go."

He reached across the bed to pat her hand. "Nobody can fault you for that, girl. No matter how you feel, you need to do what's right for the babies. And you *are* doing the right thing by putting them first."

Her eyes misted. She blinked the moisture away.

Grandma had said the same thing in just those words. She and Jed *were* trying to help, by forcing her to see her mistakes for herself.

Her worst mistake of all had come from not trusting Tyler.

Chapter 19

The minute she finished up her work, Shay rushed out to her car. This was the first day she had driven it since Tyler had picked her and the triplets up at the hospital. The outside was still shiny and clean. The inside still smelled faintly of his aftershave. She gripped the wheel and sped away from the Hitching Post.

This was also the first time she had been separated from the babies since the day they were born. The few hours apart from them had seemed endless.

The weeks Tyler had been gone felt like an eternity.

At the house, all three triplets were fast asleep in their cribs.

She could envision Tyler reaching down to lift Timothy or Jamie or Bree, always moving so carefully as he carried one of them across the room. She could see him with a bundle in the crook of his arm as he bottle-fed a baby. She recalled him changing a pair of pajamas and muttering about the tiny fastenings.

He'd resisted learning to change a diaper, though. Her laugh at that thought ended on a small sob. Now he would never learn.

By the time the babies began to wake and look for a feeding, she was more than ready to cuddle each one to her.

Grandma walked into the bedroom just as Shay kissed Bree and tucked her back into the crib. "Giving that one a little extra loving, are you?"

Yes. The extra loving Bree was missing from her daddy. She forced a smile. "You can never give too much."

"That's true enough."

Tyler had been proud of Timothy for being the strong big brother and had encouraged Jamie, the smaller of the two boys, to stretch and grow. But whether he had realized it or not, he had developed a special bond with his daughter.

Gonna be a heartbreaker someday.

Bree had become Daddy's little girl.

"And what's going on with you, love?" Grandma crooned to Timothy. She gestured to the crib. "Just see what our big boy has done, Shay."

Shay moved closer. Timothy had kicked off the light blanket she had draped over him. "I think that exercise we've been giving him is paying off." She lifted him, holding him upright with his feet just above the mattress. He flexed his legs, kicking so energetically his tiny feet pushed the covers aside.

"I do believe we've just seen him reach a milestone," Grandma said softly.

"I think you're right." Shay's voice sounded shaky. Her laugh cracked in the middle. Her eyes flooded with tears she fought to blink away. "Here, Grandma. Maybe you'll have better luck tucking him in than I did. I'll be right back."

Brushing at her eyes, she left the room.

The thought of all the milestones, of all the progress the babies would make without their daddy to see them, had broken her.

She went down the hall to her bedroom. Her cell phone sat on the corner of the dresser. She grabbed it and touched the screen to bring up the last number she had called.

The phone on the other end rang and rang, finally switching to voice messaging. Swallowing a sigh of impatience, she waited for the recorded message to end.

At the beep, she took a deep breath, brushed away her tears again and said, "Layne, when you get this, please call me. I need to talk."

The sun was just setting when Tyler pulled up and parked at the curb in front of the small two-story house. Lights shone through the front window curtains, and music floated through the open window. Flowers in boxes attached to the porch railing bobbed in the breeze, reminding him of the balloons tied to the mug he had bought for Shay. The air smelled of those flowers and fresh earth, and above that of garlic and tomatoes, probably from supper bubbling on the stove.

It was all so different from the big city and his parents' place. Here, he could breathe.

When he rang the bell, the sound of the radio lowered.

"I'll get it, Grandma," Shay called from inside the house. "It's probably Jed."

A minute later, the door swung open. She stood there with her hand gripping the door the way she had the day he'd come home...come back from his shopping trip. The day he had kissed her. Suddenly, he couldn't breathe at all.

Her eyes were huge and glowing. "You...you're here."

He coughed out a breath, looked down at himself, then up again. Not smiling, he said, "Yeah. So I am. Can we talk?"

She frowned, and his heart thudded against his breastbone. Looking puzzled, she stepped onto the porch.

"Wait," he said. "Could we talk upstairs?"

"In the babies' room?"

He nodded. "I want to see the kids."

She stared past him to the flowers blowing in the breeze, yet her gaze seemed unfocused. "They'll want to see you."

They, not *we*.

But she turned and went back inside. It was a start.

He followed her through the living room and up the stairs, his heart hammering harder than it should have after so little exertion.

On the landing, he reached out to put his hand on her shoulder to stop her from walking down the hall. Instantly, the warmth of her made him a little crazy, made him want to take her into his arms and kiss her until she agreed to everything he was going to ask her tonight.

Sanity made him drop his hand and step back. "Before we go in there, I have to tell you something. I want more than just this one visit, Shay. I want to see the babies whenever I can. I want to know I'm part of their lives." He braced himself, knowing that after the way he had left her—again—he would have to fight for his rights. Would have to face the risk of losing both the battle and something very precious in the process.

Stunned, he watched her nod.

"You *are* part of their lives. I'm not going to stand in the way of you seeing them."

It was more than he could have hoped for. More than he deserved.

In the babies' room, he went directly to the cribs. All three were awake, probably ready for yet another feeding. He lifted Bree from the crib and held her against him.

There's my little girl, he wanted to say, but didn't.

"She's…bigger," he managed.

"Yes." Shay's features softened in a small smile. "When you're only a month old, a few weeks make a huge difference."

"Are their checkups going okay?"

"They're great." And now he saw the full smile he had been waiting for.

He wanted to reach out and touch her cheek. Instead, he brushed Bree's head lightly with his fingertips. "She has curls."

"They all do, now that their hair has grown a bit."

Bree turned her head, nestling against him the way she had before he had left. His chest swelled with pride. "She remembers me." His voice shook.

"I was just getting their bottles." Shay's voice sounded wobbly, too. "Do you want to hold her while I go downstairs?"

"Yeah, I do." He wanted much more than that.

One step at a time.

Shay's question felt like a nod of acceptance. It gave him hope that coming back here had been the right thing to do.

He hadn't lied. He wanted to see the babies whenever he could. Being a part of their lives had become more important to him than he could have believed possible. But as much as that would mean to him, it wasn't enough.

He wanted his return to lead to something he might never be able to earn—a permanent place in Shay's life, too.

When she left the room, he carried the baby over to the rocking chair in the corner. "What am I gonna do, Bree?" he asked quietly. "I hurt your mom last summer. I hurt her a lot. And now I want to win her back." Bree stared up at him.

The nurse at the hospital had told him babies this age couldn't see very far. He held Bree up closer to his face. She kept her gaze fastened on him. "It's not going to be easy, I know that. First, I'm going to have to make amends…somehow. And then…your mom said I wasn't in this for the long haul. Maybe I didn't have an answer at the time, but I have one now. I'm with you and your brothers for life."

He watched her closely. "It'll take some doing to convince your mom I'm not just making empty promises. But when all is said and done, she'll believe me, don't you think?"

The baby squirmed in his arms. Her eyes crinkled shut. Her mouth pursed, then curved up at the corners. He didn't care what Cole said—his little girl had just smiled at him.

He kissed her forehead. "Thanks for the vote of confidence, Bree."

From downstairs, he heard the doorbell, followed by Shay's voice and another, deeper voice he recognized.

A minute later, he heard Jed's boots on the stairs.

The older man appeared in doorway. "Well, look who's back." He crossed the room, his hand outstretched. Tyler shook hands with him. "Couldn't stay away, could you, boy?"

"No, I couldn't," he admitted.

"I can't say as I blame you, with three little ones like these. If they were mine, I'd come home, too."

"Home?"

Jed smiled. "They say that's where your heart is."

Tyler looked down at Bree, then over at the boys in their cribs, and finally at the woman who had just walked through the doorway.

Jed was right. He had come back to Cowboy Creek because this is where he'd found both his heart and his home.

Shay watched Tyler move restlessly around the babies' room. He looked like he wanted to run, the way he had not once but twice before.

Grandma had come upstairs to greet Jed. They all chatted for a few minutes, then the two of them had gone downstairs for a glass of sweet tea before supper. By that time, Shay had fed the babies. Tyler had thought Bree was ready to go first this time, and Shay had agreed. Timothy had followed, and Jamie had eaten last.

She tucked Jamie into the crib and returned to the rocking chair. "You'll stay for supper?" she asked Tyler.

He turned to her. "Yes, I will." He cleared his throat and shoved his hands into his back pockets. "In case you were wondering where I went when I left, I went back to Texas, to the ranch where I'd been working. But things weren't the same as when I'd been there before. *I* wasn't the same."

"Becoming a daddy must make you look at everything differently. I know becoming a mom has had that effect on me."

"That's part of it." He crossed the room to her and took a seat on the footstool she had put aside. The small lamp on the dresser made his hair a glossy black. The pearl snaps on his shirtfront winked at her, and his champion belt buckle shone in the light.

"The other part is," he went on, "I've been feeling restless for a long time without knowing why. The feeling kicked in last summer, when I came here for the wedding and spent time with all the Garlands. And with you. Once I left, the feeling got worse instead of better."

She held her breath.

He smiled. "I think being around the Hitching Post made me see what I was missing. A family. And being with you made me want something I'd never wanted before. A place to settle for good."

"Then…then why didn't you come back?" Her voice broke.

"I didn't know all this last summer. I didn't know it even a few weeks ago." He wouldn't meet her eyes. "It wasn't until I left this time that I figured out what was wrong." He rested his elbows on his knees and linked his fingers together in front of him. "While I was back in Texas, I took a trip to see my folks."

"How did that go?"

He stared down at his hands. "Badly. But nothing worse than I might've imagined. I told you my parents never had my back, that my father pushed me."

When he didn't continue, she said, "I remember. You said he tried to make a man out of you."

"Yeah. But it wasn't the kind of man I wanted to be. And I wasn't the son they wanted. My father's a corporate lawyer with a big salary and the clothes and cars and condo to go with it. My entire life, my parents attempted to talk me into following in his footsteps. I tried. I tried to accept their views and their idea of success. Finally, I got to the point where I couldn't do that anymore. Because they're not *my* views."

Now, he looked at her, his eyes shining in the lamplight. "Shay, I might have grown up in a city, but I'm a born cowboy. That's the life I want. But I don't want to live that life alone." He took her hand and brushed his thumb across her knuckles. "I gave up the job in Texas—again. Permanently, this time. I talked to the manager at the hardware store here in town. He said he might have an opening coming up. He also gave me the name of a couple of local distributors he works with, said they're always looking for folks to do outside sales." He squeezed her fingers. "I'll do anything I have to, to prove to you I'm ready to settle down. I want roots. I want a family—*our* family."

Her eyes flooded. She blinked but couldn't hold back tears. He wiped them away. "Oh, Tyler." Her exhalation sounded more like a sob. "You already *have* proven yourself—to me and to everyone else who has met you here. I told you, we can all see what a good man you are, just by the way you care about our babies." She squeezed his fingers. "You must have believed me, or you wouldn't have come back."

His eyebrows came together in a puzzled frown. "You told me?"

"Yes. In my message."

"What message?"

She blinked. "On your phone. I had Layne get your number from Cole, and I called you this morning."

"I haven't looked at my phone since I left my parents' house last night. I heard a call come in earlier today and figured it was my father, wanting to ram his point home about how irresponsible I'd been." Suddenly, he laughed. "You left me a message?" he said wonderingly.

She nodded. "I told you just what I said now—that we all know you're a good man. And," she added softly, "I asked you to come back so we could talk things out."

"I'm here now."

She nodded again.

"Does that mean you've forgiven me for leaving you—twice?"

"Yes." She laced her fingers through his. "And I hope you'll forgive me for how I treated you when you came back. I'm sorry, Tyler. I was so wrong to push you away just because of what you do—of who you *are*. And you were right. I *was* holding my own experience with my dad against you. When I kept comparing you to him, I never really gave you a chance." She sighed. "I'm as bad as your parents are, not accepting your choices."

"You didn't know about them."

"No, but I know about me and how overly sensitive I am about cowboys and the rodeo. I also know you were right about my controlling the babies' future. Or at least, that's what I seemed to be doing, only because

I was too determined to justify my feelings and to win the argument." She blinked a few times, then stared at him again. "I wouldn't try to run my own children's—our children's—lives. I'm so sorry I tried to do that to you, too."

"Does that mean I won't have to give up wrangling?"

She laughed. "Yes, that's what it means. I believe in you, Tyler. And if you ever listen to my phone message, you'll know that I love you."

He smiled. "I love you, too."

He cupped her face in his hands and brushed his mouth against hers, kissing her the way she loved to begin, soft and easy and sweet. But this time there was a hint of the spice she loved, too. It felt like a promise offered and accepted, a promise that wouldn't break.

She put her hands on his shoulders and tilted her head back to look up at him. "You know," she said with a smile, "I've decided I would be content to have our babies follow in your footsteps."

"Become cowboys, you mean?" When she nodded, he laughed. "Well, it's up to them, of course." She nodded again. "But if that's what any or all of them choose, it's fine with me. Because my footsteps won't ever take me far from home."

Epilogue

Two months later

In the banquet hall of the Hitching Post, Tyler stood looking around him. Everything had turned out perfectly, according to Shay, who had told him more than once she was over the moon with happiness.

He was just glad his new bride hadn't had to do any of the work to prepare for their wedding. In fact, she had given up her job at the hotel, for now anyway, to stay home with their babies.

If her former boss resented the fact, he wasn't letting on.

Jed looked darned good in his tuxedo and cummerbund.

Tyler smiled. The man had given Tina away to Cole at their ceremony last year...at the wedding where he had first met Shay. "You're making a habit of walking brides down the aisle."

"It's great advertising for his business," Shay said with a laugh.

"The Hitching Post can use the plug," Jed agreed.

"I meant the *matchmaking* business."

Now Jed and Tyler laughed.

As Jed walked away, Tyler looked across the dance floor to one of the tables at the front of the room. Shay had convinced him to extend a wedding invitation to his parents, and to his surprise, they had accepted. They sat at the table with Mo and Sugar. All four of them had their heads bent over the baby books Mo had brought to show off to everyone at the reception.

Pictures were nice, but he looked forward to seeing the kids upstairs later, where Pete's housekeeper was minding them for the evening.

"What do you think?" Shay asked.

She was looking in that direction, too.

"For the babies' sakes, I think I can make an effort to get along." The band struck up another slow song. He took her into his arms. "Speaking of getting, you're happy you got your June wedding?"

"Of course I am. It's something I've dreamed about my entire life. And so are you."

Her unconditional support was all he ever could have wanted, too. "That's little enough to give you, after everything you've given me. Love and a home and a family. And you've made today the best day of my life."

"I've done more than that."

He smiled down at her. Her eyes sparkled. "I'll say. You carried our kids for almost nine months and brought them into this world."

"And named them Timothy and Jamie and Bree."

"So you did."

"Timothy. Jamie. And Bree," she said with soft emphasis.

"Great names. Timothy. Ja—" He stopped short in the middle of the dance floor, hardly believing the mental leap he had just made. "Timothy. Jamie. Bree. Tyler John Buckham," he said, his voice cracking. "You gave them my initials."

She nodded. "I decided on that the day the doctor told me I was carrying three babies."

"The day—?" His throat grew so tight, he couldn't speak. He waited a moment and tried again. "Even after I'd left all those months ago?"

"Even after. I wanted them to have a connection to you." She rested her cheek against his chest. He tilted his head down to hear her voice over the music. Her breath tickled his ear. "Even when I wanted to hate you, I loved you, Tyler. When the doctor told me the news, I was still upset about your leaving, about realizing I might never see you again and that the babies might never know you. But I also realized you were part of them and always would be." She raised her head to meet his eyes.

He saw her through a blur. He blinked, cleared his throat and smiled. "I love Timothy and Jamie and Bree."

"I know you do."

He held her closer. "I love you, Shay. I'll always be here for you and the kids."

She smiled. "I believe you, cowboy. And we all love you, too."

* * * * *

Tina Leonard is a *New York Times* bestselling and award-winning author of more than fifty projects, including several popular miniseries for Harlequin. Known for bad-boy heroes and smart, adventurous heroines, her books have made the *USA TODAY*, Waldenbooks, Ingram and Nielsen BookScan bestseller lists. Born on a military base, Tina lived in many states before eventually marrying the boy who did her crayon printing for her in the first grade. You can visit her at tinaleonard.com, and follow her on Facebook and Twitter.

Books by Tina Leonard

Harlequin American Romance

Bridesmaids Creek

The Rebel Cowboy's Quadruplets
The SEAL's Holiday Babies
The Twins' Rodeo Rider

Callahan Cowboys

A Callahan Wedding
The Renegade Cowboy Returns
The Cowboy Soldier's Sons
Christmas in Texas
"Christmas Baby Blessings"
A Callahan Outlaw's Twins
His Callahan Bride's Baby
Branded by a Callahan
Callahan Cowboy Triplets
A Callahan Christmas Miracle
Her Callahan Family Man
Sweet Callahan Homecoming

Visit the Author Profile page at Harlequin.com for more titles.

Callahan
Cowboy Triplets

TINA LEONARD

My heartfelt gratitude to all the loyal and supportive readers who believe in a Callahan way of life.

Chapter 1

"You can drive yourself crazy trying to outfox a Callahan. That goes double for the Callahan women."
—Bode Jenkins, neighboring ranch owner bragging a bit about his three Callahan granddaughters to a reporter

Tighe Callahan sized up the enormous spotted bull that eyed him warily. "Hello, Firefreak," he said. "You may have bested my twin, Dante, but I aim to ride you until you're soft as glove leather. Gonna retire you to the kiddie rides."

The legendary badass rank bull snorted a heavy breath his way, daring him. Dark eyes glared attitude and a *no-you-won't* warning.

"You're crazy, Tighe," his brother Jace said. "I'm telling you, that one wants to kill you."

"Feeling's mutual." Tighe grinned and knocked on the wall of the pen. "If Dante stayed on him for five seconds, I ought to at least go ten."

Jace looked at Tighe doubtfully. "Sure. You can do it. Whatever." He glanced around. "I think I'll go get some popcorn and find a pretty girl to share it with. You and Firefreak just go ahead and chat about life. Maybe a one-sided conversation, but those are your favorite, anyway."

Jace wandered off. Tighe studied the bull, which never broke eye contact with him, his gaze wise from the scores of cowboys he'd mercilessly tossed, earning himself a legendary status.

"I'm a real believer in the power of positive thinking, old son," Tighe told his horned adversary. "And I'm positive that tomorrow my name will live on as the first cowboy to ever pin a bull's-eye on you and hit it dead center. See, I figure it was destiny that I finally drew you. And what you don't know is that I've got a secret training regimen. You think you're tough, but you don't know tough until you've spent a couple years being ridden by Callahan tots. You only have to do your job for eight seconds, throw off a cowboy or two. Me? My job can go on for hours. I'm tough as nails, my spotted nemesis."

Firefreak's response was to throw a hoof his way, crashing into the wall of the pen, which thundered under the blow. Tighe tipped his hat and turned to go.

"Hi, Tighe," a feisty little darling he knew too well said, and Tighe stopped dead in his tracks.

"Sawyer Cash, what are you doing here?" He glanced around. If Jace had seen Sawyer—the new nanny bodyguard at Rancho Diablo and daughter of Storm Cash, their neighbor and a man they weren't too sure they trusted—he would have run up the red flag of danger. Jace had never mentioned it, but Tighe was pretty sure his brother had a thing for the petite redhead.

"Hi, Tighe," River Martin said, coming to join Sawyer, and Tighe felt his heart start to palpitate. Now here was his dream, his unattainable brunette princess— even though he liked to tell his family he secretly had River in the bag—smiling at him, as sweet as cherry wine. "We heard you're going to ride a bull tomorrow, so the girls and I decided to come out and watch. Your sister, Ash, is here, too, but she's chatting up some cowboys. Said she wasn't interested in watching you meet your doom."

This wasn't a good sign. A man didn't need his concentration wrecked by a gorgeous female—and right now, Tighe had a twist in his gut even a few beers wouldn't chase off. Nor did he want said gorgeous, unattainable female to see him get squashed by a few tons of angry luggage with horns. A man needed to seek his holy grail and stare death in the eyes in order to realize that he was but a speck on this earth, and if the woman he adored didn't reciprocate his feelings, well, there were worse things. Like getting stomped into dust by a rank bull.

Dante'd had his five seconds on Firefreak without the woman he loved witnessing his ultimate crash into reality.

But River was smiling at him with her teasing eyes that sent him over the moon, so all Tighe could say was, "Nice of you ladies to come out." *To witness my humiliation. I was riding on guts and bravado, and somehow that particular cocktail of courage has suddenly left me stone-cold.*

River said, "Good luck," and Tighe shivered, because he did believe in magic and luck and everything spiritual. And any superstitious man knew it was taunting the devil himself to wish a cowboy good luck when the challenge he faced in the ring was nothing compared to the real challenge: forcing himself to look into a woman's sexy eyes and not drown.

He was drowning, and he had been for oh, so long.

Ten minutes later, Tighe was sitting in his truck and considering spending the night there. He'd had an offer to bunk in with some rodeo buddies, but he was in the mood to be alone.

Actually, he was in the mood to hunt up River, but pride wouldn't allow him to chase that little goddess down. He was woefully aware he'd gotten something of a reputation among his six siblings for being a love-starved schmuck, which was odd because he'd previously held a pretty impressive record for being catnip to the ladies. Galen, the eldest, was a medical doctor, but really enjoyed touting his skills as a diviner of the heart, never more than when he was ribbing Tighe about the state of his brunette heartburn. His twin, Dante, left him pretty much alone because he knew he'd been darn lucky to catch River's best friend and fellow nanny body-guard, Ana St. John. Jace thought he knew things but didn't—though that didn't stop him from snickering at Tighe's unrequited longing. Sloan, married to Kendall and the proud father of adorable twin sons, cut him some slack because he knew how much it stank when a man couldn't seem to reel in the woman of his every waking thought. Falcon was happily married now and enjoying life with his baby girl, so he considered himself fortunate and offered no decent advice. Their sister, Ashlyn, was full of witty ripostes about Tighe's lackluster attempts to woo River, but she'd been chasing the prince of her pining, Xav Phillips, for a couple of years now, with all the luck of a sleep-struck princess.

"I'm on my own," Tighe muttered, and then a voice said, "Hi, Tighe," and he about jumped out of his boots.

"Hi, River," he said, his throat suddenly thick like a tree trunk and about as useful for talking. "Where's Sawyer?"

She glanced over her shoulder. "Torturing Jace."

"It's good for him. Pretty sure she's up to the job." He wished he could kiss her, but how would she react? "I need to head off and find a motel. Did you need something?"

She shrugged, and the gesture made her breasts move under her blue, short-sleeved dress. "You can stay with me," River said, and he had to tighten his jaw so it didn't crash to the parking lot.

"Stay with you?" he repeated.

"Mmm-hmm." She smiled at him, and it was all he could do not to shout, *hell yes!* and jump into the canyon of lost sense. "I've got my own room at Sherby's," River said.

Sherby's was a quaint B and B outside Santa Fe. He knew Sherby and his wife, Anne—they were great rodeo fans and had done a fair bit of horse trading in their day. Good, honest folk. "I'm not sure Anne would care for me lodging with you, River."

"We won't tell her I've got double occupancy." She winked at him, cute as a doe, and Tighe's blood began a pounding unlike anything he could ever remember feeling—not even when he was in Afghanistan with Dante and they were trying to keep from picking grit out of their teeth and bullets out of their appendages. He had the scar from one he hadn't managed to avoid, which had lodged itself in his biceps, right under the lightning strike tattoo all the Chacon Callahan siblings wore: the sign of their bond.

"I'm not sure where there may be a vacancy," Tighe murmured doubtfully, trying to hang on to whatever fragments of good sense he possessed.

"And you probably won't find one now. Everything is full."

Dante and he had never worried much about where they were going to stay. One or the other of them always made a reservation, or they slept in their trucks. Might have been an awkward lifestyle with anyone else, but he and Dante had been each other's shadow all their lives, and especially on the rodeo circuit. No one knew Tighe like Dante did.

In fact, it had been a little lonely since Dante had gotten married. Not that he wasn't extremely happy for his knuckleheaded twin—but Tighe did miss his shadow on occasion.

"Come on," River said, "get your stuff. I promise not to lay a hand on you, big guy." She turned and walked off, leading the way, hips swaying, the lure of the wild loudly calling to Tighe, and all he could think was *Rats. Kinda wish she wasn't so good at keeping promises.*

Riding Firefreak for the full eight seconds was more likely than him catching that hot angel.

He grabbed his duffel and followed.

* * *

River sneaked Tighe in under cover of night, through a back door so none of the other guests—nor Anne Sherby—would notice she was keeping company. For one thing, everyone staying at Sherby's was female, and River wasn't sharing. For another, what good was it to have a secret crush if the whole world figured it out?

Catching a Callahan wasn't easy, and tonight, she intended to catch this one in a snare that might interest him. She had a deck of cards and a bottle of something Ashlyn said the Callahan guys liked to sip on in their upstairs library meetings at Rancho Diablo—and a comfy bed. Oh, she had absolutely no plans to seduce this cowboy—that would be dirty pool—but it wouldn't hurt a bit if they spent a little time together away from the Callahan clan of prying eyeballs and matchmaking roulette. Just to see what would happen…

"Put your duffel there," she said, pointing to a spot under the window in the tiny room.

"Whoa," Tighe said, observing the twin bed in Miss Sherby's B and B. "Do you think maybe Ms. Anne's got a futon or a sleeping bag we could discreetly inquire about?"

River smiled. "We'll manage."

"I've seen baby cribs bigger than that bed."

"Dante says you guys have shared a truck many times. This bed is about the size of a cab, isn't it?"

"Yeah, but he's my twin."

She smiled and pulled out the deck of cards and the whiskey bottle. "I don't drink, but Ash says this is your favorite."

"Wait a minute, little lady," Tighe said. "What's going on here? I've known you for about two years, and we've rarely been in the same room, much less a bed. And you brought my drink of choice. Are you setting me up?"

Of course she was setting him up. She wasn't certain it was the best idea, but she'd been asked to play this role by the Callahans. *So here I am.*

"You mean am I seducing you?" River considered him. "Do you want me to?"

His handsome face was puzzled, maybe even perplexed. He was such a gentleman—all the Callahans were—and all that chivalry kept him from wanting to make a mistake of the sexual variety.

"Don't worry," River said. "If you're that concerned about it, I'll flip you for the bed. Or beat you at twenty-one for it."

He grinned. "You can't beat me, lady. I was born playing cards, pool and hooky."

She poured him a drink. "You're going to need a shot of this for courage."

"For Firefreak? I don't need anything to give me courage for that oversize piece of shoe leather." Still, he gulped down the whiskey.

"It's getting late," River said.

"True. I'll let you have the bed, gorgeous, and I'll take the floor. Use my duffel as my pillow."

"All right. I'm going to change." She slipped into the bathroom, took off her dress, put on a pair of sleep shorts and a T-shirt. Very modest, but still feminine. Why had she allowed the Callahans to talk her into this caper? Sawyer claimed that the only way to a man's heart was making him see you, really notice you. So that you were unforgettable to him.

River was pretty certain she'd been forgettable to

Tighe for the two years she'd been guarding Sloan and Kendall's twins. Taking a deep breath, she thought about those dark navy eyes, the longish, almost black hair that begged her to run her fingers through it, the hard, strong muscles…and then she opened the door to do her job.

"Hey," Jace said, and River nearly shrieked.

"He found me," Tighe said. "He's like a homing pigeon. An ugly one, but just the same, a pigeon."

"Hi, Jace," she said, not surprised at all to see him. The plan was proceeding as outlined, even if she didn't feel all that good about the plot on Tighe.

"He's got no place to stay, either. Mind if he bunks with us?" Tighe asked.

"I promise not to snore." Jace poured himself a drink. "Ms. Sherby sure knows how to stock the stuff a guy likes."

"Fine by me." River wished Jace hadn't shown up so soon. Secretly she'd been hoping for just a couple moments alone with her dream cowboy. She sat on the bed, waited for Jace's signal.

"You're the luckiest woman in town, spending the night with two Callahans," he said as he dumped his duffel on the floor, not sounding anything like a man who was out to derail his brother.

"Good times, good times," River said, but her insincerity was lost on the two men as they shuffled the deck, splayed the cards on the small table and began a spirited game.

"You're just determined to ride that piece of ugly spotted steak tomorrow, aren't you?" Jace asked.

"You better believe it. I'm going to ride him like a little girl's pony."

River rolled her eyes. "Sexist, much?"

"Not at all. But we give gentle rides to the ladies," Jace said. "You wouldn't want to give a woman a mount that might harm her in any way."

River rolled her eyes at the typical Callahan nonsense she'd heard many times. "Jace, why aren't you riding tomorrow?"

"Thought about it. Decided I'm too good-looking to risk injuring myself on a bull." He laughed. "My brother here is on his own personal mission to separate his brain from his skull."

"Why?" River looked at Tighe, and he glanced at her, his gaze catching on her lips, it seemed, and then lower. It was the first time she could ever remember him looking at her for more than a second. She decided to see if she could get his attention off his cards, let him slowly figure out what he was missing out on. "What do you have to prove?"

"Nothing." Tighe tossed his cards onto the table, grinned at Jace. "You lose. Deal."

Clearly, he wasn't going to take the bait. Jace poured his brother another shot. Tighe slurped it down, sighing with happiness. "This is fun. I'm finally starting to relax." He glanced at her, his gaze hitting about chest level. "Anybody else think it's hot in here?"

Jace glanced at River, surreptitiously winked. She shrugged, then got up and raised the window, which would only serve to heat the room a little more. "Maybe the breeze will help."

Tighe seemed to find her legs quite interesting as she sat cross-legged on the bed.

"I win," Jace said. "What do you know? I finally

beat you." He scooped the cards up, but Tighe didn't take his gaze away from River.

"Let's see what's in this goody basket." She rose, checked out the treats Ms. Sherby put in every room.

"I'm getting tired," Tighe said. "Think I'll call it a night. My ride's at ten, and I want to be ready to rock." He got down on the floor, shoved his duffel under his head. "This is great. Thanks, River, for letting us stay."

"Have another toddy," Jace said. "It'll help you sleep." He handed his brother another shot, which Tighe quickly downed.

"If I didn't know better, I'd think you kids were trying to get me tipsy. Won't work, you know. I've got a hollow leg."

"Excuse me," River said, "did you say you have a hollow head?"

"Ha. You sound like one of my brothers now. Actually, like my sister, Ash."

Tighe didn't say anything else, and a moment later, sonorous snoring rose from the floor.

"That's it," Jace said, "he's out like a light. Never could hold his liquor."

"Now what?" River stared at the example of her perfidy sleeping like a baby at the foot of her bed. "Seems so mean to try to keep him from riding. He says it's his holy grail. Aren't Callahans fairly wedded to their holy grails? Seems like bad juju to try to keep one from his goal."

"Trust me, Tighe can't ride worth a flip. He's really only suited for the kiddie calf catch." Jace shrugged, then grinned the famous Callahan grin. "Now you just head off to your room, and I'll take care of Brother Bonehead."

Certainly, no one could say the Callahans weren't a different breed. A job was a job, and this caper had been part of hers. Even the beloved aunt of the Callahan clan, Fiona, had been in on this gig, sanctioning Jace to do whatever he could to keep Tighe off Firefreak. "If you're sure. I'm next door, if you need anything."

"One thing about you, River, we know we can always count on you to do whatever has to be done."

She wasn't sure she felt good about that compliment at the moment. With another glance at the handsome hunk on the floor, River grabbed her stuff and headed to her own room.

It might be the only time she ever had Tighe in a bedroom, and oh, how she hoped it wasn't. But once he figured out her part in this escapade, there was no way he'd see her as anything but the woman who'd destroyed his dream, smashed his holy grail to pieces.

Which was no way to catch the man you'd been fantasizing about for the longest time.

She went into her room and closed the door. Got into bed, stared at the ceiling. As a bodyguard, she stuck to her assignment. Watching over the twins, Carlos and Isaiah, was her pride and joy.

Tonight had been a mission, no reason for regret. Tomorrow, she'd be back with Sloan and Kendall's little boys, and that was all that mattered.

Wasn't it? Not that sleeping cowboy she was helping to divert from his dream?

He was never going to forgive her for her role in his distraction.

River had nearly fallen asleep, was drifting on a cloud of guilt and soft-focus sexy fantasies of Tighe, when she heard the door quietly open. She sat up, peering through the darkness. "Sawyer?"

"Not exactly, gorgeous," Tighe said, sliding into bed, pulling her up against his rock-hard body. "You shouldn't let Jace talk you into things, babe, he's a newb." Tighe kissed her neck, and hot, dizzying tingles shot all over her. "But since you're just so darn sweet—and because I know Jace dragged you into his dumb scheme—I'm going to give you another chance to try to keep me off that bull."

Chapter 2

The next afternoon, River sat in the bleachers at the rodeo, waiting for Tighe to get himself squished. Jace seemed certain his brother couldn't ride very well. River had no reason to doubt Jace and Ash's reasoning for trying to stop Tighe, or their aunt Fiona's, for that matter, although Fiona's motives could be suspect at times.

After Tighe made love to her last night, he'd kissed her, told her she was darling and cute as a button, and that he'd think about her every second today, except when he was on the back of Firefreak.

Tighe was, in a word, an ass.

Jace slid onto the bleacher next to her, handing her some popcorn.

"Hey," he said. "Fancy meeting you here."

"Yeah. You, too." She overlooked the corny greeting, her gaze searching for Tighe among the cowboys in the arena.

"Funny thing. I lost sight of my brother last night."

"Did you?" River didn't dare glance his way. The Callahans might have hatched a plot to keep Tighe off his nemesis, but she'd been completely unable to resist his charming persuasion.

"I did. Tighe was nowhere to be found." Jace shook his head. "I think I might have sipped a little too liberally from Tighe's libation. My head's killing me." He handed her a soda off a cardboard tray he'd carried into the bleachers. "You didn't see him?"

She shook her head. It wasn't a total fib—she *hadn't* seen Tighe in the darkness. But she'd felt him, and he'd made glorious love to her that she'd remember for days.

"Don't know where he went. I looked for him near the pens, but no one's seen him." Jace shrugged. "He hasn't scratched, either, which is a bad sign that our plan didn't work."

"*Your* plan," River said. "I refuse to take further part in keeping Tighe from his…goal."

Jace glanced at her. "I don't blame you. He's a rascal."

"You're all rascals. Including your sister, Ashlyn, and your aunt Fiona."

Jace laughed. "No argument there. But we're doing what's best for him. Ever since Tighe was little, he thought he was a big shot."

"How is he different from, say, you?"

"Because I can do what I brag about. Tighe isn't Dante. He isn't smart like Galen. He's not tough like Ash. If it's true what Grandfather Running Bear says about one of us being the hunted one, the one who'll bring destruction to the family, it'd be Tighe. He's always on a quest, but he never quite achieves it. You get what I'm saying?"

"I don't want to talk about it," River said, "I've worked for the Callahans for quite a while. I know the drill."

"I wouldn't have thought you'd feel guilty, River. Your job is to be a bodyguard. Protecting Callahans is what you do, right?" Jace leaned back, a popcorn-eating philosopher. "Protecting Tighe from himself is no different from your normal job description."

"Whatever." River's nerves were jangling. "I don't feel guilty, just for the record."

"You did the best you could."

"Shush, Jace," she said, "I can't hear the announcer. I don't want to miss Tighe ride."

"True, if we blink we'll miss him," Jace said, laughing.

"You guys are mean. Tighe's on a mission." River felt compelled to stand up for him, even if she'd been part of the plot to keep him off the bounty bull. Secretly, she hoped Tighe met his desired goal, whatever it was that urged him on—because then...

Then he might want to settle down like his Callahan brothers, Sloan, Falcon and Dante.

That was treacherous thinking. One night of sexy lovemaking didn't mean anything—at least, it probably hadn't to Tighe.

But it had to her. If the opportunity presented itself again, she doubted she'd refuse another night in Tighe's arms.

In fact, she knew she wouldn't.

She might even instigate it.

* * *

It was time: the moment of truth. Either he could take it or he couldn't; it was time to find out if he could pin the tail on the donkey.

"Good luck," said Galen, who'd come out to watch his fall from grace. But Tighe had told him in no uncertain terms that he was going to stay on Firefreak for the whole eight seconds, come hell or high water.

"Thanks." He took a deep breath, approached the chute. "Is River watching?"

"I'm sure she has every intention of watching you win the buckle, bro," Galen said, and Tighe swallowed hard.

"Great." He had to make eight seconds. What price being a hero? Priceless, no matter how many bruised ribs. He got on the chute amid muttered encouragement from the other cowboys helping load up Firefreak's slayer. He mounted the massive body, which had been relatively still until he seated himself, and began wrapping his hand—then crashes, curses and fear rang through his ears in a tunnel of mindless noise. He nodded, the chute jerked open and Firefreak burst into action.

Tighe stared up at the arena ceiling, shocked to find himself on his back. A bullfighter yelled, helped guide him in a headlong rush to the corral side as Tighe gasped from the pain flooding his leg. Firefreak danced a wild jig of triumph before being chased from the ring.

Tighe glanced at the time.

Three seconds. He'd made it three seconds.

And he was pretty certain he'd done something to his leg. Heat and white-hot pain shot up to his groin. Worse, he'd proved his family right—in front of River.

"Are you all right, Tighe?" River asked, suddenly at his side as Galen checked him over.

Tighe stumbled toward a bench and let his brothers help him out of his gear. "I'm fine. Nothing damaged but my pride."

"And his leg," Galen announced. "Brother, you're going to be bed-bound for a while."

"I'm fine." Tighe was bothered that he hadn't had the epiphany he'd been expecting while on Firefreak. True, Dante had been known to exaggerate—and maybe he'd even told a wee fib just to goad Tighe on. But Dante had sworn to his siblings that for the few seconds he'd been on that bull, he'd been absolutely, mindlessly free of his demons.

"You're not fine." Galen moved a practiced hand over his leg, divining what would take other doctors X-rays to learn. "You have a fracture, brother. And a groin tear. You'll be out of commission a good six weeks."

"And we were already shorthanded," Ashlyn said, not sparing words as his other siblings grouped around him. "You'll have to learn to take care of yourself from your bed. None of us can give up ranch duties to tend you, when we told you that riding Firefreak was practically a death wish for you."

He wasn't the big zero on the back of a bull they thought he was. "I'll be fine." He looked at River, saw the worry on her face, tried to smile reassuringly. "I am fine."

"I'll nurse him." She looked at him, then around at his siblings. "Goodness knows he's a pain, but I can bring the twins and watch all three of them."

"Three children," Ash said. "Somehow seems fitting." She glared at her brother.

"You guys can be as annoyed as you want," Tighe said. "As soon as I'm healed, I'm getting right back on that ornery son of a gun."

"He hit his head." Jace shook his own numskull, not understanding his brother's determination. "You must have, or you wouldn't say something so dumb."

"I'm getting back on him," Tighe repeated, "Firefreak is a pussycat."

"Maybe you can talk some sense into my intelligence-challenged brother," Ash whispered to River.

Tighe smiled. Dante said that riding Firefreak had brought him closer to Ana, and now River was going to take care of him while he was bed-bound.

Firefreak's the best thing that ever happened to me. "Awesome," Tighe said, swallowing back a slight moan as Galen and Jace began fitting a board to his leg so they could get him to a hospital. Tighe winked at River, the woman to whom he'd made love last night—sweet as an angel—the only woman worth pulling his groin over just to get her attention.

After a trip to the hospital and then a visit to an orthopedist that didn't do much for his mental state, which at the moment was black and aggrieved, Tighe sat in Jace's truck, his leg up on the backseat, thrilled to be going home. The seven-chimney, Tudor-style mansion that Molly and Jeremiah Callahan had built long ago to house their young family of six sturdy Callahan boys— the Chacon Callahans' cousins—rose like a beautiful postcard from its New Mexico grounds. Backed by panoramic spools of canyons and gorges, Rancho Diablo was an amazing sight. Tighe didn't think he'd ever get over the breathtaking beauty of the ranch. He'd been born and raised in the Chacon tribe, then served in the military, where life was a whole lot different than here. He loved the ranch and the small town of Diablo, loved being with his family, enjoying a new closeness they hadn't been able to share in many years. Even the constant threat of danger couldn't always rub the shine off Rancho Diablo's surroundings.

But the truck didn't turn toward the main house, and Tighe's radar went on alert. "Why are you taking me to Sloan and Kendall's house?" Something was most certainly afoot.

"Since River has agreed to be your nurse—I can't imagine why—" Ash said, "Kendall says it would be best for you to be here. This way River can keep an eye on all her charges. It'll be better if the twins' normal schedule isn't interrupted."

This didn't sound good at all. "Much as I love my little nephews," Tighe said, "I don't want to stay at Sloan and Kendall's. I'll stay in my own room in the bunkhouse." How could he ever be alone with River if he was sharing space with little Carlos and Isaiah? They were active, trying to pull themselves up on unsteady feet, eager to find their range and explore.

There would be no time for romancing the tall, delicious bodyguard with two busy rug rats taking up her every second. "Not to be selfish or anything," he said, and Ash said, "Go ahead and admit it, you're selfish. I can hear the wheels turning in your head. 'How can I be alone with River if I'm laid up with my darling nephews?'" she added in a high voice, mimicking what she thought he was thinking, and in fact, what he had been thinking.

"I am selfish." Tighe sighed. "Something's happened to me. I used to be footloose and, well, footloose."

"Now it's just your head that's loose. Come on, brother. Let me help you inside." Ash hopped out, opened his door.

He glared at her. "No. Take me to the bunkhouse, or the main house. I would rather suffer in silence than be just another—"

"Helpless person River has to keep an eye on?" Ash prodded.

"The trouble is, you don't suffer in silence. Come on." Jace put his shoulder under Tighe's to give him support as he unsteadily maneuvered himself out of the truck. "You're lucky we don't just leave you out in the peacock pens to heal, where we can't hear you moan and groan."

It was too humiliating. He wouldn't look like a warrior, wouldn't be a hero with badass courageous qualities if his woman tossed him in with the kiddies as an extra responsibility.

"Either you take me to the bunkhouse or I'm going to the canyons." After making fierce love to that little lady practically all night long, he wasn't about to appear anything less than a stud—and he couldn't be that if he was laid out on a sofa. "The weather's fine. The canyons suit me just as well as anywhere."

"Be a sitting duck for Uncle Wolf and his cretinous crew," Jace said. "Come on, be practical, bro."

Jace didn't understand practical. Practical was when you could think past the sirens that screamed in your head every time the woman you had a thing for got within ten feet. Tighe had lost his practicality a long time ago. "Canyons or bunkhouse. Take your pick. Can't promise to stay either place."

Ash sighed. "Flip a coin. Either decision is bad. Fiona will roost on the bunkhouse if you stay there, she'll be so worried that you're an easy mark. The canyons and you're even more of a sitting duck."

That sounded very much like conditions he'd lived under in Afghanistan. He could survive there by his wits, and wouldn't be taking up any of the family's time. Tighe brightened. "The canyons. Who's riding canyon right now?"

"You were supposed to," Jace said sourly. "It was your shift. Now Xav Phillips says he'll come back and take over, which isn't a good idea." Jace glanced at Ash, who was talking on a cell phone to River, complaining that Tighe was a stubborn ass. "We don't need Xav in the canyons, dude, as you well know, because Ash will find a thousand reasons and ways to get down there to haunt her favorite cowboy."

"Who's got a favorite cowboy?" Ash asked, returning. "Apparently, not River right now. She's annoyed with you, Tighe." Ash grinned. "She says you have to go to Sloan's, because she can't leave the twins to visit you in the bunkhouse."

Even better. He didn't want River around while he healed. A lightning flash of intuition told him he'd be better off returning when he was all better, a hero again—not the poor sap everyone was annoyed with. "Really, I'm such a pain in the ass, the only place I can be is the canyons."

"I agree completely. Still, a bad idea," Jace said.

"But—" Ash began, and Tighe waved her to silence. "I've made up my mind." What use was he as a man if he was on par with the twins? "I got myself into this mess and I'll get myself out. As a matter of fact, just take me to the stone and fire ring. All I need is a bottle of whiskey and some girlie mags. I'll be fine."

Ash and Jace stared at him, their expressions dismayed.

"Okay, no girlie mags," Tighe said, loving messing with his siblings. They thought he wasn't big and bad right now. Well, he was; he was a monster pain in the butt, and that was just the way a man should be.

"You'll be unprotected," Ash said. "Much as you're the only one among us with such disregard for yourself, you still do not want to put yourself out there with a bull's-eye on you for Wolf and his gang. Listen to me," she pleaded. "I'll worry myself sick."

"Sick about what?" River asked.

The three Callahans stared at the tall woman who'd just walked up, catching the last words of their conversation. Just the sight of that gorgeous creature made his blood pound. River gave him the wild, mad dreams of a man who'd tasted heaven once and was determined to do it again. Once he was healed, he was coming back for her.

"Nobody's worried about a thing," Tighe said.

"I'm worried." Ash looked at River for help. "My jackass of a brother wants to camp out in the open instead of stay in the house with you and the twins. In the *open*," she emphasized.

River didn't miss Ash's message. She met his gaze, didn't look away. Peered deep inside him, until he felt her reaching into his soul.

The woman practically stole his very breath.

"I'll drive you out there," River said.

Chapter 3

After he'd packed up some gear and run the gauntlet of a protesting aunt Fiona and family, River hustled Tighe into the military jeep and steered it toward the canyons. He glanced over at the goddess next to him, trying to decipher the change in her mood. She certainly wasn't the cooing, sexy tigress he'd had in his arms last night.

He'd have to call River's mood elusive, which didn't sit well with him at all. It almost felt as if she was abandoning him without a thought.

"Thanks for the ride. My siblings weren't going to bring me."

Glossy dark strands of hair blew around her face as she drove, rather speedily, he thought, given the uneven terrain. She could at least quit mashing the pedal.

"It's not my worry if you've got a death wish. I have no desire to keep you from your fondest desires, Tighe."

That didn't sound right. *She* was his fondest desire. "I don't have a death wish."

"Don't you?" She leveled him with brown eyes that held not a care in them. "First Firefreak. Now sleeping in the open, when you know that the ranch has been under siege for forever. For longer than either you or I have even been here."

Aw, she was fretting about him, the cute little thing. He reached over and gave her shoulder an affectionate squeeze.

She batted away his hand. His brows rose. "Regretting last night?"

She turned to him, her forehead pinched in a frown. "Regretting what?"

He hardly knew what to say, since this darling angel seemed to have suddenly sprouted a ten-inch layer of cactus needles around herself. "You and me."

"Hardly," she shot back. "It didn't mean a thing, cowboy."

He tried not to let his jaw fall open. "Nothing?"

"Should it have?"

It certainly had to him. Hell, he'd gotten on Firefreak for her! Making love to her, plus facing his greatest challenge since coming to Diablo—well, it was the greatest cocktail of adrenaline and gut-punching life he'd ever experienced. "You know me. It's just all about getting naked," he bragged, trying to sound like his old self, the self he'd been before they'd made love. His whole world had changed—shouldn't hers have, too?

"Where am I dropping you off?"

She sounded completely unworried. Tighe comforted himself that that was because everyone knew he could take care of himself. "At the stone ring, please."

At that news, she did look a little alarmed. "You'll be out in the open. I think your family assumes you're at least taking shelter in one of the caves or overhangs."

"Wouldn't do any good. Wolf will find me if he wants to, and frankly, I don't care if he does."

"You're injured, Tighe. I know you don't like to admit to mortality, but you do recall that seven goons tied up your sister and Xav Phillips just last month?"

Tighe had no intention of hanging out in a cave like a cowering dog, away from the stars he loved and the fresh breezes that stirred his soul. "It's just a little groin pull, darling. No worries. However," he said, perking up, "maybe you'd like to hang around and nurse my groi—"

"And a hairline fracture," River interrupted.

"I mend best in the open. I lived in the tribe. Was deployed to some hellish places. Don't you worry about me, beautiful."

"I'm not," she snapped. "I think you're an idiot."

Well, that wasn't how a man wanted the angel of his dreams to view him. "Harsh."

"Honest."

She pulled up to the stone ring. Large rocks, one set for each of the seven Chacon Callahans, encircled a small glowing fire. His grandfather, Chief Running Bear, tended the blaze. The chief said this place was their home now, while they protected Callahan land, and the mystical black Diablos, the spirit horses that lived in the canyons. They were the true wealth of Rancho Diablo.

"Home sweet home," Tighe said.

"Then get out," River said, "if this is where you want to be."

He turned to look at her. "Gorgeous, I'm pretty sure I showed you a good time in bed. Is there a reason you're all prickly suddenly?"

She met his gaze. "I told you. I'm pretty sure you're the loose cannon I always believed you were."

He winced internally. This was true. But it wasn't necessary to rub in the fact that he'd clearly failed to change her mind. "All right, sweet face. Try not to miss me too much," he said, getting out of the jeep and managing his crutches a bit more slowly and painfully than his jaunty tone implied.

"I won't miss you at all." She wheeled the jeep around and drove away, apparently not even curious as to where he planned to lay his bedroll.

"Guess that means we won't be sharing the old pillow tonight. It's a shame, because I'm pretty sure you're kidding yourself, my hottie bodyguard." He hobbled around, trying to find a place to settle, not altogether surprised when his grandfather appeared.

"Howdy, Chief." Tighe tossed his bedroll down. "Haven't seen you since Dante's wedding."

"I've seen you." Running Bear picked up the bedroll. "Come."

Tighe followed as fast as his crutches would allow. "Where are we headed?"

The chief disappeared behind some thick cacti. A threadlike stream encircled a wide stone dugout tucked back and hidden so well that Tighe would never have seen it even if he'd been looking for it. He had a feeling his brothers and Ash had no idea about Running Bear's lair. Well, Ashlyn might; she seemed to know more than most. But he thought Galen, Jace, Falcon, his pinheaded twin, Dante, and Sloan were just as in the dark as he was. "Nice digs, Grandfather."

Running Bear grunted. Tighe felt honored that his grandfather had brought him to his private sanctuary. They sat near the opening, staring out over the curling canyons below. "Wow, this is quite a view."

"Yes." Running Bear didn't look at him as Tighe gingerly settled himself against the rock ledge so his leg could jut forward for support. "We need to discuss your time at Rancho Diablo."

"My time?"

His grandfather gazed out into the distance. Sudden fear clenched Tighe's gut. The old chief had warned the seven Chacon Callahans that one of them was the hunted one, the one who would bring harm to the family. Was it *him?* Was that why Running Bear had brought him here? Somehow Tighe had known this was where he belonged, almost from the moment he'd realized River had gone chilly on him.

"Tell me what I should do, Grandfather," he said, and the old man closed his eyes, though Tighe knew he wasn't dozing.

"Meditate on who you are," Running Bear said. "You are not yet who you will be."

Tighe didn't know how to be anything other than what he was. Some—like River—claimed he was a bit wild. Maybe he was. Certainly he liked to live on the edge, but wasn't that part of enjoying life to the max? His family teased him, calling him more taciturn than his talkative twin, but that had been when they were kids. The military had thought he was fairly accurate and single-minded when it came to sniper skills. Tighe had earned the moniker Takedown. He'd liked living almost alone at times, when he was on an assignment. Other times he'd appreciated the camaraderie and brotherhood of his platoon. It had been a close bond, reminiscent of his tribe. "Chief, I don't know how to be anything different than what I am."

His grandfather looked at him. "You will learn."

Then he left the stone crevasse, disappearing without a sound. Tighe leaned back against the rough wall with a sigh. He looked out over the canyons from his grandfather's aerie, and wondered if he would ever get River to kiss him again. She seemed to think he needed to change somehow, too.

He was pretty resistant to that. "Twenty-seven years of being the opposite of Dante wasn't so bad," he muttered. "I'd rather be me than him."

He liked being wild and free. What exactly was wrong with that?

Even River wouldn't want him to change that much. She had to have liked him the way he was or she wouldn't have allowed him to make love to her.

Then again, he could consider changing just a little if she'd open her arms to him again. Problem was, he didn't know what he was supposed to change. Tighe closed his eyes, willed himself to meditate.

"Every journey changes your soul. Each journey is a path to self-knowledge," Running Bear said. "There is no life without this."

"I know, Grandfather, I know. I remember your teachings." Tighe opened his eyes, glanced around. Running Bear was nowhere to be seen. But his words remained in Tighe's mind, delicate as air.

Closing his eyes again, he allowed the mysticism

he knew so well to envelop him, something he hadn't done in a long, long time.

"What are you doing?" Ash asked River, who was looking out a window in the main house, toward the barn. River had specifically chosen this room for her project.

"I'm spying on your brothers. And Sawyer. There's something strange about her. I don't believe for a second that she's had real training as a bodyguard. Not like Ana and I had."

"The little twins seem to like her."

"Isaiah and Carlos like her because they're Callahan males. They're predisposed to like pretty girls from the moment they're conceived. That doesn't make her a bodyguard. It makes her a decent nanny. Maybe."

Ash flopped into a chair. "When I asked Kendall why she'd hired Storm Cash's niece, she said Sawyer had the right training, and that she'd spent time in the desert honing her skills. Kendall said she checked her background, and Sawyer and Storm hadn't been close during Sawyer's childhood. So in Kendall's maternal opinion, there was no reason to eliminate a perfectly good bodyguard just because of some stinky family relations. And Kendall said sometimes it was best to keep your enemies tucked tight to one's bosom."

"I like my bosom enemy-free. I'm not leaving until I know the twins are in capable hands," River stated.

Ash watched Sawyer below, chatting up Jace, as little Isaiah and Carlos happily sat in their double stroller. "I didn't know you were planning on leaving. And yet, I guess I did know. I was just hoping my hunch was wrong." Ash sighed. "You're going to find Tighe, aren't you?"

"It's time someone does." It had been three weeks since she'd driven Tighe to the stone fire ring. She had no idea what he was eating or drinking, or if he was miserable from his leg injury. None of the Callahans, including the protective aunt Fiona, seemed all that worried. When River had mentioned to Fiona that maybe her husband, Burke, might need to go check on Tighe, she had shaken her head and said she didn't have time for such monkeyshines.

"Oh, Tighe's fine. Don't worry about him. When he was a boy—"

River glanced at Ash, who seemed to suddenly have swallowed her words. "When he was a boy, what?"

"I was just going to say that once when we were young, Tighe went off for a while. I was six," Ash said, "so I remember it well." She smiled at River. "It's all right. We're used to him being independent."

"If you were six, Tighe was eight when he went on this adventure. How long was he gone?" River was curious as to how he had fared in his childhood. "Five, six hours?"

"Two months," Ash said softly. "He was gone two months, in the coldest part of the year. Most of us wanted to stay close to the fire at night. Tighe wanted to find out if he could build his own fire and survive on what he found and caught."

River sucked in her breath. "No parent would allow that."

"Oh." Ash shook her head, got up. "No worries about that. Tighe was never really alone, though he doesn't know that, so don't tell him. It would totally crush him and blow his wild man conception of himself. But there were always scouts watching him. Not that the scouts would have interfered, unless there'd been severe danger. A test is a test, and Tighe wanted the chance to test himself." Ash fluffed her silvery-blond, shoulder-length hair, not concerned in the least. "Grandfather said Tighe had the soul of a tiger, and that he would make many kills when he left the tribe. And he did. He was a pretty good sniper. Don't worry about my pinheaded brother," she said. "He's more wolf than man. Tighe's problem is that is he's scared, maybe for the first time in his life."

"Scared of what? Not rattlesnakes, or becoming a dried-out skeleton, with no food or water in the canyons."

"My guess is," Ash said, "he's been a little scared ever since you came here."

"Me?"

"Maybe. Tighe's always seen himself as the uncatchable male. Also, I think it's come to his mind that he might be the hunted one."

"You know," River said, looking back out the window, "it could be you, Ash."

She shook her head. "Not me. But if it is, I hope someone shoots me and puts me out of my misery."

"Shoots you?" River was horrified. "Who would do that?"

"I'm hoping you," Ash said softly, looking at her. "You've always got your Beretta strapped to your thigh, don't you?"

"I would never shoot you," River snapped. "And how do you know about my gun?"

"I know everything," Ash said, wandering out the door.

"I see," River muttered, watching Sawyer stretch up to kiss Jace on the cheek on the ground below her second-story window. "Really nice to know I've fallen for some kind of hard-core survivalist wolf-man. And that woman is working an angle," she said of Sawyer, watching her slink off, leaving a seemingly stunned Jace behind. "Don't fall for it, handsome."

Jace would probably fall like a ton of bricks. She watched Jace almost strut, all peacocklike, his gaze fastened on Sawyer's backside. River sighed and got up from her perch. Ash's wealth of information had unsettled her to some degree. Tighe wasn't afraid of her—not in the least. That could be ruled out. He was stubborn and opinionated, but not afraid of a woman.

Now the other business…was he the hunted one? Ash was crazy if she thought River was going to shoot her, if it turned out to be her. "The only shooting I'm doing is at bad guys, and there may not be any of those," River said, watching Jace rub his cheek where Sawyer had pecked him. "Just gullible ones."

She went to hunt up Tighe, the resident wolf on the loose.

The stone circle showed few signs of anyone living there, though a small fire flickered, the embers glowing. There were no signs of foul play, but River felt uneasiness in the pit of her stomach. A man with a sore groin and a fractured leg should be right here where she'd left him.

"Hello, beautiful," she heard someone say, and River turned.

"What are you doing?" she demanded. "Why are you standing up?"

Tighe smiled, feeling very much in control of the situation, obviously, by the devilish light in his eyes. "You were worried about me."

"No, I wasn't." Why add to his already overburdened ego?

"You were." He stumped forward, resting his weight on a crutch crudely fashioned from the forked limb of a tree. "I'm glad you were worried about me, but I could have told you there was no need."

"Then I'll be going." She didn't feel like putting up with his macho attitude when he'd worried her half to death for days. "I'll let your family know you're fine."

"I may return with you for a bit. You got room in your ride?"

She'd driven the military jeep, which had plenty of space for cargo. "I suppose."

He got in without needing assistance and grinned at her. "Unless you want a tour, I'm ready to head back."

She looked at the cowboy, the man who invaded her dreams and kept her breathless whenever she thought about him. "Are you sure this is what you want?"

"For the moment. That's how I live—I'm totally in the moment." He grinned, pleased with his lone-wolf persona.

She gazed at his rangy body, and his long hair, which hadn't seen much of a brush in the three weeks he'd been gone. He looked as delectable as ever. It was annoying that a man could hunker in the wilderness and not suffer ill effects. "I have to admit I was afraid of what I'd find."

"You don't think I can live without Fiona's cookies." Tighe laughed. "I miss the comforts of home, but mostly the children, I have to admit." He caught her hand as she put it on the shift. "Sometimes I even missed you."

"Did you?" She shifted, moving his hand away. "I didn't miss you a bit."

It was a lie, of course, to save face.

"I think you did," he said cheerfully. "But I understand you want to keep it to yourself. It was sweet of you to come find me. I'm surprised my family didn't tell you there was nothing to worry about."

He was so annoying she wanted to dump him out of the jeep. The thing was, everything he was teasing her about was true—she *had* missed him, and she *had* worried. Did anything ever get under his skin? "Hey, fun fact," River said, "I've skipped my period."

Oh, for a photo of Tighe's expression. He looked... stunned. River kept driving, curious to see what he'd say, pretty pleased that she'd found the one thing that would shut him up for just a moment.

A loud whoop erupted from him. Tighe threw his straw Resistol into the air and laughed out loud, loudly enough to startle birds from trees, if there'd been any around.

Apparently he wasn't so much the silent type as his siblings had claimed.

"That's awesome! When will we know for certain? How long do these things take?"

"In a couple of weeks I'll go to the doctor. I keep telling myself maybe I'm late because of worrying—"

"About me—"

"No. About things at the ranch," River interrupted, "but I've always been completely regular."

"You cute little thing," Tighe said. "That night you

and my brother and sister were plotting against me, you had your own little plot going."

"Not hardly." River was getting mad. "Perhaps you didn't do a decent job wrapping up."

"You helped, as I recall," he said gleefully, "and I remember you seemed to be impressed."

"Oh, for crying out loud." River parked the jeep at the house, jumped down. "You can just wait there until one of your siblings finds you. Or Wolf. Right now, I don't care."

She went inside, aggravated beyond belief.

"Did you find my brother?" Jace asked.

"I found a jackass. It might have been your brother. You can go out to the jeep and see for yourself."

With that, she went to check on the twins.

Chapter 4

"Whew. What'd you say to River to get her in a knot?" Jace asked, as Tighe helped himself down from the jeep, still grinning from ear to ear.

"That amazing woman is highly annoyed because she's caught herself a man."

"Who?" Jace glanced around. "Why is that annoying? Don't women want a man like a bee wants a flower?"

"Yes, they do. They just don't want to admit it." Tighe's heart was singing. "There's a good chance I'm going to be a father." He laughed, pleased.

"How did that happen?" Jace frowned. "You mean you may have gotten River in a family way?"

"I think she got me in a family way. As I recall, the two of you plotted against me. I just fell willingly into the trap." He went inside to hit the cookie tray and gloat.

"What are you going to do?" Jace sat down at the kitchen counter next to him. "I don't envision you settling down."

"I didn't say a word about settling down." Tighe munched on a sugar cookie. "She didn't say anything about that, either." He looked at his brother. "We'll know for sure in a couple of weeks, but I know now what the spirits were trying to tell me. I'm definitely going to be a dad." He let out a wolf howl, bringing Fiona into the kitchen.

"Mercy!" She glared at her nephew. "I thought a wild animal got into the house!"

"One did. My brother," Jace said drily. "He thinks he's going to be a father."

Fiona's jaw dropped. "A father? Weren't you supposed to be on a wilderness sabbatical, resting and considering the stars?"

"It's what he did *before* the sabbatical," Jace explained, and Tighe reached out to hug his aunt.

"I have you to thank, Aunt Fiona. If you hadn't been so determined to keep me from my destiny—"

"Your destiny?" She frowned.

"Firefreak," Tighe said reverently. "You sent an angel to keep me from my destiny, and my destiny was the angel. What a wise aunt you are."

"Yes, well," Fiona said, her voice uncertain. "You sound like you have dehydration symptoms and perhaps starvation issues. I'll put in a meat loaf."

She crossed the kitchen and pulled out some pans, not proffering him the excited congratulations Tighe thought he'd earned. "Aren't you excited that there will be another Callahan tot around, Aunt Fiona?"

She looked at him as she unwrapped some meat. "I'll have to talk to River."

"My baby mama is going to be beautiful when she's in full bloom," Tighe said, very satisfied. "I'm going to love being a dad."

"You're going to have to figure out a way to get her to the altar then," Fiona said.

"Piece of cake."

"That's what you'd been saying for the past year, that you had River all wrapped up," Jace pointed out. "But then we figured out she didn't have a boyfriend in Tempest, that she was just trying to stay away from you. And just because she slept with you once doesn't mean she's inclined to do it again. Especially since you showed deficient skills at simple tasks, like wearing a—"

"I have plenty of skill, thanks." Tighe got up. "I'm going to go find her. You doubters will see, the woman is crazy about me. She's just a little shy, doesn't want to seem too eager about catching her a Callahan cowboy. But I like her eager," he said, remembering the night he'd made love to her. "In fact, if you don't see me again tonight, don't come looking for me."

"Best of luck," Jace said, and Fiona flapped a dish towel his way, shooing him off.

He didn't need luck. He had what his little lady liked—and it had nothing to do with luck.

"Go away," River told Tighe when he walked into Sloan and Kendall's house. She was playing with the twins, about to start their baths. "If you're here to talk to me, I'm not in the mood."

"Don't be prickly, beautiful. You and I have things to

discuss. Hey, boys." He ruffled the hair on Carlos and Isaiah's heads, a fond uncle, even if he was still gimping around and not able to get down and play with them the way he liked.

River put away the toys. "I've thought long and hard about this, and if we're going to be parents, you're going to have to do this my way."

"Meaning?"

"Separately. Just because Falcon and Sloan and Dante got together with their—"

"Baby mamas?" Tighe said helpfully.

"I really don't like that expression. How about mother of your child?" River said.

"Kinda formal, don't you think?"

She refused to look at the handsome cowboy who might be bound to her forever now. "Let's not discuss it more until we know for certain. I don't have any intention of tying you down."

"That's fine," Tighe said, "I'll do the tying down, sweetheart, if there's tying to be done."

Her body seemed to lighten and expand at his words. Her friend Ana had mentioned that Dante had been forthright in his pursuit of her, and that she didn't expect Tighe to be any different.

River didn't want to be pursued, and she wasn't certain how to get that through his head—or hers. She'd felt the unmistakable surge of excitement at the thought of being romanced by him. When he'd made love to her, it had been like magic, pure magic, and she'd adored every minute of it.

"You know you want me," Tighe said, his voice teasing, and River looked at him, and thought, *Yes, I do. But it's just not going to happen.*

* * *

"This is so going to happen," Tighe said, following River to her room. "We need to get to know each other much better since we're going to be parents."

"We don't know for sure."

"I know for sure. And I can't wait. Pack up your stuff, doll face. I need a night nurse."

"You need nothing and no one. I have this on good authority from your sister."

River wouldn't even look at him, the cute, shy little thing. "Don't listen to Ash," Tighe told her. "She thinks she's the family font of all knowledge, but we humored her growing up. She was sheltered, babied. She doesn't know a thing." He settled on River's bed. "I can't sleep here with you. It wouldn't be appropriate for the twins."

"Yes, I know," River said sweetly, but he wasn't fooled in the least.

"You'll have to be my night nurse at the bunkhouse."

"If you need a nurse, ask Fiona. I have a job. In fact, my job is the exact reason why nothing further is going to happen between you and me."

He frowned, not liking the sound of that.

"The thing is, it's unprofessional. In fact, it was unprofessional, what I did with you," River said, her cheeks turning a becoming pink Tighe thought was adorable. "I shouldn't have allowed your aunt and family to talk me into that little adventure, and I should have…turned you away when you came to my room that night."

He laughed. She was just such a sexy fireball. "Sweetcakes, you wouldn't have turned me away. As I recall, you scooted over and made room for me in that tiny little bed."

Her face went bright red. He grinned. "I liked it. Made me feel very welcome. And that's what I'm going to do for you tonight, when you come to my bed."

"I won't be doing any such thing," she said, a little snappishly, but he wasn't afraid of a girl with spirit.

Tighe got to his feet. "See you later."

"I don't think so."

He headed out the door to the bunkhouse. He'd be seeing River all right—the lady liked him.

But not as much as he liked her.

Give me time. I'll change her mind.

Tighe heard his door open about midnight, and smiled in the darkness. This was awesome. He'd known River would come. She couldn't resist him. Whether she wanted to admit it or not, they shared something special. He pretended to be asleep, so he wouldn't ruin her surprise.

He'd act so surprised, and then make love to her until she admitted she was crazy about him.

The light flipped on, jarring his eyes open. River stood there, wearing a robe and high-heeled slippers. He grinned. "Well, hello, gorgeous. Come to nurse me back to a full-strength wild man?"

He watched her move his crutch away from his nightstand, a bit out of his reach. Of course, he wouldn't need that tonight. River gave him a long gaze, then opened her robe, and he swallowed so hard he thought he might choke. Not a scrap was on her body.

"Holy smokes," he said, "come to Daddy. And don't take the long route. Jump right into my arms."

River closed her robe.

He looked at her. "If you're cold, I'll be happy to warm you, darling."

She gave him one last look, took his crutch and left the room.

"That little devil. What was that all about?" He hobbled out of his room, glanced around the bunkhouse. His nocturnal angel had gone, taking all the sexy joy away.

Now he was stiff in several places.

"That little lady and I have got to work some things out," he muttered, and climbed back into bed, completely disgruntled.

And then he got it. She was trying to drive him mad. That was the plan, while he was in no shape to give proper chase. She was going to make him crazy, make him want her, until he begged her to be his woman.

"No, you dope," Jace said the next day when Tighe mentioned that he'd had the strangest dream in the night, wherein River had nearly killed him with a vision of divine beauty, then cruelly snatched it away. "She's not softening toward you. I heard Ash and her discussing it. She was showing you how cruel it had been that you sandbagged her in her hotel room that night. Ash told her you had to realize that what happens in the night doesn't necessarily translate to real life. Sort of what happens in Vegas stays in Vegas."

"My sister put my girlfriend up to giving me a relationship lesson? Isn't that the blind leading the blind?" Now that he understood what had happened, Tighe felt a whole lot better. It explained the wild look in her big eyes, as if she wasn't totally committed to the caper, perhaps might have even been nervous.

"I wouldn't put it so harshly. Ladies cook up these plans all the time. Guys do, too, but we're more interested in getting into ladies' drawers than staying out of them. River wants you to know that the two of you don't have anything that translates to real life." Jace kicked back in the bunkhouse, grinned at his brother. "This one's gonna be tough, bro. And you've only got one leg to chase her on."

"Won't matter." Tighe felt a bit deflated suddenly. Maybe River didn't want him. Was that possible?

Nah. No way.

"Hey, give me a ride, will you?" he asked Jace.

"Heading back to the canyons?"

"No. Not yet." He stumped toward the jeep. There was only one place to go when a woman was on the fence about a man, and if a man was smart, he got himself there and did the thing right. Big. Huge.

He could do impressive.

"This isn't a good idea," Ash said, poking her nose into his business as she loved to do. "What message did you not receive during her midnight visit? What happens at night isn't real life, bro."

"Why did you come with me to Diablo, anyway?" Tighe muttered, wondering if his sister was right as he stared into the jewelry case at all the twinkling engagement rings. He was suddenly doubtful, and Ash wasn't helping.

"You don't even know if River's having your child," Jace pointed out. "This is premature. Maybe."

"I want River to know that, baby or no baby, I want to marry her. Whatever happens, I'm the man she wants."

"I don't think so," Ash said. "Not that I'm trying to

knock your good leg out from underneath you, but I'm pretty sure she hasn't changed her mind about you."

Tighe shook his head. "She has a great poker face." And a great body, but he forbore adding that.

"She's not faking it," Ash told him. "I believe in my heart that River thinks a real relationship isn't built on nighttime shenanigans."

"I'll take that one," he said to the jeweler, pointing to the biggest sparkler in the case. "Bigger is always better."

Ash sighed. "Your head is bigger than most men's, and that's not better."

"True," Jace said. "Why don't you wait another month, so you don't crowd her? You know how sometimes if you try to rush an animal, it goes in the opposite direction?"

Tighe debated whether he was getting good advice from his siblings. If he was, it would be the first time.

"Since our family came here to Rancho Diablo," he said softly, "we've changed. All of us have worked hard. We've done what Running Bear wanted us to do. The mission was understood, and we've kept to it. But River is outside of the mission. And she makes my heart whole. That's the only way I know how to explain it."

Ash nodded. "I know. But we were just trying to keep you off of Firefreak," she said gently. "We didn't expect that the plot would go as far as it appears it did."

He swallowed hard. "River didn't sleep with me to keep me off a bull. Nothing and nobody could have kept me from that ride."

"I know." Ash sighed. "Never mind. Forget I said anything."

Tighe looked at the ring he'd selected with some regret. "Maybe you're right."

"Probably this once, she is," Jace said. "You hate to jump the gun. Ladies can be so giddy."

"Not really," Ash said. "We're just practical. We can see the forest for the trees. We can—"

"Come on," Tighe said. "Drive me back, Sophocles."

He felt a bit roughed up and heartbroken. No man wanted to think a woman wouldn't be thrilled with his proposal and a beautiful ring. But Ash knew River better than he did. Feeling like a dog with a tucked tail, Tighe allowed his brother and sister to usher him out of the jewelry store.

By the jeep stood their uncle Wolf, grinning at them with his typical up-to-no-good grimace. Tighe wished he wasn't using a crutch, hated to appear weak in front of the enemy. "Look what the summer wind blew in. Pollution."

"Well, if it isn't my favorite family members," Wolf said.

"Spare us," Ash said, getting into the jeep. "When are you going to give up? We're not going anywhere. Rancho Diablo is our home."

"Just wanted to warn you that we saw some strange things in the canyons, me and my men." Wolf looked at them. "Might have been some birds of prey. Never can be sure at a distance."

"What are you getting at?" Tighe demanded.

"Have you checked on Running Bear lately?"

Tighe settled into the back of the jeep, and Jace got in the passenger seat while Ash switched on the engine. "No one needs to check on the chief. He checks on everyone, including you. Even black sheep get watched by the shepherd."

Wolf's expression turned peeved, though he shrugged. "Just a thought." He walked away, went inside the Books'n'Bingo Society bookshop and tearoom. Up the main street, Tighe saw a few of Wolf's merry stragglers staring them down.

"I've got a bad feeling about this," he said under his breath.

"So do I," Ash murmured. "For one thing, Wolf's gone into Fiona's tearoom, which means he plans to stir up trouble. But that bit about Running Bear—"

"Is a trap," Jace said.

"Agreed. Head for home." Tighe shoved his hat low on his head, settled his leg more comfortably, trying to ignore the sudden yawing pit in his stomach. No one could get to Running Bear; their grandfather was part of the canyons and the wind and the sun.

They knew Running Bear wasn't immortal. He just seemed like it.

Closing his eyes, Tighe tried to envision his grandfather as Ash sped toward Rancho Diablo. Searched his mind for the old chief's spirit.

Something didn't feel quite right. He just couldn't put his finger on it.

It felt as if change was coming.

The ranch was alive with women when Tighe returned with his siblings. Ladies of all shapes and sizes filed into the house, carrying bags and boxes and notebooks.

"Wow." Ash parked the jeep, staring. "Has Aunt Fiona got one of her meetings today?"

Jace grunted. "Looks like every woman in Diablo is here. Maybe she forgot to tell everyone the meeting is at the Books'n'Bingo tearoom, as they always are."

Tighe got down out of the vehicle, ignoring his brother's help. "I've got a crutch," he snapped. "Anyway, my leg is almost healed."

"Not until Galen examines it and says so. No heroics. We've had enough of those." Jace headed toward the house with Ash, leaving Tighe to stump along behind.

Inside, the ladies were an excited gaggle of happy faces and energetic voices. His aunt was in her element in the middle of the crowd Tighe estimated to be somewhere around thirty. He kissed her on the cheek. "Aunt Fiona, did you forget to send me an invitation to the party?"

River stood nearby, gorgeous but not pleased, if he gauged her mood correctly. She wasn't smiling, though to be fair, she was beautiful even when she frowned. "I sure do have a thing for you," he said to her, and she shook her head and drifted into another room.

"What's going on, Aunt Fiona?"

"I think you better talk things over with River," Fiona said.

His heart fell into his boots.

"You always were the unpredictable one," his aunt said with a grin.

"Oh, no, Aunt Fiona, this baby shower isn't for River, is it?" River already had a tiny touch of cold feet. This wouldn't help. He strode out of the room to follow her.

"River?" She was putting some small, crustless sandwiches on a tray in the kitchen. "What's going on?"

"Well," River said, "apparently we're definitely pregnant."

His heart leaped for joy. Yet she wasn't smiling, so he sensed a heartfelt "Hurray!" wasn't appropriate. "And Aunt Fiona already planned a baby shower?"

She shook her head. "This isn't for me, although the word is definitely out and plans are in full swing. I'm surprised you weren't mobbed with congratulations when you walked into the house."

He glanced over his shoulder to where the women were corralled in the den, chatting. "You could have called and let me know. I'd have liked to be first and not last."

"Don't worry. This is just a planning meeting for the upcoming Christmas ball." River handed him the tray. "Six months is hardly enough time for Fiona to get everything done she wants, so the planning must begin now. Volunteers must be pressed into work, committees formed."

"Yes, yes," Tighe said, impatient, "but what did the doctor say?"

River shrugged. "That I'm healthy. The pregnancy is right where it should be, considering."

He frowned. River really wasn't happy about carrying his child. Somehow he was going to have to fix this. "That's good. We'll get you on some good prenatal vitamins, make sure you get lots of rest...." He glanced out at his aunt, who had called her committee to order. "It's quite a coincidence that Fiona gathered all these ladies on the spur of the moment, just for an advance meeting about the Christmas ball."

"They're holding an emergency meeting because we're expecting a baby. Which makes you ineligible for the Christmas ball raffle. If you recall, Dante was the grand prize last Christmas. Your aunt had already determined that you were this year's sacrifice—I mean, prize. They'd planned advertising on barn roofs and everything, with slogans for you." River smiled. "Too bad you'll miss the fun."

"Not at all." Tighe was secretly relieved. "Who's the backup sacrifice?"

She shook her head. "I didn't ask."

"It's Galen's turn, if you ask me." He looked at Ash, who'd just walked into the kitchen. "You realize your turn at Fiona's chicanery will arrive one day. The bachelors will swarm this county."

His sister blanched. "I don't want to be swarmed. Don't talk about it."

"Don't worry. It'll be Galen or Jace on the griddle this year." Tighe looked at River. "Good to hear about the baby. I'll have Galen make you up a holistic protocol, if you'd like."

"Oh, you told him!" Ashlyn grinned at River, then Tighe. "Congratulations!" She threw her arms around his neck, giving him an octopus-like squeeze.

"Ash—" River began, and he gazed at her over his sister's shoulder.

"How does it feel to know you're going to be the father of triplets?" Ash asked, and Tighe watched River close her eyes as if she was in pain.

"Triplets?" He put Ash away from him gently.

River nodded, distinctly uncomfortable.

Joy swept Tighe fast, and amazement, and maybe even a little light-headedness, so that laughter burst from him. He couldn't stop laughing even if he'd tried.

"Whew," Ash said, "he's finally gone around the bend. One tap too many to the old brain stem."

River looked concerned. "Is he going to be all right?"

He wrapped her in his arms, kissing her on the forehead. "This is great! I win!"

His sister shook her head as if he were mentally slow. "This isn't Firefreak. You didn't just win a buckle. I'm pretty sure you haven't won anything—yet."

"Three kids—that's more than anybody else in the family. Just call me 'straight shooter' from now on." He laughed with delight. "If I was playing the one-armed bandit, I just hit Jackpot!"

River pushed him away. "Tighe, I have to get back to the gathering."

"We're going to visit later," he told her. "We have to talk this out, River."

She disappeared into the den. Ash looked at him. "I remember the days when you claimed you had her in the bag."

He did. Surely he did. He had to. "Are you part of Fiona's whiz-bang planning committee?"

"To give away my brothers? I wouldn't visit any of you on some poor unsuspecting female."

He shrugged. "So let's head out to find the chief."

River walked back into the kitchen and put teacups on the counter. "Oh, no, you don't. You're not leaving me here with the gang of matchmakers. I'm going, too."

Tighe blinked. "I don't think the babies should ride over rough terrain, do you?"

Ash took his arm, led him toward the door. "I think it's best if we head out before your feet get permanently stuck in your mouth, brother. Come on, River. We'll put him in the back."

River was plenty annoyed with Tighe, but more than anything she was annoyed with herself. Triplets! She still hadn't gotten over the shock. The physician said if she was very careful, she might last until February or even March. That meant giving up her bodyguard position soon. The doctor wanted to take every precaution.

She looked at Tighe, who'd chosen to seat himself next to her where he could situate his leg most comfortably. He grinned at her from under the brim of his cowboy hat.

"It's awesome, babe."

"It is not awesome. I mean, it is, but you're not, so don't tweak me."

He laughed. "In a week or two, you'll be trying to drag me to the altar."

"I don't think so."

His navy eyes practically danced with pride. He was really impressed with himself. River sighed and looked away.

"I'm so amazed by you," Tighe said.

She turned to face him. "Why?"

"Because you're such a fertile goddess. I would never have suspected you'd be the Callahan woman to turn up a three-in-a-row."

He grinned again, the handsomest man she'd ever seen, and River wanted ever so badly to smack him. She went back to perusing the scenery as it rushed past. "Why are we checking on Running Bear, Ash?"

"Because we just thought we would." She was noncommittal, which was typical Callahan, and meant she wasn't going to give the real reason for the drive to the canyons.

"Hey." Tighe gave River's arm a little squeeze. "I couldn't sleep after you visited last night. If that was your goal, you succeeded, gorgeous. I may not sleep for a week. And you know," he said, his eyes laughing and devilish, "you'd best not waste any time visiting me again with the old naked-under-the-robe trick. I want to remember how you look now, before you're big as a house."

"Whoa, Tighe," Ash said. "Careful where you step with those big feet of yours."

"Course, you'll be beautiful when you're enormous, too," Tighe said, and River glared at him. "But everyone knows the body changes forever once—"

Ash slammed on the brakes, and Tighe pitched forward. "Nice driving, Ash."

His sister hopped out of the jeep. "Just trying to help you out, brother dearest. Come on, River. Peg leg can follow us at his own slow pace. That way we won't have to listen to him."

"That will be a relief." River sent him an irritated glance and went off with his sister. Tighe grabbed his crutch and made his way out of the truck toward the stone circle, aware that his sister was trying to warn him that he wasn't scoring with River.

He really didn't know how to score. The woman had been distant toward him for so long—except the night he'd made his way into her bed—that he hardly knew how to woo her.

But she was having his children—and that was nothing short of glorious.

Chapter 5

By the time Tighe caught up with his sister and River, he found them facing Wolf at the stone circle. River glanced at Tighe, watching for his reaction.

"Didn't we just see you?" he asked his uncle. "Not any happier about this meeting than I was in town."

"Just checking on the chief. Is it a crime to check on one's father?" Wolf said.

Tighe gave his uncle a long, level look. Perhaps this was the source of his recent sense that all was not well. "If you've harmed him, you'll answer to me."

Wolf laughed. "You're not exactly standing on two legs right now, nephew."

"Don't worry about me." Tighe glanced about, searching for any indication that Running Bear had been there before Wolf's unannounced arrival. "Why are you hanging around so much suddenly, anyway?"

"Just making sure all is right at Rancho Diablo. That's what family does, isn't it? Sticks together?"

Ash squared her shoulders, jutted her chin. "You're not family. Turns out blood isn't always thicker than water."

"That hurts, niece." Wolf smiled at River. "Heard you're expecting, young lady. I hope you'll accept my congratulations."

River didn't say anything, but it was all Tighe could do not to lose his temper, which was what Wolf wanted. "We don't need any congratulations."

"Oh," Wolf said. "Is she having your children?" He gave a short, terse laugh. "I thought Jace had spent more time with the bodyguard—"

"That's enough," Tighe stated, cutting in. "Move along, Uncle, before things get ugly. It's getting close, if you know what I mean."

Wolf's seven men appeared from out of nowhere. "Not too close," Wolf said. "Think the odds are on my side."

Tighe heard the whistling sound of an arrow flying before it split the ground, shaft up, right between Wolf's boots. His men backed up a pace, looking to him for direction.

"Seems we've overstayed our welcome," Wolf said. "Just remember, I'm keeping my eye on you. In the end, I'll get what I want."

"Which is what?" Tighe snapped.

"The land. The Diablos, the silver. All of it. Once again, the cartel will run this area." Wolf grinned, but his expression didn't have any warmth in it. "Don't think I won't sacrifice the lot of you for what I want."

Another arrow whistled, piercing the ground at the toe of Wolf's boot.

"We're well-trained, Uncle," Ash said. "We've trained all our lives for this. Running Bear's kept us on a path to survive whatever you've got."

Tighe's insides curled a bit as his blond-haired, gamine sister glanced at Wolf's small army, her hands on her hips.

"You don't have enough men to take us out," Ash said.

"That's right," River stated, and Tighe's heart dropped into his boots. "The Callahans have backup."

"You?" Wolf laughed. "You won't be doing much of anything in a couple of months. You'll be lying in bed, no use to anyone. Just a host for your parasites."

Tighe started forward, but a war cry shattered the air, stopping him. Astonishment crossed the faces of Wolf's men.

"Time to go, boys," Wolf said, and they trooped off to a black truck with a double cab. Two men rode in the back, their guns pointing at the Callahans, covering their departure.

Tighe wanted to put his arms around River, but he could tell by the outraged expression on her face that all men were probably unwelcome in her space at the moment.

"That goon insulted me," she said, disgusted. "How dare he?"

"Pay no mind to Uncle Wolf," Ash soothed. "He's all sound and fury."

River looked at Tighe. "It was all I could do not to shoot him."

"I know. I could feel you quivering. I'm glad you didn't," Tighe said. "He's really not worth it."

"He doesn't like you. I'm going to have to keep an eye on you while you're incapacitated."

Tighe grinned. "Oh, darn."

"You can laugh," she said, "but as we know, you don't always make the best decisions. Witness your jaunt on Firefreak."

He felt his jaw drop. "That was the best decision I ever made!"

Ash laughed. "Come on. Let's go dig Grandfather out of the shadows and find out how he wants us to proceed."

"I'm serious," River said. "You can't fire a gun while you're balancing on one good leg, Tighe."

He frowned. "I can shoot a needle off a cactus. You just start thinking about the rest of his conversation. That's the more immediate problem."

"Which is what?" River glared at him.

"You're going to be bed-bound soon," he pointed out, and Ash said, "Incoming. Lightning strike for brother with unfortunate mouth problem."

"And while we're on the subject of your pregnancy," Tighe said, feeling very righteous at the moment, "I don't want anybody thinking Jace is the father of your children. We're going to have to get married immediately."

"Why do I have the dumbest brothers on the planet?" Ash moaned.

The trio made their way to a rock ledge, heading toward where the last arrow had originated. It was hard to tell where they might find the chief, since the arrows had come from opposite directions.

"Your uncle was just trying to get your goat," River

said. "He succeeded. But that doesn't mean I'm going to do anything about it."

"The boys will want their parents to be married," Tighe pointed out, doing his best to think of any reason to convince the beautiful woman at his side to think of him in a romantic light.

"Grandfather!" Ash exclaimed. "Am I glad to see you! Break these two up, will you?"

Running Bear smiled. "They are meant to be together. Hello, Tighe. River." He looked at his grandson. "Now you understand the path of your spirit."

"Do I?" Tighe frowned. "She won't cooperate."

"No, I won't." River matched his frown. "And the only reason I'm having your children is because you wouldn't cooperate with what your family wanted!"

"A marriage ceremony can be performed now," Running Bear said with a pleased smile.

River sent Tighe a startled look. "Now? As in, right here?"

"I get to be the maid of honor!" Ash exclaimed.

"Now, wait a minute," River began, and Tighe took her hand in his.

"Thank you, Grandfather. It would be an honor if you would join us," Tighe said.

"Hang on," River said. "First, I never said I would marry you. And you haven't asked."

"I did," Tighe said. "You just said no."

Running Bear and Ash laughed.

"She's a good match for you," the chief stated.

"I know, Grandfather." He considered the bodyguard with the whiskey-colored hair and the lifted brow challenging him. "She's strong."

"And don't forget it," River said. "When I finally do

have to stay in bed, I don't want to hear one word about my delicate state or weakened condition. I'm a body-guard, and I always will be."

"I know. Will you say yes now?" Tighe asked, hoping against hope that River would accept him. She could be stubborn, more so even than Ashlyn or Fiona, and that was saying something. His sons would inherit a huge stubborn streak! It would work well for them.

"No, thank you," River said. "I'm sorry, but I hate being rushed. And I'm not happy about your uncle and what he said. I don't like to make big decisions when I'm not happy." She looked at Running Bear. "Thank you for the offer, though, Chief. It would be a great honor to have you bless our marriage. But your grandson is too wild-eyed for me. We don't know each other very well. I hope you can understand, Chief." She went back down the trail the way they'd come.

"Shot down," Ash said with a sigh. "I'm so sorry, brother. On the other hand, I'm not really surprised. That Jace business annoyed her, but she has spent more time with him over the past year. She and Ana both. Of course, we know they just see him as an irritating kid brother, but…" Ash shook her head, sending him a sorrowful look. "Even Storm Cash's lady friend, Lulu Feinstrom, asked me if Jace and River were an item when I was in town today. So you see why Wolf easily found your underbelly on that one."

Tighe sighed. "It's all right. Well, it's not all right, but it will be soon. I hope." He'd work on River a little more, try to get her to see that he adored her from her toes to her nose, and then, maybe, she'd realize she just simply couldn't live without him.

He certainly couldn't live without her.

* * *

In the upstairs library where the private Callahan meetings were held, Tighe didn't fare much better than he had with River. His brothers and sister gazed at him with sympathy, approbation and some disappointment.

"We need every one of us to be clear-eyed and clear-minded," Galen said. "No more risky behavior."

The gazes landed on Tighe again.

He didn't say anything for a minute, but when it became clear that his siblings expected to extract a promise of better behavior from him, he sighed. "My leg will be fine in a week or so. Then I'll be right back to my old, lethal self."

"Good." Galen nodded. "Jace, until then, you stick close to the women."

"No," Tighe said. "He can manage every other woman on the ranch. I'll handle River."

"No one's managing or handling anyone," Ash said. "Galen wants one guard near the houses, and one on Fiona and Burke. He wants the canyons staked out, and the outlying bunkhouse, and so on. Don't make this difficult, Tighe."

There'd been enough gossip about Jace and River. Tighe aimed to set folks straight on that really quick— just as soon as he could figure out how to get his elusive girlfriend to an altar. Girlfriend? He pondered his brandy. Would River call herself his girlfriend?

He doubted it. "River's having my children, so it makes sense for me to stay close to her."

"I wouldn't put it exactly that way to her," Ash reminded him. "River thinks she's looking out for you, and I can't argue with her, considering your physical condition."

"There's nothing wrong with my— Never mind." He was darn tired of everyone reminding him that he was the weak link. "You guys can keep ribbing me about Firefreak, but I'm telling you, riding him was the moment I found my destiny. Just like Dante." He glared at his twin.

Dante shook his head. "I didn't find my destiny on the back of a stupid hunk of meat. I found my destiny in Ana's bed."

His brothers all whistled, and Ash looked disgusted. "I hope whoever I end up with doesn't talk about me the way you meatheads talk about the women in your lives."

"I'll chat with Xav Phillips about it. Let him know you don't go for possessive, alpha males." Galen ruffled his sister's hair, and she spared him an aggrieved glance. "Back to business. It probably would be best if you stayed here at the ranch, Tighe. You're not much use at the fence or in the canyons, since you can't ride a horse. So you'll stay with the women and children."

"Oh, for the love of Mike," he grumbled. "Leave me a shred of dignity?"

"Jace, you ride fence. Ash, you stick with Fiona." Galen looked at Sloan and Falcon. "I'll cover the outlying bunkhouse and talk to the foremen." He glanced around the room. "Does anybody have anything they want to bring up?"

"Yeah," Tighe said. "As soon as I'm able, I'm planning to ride Firefreak again."

They all stared at him.

Ash smacked her forehead with her palm. "Next time, I hope you land on your head!"

"If you hadn't sent River to my room to keep me

from riding—" he reminded his siblings, and they all booed him down.

"I'm going to be a father now, and my lady won't marry me. It's because I didn't finish exploring my calling. I'm playing matters too risk averse."

"Nope. It's because of the wish I made of the universe," Dante said with glee. "It's going to happen to Jace, and Galen, too. To all of you, because you all made my life such a living heck on my way to true love."

"What wish?" his siblings demanded.

"I wished you all would fall for partners who understand the thrill of the chase, and would give you a good long slippery run, where there's lots of crow to be eaten at every bend in the road." Dante looked pleased with himself. "I said it into the wind, and the words took life. Obviously."

"That's terrible," Ash said. "How could you?"

"I don't believe in that kind of nonsense," Tighe said. "My problem has nothing to do with you. River is superindependent, and she thinks our one night together was a mistake. A setup."

Ash sighed. "This is all my fault."

Tighe nodded, glad to see someone taking responsibility for his situation. "You didn't stop me from riding."

"No, I didn't, but not for lack of trying. I hope you'll be a better father than you are a bull rider," she said. "I hope you have three darling little girls to run you ragged. It would be your just deserts."

His mouth turned down. "I'm having three boys. I'm positive that's what I'll have. I like the color blue, and I like boy sports. I don't think I could handle three Fiona-type youth-size blessings in my life." He gazed at his sister, taking in his petite firecracker of a sibling. "Or a female like you, for that matter."

Galen stood. "Let's get back to our ranch issues. Running Bear is worried about the fact that Wolf has practically made himself at home on our land."

"Home is where the heart is," Tighe muttered. "Wolf's heart isn't here. He's just greedy. And I believe scared."

"Scared?" Jace demanded. "How do you figure that?"

"I think the cartel's hanging something over him. My gut tells me he cut a deal with them and now he needs to deliver. The fact that Wolf's followed this thing for so long makes me think either the payoff is huge or he made too large of a promise to the cartel and now they're forcing him to ramp up his activity here—or both."

"Either way, it's not good," Sloan said.

"No. I keep trying to figure his next move, but he always surprises me," Ash said.

"What are we going to do about Storm?" Tighe asked. "Sloan, you honestly feel good about having Storm's niece, Sawyer, guarding your twins?"

Sloan shrugged. "River keeps a pretty tight eye on Sawyer, if you haven't noticed."

He hadn't, probably because he was too busy trying to keep a tight eye on River without looking like an overpossessive, sex-hungry doof. "River's not going to be able to do that for long. She'll be housebound before she wants to be." There was no question River wouldn't be the kind of woman who enjoyed sitting in her bed watching TV and reading books, even for a few months. Or a few hours.

She'd probably think it was the nearest thing to in-carceration. No doubt she wouldn't look on him any more kindly than she did now, once she hadn't seen sunlight and ridden a horse in the fresh air for a couple of months.

"Earth to Tighe," Ash said. "Are you listening?"

"Probably not too well," Galen said. "Does he ever?"

"It's true," Tighe agreed. "I don't always have the best auditory skills."

"Selective hearing is what ails you, bro," Jace said.

"Maybe. The key is to say something important. That's the way to command my attention," he said helpfully.

Ash sighed. "Let's adjourn this meeting. We're all strung too tightly to make much headway."

"I'm not strung tightly. I feel just fine." Tighe got up, limped to the door. "But I don't have a problem with adjourning."

"Because you want to go find River," Ash said.

"True. Seems like something a wise man would do at this moment." He thought about the beautiful body-guard and wished he knew how to romance her better. "Just can't figure out where I'm going wrong with that little lady."

His brothers and sister gathered around him, thumping him on the back. They stared out the windows of the upstairs library, gazing out over the ranch.

"Listen!" Tighe said suddenly, his ears on alert. It was unmistakable, the sound of hooves pounding, rushing along rock trails that time had cut into the canyons. "The Diablos."

The Callahans glanced at each other, standing together united. The mystical Diablos were a portent of things to come, according to legend. Tighe's scalp prick-led. There had already been so much change—but he'd felt the signs in the wind, too. He'd known something was coming.

Running Bear had warned of impending darkness. He'd warned of a hunted one. Was the warning coming to pass now?

If it's me, I'll go off and live in the canyons where no one can find me. I'll never hurt this family in any way. I was brought here to save it.

Ash leaned her head against him. "Whatever it is, we stand together."

He nodded, and their brothers murmured their agreement.

The bond was unbreakable.

Chapter 6

Tighe was pretty shocked when his bedroom door creaked open, the sound somehow loud in the still bunk-house. He didn't move while the intruder crept slowly, deliberately toward his bed. Tighe's gun was under his pillow, and the element of surprise would be on his side. By his military watch, he could see the time was 2200 hours. Late. So he waited, holding his breath, coiled like a spring.

His nocturnal visitor bumped the bed, and still Tighe didn't move.

The sheet and blanket lifted, and a warm body slid in next to him.

"Hello?" he said, just as River's sexy form melded against his side.

"Hi. Do you mind?"

"Not at all." His brain raced with relief and the good

fortune that something had brought her to his bed. "What's going on?"

"I want to talk to you. This is the best place to do it. No prying eyes and listening ears."

So much curvy softness pressed up against him it was smoking his synapses. It was hard to think about conversation when her perfume teased at him. "Sawyer watching the twins?"

"They're with Sloan and Kendall. I think Sawyer went to see her uncle. I'm off duty, Kendall says, because she wants me to rest." River sighed. "I don't want everyone babying me just because I'm carrying triplets."

He hadn't expected her to feel any differently. "So what can I do for you?"

"Fiona wants me to try on the magic wedding dress. She says I'm running out of time if I want to know the truth."

He frowned in the dark. "Truth about what?"

"Whether we belong together."

"Listen, you know you belong to me, because we're having three babies. It has nothing to do with Fiona's myths."

"Ana says it's not a myth."

He sighed. "Trust me, I've heard this tale over and over again. I'm a big believer in spirits and angels and things that guide us. Probably no bigger believer in the family than me. Tell me a story about things that go bump in the night, and I'm all over it. But a magic dress is too much for me."

"I thought you'd feel that way. So I told her I'd try it on if you didn't object."

He sat up to lean against the rustic wood headboard.

"Anything that gets you to thinking about a wedding is worth encouraging. So now that I'm wide-awake and thinking about it, I vote yes on trying on the infamous gown. I've got a fifty-fifty chance it goes my way, right? Either I'm Prince Charming or I'm not. I'm feeling good about it." He smiled, pleased with himself. If there was truth to the gown's fantastical leanings, then it would definitely reveal him to be River's one true love. She was having his triplets, and nothing could deny that. There wasn't a charm on the planet that could take away the fact that he and River were together forever.

Maybe she'd fall so in love with the gown she'd be anxious to head straight to the altar. The sooner the better. There was a time constraint issue here. Tighe knew River pretty well, and figured if he wagered on her being the kind of woman who wouldn't get married once the three little boys added their sweetness to her already sweet figure, it was a wager he'd win. "The more I think about it, the more I believe you ought to listen to Aunt Fiona."

"Why do I have the feeling that your initial reaction was your gut, and true, reaction? Even though I can't see your face, you're not that hard to read, Tighe."

"I'm an open book," he said cheerfully. "Is that all you came to visit me about? Get my permission to try on the family gown?"

"I don't need your permission."

"So go for it. I don't hold much stock in it, but the other Callahan ladies swear by it. Although they never share their experience, so all I know is that the gown seems to be a good luck talisman of some kind, since all my brothers end up at the altar. Including Dante, which was a miracle, in my mind." Tighe tucked his arm around her, pulled her up against him, but she wriggled away. He felt her leave the bed. "Hey, where are you going?"

"Back to my room."

"I enjoyed you flashing me the other night. I wouldn't mind a repeat performance, beautiful."

That didn't win him anything but a raised brow, so he shifted gears as fast as he could. "Stay awhile longer. I've got some things on my mind, too."

She slid back in, but he could feel her tension, so didn't try to wrap her against him again. "I want to go with you to your next doctor's appointment. If you wouldn't mind."

"That's fine."

Easy. Almost too easy. Tighe decided to press his advantage. "I'm hoping you'll let me give my children my name."

"You mean if we don't get married."

"Right. Does seem the right thing to do." He was asking as nicely as he knew how without downright putting his foot down.

"I think that would be best. Thank you."

Great. All hurdles cleared—except the big one. But now wasn't the time to press her about marriage. He'd have to be satisfied with tiny steps.

"Tighe, I don't want you riding bulls anymore. Including Firefreak."

He blinked in the darkness, surprised. "Why not?"

"Because you're apparently not that... I mean, I'm going to need help with the children, after they're born. You'll have healed in the next several months, before I give birth. After that it will probably be as exciting around here as riding bulls."

"You're right. I agree."

He felt her turn her face toward him, longed to put his arms around her and kiss her thoroughly.

"So you'll stay away from the rodeo?"

"If you'll stay out of the canyons and close to the house, where one of my brothers—or preferably me—will be with you at all times."

"That won't be a problem," River said, "if you put a recliner near a window for me. I don't think I can bear to be in a bed for a month without looking out the window."

"I'll buy you a top of the line, brand-new recliner. You'll feel like a queen."

She slid out of the bed. He didn't ask her to remain—he knew she wouldn't. But at least she'd come to see him, felt comfortable getting into his bed.

"Good night, Tighe."

The words flew out of his mouth before he could stop them. "Make love with me."

He felt her hesitation.

"How?"

"Well, first, you get back in my bed," Tighe said, "and then I'm going to kiss you. Then I'll probably slide your clothes off one by one, with my teeth, no doubt, just because it sounds like fun and we didn't do that last time. And then—"

"I meant," River said, interrupting his wistful soliloquizing, "if we're not getting married, how could we make love? Why would we repeat what got us into this mess?"

"Details, details." Reaching out, he pulled her back into his bed. "We don't have to make love tonight. Let's just sleep together. Get to know each other better. It's hard to get to know someone very well unless I'm in a bed with them."

"I'll bet," River said, and he laughed.

"You're going to be such a feisty little mother."

She sighed, but he noticed she didn't wriggle out of his arms. "I'll try not to let the females of this family down."

"That's right. Tradition is very important to us." She felt so good he could barely stand to keep his hands to himself. "Any chance you're cold? Need a tall, dark, handsome blanket to warm you up and maybe make you the happiest woman on earth?"

She giggled. "You don't think much of yourself, do you?"

He snuggled into her neck, smelled the flowery scent of her hair. "I believe I recall it was all you could do not to yell down Ms. Sherby's B and B, beautiful."

River pinched him. "You were the only one making noise, cowboy."

This was true, as he recalled. Making love to River— finally, after months and months of dry-mouthed moon-ing—had been a dizzying, crazy ride. "Let me relive that moment. I promise not to yell this time."

"Personally, I think you'll always be noisy, Tighe. Because of your reputation for being silent, you've re-pressed a lot of sound."

He kissed her cheek, inched a hand across her stom-ach, slowly making his move. "Let's find out."

"You just want to make love to me before I get big as a house."

"Indeed. And then, too." He kissed her neck, stole across to her lips. "I promise that no matter how large you become, I'll always be able to handle it."

"You're about to get yourself in big trouble, cowboy," River said. But he noticed she wasn't pushing him away, so he decided kissing her needed to be done at once.

She opened up to him like a sweet flower. A groan escaped him, and she giggled.

"You see? You're the noisy one."

He slid a hand up, captured a breast. "Give me a couple hours. If I don't yell, you can come back tomorrow night. How's that for a deal?"

"We'll see," River said.

After the night River spent in Tighe's arms, she knew she had to take the path the other Callahan women had journeyed.

There was no reason to wait. Either she and Tighe were a one-night fling that had resulted in children, and therefore she'd had no business being in his bed last night—or they were meant to be together. Either way, there was no time to lose. It felt as if her waistline had already put on a couple inches—though when she measured, it was more like one. Tighe hadn't seemed to notice, although she did think he'd been much more careful—less wild sexually—than the previous time they'd made love.

She didn't believe the treasured family gown would tell her whether Tighe was her man, but she did wonder if putting the silly thing on would make her feel more as if becoming a bride was the right thing to do. That bothered her most of all—the itching, nagging feeling that maybe marrying in haste would mean a lifetime of regrets.

Her parents had been divorced. She was going to try to avoid that uneasy route.

"Hello, River," Fiona trilled. "You're up bright and early, aren't you? Shouldn't you be resting?"

She had a feeling Fiona would be tickled if she learned River probably hadn't had two hours of sleep last night, thanks to Tighe. "Fiona, you offered to let me try on the magic wedding dress, and—"

"Oh, my dear!" The older woman beamed. "Are you warming up to my wonderful nephew?"

"Perhaps. Slowly," River admitted, not wanting to put Fiona into full-tilt wedding machinations.

"Slowly is fine. Can't rush a good thing. The best things in life are worth waiting for and all that." She pointed with her spatula to the stairs. "You just go on up into the attic, close the door so you'll have privacy and try it on. I'd show you where it is, but I'm deep into making waffles for the crew." She smiled again. "I'm so happy you've decided to give the dress a try."

"Thank you." River went up to the attic, amazed that anxiety set in as she ascended the stairs. Her steps slowed as she entered the enormous room made homey by window seats and a dangling chandelier. It was only a dress, and a myth. A legend that made the Callahans happy.

Ana had had a bit of a rocky time with the dress, although River didn't know the particulars. She just knew the dress wasn't a panacea, a magic wand, for her relationship with Tighe.

When he made love to her, it was hard for her to think there was anything wrong with their relationship—which was the problem. It was all about sex, and a purely sexual relationship didn't last.

Although she could easily imagine wanting to make love to Tighe for the rest of her life.

She glanced around the room, noting a cheval mirror, a couple of small chairs and tables, a cozy nook in which one could read—or plot, in Fiona's case. River opened the door to the long closet, easily locating the bag that contained the gown. It was the only item hanging in the cavernous walk-in space.

She took the bag—it was surprisingly light for holding a fabulous, magical wedding dress—hung it on a hook near the cheval mirror and with sudden excitement, gently drew the zipper down.

Chapter 7

Tighe hurried into the kitchen, spotting his aunt Fiona with relief. Maybe there was still time to stop River from trying on the magic wedding dress.

"Hello, favored nephew. How about some waffles?" Fiona asked. "And maybe some eggs?"

"No, thanks, Aunt Fiona." He glanced around quickly. "Has River been here?"

"A little bit ago. But she's not here now. Bacon?"

"It looks great, but I'm kind of in a hurry. Did she say where she was going?"

"She did," Fiona said, "but I don't know if I'm to divulge her location."

He glanced up at the ceiling toward the attic. "She's up there, isn't she? I'm too late."

"For what?" Fiona gave him a curious look.

"To stop her."

"Gracious me, why would you want to?" Fiona shook her head, her eyes rounded. "I thought you were all hot to get River to the altar."

"I am. But Dante just told me that the dress backfired on him in rare fashion.

"Oh, pooh. Don't listen to your twin." Fiona laid a plate in front of Tighe to tempt him. "You and Dante may be from the same zygote, but truthfully, you're total opposites."

"This is serious, Aunt. Dante said it was months before he saw Ana again after she tried on the gown. He said it messed everything up for him." Tighe felt very desperate on this score. "I've got enough trouble on my hands with River without that kind of supernatural assistance." He'd just sweet-talked her into his bed, and the pleasure had been mind-bending. He wanted more of that! Intimacy was the way to get his woman to the altar, not a gown. "Trust me, I've got this covered."

"I believe that's what you said about Firefreak, and about River," Fiona observed. "I do believe you could do with a little help in some matters, nephew."

His gaze fastened on the ceiling. "I don't suppose there's any way to stop her?"

"You could," Fiona said, "but I wouldn't recommend seeing her in the gown. If you go charging up there, that's what might happen. And I don't know how that would affect matters." She shook her head. "Every woman has had her time alone with the gown. Her time to figure out what she really wants."

"Damn it." He sank onto a bar stool, contemplated the delicious eggs, waffle and bacon without enthusiasm.

"Oh, no! Whatever you do, don't curse the gown," Fiona warned.

"I'm not. I'm cursing myself. I'm sort of cursing why I didn't just keep her in bed with me this morning. I could have told her my leg was acting up. I could have told her—"

"Pardon me," Fiona said, her face wreathed with sudden delight, "not to be indelicate, but you did just let something slip."

"Sorry," he muttered. "I didn't mean to be unchivalrous. I do apologize, Aunt."

Fiona cleared her throat. "However, all that being said, you and River have something of a rapprochement, then?"

"All I can tell you is that I'm gaga for her, and I'm real nervous about her being in your attic of drama."

Fiona patted his hand. "Everything will work out."

He couldn't stand it. Dante had scared the heck out of him. Tighe didn't want to be separated from River for months. He had enough problems—why had he endorsed Fiona's magic bag of tricks?

Still, a man couldn't deny his lady a chance to try on a beautiful gown, could he?

"I'm scared. I've never been scared like this before."

"Nephew!" Fiona ladled more food onto his plate, though he hadn't touched a bite. "I've never seen you like this! For a man with a huge adventurous streak, you're a nervous wreck!"

He slid off the stool, went to the stairwell. "It's too quiet up there. I'm going up."

"I really cannot counsel you to do so," Fiona said, worried. She came to stand at his side. "Just call up there, if you're so concerned, but I won't vouch for what happens. I'm pretty sure it's a man-free zone. And I don't know if River will appreciate you being a Nervous Nelly."

Maybe he overestimated the gown's importance. But what if he had the same misfortune Dante had suffered? Tighe had just lured River back into his arms! He wasn't letting go of her again, not after he'd waited like a dying man for her to soften toward him.

Making love to her was the sweetest thing he'd ever experienced in his life and there hadn't been a whole lot of sweetness in his twenty-eight years. He'd waited a very long time for River to even look his way. Dante and he had waited a long time for the nanny bodyguards to do more than say hello—and the night Tighe had caught River and his siblings plotting to keep him off Firefreak, he'd felt no compunction whatsoever about turning the tables on her and seducing her.

Only the tables had been turned on him big-time—and he'd tumbled like a rock into a pond. Now he'd been given a second chance, and that second chance had been ever so delicious and tantalizing last night.

He just couldn't risk it.

He charged up the stairs.

River sat in one of the window seats, staring out the window, thinking. She'd put the dress bag away, closed the closet door.

It had been the most amazing thing. Yet somehow unsettling. Very unsettling.

She'd try again in a moment. Try to work up her courage to do it. She had drawn the zipper down, and just as quickly, zipped the bag back up.

She heard boots thundering on the stairs and jumped when Tighe burst into the attic. "Tighe!"

He came to a dead halt. Gave her a funny look when he spotted her sitting in the window seat. "Am I too late?"

"Too late for what?"

"To stop you from trying on the dress."

Her brows rose. "Why would you want to?"

He seemed upset, which confused her. "I just had a funny feeling you shouldn't. It was like something came over the wires, if you know what I mean, that told me this wasn't an idea that was going to go in our favor."

"You told me to go for it."

"I know," Tighe admitted, "but like I said, it was like I received some kind of weird message from the ozone."

"It doesn't entirely surprise me that you'd receive a weird message," River said with a sigh, "because sometimes you do seem a bit weird. Like the other Callahans, at times." Still, he did seem bothered about something. "Anyway, I didn't try it on. I never even looked at it."

"Why not?"

She shrugged. "Maybe I got the same message you did."

He seemed relieved. "That's a good sign, if we're getting the same thoughts."

"Maybe. I wouldn't put money on it." She looked at Tighe. "I've decided to throw caution to the wind and marry you regardless of what the magic wedding dress might have to say."

"Really?" He was obviously surprised.

"Yeah." River went to turn off the lamp. "Marriage isn't a decision to be made by a magic eight ball. I don't want a gown to tell me what to do—even if I did believe in such things."

"You're going to marry me?"

She sighed. "Yes, Tighe. But it's a practical decision, not a romantic thing."

"I don't think so," he said. "I don't think we were being

practical last night when we made love. In fact, I'm pretty sure we were being romantic. At least I was. And I intend to be even more romantic, especially because in a couple of months, you're not going to care about romancing."

She glared at him. "I don't know what you mean about last night."

"What I mean is that the earth moved for both of us last night. And I was not silent. Neither were you. Birds flew out of trees. Critters ran from the ranch. You, my love, express your pleasure loudly enough that we're going to have to move into the bunkhouse near the canyons, and even then, I'll have to soundproof the house."

She felt a blush steal up her cheeks. "You're embarrassing me."

"Don't be," he said cheerfully. "I liked it."

She walked to the top of the stairs. "It's a practical matter, Tighe. We're having children. It would be best for them if we married. I'm not repeating last night."

He stepped over to her, took her in his arms, closed the attic door. Kissed her long and hard, then his kisses turned gentle. River felt her knees weaken. Her fingers stole into his hair, then gripped his shoulders. He made short work of her skirt, murmured something about "magic wedding dresses being no help," then sat down and moved her into his lap. She grabbed the zipper on his jeans, and faster than she'd undone the dress bag, had his zipper down, gasping when he entered her. She tried to cover her moans of pleasure by burying her face in his neck while he dug his hands into her buttocks, pulling her tighter against him.

Glorious heat exploded all through her, and she couldn't help moving, rocking, hard against him. Tighe groaned, held her tight and still, and collapsed against her, the two of them gasping with pleasure.

"No more talk of practicality," he said after a moment. "I can't stay away from you long enough to be practical."

"All right," River gasped. She felt so bone-meltingly lovely she would have agreed to just about anything at this moment. "But it's not romance, either."

"Not everything is a business decision," Tighe said, cradling her against his chest, supporting her weight as he relaxed against the window seat. "You just let me make you happy like this every day, and we'll worry about what to call it later."

He wasn't listening. Their relationship wasn't romantic. It was sex.

Yet it wasn't just sex. She'd been crazy about this cowboy forever. "Whatever you say," she finally murmured, too satisfied to argue.

"That's my girl," he said, and River giggled.

"You're going to get in trouble with me, cowboy. Chauvinism is not romantic nor practical."

"I'll work on it."

"You do that." She fell silent, feeling slightly guilty. She hadn't been totally honest—not honest at all. She had unzipped the bag. She *had* looked at the gown.

But when she'd pulled it from its covering, it had turned black. Black as the ace of spades. And turned into tactical gear, something to be worn in a war zone, or at least a very dangerous place.

Frightened, she'd stuffed it back in the bag and rudely shoved it into the closet.

She wasn't going to tell a soul. But even she knew that a magic wedding dress that turned black was a bad omen. Chills ran over her skin.

"Cold?" Tighe asked.

"A little," she said. "Let's go downstairs."

They moved slowly away from each other, rearranged their clothes. She could hardly look at him, even when he touched her chin, held her close to him. Kissed her, long and sweet. "I'll talk to Grandfather. We can marry this weekend."

"Fine," River said, and went to the door.

No enchanted gown was going to cost her the chance to marry the father of her children, the cowboy of her dreams. Maybe he'd regret their marriage later—after all, the gown was a Callahan gown and probably was fine-tuned to Callahan emotion—but after worrying and wondering over what she should do, River decided to catch her cowboy.

Making love with Tighe had convinced her.

She wasn't about to give him up, even if she had to battle a disapproving magic wedding dress to do it.

Tighe felt as if the world had just smiled on him. Everything was going better than he'd hoped at this stage in the game.

This was awesome.

"Let me take you downstairs. Fiona's made breakfast," he said, leading River out of the attic. "I'm sure my little boys would love a waffle right about now."

"No one has said we're having boys."

He loved teasing her. She probably wanted three little girls. He didn't care, as long as he was getting three of everything she wanted to give him. How many men could say that a woman gave him three babies?

He stopped on the stairs. "Do you hear that?"

She stopped beside him. "I don't hear anything."

"Exactly. And something's burning."

She grabbed his arm. "It's the food!"

He practically broad-jumped the rest of the stairs to hurry into the kitchen. "Find my aunt," he said. "I'll put this fire out." Bacon grease smoked in the frying pan, the bacon black. Eggs lay cold to the side, and the waffle iron held a blackened waffle. He shut that off, too, glancing over his shoulder as River hurried back into the kitchen.

"I can't find her," she told him.

A horrible feeling crept over him, spreading like spilled ink. Grabbing his phone, he texted an alert to his siblings. *Think we've got trouble. Can't find Fiona.*

It didn't take long for the back door to blow open. Jace and Galen came charging in. They looked at the ruined food, saw River trying to air the smoke out of the kitchen.

"This is not good," Galen said. "I've never known Fiona to burn anything."

"No kidding." That was the understatement of the year.

"She can't just disappear," Jace said as the door flew open again and Ash hurried in.

"What's happened?" She looked at River. "Weren't you here with her?"

"I was upstairs," River said.

"And you didn't hear anything?" Ash demanded. "Didn't smell the kitchen practically burning down?"

River gave Tighe a startled look, and he said, "Easy, Ash. Neither one of us noticed anything out of the ordinary. Fiona was her usual cheerful self when I walked through, and I was the last to see her."

Sloan and Dante hurried through the den into the kitchen. "She can't have gotten far," Sloan said. "Someone have Falcon start tracking her."

"I'll do it," Jace said. "I'm the best tracker in the family."

"Not better than me," Ash said, pushing past him.

"You two stick together," Tighe said.

"Got it," Ash called back.

"Okay, fan out. River, you stay here, in case she comes back," Tighe began, but she scowled at him.

"I'm a bodyguard, Tighe."

"And pregnant," he said. "Stay here, please. Just in case she returns."

"Who's going to watch *her?*" Galen asked, tipping his chin toward River. "If something has happened to Fiona—"

"Where's Burke?" River suddenly asked. "I checked their room, but he's not there."

"I just saw him out in the corral," Sloan said. "I'll go tell him." He trudged off, not eager to relay bad news.

The brothers divided up the rest of Rancho Diablo to search for tracks, and they all took off. "I'll be right back," Tighe told River, who favored him with another scowl. "I'm sorry. You can't ride with us. It's dangerous, and this isn't your fight. Be home base for us, and let us know if Fiona shows up here. All right?"

River nodded. He brushed a swift kiss against her lips, and she threw her arms around him. "Find her, Tighe."

"We will."

"Do you want me to call Sheriff Cartwright? Just in case she's been in town for some reason?"

Fiona wouldn't have left a mess. Yet Wolf had been frequenting town more and more. "It's a great idea. Thanks."

Tighe kissed her one final time and headed out.

Chapter 8

By nightfall, everyone in the town of Diablo and the surrounding county knew Fiona Callahan was missing. They also knew she hadn't simply wandered off—the sheriff and his deputies had pointed out signs of struggle in the dirt outside. Running Bear had come by, gravely examining the scene in the kitchen, then standing quietly for a long time, his eyes closed. River hadn't known what to say—she'd felt guilty every time the sheriff or his deputies had asked her if she'd heard anything strange.

She hadn't noticed a thing. Lost in her daydreams of Tighe, she'd been focused on the gown, and him. Not doing her job of guarding the Callahans.

Worse, she'd left the twins with Sawyer Cash—and no matter what Kendall said, River couldn't help wondering if Sawyer might have signaled to her uncle Storm or someone that no one was on duty except her, making it the perfect time to strike.

If the Callahans weren't worried about Sawyer, why should she be? Anyway, it seemed as if Jace was keeping a fairly close eye on Sawyer.

River sank onto a bar stool in the kitchen, considered the counters she'd scrubbed until they shone. After the sheriff and deputies and Running Bear left, she'd cleaned the room, throwing out the ruined food and mopping the floor. It was still a pretty sad space without Fiona's cheerful mess in it.

Ana walked into the kitchen and plunked down next to her. "You should be sitting in the den, relaxing on that nice comfy leather sofa."

"I can't relax. I'm so worried." She looked at Ana. "I feel terrible that Fiona needed me and I was up in the attic." She closed her eyes for a moment. *Being utterly, wonderfully seduced.*

"Don't fixate on that. Whoever grabbed her had been watching the house, saw an opening. Everybody here is some kind of operative or bodyguard, and still, they managed to grab the one of us nobody expected would ever be under threat. Fiona isn't exactly new to this rodeo. She knows how to be careful." Ana hugged River. "There's nothing you could have done."

"Except be in the kitchen with her. Where I should have been, and not in the attic."

"All of us visit the attic on occasion. And the basement, to find the holiday lights and Fiona's delicious preserves. Basement, attic, makes no difference. We had our guard down, and someone noticed. We can't beat ourselves up about it." Ana sighed. "It will all work out, anyway. The Callahans aren't going to let anything happen to their aunt."

"I feel horrible for Burke. He looked like he aged five years when they told him she was gone." River felt as if she might cry, forced the tears back. "He's in his room right now. The sheriff told him to stay put. I think he's afraid Burke might have a heart attack from the stress."

"I'll check on him in a minute." Ana looked at her best friend. "Come on. I insist you lie down on the sofa."

"I can't." Still, she followed Ana into the other room, glad to get away from the kitchen, which was depressing without Fiona. "Wait. You're here to guard me, aren't you? Did Tighe send you?"

"Yes, and yes. And don't argue. Lie down." Ana forced her to do so, then tossed a soft afghan over her even though it was hot as blazes outside.

They didn't speak for a long time. Ana probably hoped she'd fall asleep, but River couldn't, not while Fiona was in danger. Too many worried thoughts ran through her head. She tried not to think about the what-ifs, but it was hard.

"So, triplets," Ana said. "That'll put Tighe in the race for the ranch." She laughed, shaking her head. "Not that any of us believe there is such a thing. But Fiona will do anything to see her nephews happily married."

If Fiona came back. River could hardly bear to think of it. "Did you ever imagine when we came to work here that we'd end up married to two of the brothers?"

Ana shook her head. "Kind of nice, though."

River got up from the sofa, paced to the window. "I wish we'd hear something."

"Me, too."

"You left Sawyer with the twins?"

"Kendall's got them. She wanted to come over and keep you company, but Sloan said no. He's too worried, since Fiona was kidnapped from here. Unless she wandered off…"

The comment hung in the air. They both knew Fiona wouldn't have wandered off. Her mind was fully clear, and never more clear than when she was cooking for her nephews. "She didn't. She had fresh dough for waffles, and eggs sitting out."

Ana came to stand beside River. "Worrying won't help, and it's not good for the triplets."

"I know."

"Ever since Tighe found out you're expecting, he's been a different man." Ana laughed. "These Callahans insist they'll always be single, until they find out they're going to be a father."

"Don't remind me." She wanted to believe Tighe would romance her this way even if she wasn't pregnant with his children.

He wouldn't.

Running Bear walked into the den, and River saw pain on his face. "How are you doing, Chief?"

He looked drawn. "I know where they took her."

River gasped. "Where?"

"They took Fiona to their hideout in Montana. Same place they took Taylor."

"Oh, no!" River looked at Ana. "But why?"

"They mean to keep her through the winter. They figure she will break." Running Bear's face looked older with each word he spoke. "It's far from her family. It will get cold early. Her family is her life, so they know this is her weakness."

River went into the kitchen to get Running Bear a

cup of tea. He'd probably spent hours sitting in this kitchen, chatting with his dear friend. Actually, Fiona did the chatting, and more often than not, Running Bear sat silently. It was their way.

He perched on the bar stool, his shoulders slumped a bit. River put the tea in front of him, rummaged around for some of Fiona's cookies she knew he favored.

He touched neither, but nodded his thanks.

"So now what?" River asked.

"I am not sure."

Tighe came in the back door, glanced at River and Ana, then Running Bear. "What's happening, Grandfather?"

"Fiona is in Montana."

"Montana?" He looked at River, his brows raised. "Wolf's got her?"

Running Bear nodded silently. River looked at both men for a moment, then poured Tighe a cup of coffee and went back to the den. Ana followed, and they sat down to talk privately.

"If Fiona's in Montana, Burke's going to—"

"Don't think about it," Ana said. "The Callahans will figure something out. They did for Taylor."

"We could go get her."

Ana blinked. "Go get her?"

"Sure. We're not Callahan. Wolf would never suspect us." The more she thought about it, the more River was convinced it was a smart idea. "We're both trained bodyguards. We can take care of ourselves."

"You're pregnant," Ana reminded her.

"This is true," River said, "but I haven't noticed it yet. I'm still in fighting form."

"Tighe would lose his mind if you left. He wants you resting."

River nodded. "We wouldn't tell him. Not immediately."

"I want no part of this. None."

"It may not be necessary. Running Bear always has a plan." River thought about that for a few moments. "But Fiona's not staying there for months like Taylor had to, not if I can help it."

"River," Ana said, sounding very worried, "Tighe would freak out."

"That's okay. He freaks out on occasion. It's part of his psyche." River crossed to a window, stared out. "I know she's frightened."

"I doubt very seriously Fiona is frightened. Mad as a hornet, but not frightened. After you've raised a basketball team's worth of boys, you don't scare easily."

"This was what Wolf wanted all along. He knew he couldn't get any information out of the others. It was all scare tactics." River looked up at Tighe and Running Bear as they walked into the den. "Wolf wanted Fiona all along."

"I agree." Tighe nodded, went to rub River's shoulders.

"Don't agree too much," Ana said. "River wants to go get Fiona."

Tighe's hands tightened on her shoulders, then abruptly dropped. "Absolutely not. Out of the question."

Running Bear glanced at her. "Maybe in the spring."

"Spring!" River was horrified. "Why the spring? Fiona can't stay there with those thugs that long!"

Ash walked in, looking depressed. "Whoever took

Fiona covered their tracks well. I pride myself on tracking, but I'm not finding much to go on."

"Running Bear knows where Fiona is," River said.

"You do, Grandfather?" Ash looked surprised.

"She is in Montana." Running Bear's eyes were dark with some emotion River couldn't really define.

"Montana? Where they took Taylor?" Ash demanded. "Let's go get her! And this time, we'll burn that shack down. I'm sorry, Grandfather, but we can't go on living in fear."

"Whoa," Tighe said, going to comfort his sister, which River was glad to see. "We need a plan. We can't just go burn Wolf out of there."

"Yes, we can," Ash said. "Yes, we most certainly can! *I* can, if no one else wants to."

"I can, too," River said. "I've got your back. In fact, I'll drive."

Jace and Galen came into the room. "Where are we driving?" Galen asked.

"I want to go rescue Fiona and burn Wolf right out of his lair." Ash's arms crossed, her posture stubborn. River silently applauded her, more than ready herself to drive the truck to rescue Fiona.

"Tonight," Tighe said, "we'll sit down as a family and discuss this. Right now, everyone go back to your posts. No one, and this means you both," he said to River and his sister, "will be doing any sneaking off to do any burning, torching, rescue attempts or any other mission. Is that understood? We need a battle plan, not a herky-jerky attack."

"It's not herky-jerky." Ash glared at Tighe, then turned to her grandfather. "Running Bear, we've always adhered to your rules. We understood we were never to harm Wolf. But this is troubling."

The chief nodded. "Troubling, indeed. But it will not solve the problem of the cartel, and right now, Wolf is the liaison. My son is the devil we know."

River went to warm Running Bear's cup. Tighe followed her into the kitchen. "You will not be going to Montana."

"I'm willing. Someone needs to get Fiona. I'm trained for this, Tighe."

"And you're carrying my children."

"I'm barely showing. Not at all, really. An ounce of stomach I didn't have before."

"It doesn't matter." He pulled her into his arms. "You're not putting my sons in danger."

"Daughters."

"Do we know that?" He leaned back to look at her.

"No. I just feel like torturing you because you aren't already on the road to rescue Fiona!" Tears suddenly sprouted from River's eyes. "Oh, my God, I'm so sorry. I've never been a crier. I have no idea why I'm suddenly crying." She grabbed a tissue from the box on the counter.

"Treading carefully here, but isn't it normal for women to be emotional when they're pregnant?" Tighe asked.

She blew her nose. "I'm a well-trained bodyguard. I'm not emotional. I'm simply annoyed with you."

He smiled, held her against his chest. "Thank you for loving my aunt so much."

"Well, I do." River pulled away from him, not pleased that he was seeing her with her nose running and sounding like a dented trumpet. "I can't bear the fact that they took her. I would trade places with her in a flash! She's too old and fragile to be in Montana with Wolf and his minions."

She blew her nose again and he laughed, kissed the top of her head. "Aunt Fiona's the least fragile person I know."

"She has you fooled."

"I guarantee you she's giving Uncle Wolf fits."

"Good for her. I hope he has an infarction of epic proportions." River looked up at Tighe. "I know the chief doesn't want us to be violent, doesn't want you to exact any justice on your uncle, but I would just like to say that I'm not part of this family. That makes me an obvious rule-breaker." She gazed at him earnestly. "Send me up there, Tighe."

"No. But I can tell that I'm going to have a really interesting married life."

"No, you're not," River said. "I'm not agreeing to marry you until you get Fiona back. I feel quite stubborn about this. It wouldn't be a wedding without your aunt."

"No, it wouldn't." He looked thoughtful. "I'm going to order some dinner for this crowd. Then I want you to rest."

Her jaw dropped. "How can you think about food at a time like this?"

"Easily. No one has eaten all day." He allowed her to move out of his arms, went to poke around in the fridge. "I'm nothing if not practical. I've always been practical."

She followed him to the refrigerator. "I think you're in shock."

"No." He shut the fridge door. "I just know that this

will be a long mission. Planning will need to be done carefully. And that requires food."

She sighed. "Why do I get the funny feeling that you're trying to give me a subtle hint that I should take over Fiona's kitchen duties, or else everyone on this ranch will starve?"

He laughed. "No. We're all capable of scrambling eggs for ourselves."

"We really are going to starve." River perched on a bar stool, watched him rifle through the cabinets, searching for containers Fiona had stored. "If you get your aunt back—like, say, tonight, tomorrow—you won't have to worry about your stomach."

"Good point," Tighe said, "but—"

He froze suddenly and looked at her. "This is my journey." He sounded stunned.

"What journey?"

He pulled out some cookies, crackers, fruit. River watched with astonishment as he prepared a large snack for the family.

"The journey I'm supposed to take. I learned about it during my time with Running Bear." He made a small plate for her. "Eat, please."

She didn't really feel like it, but picked up a piece of fruit to pacify him, keep him talking. "The journey?"

"It started on Firefreak."

"Quick journey," River observed with a wink.

He waved a cookie in her direction. "Sarcasm isn't allowed when one speaks of their visions."

"Sorry. Truly." She ate a cherry and then a strawberry. "So, in the beginning, there was Firefreak."

"Actually, in the beginning, there was you." He sat

by her, started a different kind of journey leisurely kissing a trail down her neck. "You put me on that bull."

"I was part of the plot to keep you off, if you recall. Continue."

"Believe me, I will." He kissed the cradle of her collarbone.

"Tighe, someone's going to come into the kitchen." Still, she didn't push him away.

"I know. I think it excites me. If I compromise you, you'll have to marry me."

"I think we already compromised each other." Regretfully, she pushed him away. "Can we stick to the journey? Stop trying to change the subject."

"Soup's on!" he called into the den. "Or at least all you're getting to eat without you fixing it yourselves."

The family trooped in, stared at the repast.

"Thank you, brother," Ash said. "You tried. I can tell you made a sincere effort."

Tighe smiled. "Thank you."

"We think we have a plan," Galen said. "Running Bear?"

"I will go," the chief said. "Wolf is my son. He will not harm me."

River saw concern jump into Tighe's eyes. "You're exactly the one he would harm, Grandfather," he said. "I'll go."

"I'll go with you," River said quickly.

"No," he stated, and she bristled.

"Listen, you don't get to have all the harebrained plans in this relationship, Tighe."

"Harebrained?"

"Harebrained. Like riding Firefreak as the beginning of your journey." She glared at her handsome cowboy, whose ego could barely fit in the same room with his body. "Riding Firefreak was an ego thing. You were trying to keep up with Dante. So you hurt yourself, just like your family knew you would, and went and sat in the desert for a few weeks. I'm not sure if you had an epiphany of the soul out there or not, but what I do know is that on this journey to Montana, I am going with you."

Tighe opened his mouth to protest, and she looked at the chief.

"She has a strong heart. She will go with you," Running Bear said.

"She is also pregnant with three babies. Did she tell you that, Grandfather?"

Running Bear smiled. "All the more reason River should go."

"I don't understand," Tighe said as the old chief exited the kitchen. Thunder rattled the windows, though there was no storm outside. "You're stubborn. Do you know that?"

"Not as stubborn as you are," River said. "I consider that a compliment." She slid off the bar stool and headed out the door Running Bear had exited.

"Where are you going?" Tighe asked.

"To pack. See you at first light."

Chapter 9

"I'm still not sure how I got talked into this," Tighe said as they left New Mexico behind. River sat next to him in a black stretchy skirt she said gave her belly plenty of room to grow, and a cute black lacy top. Her hair was pulled up on top of her head in a bouncy ponytail that made him want to kiss her.

Actually, just about everything about River made him want to kiss her, and then some.

"It's the next leg of that journey you're on," she said. "No worries. We're just taking the journey together. I hope that won't make you feel crowded." She giggled, enjoying teasing him.

He wished her being along for the ride made him feel better. "You should be resting. Your feet should be up, and you—"

"Tighe, this is probably a good time for you to keep

those cute little opinions and phobias to yourself," River said, patting his arm, "or this is going to be a very long, very tedious trip."

"I can take a hint."

"That's good news!" She peered at her phone, going over directions. "The route looks pretty straightforward, so let's develop our battle plan."

"I think any plans I ever had went completely out the window." He wondered if it had been wise to make this rescue attempt with no other backup than his pregnant significant other. "I have an idea," Tighe said. "Since I agreed to bring you with me, let's get married in Montana."

"Once we rescue Fiona."

He blinked. "Does that mean that you won't marry me if our mission doesn't succeed?" It had taken Falcon months to get Taylor back home. He didn't think he could wait that long to make River his. On the other hand, it didn't seem he had much choice.

She turned her head and stared at him. "We *will* succeed in rescuing Fiona. If you don't, I will."

"I knew when I first saw you, slinking around Rancho Diablo, walking like a sexy panther, that you were the woman for me," he said, happy to get that off his chest.

"You think I walk like a panther?"

He nodded. "Even though you and Ana have changed your hair color a few times since you first arrived, one thing that hasn't changed about you is that sexy walk."

"Wait a couple more months. I hear a waddle sets in."

He laughed. "You're going to get sexier with every passing body change. I can't wait to see my triplets transform you."

"Your boundless enthusiasm for my pregnancy is very manly."

"It's your determination that warms my heart. The fact that you set a task and do it. Like the night you seduced me."

"I didn't actually seduce you," River said.

"You did. You got me tipsy and had your way with me." He grinned. "Anyway, I believe this journey we're on will bring us closer together. We'll have lots of time to get to know each other on the drive, anyway."

"Yeah, about that," River said, "there's something I need to tell you."

He felt a slight warning tickle, dismissed it. "I'm listening."

"I think I brought bad luck to Fiona."

"Not possible, gorgeous."

"I opened the magic wedding dress bag."

The smile slipped off his face. "I thought you said you didn't."

"Well, I did."

"That doesn't have anything to do with Fiona." His uneasiness grew. "It just means you weren't comfortable with whatever was in the bag." He slid a glance her way. "Am I guessing correctly?"

If he was right, that didn't bode well for him. He drummed on the steering wheel, noted River wasn't swift in answering him. "This getting to know each other on a long drive is going to be a brilliant idea."

"We'll see."

Maybe not that brilliant. "So are you going to tell me what you saw?"

"I believe what happens in the attic, stays in the attic." River looked at him. "Isn't that the rule?"

"I don't exactly know the rules of the attic."

"But you were the one who said the Callahan brides never discussed what happened up there. It was their own personal emotional journey, you might say."

She was turning his own words against him. "You pride yourself on being a rule-breaker. I'm listening if you want to talk."

"It might be bad luck. Perhaps after we find Fiona I'll tell you."

"But suffice to say it wasn't your dream-come-true moment?"

She sighed. "Aren't I supposed to see my handsome prince? Isn't that the wedding tale?"

"I'm not exactly certain on all the ins and outs of the magic wedding dress, but I think it's safe to say that most brides at least have some feelings of warmth and perhaps delight when they encounter their perfect dress. And then I think there's something about the prospective bride—that would be the lady trying on the gown—perhaps seeing the face of her true love." Tighe glanced at River. "You sure you didn't see me?"

"If you were the silent brother, you sure have changed."

"You're avoiding the subject." He felt a huge stone lodge in his chest. "You didn't see me, did you?"

"I didn't see anything. I didn't try it on. I assume that's when the magic occurs. Unless something was supposed to happen when I unzipped the bag." She shrugged. "Nothing did. Maybe you and I don't meet the standards of the magic lore."

With some discomfort Tighe remembered Dante had said Ana had a similar disconcerting experience with the gown. He hadn't paid too much attention to his twin's ravings at the time. "Maybe I should have paid better attention to my brother's misery."

"Probably not. Dante is really happy now. Sometimes it's best not to get involved with sibling misery. Let people figure things out for themselves."

Tighe straightened. "River, do you have any brothers or sisters? Family?" He supposed somebody at the ranch knew all the particulars about her but he'd never heard any details. "I mean, is there a father whom I should ask for your hand in marriage?"

"Tighe," River said, "that's really sweet. But it's not necessary."

Why wasn't it? Because she wasn't going to marry him? There were moments with River when he had to breathe deep, look inside himself, to stay calm. The woman had more twists and turns to throw him off than a river, like her namesake. A long, winding river he couldn't seem to tame. "When we get to Montana I want you to let me take care of everything. On this I insist."

"You just want me to sit here and look pretty?"

"Could you?" He met her gaze. "Just this once?"

"Not likely. I'll probably have your back and still look pretty doing it."

He blew out a long breath of frustration. "It's *my* aunt who is in trouble. You're pregnant with *my* children. You see my problem?"

"Yeah. You've got yourself in a real pickle, cowboy."

She was laughing. Completely confident in her ability to take care of herself, and him, and rescue Fiona, if she had to. And this wasn't the kind of female to whom one could say "Stand down" because *stand down* wasn't in her vocabulary.

It was as if he'd met himself, in female form, only

a bit wilder, a little more brave and courageous than maybe he'd ever been. The dark days of war were long behind him now, hidden places he didn't really visit in his soul. Not very often, anyway. He remembered he'd been tough, and was comfortable being in survival mode—but he didn't want River to have to be. "I view this trip as early recon, babe. Reconnaissance. That's it, and nothing more. Once we get the lay of the land, I'm calling for backup. Lots of it. Everything I need to get Fiona out of there. And you're not going to play hero. Not with my babies. You agree to that, or I'm turning around right here, right now."

"Stop the truck."

He pulled off the highway at a beautifully wooded rest stop, switched off the truck. "You okay?"

"I'm fine." She put a hand on his arm, slid it to his chest. "Tighe, I'm not making any promises."

"You have a problem with promises, don't you?"

"The kind you're asking for, yes."

He took that in, allowed himself to drown in her eyes for a moment. "This was a mistake. I should have tied you to Sloan and Kendall's twins so you couldn't follow."

She glared at him. "Still enjoying getting to know me better, cowboy?"

"It had to happen sooner or later."

"Yes, it did. I just want you to know that if I see a chance to grab Fiona, I'm going to do it, and I expect you to rev the engine and haul cowboy butt down the road. Are we on the same page now?"

He gritted his teeth. Never had he wanted to kiss her so badly; never had he wanted to turn the truck around and head back to Rancho Diablo more than now. "I'm not letting anything happen to you."

"And I'm not letting anything happen to *you*." She leaned over, kissed him lightly on his lips. He held very still, enjoying what she was doing to him, not about to move in case she stopped. He never wanted her to stop. But then she did stop, and stared into his eyes. "We're a good team, even if I didn't see you in Fiona's enchanted attic."

"Maybe you didn't really look," he said hopefully, wanting to keep her close, wondering if he dared pull her to him and kiss her like he wanted to. "You could always try again. See if you get a different result."

"I don't really believe in magic. So I didn't expect to see anything. Trying again won't change that, I think."

He gulped hard, remembering his brother's angst over cursing the wedding gown. "I believe in magic, and spirits, and everything that can't be explained."

She leaned her forehead against his. "I know. It's one of the reasons I'm crazy about you."

His spirit soared. "You're crazy about me?"

"Yes, I am. When you're being normal, like you are right this moment. Not when you start telling me how you think I should do everything. And most certainly not when you try to run my life."

He couldn't help himself. She was so close, she smelled so good and he'd waited so long to be able to touch her that every chance he got was a chance he didn't intend to waste. He moved to her lips, kissing her, lifted his hands to her shoulders and up into that beautiful hair. She was his life preserver, his reason for being—his reason for his journey—and he had no intention of ever letting her go.

If anything happened to her, it would kill him.

"Can I lock you in the truck when we get to Wolf's hideout?" he murmured, after he'd reluctantly pulled away from her sweet lips.

"Put that out of your mind, cowboy. Now get this truck in gear and let's go. We're a team, and you need me."

"I need you," he agreed, and started the engine. He needed her, and his babies, and everything River meant to him.

If he had to kill his uncle to keep his woman and his children safe, he'd do it in a heartbeat.

He heard his grandfather's voice echo *"No"* in his mind, loud and clear and so sharp he glanced at River to see if she'd noticed anything. She was deep into staring at the map on her phone, plotting.

If it meant going against what he knew of life, and the spirits, and even his grandfather, Tighe would take the life of his uncle. To save what he loved most, it might be the only way.

And that's when he knew the truth.

He had to be the hunted one.

Chapter 10

The lair lay in an area so remote and distant, so shrouded from the main roads, that Tighe was amazed Taylor had lived here for months. Falcon had to have lost his mind while she was gone. Tighe couldn't imagine River being away from him that long.

It probably would do him in.

"This is it." River peered through some high-powered binoculars she'd pulled from her black backpack. "This is definitely the place. Guess who's outside feeding the birds." She handed him the binocs.

He stuck them up to his eyes. "Aunt Fiona. She just went back inside the house."

River nodded. "And just behind you'll see those two female bodyguards Taylor talked about. We know they're the weak link in Wolf's plans. We'll work them over."

Tighe lowered the binocs and stared at the mother of his children. "Where did you get these? They're military grade, with night vision."

She shrugged. "You wouldn't have expected me not to come prepared, would you? *You* didn't, surely."

He had a few guns, a hunting knife, nothing he thought he'd use. Some rope, some other odds and ends, a small explosive device Jace had tucked away in the truck bed at the last minute, saying it was "just in case the opportunity presented itself." Meaning, if he got the chance to lay an explosive and blow Wolf's hideout to kingdom come, the siblings wanted him to press *Blow.* "I've got a few things. Why? What do you mean, you came prepared?"

She opened her pack. "Just a few equalizers."

He looked in it at the array of armaments, his jaw dropping. "You didn't pack any clothes?"

"We're not here for tea and cookies, are we?"

"No, but—" She was going to give him a cardiac event of epic proportions. "You're not on the payroll at the moment!"

"I believe I draw a salary at Rancho Diablo."

"Yes, but I mean, you're just along for the ride, beautiful. Your role is to keep me company, not—" He glanced inside the bag again. "Holy crap, you've got enough stuff inside here to take out a lot of bad guys."

She zipped the bag closed. "We won't need most of it. My specialty is getting in and getting out, sight unseen. That's why I said I want you prepared to roll cowboy butt if I get the chance to grab your aunt."

He swallowed hard. "River, you're going to have to marry me. You need to make an honest man out of me. You're the only woman who thinks like I do."

She laughed. "Don't flatter yourself. I think on a much higher plane. You're too bogged down by worries. Compartmentalizing doesn't appear to be your thing." She got out of the truck.

"Great Spirit," he whispered. He looked out the window at River stretching the kinks out of her back and legs, and felt himself get turned on and fearful all at the same time. "That lady is my path, my life. And the stress just may kill me."

He got out to join her.

"Okay, I think I've got a handle on this now," he said, squatting next to her as she took cover behind a large boulder, spying with the binocs on the wooden cabin surrounded by trees at the top of the muddy road.

"Good."

"Here's the thing." Tighe moved the binoculars from her face so she'd look at him. "This time, right now, you're not a bodyguard. Not *my* bodyguard. You're man number two, and I'm not a chauvinist. Can we agree on that much?"

She smiled. "Now you're catching on."

"Yes. Slowly." He kissed her, because he couldn't stand to look at her lips and not possess them any longer. "We're equals, but you let me have override status on this mission."

"It's your aunt, and your fight. I can agree to that."

"My God, you're sexy." He'd give a million dollars to get Fiona out of there, toss a small grenade into the dump, put Fiona on a plane home and take River to a quiet place in the woods to make love to her until her pregnancy would no longer allow it.

"Focus, Tighe." She handed him the binoculars. "Everything else can wait."

He looked toward the cabin. "There's Uncle Wolf. I'm pretty sure he's made us."

"He made us two minutes ago. That's okay, we weren't really trying to hide. And he was expecting us. We don't want to disappoint him."

Tighe looked at River. "How do you do this?"

"I'm highly trained. And unlike you, my mind is on the mission."

"You've blown my mind so badly it's all I can do not to just sit and stare at you. All I think about is getting you in bed with me again."

"Tell you what." She smiled at him, laid her head on his shoulder. "You rescue Fiona, and I'll leave my nightstand light on for you."

His heart beat hard. "All I have to do to get back in your bed is break into a camp, overcome half a dozen bad guys and a couple of bad girls, and rescue a little old lady? And you'll sleep with me?"

"All night long."

He grinned. "River Martin, I'm madly in love with you. Just remember I told you that." He kissed her one last time, handed her the binoculars and walked into the open field to meet his uncle.

If he was the hunted one, then Fiona should not be the one to suffer.

River watched Tighe walk away, wondering if facing Wolf down was the best plan. Just to be certain, she got out a gun with a silencer and aimed it toward Wolf. Running Bear might be against shooting his son, but that didn't mean she couldn't do it. She could wing him, give Tighe a chance to retreat.

She lowered the gun. Tighe wouldn't retreat—he would fight. And it wasn't her place to shoot Wolf.

"But I can rescue Fiona." Taylor had told her the location of the bedroom she'd been assigned, as well as that of its window, and how Running Bear had managed to communicate. Getting up, River skirted around through the woods to the back of the house while Wolf's attention was on Tighe. She found the window Taylor had described to her, and peered inside. Sure enough, she could see Fiona's rubber-soled boots next to the bed, though Tighe's aunt wasn't in the room.

This could be a setup. Wolf would expect them to look for Fiona in the most obvious place. "Which is why we're not falling for the boots-in-Taylor's-room trick," River muttered. She moved to the next room, peeked in the window. Two twin beds, both unmade, were cluttered with a few changes of ladies' clothes. Some shoes and socks lay scattered on the floor. This would be the bedroom of the two women who'd been kind to Taylor, after a fashion. "Messy. It's a wonder Fiona doesn't whip their butts into shape."

River moved to the final window on this side of the hideout. The shades were tightly closed, so there was nothing to see. She wondered if this was Fiona's room, well protected against prying eyes.

"Hi!" a voice whispered next to her, and River nearly jumped out of her skin.

"Fiona! For heaven's sake!" She put a hand over her hammering heart, then threw her arms around the older woman. "I'm so sorry I let you get taken! Are you all right?"

Fiona's eyes twinkled after River finally released her. "I'm fine."

"Good. Come on." She grasped Fiona's hand and pulled her toward the woods, but Tighe's aunt resisted.

"I can't go."

"Why not? Now's your chance! I've already instructed Tighe to be ready for a fast getaway."

"I like that plan!" Fiona shook her head. "Alas, I can't."

"Why not?" River hated to rush the head of the Callahan clan, but if Fiona didn't quit dithering, she was going to toss her over her shoulder and carry her off.

"Because they'll come after us. I heard Wolf discussing the plans with his gang of trolls," Fiona whispered back. "This is a setup."

"I figured as much. It's too easy." River thought quickly. "Tighe's out there jawing with his uncle even as we speak."

"I know. Tighe's brave. Not always the brightest, but always the bravest." Fiona looked satisfied. "It isn't very bright to try to beard Wolf in his den, you have to admit."

"There are a lot of fine points about your family I might be willing to admit, but we should discuss them another time, Fiona. Even if this is a setup, we can go hide in the woods! They won't be expecting that!" River pleaded.

"True." Fiona considered that. "But I can't. If they catch you before we're able to meet up with Tighe, they'll keep you here, too. And that won't be good for those precious babies you're carrying."

"I can't bear to leave you here."

Fiona fastened bright eyes on her. "Now listen, we have no time for sentiment. I need you to take over my committee for the annual Christmas ball. Talk to my friends at the Books'n'Bingo Society. Those three ladies will be happy to help you plan the thing. Be sure you don't forget the advertising on the barn roofs." Fiona tapped her mouth with her finger. "There's only Jace, Galen and Ash left to manage marriages for. I say you advertise Jace this year on the roofs. I guess the ladies would consider him a decent raffle prize."

River glanced over her shoulder. "Fiona, if you're not coming with me, you need to go back inside. I don't want them catching you out here." She gave her another hug. "Are you sure you won't come with me?"

"I'm perfectly happy here. Not as happy as I'd be at home," Fiona said, straightening her shoulders bravely. "I'd rather be in my own kitchen, around my own family, and the children. But Wolf is trying to get to the family through me, and I won't let that happen."

River nodded. "Okay. Go inside."

"Tell Burke I love him." For the first time, Fiona's eyes got a little sparkle in them from unshed tears. "Tell everyone I love them. And they're not to worry about me. I'm a tough old bird. I've handled far worse than Wolf in my life. Be sure they know I expect them to be warriors."

"I will. Go."

River watched Fiona head back around the side of the house, heard a door quietly shut. She needed to sneak back to the truck, check to see that Tighe was getting the best of Wolf. At least she'd seen and talked to Fiona, and that would reassure Tighe until they could think of a good plan to get her out of here.

River carefully retraced her steps, making certain not to leave any trace of a footprint in the loose dirt. Once safely in the woods, she looked out toward the field, saw Tighe and Wolf still soaking up some sun while they chatted—although based on the stiff, angry postures, it wasn't the world's friendliest conversation. Yet it didn't look as if any blood had been spilled or bones broken. River didn't think either man had moved since she'd surveyed the house.

Three minutes later she was back at the truck, crouched down, covering Tighe's back. She held her breath, watching as Wolf turned around, headed back toward the house. Tighe stared after him, his hands on his lean hips, his wide back strong and stubborn. "Come on, Tighe. Don't stand out there all day catching rays. Let's hit the road and regroup," she muttered.

After a moment, he turned around, headed to the truck. Pretended he didn't remember that she was there. Started the vehicle, backed it up, wheeled it around, giving her enough cover to jump in the passenger side. She was in the truck so fast that he simply made one smooth backup and then pulled away.

"Well done," Tighe said as she tossed her backpack into the backseat.

She kept low so Wolf or one of his many henchmen wouldn't spy her from a window. "Thanks. What were you two shooting the breeze about?"

"Nothing of real interest. Mainly I didn't want him to see you sneaking around the cabin. You nearly gave me heart failure!" He glared at her. "What were you thinking?"

"That while you two were busy reminiscing about old times, I'd rescue your aunt. I found her and I talked to her." River sighed. "But she wouldn't leave."

"I could have told you that," Tighe said, his tone irritated. "This is Fiona we're discussing. She's never going to do what anyone expects or hopes she will. You put yourself in jeopardy! What if you'd been captured?"

River shrugged. "I wasn't worried about that. Now help me think of a way to get Fiona out of there."

"I can barely concentrate! You've got me so rattled I can't string two thoughts together. You're supposed to ride shotgun, not be the spy who loved me!" He sighed, and River thought it was very heartfelt.

"If it makes you feel any better, Fiona looks awesome. I think she's enjoying her role of family plant."

"We did not plant her there to spy on Wolf."

"But she's a counterbalance to his operation, and I think she relishes that."

"There are days," Tighe said, "when I wonder why I couldn't have fallen for a mousy bookworm who only wanted to stay home and cook and bake for me."

"Because the sex probably wouldn't have been as awesome. I'm pretty sure you're not interested in my cooking skills as much as some other skills."

She could tell he was trying not to laugh, despite his aggravation with her. "I do, however, make a mean lasagna, and I've read all the Five-Foot Shelf books— every one. I can keep your interest, cowboy."

"Impressive, and yet in spite of that, I'm still trying to recover from the sight of you creeping up on Wolf's hideout." Tighe let out a long breath. "On the other hand, I find it awesome that you care enough about my aunt that you'd put yourself in danger to rescue her. That's very sexy."

"It is, isn't it?"

"But," he said, wagging a finger as the truck bumped over ruts in the road, "you have to be careful about putting yourself in danger. You have to think of the babies."

"So you prefer me making lasagna and reading *How to Please Your Man* for when you get home at night?"

"Is that so much to ask?"

She laughed. "That sneaky look on your handsome face tells me that even you know you're not going to have that pleasure, cowboy. You'll have to stick with the real me."

"I'm sticking like glue. Uh-oh," he said, and the smiled disappeared off his face. River turned to look at what had his attention.

Four armed men blocked the road ahead.

Chapter 11

"Wolf's henchmen," River said. "Run them down."

"I can't do that!" Tighe slowed the truck, came to a halt in front of the armed guards. He couldn't risk getting shot at with River in the vehicle. Tighe was sure Wolf would have the road blocked behind them, as well. Woods stretched on either side of the road, thick and impenetrable. "We're going to have to hope for the best."

He had a sick feeling in his stomach, though. Henchmen carrying AK-47s indicated his uncle meant business.

River pulled her backpack up beside her. "Don't do anything crazy," Tighe warned. "Let me see if I can talk my way out of this."

Even he knew that probably wasn't likely. But if River started shooting, they'd fire back. He shouldn't have brought her with him.

The passenger door jerked open. "Out, little lady," one of the thugs said to River.

"I'm pregnant," she replied. "At this moment, I'm carsick and likely to vomit."

"That sounds like a personal problem to me." He gestured with his gun toward the jeep hidden off the road. "Take a seat over there, princess."

"Tell my uncle he doesn't want her. He wants me," Tighe said.

"No." The ugly brute with the facial scar staring in the window shook his head with a sick smile. "He specifically said he wanted you to go home and ruminate on your bad manners."

Tighe cursed his softness in allowing River to accompany him. He should have foreseen this moment. His uncle and he had said nothing out of the ordinary to each other. Tighe had asked him to release Fiona; Wolf had said no. The conversation had merely been the two of them circling each other.

"Go, Tighe." River said. "I'll be fine."

She marched off with her backpack. When one of her guards tried to take her arm to help her into the jeep, she shook him off. Tighe swallowed hard, knowing the arsenal she was carrying. River was likely to leave the place in bits and pieces. His stomach clenched and he could barely breathe past the fear in his chest. She was stubborn, she was fiery and she had Fiona as an accomplice.

Nothing good could come of those two ladies being on the loose and in cahoots. And spirits help her if Wolf decided to have her bag searched.

Tighe looked at the goon next to him, studying the

scar. "I know who you are. You're Rhein, Wolf's right hand."

"That's right. And you're the nephew that used to be such a ladies' man. Funny thing, but Wolf's just been dying to pick off a Callahan female to drive you boys nuts. And now that you've decided to settle down with just one lady, that's the lady Wolf gets to hold as a bargaining chip. I call that irony." Rhein laughed out loud.

"Now drive on, if you know what's good for you," the guard to his left said. "And don't look back, if you don't want to make trouble for the little lady and the old woman."

"I don't suppose you'd take me instead and let them go?"

The ugly man shook his big head. "Boss man says he's got the big fish now. The old lady'll break eventually, and she's the one who knows every secret Running Bear's hiding." He smiled, and Tighe felt ill. "With the little pregnant lady as a hostage, Wolf's got all the leverage he wants. Somebody'll sing like a bird sooner than later, I reckon. And then we'll know where to find your parents, won't we? Both sets of 'em. We've waited years for this."

"River doesn't know anything," Tighe said, trying not to sound as desperate as he felt. It was eating him, driving him out of his mind.

"Your lady might not know anything, but the old lady knows everything. Wolf says there's only one captive with higher value than her, but we don't need to play that card yet."

Tighe wanted to keep his talkative friend dropping clues. "Who's a higher value target than Fiona? Running Bear?"

"Wolf wants nothing to do with his father. If he ever gets the chance, he'll shoot Running Bear dead."

"Seems like a pretty harsh way to treat one's dad."

"Not my problem. I just draw my weekly pay and do my job. Now, move along, and no heroics. We shoot heroes on sight."

Tighe glanced toward River one final time, though he didn't move his head. Didn't want Rhein to suspect her importance to him. River sat in the jeep, tying her whiskey-colored hair up into a tighter ponytail, acting as if she wasn't a hostage, as if it was just another day in an unexciting life.

Trying to keep him calm.

He was anything but.

Tighe called an emergency family meeting upstairs in the library as soon as he returned. He'd even sent Ash to locate Running Bear—although he made Jace ride at her side for protection.

As his brothers and sister and Running Bear took their places, he waited, his heart beating hard. Tighe didn't think his pulse had quit hammering ever since he'd driven away, leaving River in Wolf's clutches. He'd sped home, barely stopping for anything, to consult with his family and develop a plan.

The plans they'd had so far had gone horribly wrong.

Running Bear sat in silence, shaking his head when Galen offered him a drink. The rest of them accepted a crystal tumbler of whiskey, their eyes on Tighe the whole time.

"Where's River?" Ash demanded.

"River and Fiona are both with Wolf in Montana." Tighe watched his family take in this news with dismay etched on their faces. "I didn't want to leave either of them. I had no choice. We have to figure out how to bring them home."

"What happened?" Galen demanded.

"I talked to Wolf in person. He said he has no intention of letting Fiona go. She's his ace in the hole for making sure he finds out where our parents, and our cousins' parents, are in hiding. None of us know that information, but Fiona might. At least Wolf's banking on that."

Tighe looked at the chief, but Running Bear's gaze was flat, emotionless, giving away nothing. "His goal, of course, is to make them pay for informing on the cartel. That's what he's been hired to do, and he won't rest until that happens. Eventually, he says he'll take over Rancho Diablo. The cartel has promised him this in exchange for our parents, Molly and Jeremiah, and Julia and Carlos."

"How could you leave River?" Ashlyn demanded. "She's going to be confined without prenatal care!"

"There wasn't an option. I even offered myself in exchange." Tighe wanted to kill Wolf at the thought of River being held hostage. "Trust me when I tell you I've never been so scared in my life."

Ash flew to him, throwing her arms around him. "I'm so sorry!" she whispered, hugging him hard.

He let his sister comfort him for a moment before he moved away. "While I was talking to Wolf, River managed to get to Fiona and talk to her."

"That was brave," Sloan said. "Scary, but brave."

Tighe remembered the startled fear he'd concealed when he'd seen her moving stealthily through the trees. He'd kept his gaze on Wolf, barely allowing his peripheral vision to acknowledge what River had been doing—but his heart had fallen into his boots. "She said Fiona is fine. She says to tell everyone not to worry."

"Not to worry?" Falcon challenged. "Like hell!"

"I want to kill Wolf," Ash said, "Grandfather—"

The chief held up a hand, and she fell silent. "That is not the answer."

"I personally think it would solve all our problems," Ash muttered, "at least ninety percent of them. And we could get Fiona and River back!" She gazed at her brother. "What are you going to do, Tighe?"

He remembered River tying her hair back, ignoring her captors. Many women would be scared. Many men, too, up against what she was facing. "I don't know. The part that frightens me is that I know that, carrying triplets, she won't be easily moved forever. At some point, she'll be confined to bed rest." It would be a whole lot harder to rescue her then.

"This is a dilemma," Dante said. "I'm sorry as hell."

Tighe looked at his twin. "River was carrying a backpack full of things I can only describe as bodyguard goodies. I'm concerned that Wolf will search her bag. Either that, or she'll blow the place sky-high."

"I hope she grabbed the charge I put in the truck for contingencies," Jace said. "It's for one of those just-in-case moments, when you want to make a really big exit."

"Oh, great," Tighe said, closing his eyes with exasperation. It wasn't in the truck now, so River had in fact packed it into her little black bag of fun and games. He opened his eyes and glared at Jace. "There's no reason to encourage her, so don't even say that out loud. She's carrying my children!"

"Yeah," Galen said. "You've got to admire a woman

like that. Uncle Wolf has no idea what he bit off by taking on Fiona and River. Those two could hound the devil himself."

"I don't want to think about it." Tighe finished his whiskey and Ash refilled his glass in a hurry. The liquid burned through him, bracing him, but not giving him any creative ideas on how to rescue his woman.

I can't even really call her my woman. She's not exactly overly enthusiastic about marrying me.

"I never thought the day would come when I couldn't defend my own family. And there I sat, with no options, while my family, my whole world, went off with a bunch of armed thugs." Tighe felt as if he'd been smashed to bits, stomped by something stronger and meaner than Firefreak.

"We will wait," Running Bear said quietly, and they all stared at him in surprise.

"Wait for what?" Tighe demanded. "I don't have long to wait. River's a couple months pregnant. I need to get her *home*." *In my arms. Where she belongs.*

"Well, you can't go after her," Ash observed. "You're still limping. Bet you wish you hadn't tried to ride that stupid hunk of meat, huh?"

"I'm fine," he snapped. "I just came home to get backup." Tighe looked around at his brothers expectantly.

"No," Running Bear said. "You're too hotheaded right now. When passions rule, danger is near. Wolf will expect us to come to him. Yet we will not."

Tighe gulped hard, his throat so tight he nearly couldn't draw a breath nor swallow with ease. "I can't agree to that. I'm going back, either alone or with help.

If no one here wants to go with me, I'll hire mercenaries."

"No," Running Bear said again. "Time is on our side. Eventually Wolf will make a mistake."

"I don't have time to wait for mistakes! The mistake has already been made, by me." Tighe looked around at his brothers. "What would you do in my place?"

"Listen to Grandfather," Jace said. "He's suffering more than anyone."

Tighe looked at the old chief, realizing he was, indeed, extremely grieved over this situation. He looked older, sadder, no longer serene. His dark skin seemed to sag a bit with age, and Tighe couldn't remember their energetic grandfather ever looking defeated. But it made sense. Fiona was his best friend in the world. They'd been a united front for years, plotting and keeping lots of people alive. Keeping the land alive, and the Diablos safe. Making sure no one ever tore the family apart. "I'm so sorry, Grandfather," Tighe said. "I spoke in haste. Forgive me."

"I understand," Running Bear said. "We always knew the fight would be difficult and long."

That was true. No journey was ever easy. Tighe's Callahan cousins had been fighting the good fight longer than he. For that matter, Fiona and Running Bear had been trying to save the family and the land for even longer, and before that, Jeremiah and Molly, and Julia and Carlos. "I'm sorry," Tighe said again, the words inadequate. He sat back down on the long leather sofa, forcing himself to take a deep breath. "I am hotheaded."

"It's only natural," Dante said. "When family's in danger, the reaction is to rush in where angels fear to tread."

"Still, we need to have a plan." Ash rubbed Tighe's back. "We're just going to have to wait until the right time comes." She looked at Running Bear. "I do agree with Tighe on a couple of things, Grandfather. I don't want Fiona to be up there during the winter. It would be too hard on her. And I don't need to tell anyone that River needs to be here, resting."

They all took that in for a long time. There was no good answer. Tighe could hear his own heart beating with stress.

"Calm," his sister said. "We all must stay calm. Wolf is expecting us to come back, guns blazing. It's a pretty good trap."

Tighe paced to a window, stared at the dark landscape beyond. There had to be a way out of this he wasn't seeing.

"By Christmas," Running Bear said, "they will be testing each other's patience."

Tighe whipped around. "Christmas! That's five months from now!"

"There'll be no Christmas without Fiona and River," Ash said sadly. "There will certainly be no Christmas ball."

He couldn't worry about holidays and matchmaking balls. "Grandfather, we can't wait that long!"

"How much time until River probably needs bed rest?" Sloan asked Galen, the doctor among them.

"It won't be longer than December. Not with triplets," Galen replied. "Possibly January, if her weight stays down and she stays healthy. We can always ask our cousins how they fared. There are two sets of triplets in their family."

"Christmas," Running Bear said again, more definite

this time. "We plan our raid for Christmas. They won't be expecting us then. The roads will be more difficult."

"Can't we make it Thanksgiving?" Tighe asked. "The sooner I get them home, the better."

"If we go now," Falcon said, "people are going to get hurt."

Tighe feared someone was going to be hurt even if they waited. He thought about River's backpack of surprises and thought he was going to lose his mind. "Am I the hunted one, Grandfather?"

Running Bear's gaze settled on him. "Why do you ask me?"

"Because you said the hunted one would bring danger and destruction to the family. And I have."

His siblings stared at him with sympathy. The chief closed his eyes, shook his head before turning his gaze back on Tighe. "I don't know."

"Sure feels like I am," he muttered.

"Oh, brother." Ash laid her head against his shoulder. "You're a prince."

"I'm not a prince. I'm a guy who's lost the only thing he ever wanted."

"But you'll get her back," Ash said. "It just won't be any quicker, I guess, than when Falcon lost Taylor."

"Yeah, but this is my fault. I let River go with me." Tighe played every moment over again in his mind, wondering if there'd been any way he could have stopped Rhein and his men from taking her. There wasn't. He'd done the only thing he could to ensure her safety. He went to stare out the window again, thinking hard. "Where's Sawyer?" he suddenly demanded.

"Watching little Carlos and Isaiah with Kendall," Sloan said. "Why?"

"Just wondering." Tighe watched a tall man ride up on horseback, settle his horse near a tree, tie the reins to a post. "Storm's here."

"Storm?" Dante asked. The family crossed to the window to stare out at their neighbor.

"Reminds me of the night the rock got tossed through our window up here," Galen said. "We never did prove that he didn't do it."

"I was thinking the same thing." The doorbell sounded, and Tighe said, "I'll go see what he wants."

"I'll go with you," Ash said, scrambling to his side. "And I'll bring up a plate of cookies for the rest of you when we come back. We have a lot to discuss."

They went down the long, beautifully carved staircase.

"Brother, you're going to have to keep it together, for River's sake."

"I'll try. But I'm making no promises."

"I figured as much." Ash bounced to the front door, flinging it open. "Hello, Storm. What brings you here?"

Tighe stood behind his sister. Storm eyed them both, his wide, handsome face framed with silver-gray hair and stubble-rough cheeks.

"I've come to offer to sell you the land your aunt Fiona wanted to buy," Storm said. "I feel I've gotten involved in something I want no part of, and this is the only way to make things right."

Chapter 12

River was annoyed, and when she was annoyed, she wasn't the friendliest person to be around, which Rhein quickly found out when he tried to carry her backpack.

"Do I look like I need help?" she snapped.

"Sorry," Rhein said. "Didn't know if pregnant women were supposed to carry stuff."

"Look, you're kidnapping me, right?" She stomped toward the house with five men on her tail. The other two—she knew there were seven, because Xav Phillips and Ash had been tied up in the canyons once by what Ash referred to with great disgust as "the seven birdbrains"—were likely off keeping an eye on Rancho Diablo, reporting back to wicked Wolf. "As long as I'm a hostage, don't even look at me. Don't try to help me, don't be nice to me, because I'm not going to be nice to you. Deal?"

"Sure. Whatever." Rhein went off with his band of

uglies, and River sat down on the porch alone, irritated beyond belief that she was now good and stuck.

On the other hand, it was a great opportunity for spying. And it would be easy to report back to Rancho Diablo, because in her backpack she had a cell phone. She looked at the surrounding woods and deep violet twilight sky, and shivered a little as cold tendrils of breeze touched her. She had one change of clothes, a couple of pairs of panties and lots of things Wolf wouldn't be too happy about if he knew she was carrying them.

Fiona came out and joined her on the porch. "At least I have company now."

"You were supposed to be rescued. I botched that."

"No need for a rescue. I sort of like it here." Fiona turned her head up to look at the stars just peeking out in the velvety sky. "I keep everybody in line. I've taught the guard girls to cook a little. They're pretty useless otherwise, not trained to Callahan standards as bodyguards, or in general protection. Nobody is allowed to wear their boots and shoes in the house, and everybody has to make their bed. The toilet lid is always to be put down, and no one leaves water spots on the mirrors."

"How did you accomplish all that? They strike me as a pretty thuggish crew."

Fiona laughed. "Listen, I've raised six wild nephews, and have crewed for seven Chacon Callahans. You get the hang of herding cats. Anyway, if my rules aren't obeyed, I don't cook. Or bake. Not one cookie, not one batch of chili. Trust me, nobody wants to go back to the slop they were eating before my coerced arrival."

"That's awesome." River smiled. "Fiona, you amaze me."

"It's easy when you know what people want." The

older woman looked at her. "So, I never did hear what happened when you tried on the magic wedding dress."

River wasn't certain how much to tell. There was a fairy-tale element to the Callahans' precious gown, and maybe that was all it was supposed to be: fairy dust and romance. "Not much," she hedged.

"There's never been *not much* that happens with the dress. You might as well tell me. We've got a long time to sit here and rusticate."

River felt a small chill. "How long do you think we'll be here?"

"Well, if I had to guess, I'd say something will either happen quickly, or not till after winter."

River gasped. "After winter! My babies might be born here!"

"Luckily, it's a beautiful place for babies to be born," Fiona said, trying to sound positive. "Although I'm sure it won't come to that."

They couldn't be sure of anything. "I'm not going to try to see the future," River said bravely.

"Wise choice. So, back to the gown. Tell me what happened!"

Fiona looked like a young girl pleading for a treat. River decided to give in gracefully. "I took the dress out of the bag and hung it on a hook so I could unzip the zipper. But when I touched the gown, it changed."

"Changed?" Fiona repeated, her eyes huge.

"It changed into combat gear. Like something a military operative would wear. Your basic little black dress, except very after-midnight casual." River frowned. "I have no idea why."

"Odd," Fiona murmured. "I can't figure that out at all."

"Nor I."

"Well, did you see anyone?" she asked, eager for more details.

"Not a thing. No one and nothing. I was a bit let down," River admitted. "Actually, I was *very* let down."

"I bet." Fiona looked into the distance. "It wasn't in a very cooperative mood, was it? As wedding gowns go, it certainly was being cantankerous. Combat gear, indeed!" She looked at River. "What would a woman who's pregnant with triplets want with that?"

"I no longer try to understand everything that happens at Rancho Diablo. I just accept it and move on. Or try to." River took a deep breath. "As much as I hate to say it, I have a bad feeling about this mission."

"Well, don't. There's no point in having bad feelings. We have to focus on what we need to do." Fiona reached out and took her hand, and River felt the older woman's fingers tremble slightly.

And that's when she realized the toll the situation was taking on Fiona. She was putting on a brave face to spit in Wolf's eye and to control the way they treated her while she was captive. She might be a prisoner, but Fiona had them convinced that they had to please her; hence the clean floors and shiny mirrors. But she was also putting up a brave front for River's sake. Yet her trembling hand gave her away.

"It's going to be fine," River said. "We're Callahans. And we're the good guys." She patted the older woman's hand. "And when you're absolutely ready to go home, Fiona, you just let me know."

Fiona's eyes widened. "What do you mean?"

"I brought a few magic wands with me," River whispered. "I'm pretty sure I can cause enough distraction to give you time to get away."

"I'm not leaving you! You're expecting my nephew's children!" Fiona shook her head. "No, we're in this together, my girl. All for one and one for all, as they say."

"Then if we have to, we'll teach Wolf and his gang of miscreants Christmas carols."

Fiona laughed. "I can just see Scrooge and his seven dwarves singing carols."

River smiled, desperately hoping they wouldn't be spending Christmas in Montana. Christmas should be at Rancho Diablo—with Tighe.

"We have to have a Christmas ball," Ash told her brothers as they slumped on the sofas in the library. Four weeks had passed since River and Fiona had been gone, and the mood was very low. Tighe thought they'd never been so dispirited. Falcon, Sloan and Dante had become so overprotective of their wives and children that the wives had finally snapped at them to quit being such horses' asses.

Everyone was on edge.

Yet Tighe thought Ash was right: Wolf had what he wanted. The jewel in the Callahan crown was Fiona— it had to be. She alone, besides Running Bear, knew all the secrets of the vast ranch, and all its holdings. She knew where the fabled silver mine was, and where its treasure was buried. They knew this, too, now, but their aunt was directly in charge of the finances and all the sources of wealth Rancho Diablo held. Therefore, she was the most important fount of information Wolf could have happened upon.

River was just icing on the cake. Wolf knew she was

pregnant, and that the fact would eat at Tighe. Which it did, night and day. He didn't think he'd slept decently since the day she'd been taken. He hadn't, and if he had, he would have felt guilty, knowing that River was a prisoner. What man could ever sleep knowing his woman was a captive?

"I don't give a flip about Christmas balls," Tighe growled. "It won't be a ball without Fiona, and there's no point in pretending it is."

"That's just the point," Ash said crisply. "Fiona wouldn't want us to act like anything is out of the ordinary."

"Everything is out of the ordinary," Galen muttered.

"No one can plan a party like Fiona," Jace said. "I agree. No ball this year."

"Then Wolf wins." Ash stared around at her brothers. "It's about time we try to fill our cagey aunt's boots. We can do it." She took a deep breath, stared at Tighe. "There's no point in sitting around here losing our minds."

"It's not going to get better just because we party." Tighe shook his head, filled with a gnawing agony over what his woman might be suffering. "I'm going back to Montana," he declared abruptly, catapulting out of his seat.

"No!" his brothers all said, and Falcon and Sloan pressed him back onto the sofa. Dante handed him a whiskey, and he gulped it, trying to collect his shattered wits.

"You can't, bro. Trust me, I know it's not easy having your woman gone," Falcon said. "It was hard as hell when Wolf had Taylor. The thing is, Wolf's trying to get to us. This is how he does it. It's a mind game. All he has to do is keep us rattled, and we'll crack."

"I'm cracking," Tighe said. "In fact, I think I'm past cracked."

"I assign you to finding volunteers," Ash stated. "And you can do whatever deep thoughts and meditation and bookkeeping you need to do to consider Storm Cash's offer to sell us the twenty thousand acres across the canyons."

Everyone stared at her. "What?" Tighe said.

"When did you become the head of the household?" Galen asked.

"Since we're all too down in the mouth to be effective," their sister snapped. "Since he's turned pale and thin," she said, pointing to Tighe. "Since nobody can think of anything but the fact that our aunt is being held by the enemy! And River, too!" Ash glanced around the room. "All of us need to keep busy. We have to live our lives. The die is cast, the way Running Bear says it should be. So we're not going to attack. We're not going to try to get them back. We're going to wait for Wolf to come to us, and that means doing what we have to do." She glared at Jace. "I assign you to setting up cooking schedules. We'll all take one day a week. Every night we all do KP," she told Galen.

"That's probably a good idea," Tighe said with a sigh, thinking that if they all had a healthy meal for a change, instead of the thrown-together grub they'd been snatching from the pantry and Fiona's freezer—mainly cookies and pies, and some frozen casseroles—maybe they'd be able to think better. For his part, he'd mainly been on a liquid diet of whiskey, whiskey and more whiskey. Sips here and there, but he'd known when he got up and poured whiskey instead of sugar into his coffee mug this morning that he was going to have to back off the liquid courage.

"Ash has a good idea," Tighe said. "The more I think of it, the better I like it. We'll each take a night of cooking. Basic meals, no desserts, no frills, but healthy, fresh, living food. An occasional salad would be cleansing."

"Oh, boy," Jace said. "Here we go. Dr. Nutrition speaks."

"I'll talk to Fiona's friends at the Books'n'Bingo Society. They'll be able to give us the blueprint for when invitations need to go out. We'll need some victims," Tighe said, considering his brothers. "Who's going to be the grand prize this year at the bachelor raffle? And to what charity will we donate the proceeds?"

"Fiona loves the school and library so much that I say we split it between them," Galen suggested, and everyone nodded. "They always need supplies and equipment. Maybe we won't make enough to buy a roof for the elementary school, like we did last year, but we'll be contributing something."

"That's right." Falcon nodded. "And then Wolf isn't beating us. We can't allow him to cut the lifeblood of Diablo, or Rancho Diablo. That's his goal."

"That's right," Tighe murmured. "The cartel will get to us when we're weak. We have to stay united as a family, and as a community." He felt strength surge inside him as his brothers and sister murmured in agreement. "Great. Then we're together on this. Jace, you're the grand prize. Galen, you're going on the block this year. Who does that leave?"

They all stared at Ash. She went paler than her hair. "Oh, no. Not me. I'll never be raffled."

"Why? We've all had to do our bit to raise money for the town."

She shook her head. "No. You don't understand. None of you wanted to settle down. All of you fought it hard, or did fight it until you got caught fair and square. But I don't want a man."

"Oh, you want a man," Tighe said, enjoying pricking at his sister's shell of superiority for just a second.

"I've got my man," she murmured.

They all smiled at her as she fidgeted.

"You have your man?" Tighe asked. "Are you sure? Has Xav Phillips been around? I haven't seen him in months."

"That's mean," Ash said.

"If you're not spoken for, you're part of the raffle. It's all for one and one for all," Jace said. "That's what Fiona always says."

"Yes, well, she's speaking of the Three Musketeers type of stuff, but I'm surrounded by the Many Stooges," Ash snapped. "I'm not doing it. I'll support all of you while you raise money, but I prefer to man a lemonade stand or something for my contribution."

They all smiled adoringly at their little sister. "You know," Tighe said, teasing her, "maybe we should invite Xav to be part of Aunt Fiona's custom of being raffled off to raise money for Diablo's—"

Ash hopped to her feet, her hands on her hips. "Go right ahead. I'll buy him."

Her brothers whistled and clapped, and roses bloomed in her cheeks. Tighe looked at his family, enjoying the teasing and closeness, but as he looked out the window toward the moon—the same moon and stars that were surely visible in Montana—he wished he could be with River tonight.

A falling star flew across the sky, bright and brilliant as it flamed on its path.

Tighe turned away. He no longer believed in magic, dreams and wishes cast into the air. He didn't believe in spirits, or connections to the elemental or supernatural. He believed in right and wrong, that was all. White and black. Dark and Light. Good and evil. It was a battle he was no longer certain they could win.

And he had very little patience for the journey he was on.

Chapter 13

It was late October when River heard a light tap at her window, likely snow and sleet hitting the glass. She glanced at her watch to find it was nearly three o'clock in the morning. Snow had blown for days in the wild piney woods surrounding the hideout. Fiona had told Wolf's two female guards they had to put in supplies for hard weather, and they'd gone to the store, bringing back everything Fiona wanted. River and she had started cooking, but when Wolf snapped at Fiona from the tension of cabin fever, as well as no Callahans showing up for a rescue attempt, she had retired from the kitchen for a week, not preparing a thing.

Then everybody in the house and bunkhouse gave Wolf the silent treatment, born of deep resentment. River and Fiona had thought it was funny, because they'd stored plenty of snacks in a barrel outside their window. They were doing fine.

The tap came again, a bit louder, and River realized it wasn't sleet. She crept to the window, slowly raising the shade. "Tighe!"

She slid the window up as silently as possible, not easy because it was wood-framed and swollen. He crawled in, and quickly sprayed the hinges of the window with something before closing it. River couldn't wait any longer—she kissed him like she never had before. "You're freezing!" Pulling off his coat, River pressed herself against him.

"I'm fine, babe. No sense in getting you cold, too." He pushed her away, and pulled off one of his boots. She helped him with the other one, and then dragged him into her bed to warm him.

"You've been outside for a long time," she murmured against his throat. They held each other tightly, and after a moment, his hand stole to her rounded belly.

"I've been there a few hours, waiting for the right moment." He kissed her forehead. "I don't want to endanger you."

"I doubt anyone will notice. They're all upset with each other because they haven't had a decent meal in a week." She giggled against Tighe's chest, loving how it felt to be in his arms again. "Fiona hasn't cooked. She's training Wolf to ask how high when she says jump. The whole gang is about to mutiny because they're hungry. Fiona says they have no survival skills."

"What have you been feeding my babies?" Tighe murmured against her hair.

"We stocked up on healthy goodies, which are hidden in a barrel outside in the snow. They've gotten pretty lax about keeping tabs on us because they're so unhappy. You Callahans haven't ridden to the rescue, and now the weather is harsh for living in this cabin. Wolf doesn't want to pay heating bills, so we're surviving with log fires. But that's only in the den."

Tighe's hands circled her belly. "I brought you prenatal vitamins."

"I have some. The girl thugs bought them for me. Fiona told them to sneak them in and she'd make her special muffins. But thank you." River kissed his chin, then his lips. He hesitated for a moment, then kissed her long and sweetly. She sighed against him. "It's really not that bad here. I guess because Fiona's with me."

"I don't like the thought of you being cold and not having medical care." His hands stole down to her bottom, cupping her against him.

"A midwife comes out every two weeks. And I'm never cold."

"It's like an iceberg in this place. Almost as cold as outside."

"I got to a certain point in my pregnancy where I'm warm all the time. In the night, I kick off all my covers and lie on top of them. I wish I had a fan, I really do. I'd blow it on me constantly."

"That's my boys," Tighe said. "Raising your body temperature."

"Maybe. I'm like a polar bear." Now that she'd warmed him a bit, she wanted to hear the plan. "Why are you here? Are you rescuing us?"

"No. Not yet. Running Bear says maybe after Christmas." Tighe kissed her forehead. "He says Wolf's minions aren't stir-crazy enough. But this storm is going to dump four feet of snow, and then the nerves will really start to fray around here. That's when they'll make mistakes."

River was a bit crushed. Yet she also understood. "I hope it can be by Christmas. The midwife says I'll probably be on absolute bed rest by next month."

Tighe raised up on an elbow. "Okay. Then I'm busting you out of here."

"I'm not leaving Fiona! And if I leave, Wolf will be angry. He might take it out on her." River slid her hands into his pants, feeling his warmth and his strength.

"Whoa," Tighe said, "none of that, young lady."

He tried to remove her hands, but she put them right back, holding the part of him she wanted to hold, while she kissed his mouth, feverishly luring him to make love to her. If she couldn't be rescued, then she definitely wanted him to kiss her, hold her, romance her.

"You're coming with me."

"I will not." She pulled him free of his jeans, massaging him. He groaned, so she kept doing exactly what she was doing—tempting him.

"I brought you a cell phone," he said, making a last-ditch effort to resist her. He tried to put himself back in his jeans, but she'd gotten him into such a state that nothing was fitting in place easily.

"I have one." She climbed on top of him, straddled his stomach, kissed his chin.

"You have a cell phone?"

"Yes. Didn't I tell you? It's in my bag of tricks."

The conversation was conducted in whispers, but River thought that if Tighe could yell at her at this moment, he probably would. He seemed so dumbstruck. Though she couldn't see him in the dark—turning on a light might alert the night watch—she could feel that his body had stiffened. Yes, he was a bit annoyed.

"If you have a cell phone, it would have been nice if you'd texted us how you were doing."

"I could have," River said, noticing that his hands had crept back to her hips. She wore a stretchy pair of pajama bottoms that were light and thin, and a matching top. It wasn't fancy, but for modesty's sake in a house full of eight men and two strange women, she'd wanted pajamas.

Tighe played with the elastic, almost seeming to ignore her bare skin.

"I could have texted, but I was afraid they've got some kind of communication device that looks for cell messages and phone calls. It's not that hard to trace such activity. I never dared to switch the device on. They don't know I have it."

"Smart," he said gruffly. Then his hands slid around to her stomach once more. "You definitely have to leave with me. I can't risk you needing medical help that this area can't provide, especially under Wolf's auspices. This might be a high-risk pregnancy. I can't imagine that having triplets isn't."

She worked him entirely free of his jeans. "I'm not leaving Fiona. And that's that. End of discussion."

"Then she'll come with us."

Her man was dreaming. He was talking big. This was the same guy who'd tried to ride Firefreak when he lacked the skills—according to his siblings—to do so. "No, Tighe," she said, and then did what she had to do to make him forget all about rescue attempts.

River's belly was huge! Tighe had kissed every bit of her once-flat stomach, astonished by the size his sons had stretched her to. And matters were only going to get worse. His growing boys weren't going to stop supersizing. It seemed to him that she was the shape most women were at the nine-month point of a single pregnancy.

In fact, he shouldn't have allowed her to make love to him. That was not a good idea. But her soft hands had been so busy, teasing and tormenting him, and he'd missed her so terribly. She'd moved so quickly, straddling him, that he couldn't resist. He felt comfortable about her taking things at her own pace; still, he'd worried that pleasuring her would bring on an early delivery.

She'd laughed at him, and taken his mind right off anything sane.

Now she slept in the crook of his arm. He hated that he had to leave. An hour had passed; there was no reason to tempt the devil. Tighe got up, kissed her goodbye. Kissed his sons goodbye. "I'll be back in a couple of days. Be ready. Tell Fiona, too."

"But Tighe—"

He put a finger against her lips. "Just this once, I want you to say, *'Whatever you want, darling.'*"

"No one talks like that," River said, and giggled.

"Try it. It's my fervent desire to hear those words on your sweet lips."

"I'll do whatever you want."

"Darling."

"Darling." She giggled again, and he wished he could see her face.

Within a week, they'd be back at Rancho Diablo. With a new moon, they'd celebrate Thanksgiving together, as a family. Then he'd put River in a rocker and make her stay still as a bowl of fruit until his sons were born.

He went out the window and disappeared into the swirling snow.

Tighe returned to Rancho Diablo for a rescue party. He went to Ash, because he could trust her to be up for an adventure. "I've got to get River out of there."

His sister turned to look at him from her perch atop the bunkhouse. She'd had binoculars glued to her face, peering toward the canyons. It was a great vantage point, but he was pretty certain she was looking for Xav Phillips just as much as any trespassers.

"What are you talking about? Running Bear isn't ready."

"I saw River last night. The chief's going to have to be ready."

"How did you see her?"

"I staked out the cabin for a few days, figured out the routine and which window was hers." He shrugged. "A big storm moved in, and I took advantage of the situation."

Ash's eyes were huge. "Running Bear is going to gnaw on you for that."

"I don't care. River's enormous. She'll be on bed rest soon. We've got to get her out of there. Fiona, too. River says Wolf's men are fighting among themselves, and Fiona's not feeding them right now. They're like hungry animals."

Ash smiled. "Sounds like Fiona has everything just the way she wants it. Everybody eating out of her palm." His sister shook her head, the smile fading. "But I want no part of what you're planning. Not unless you talk to Running Bear first."

"Ash. River is my woman, and she's carrying my sons. Or my daughters." He didn't care which; he just needed her home safe. Tighe took a deep breath. "I'm getting her out of there. I'm getting her real medical care. This is a matter of my family's lives. My wife's life."

"You're not married," Ash said, with a sneaky smile.

"I'm married in my heart. And River's coming home."

"You talk to Running Bear and tell him the problem, and I'll help you any way I can. I promise." She patted Tighe on the back. "Poor brother. I know this is so hard for you."

"Not hard on me like it is on Fiona and River." He felt terrible about that. "The cabin is freezing. There's no heat. River's brave, says her body temperature changed with the babies and now she's hot all the time, so she's fine. But what if Fiona gets pneumonia? Or River?" He was worried sick. "It can't be healthy to live in those conditions. And though Fiona has everybody doing house chores, it's not like being here."

"I'm so sorry." Ash laid her head on his shoulder. "When Running Bear gets back, discuss it with him."

"Where is he?"

"He's gone somewhere. I don't really know where. I have my suspicions, but if I'm right, he's on a mission. My guess is he's gone to visit the unmentioned part of our family tree. Might not be back for a while. Obviously, we didn't foresee you trying to move up the timetable on the rescue."

Tighe's heart felt as if it might beat out of his chest.

"I don't have that long to wait. It's got to happen now." He climbed down the ladder from the roof and headed to find Dante and the rest of his brothers. He and River would be at an altar in the next few days if he had to stop and marry her in Montana on the lam from Wolf. Tighe had looked it up. There were very few restrictions on getting married in that state. No blood work. It could be done.

Or Running Bear might return, and could do a traditional wedding blessing.

Tighe's brothers were out handling their duties. They'd be back by early twilight. It'd be easier to herd them all into the library and state his case then.

Maybe he'd go hunt up that stupid wedding dress while he waited for their return. He wanted to see what it was that had freaked River out.

Had any of his brothers or cousins laid eyes on the fabled magic wedding dress while in its ephemeral cocoon?

Was it to be handled only by hopeful brides seeking knowledge of their one true love—or could a man touch it? Would it still be a supernatural gown, or would merely holding the charmed fabric turn him into a gargoyle?

It was time they all stopped tiptoeing around the bewitching fiddle-faddle Fiona endorsed. There was no such thing as magic. The thing was, they'd drunk in the stories and the mystery and the mysticism.

He silently crept up to the attic, even though no one was in the main house. At the top of the stairs, he flipped on a lamp and closed the door behind him. Then he went to the closet where the gown supposedly hung, and took a deep breath before looking inside.

There was the shimmery white garment bag, just as he'd always heard. It did seem to twinkle a bit in the dim closet, but that was just his eyes adjusting to the low lighting.

He brought out the bag, hung it on a hook. Stepped back, pondered what he was hoping to learn.

"All right, dress," he muttered. "You're just a fable in this family, a story that was created to get anxious brides to the altar."

The bag twinkled at him. He held his breath and took hold of the zipper.

Chapter 14

There was nothing there.

Tighe stared at the empty space where a magic wedding dress should be. This made no sense. It wasn't at the cleaners, because Fiona wasn't here to take it. No doubt she'd had it properly put away after Ana's wedding to Dante. Yet River had told him she'd seen it. He couldn't think of a single reason that the gown would be out and about without its special garment bag.

This wasn't good.

The thing was around here somewhere. He just had to find it. He'd put it back in the bag, and when he brought Fiona and River home from Montana, everything would be as it should be.

He searched the attic, then every room of the huge house.

The dress was nowhere to be found.

Ash approached him with a puzzled look when she found him rummaging through the basement. "What in the world are you doing down here, brother?"

"I'm looking for something."

She glanced toward the long scar in the floor where the Rancho Diablo silver treasure was hidden.

"No," Tighe told his sister. "It's not there. I wouldn't dare dig anything out of that hole."

"What's not there?" Ash asked.

"The Callahan wedding gown."

Ash blinked. "What Callahan wedding gown? The magic wedding dress?"

"I refuse to call it that," Tighe said. "I don't believe in magic."

Ash shook her head. "Why would it be in the basement?"

"Because it's not in the attic," Tighe explained.

"Of course it is." Ash gave him an impatient look. "Typical male. Can't find anything that's right at hand, in the most obvious place."

"Fine," Tighe said. "Go see if you can find it."

Ash jutted her chin into the air. "I will."

She trotted up the stairs. He went into the kitchen to see who was making dinner tonight. All seven of them had been assigned dates on a dry-erase board, and if anyone needed to swap their night, they erased their name and exchanged with their substitute.

"Blast. It's Galen's night for dinner. That means sloppy joes. I think that's all he knows how to make."

Tighe heard Ash's feet on the stairs. "It's up there, you dork," she said, coming into the kitchen.

He was stunned. "In the bag?"

"Yes. The garment bag is there."

"But did you look in it? Actually unzip it?"

Ash pulled some of Fiona's cookies from the freezer. "I did not."

Tighe looked at his sister. "Then how do you know it's there?"

"Because the bag is there. Where else would the dress be?" She put some cookies on a tray. "I can't unzip the thing, Tighe. It would be bad luck for me to see the dress before my time comes. But I felt the bag. It's in there." She looked pleased by her cleverness.

"Something is inside?"

"Yes. It's definitely a wedding dress. It's kind of long and heavy, and a little poufy."

Tighe shook his head. "It doesn't make sense. I tell you the bag was empty. I unzipped it and looked inside, and I don't believe in magic, so it didn't bother me at all to take a peek. And what was in there was nada."

She studied him curiously. "I realize this is a dumb question, but what exactly were you doing rummaging through the magic wedding dress bag?"

"What do you care?"

She hopped onto the counter and munched her cookie. "Well, it's not the typical thing a man does. Not even you. That type of behavior strikes me as a bit desperate."

He sighed. "Ash, I just wanted to make certain it was there, okay? So that when River comes home, she can wear it and see me in a vision and sit around the fire with the other Callahan brides and tell magic wedding dress campfire stories, all right?"

"You're truly weird. Anyway," Ash said, jumping down off the counter, "if you don't believe me, go back up there and see for yourself, if you have your panties all in a bunch about it being here for River. I haven't heard that she accepted your proposal, but if you're looking for a good luck charm, go ahead and get it off your chest. It's there."

He trudged up the stairs, feeling a bit of an ass.

The bag wasn't in the closet. Wasn't anywhere to be found in the attic. Nor was there a shimmery dress suited for a bride. "Nuts," he muttered. Ash was playing a heckuva trick on him. She'd hidden it, and was downstairs sniggering, just waiting for him to come jogging down the stairs with "his panties in a bunch."

He was a little tired of being the source of family fun. So he went down the stairs, decidedly calm, and not looking like a man who was having a Callahan prank played on him.

"Find it?" Ash asked.

"Yes, I did," he said, and kept walking through the den.

"I told you. I don't know why men have to make everything so hard." She disappeared into the kitchen, and Tighe took his bad mood upstairs into the library, to wait on his brothers to show up.

Magic wedding gown or not, they were going to help him enact the perfect, foolproof rescue for River and Fiona.

He'd worry about what had happened to the erstwhile dress later. There would be some explaining to do once his chosen lady and Fiona returned, but for now, he couldn't worry about dresses.

He had to get his bride home first.

"This rescue party is going to have to start earlier than expected." Tighe looked around at his brothers and sister, who were sitting on various chairs and couches studying him with grim faces. "River is huge. There's no way she can be moved if we wait until Christmas to raid Wolf's hangout."

Galen spoke first. "Overlooking the fact that you went off post without notifying any of us, and also over-looking the fact that Running Bear specifically told us to stay away, and that you could have gotten caught—" his eldest brother glared at him "—you're not a doctor. How can you tell River's going to need to be on bed rest soon?"

Tighe gulped, remembering River's stomach as she lay on top of him. "I think my babies are going to be linebackers. Her stomach pokes out a good, well, like this." He gestured with his hands to show the size to which River's tummy had grown.

His family appeared to be suitably impressed.

"She hasn't had proper medical care," Ash pointed out. "There's every chance River could soon require high-risk assessment."

Tighe looked at Sloan. "You had the first set of twins. How long was it before Kendall needed to be in bed?"

"She lasted a good while," Sloan said, "but River's carrying one extra. I say we raid."

"I do, too," Falcon said. "We have nothing to lose by bringing her home early."

"Besides," Jace said, throwing his two cents in, "it's not like we all haven't had missions moved up or back on us. We've gone into rough places at the drop of a hat, based on new intel that's been provided to our com-manders." He shrugged. "I vote we raid."

"I'm in the mood for a hunting party," Ash said. "I miss Fiona. And River. Fiona's too old to be hanging around without sufficient heat." She frowned. "And frankly, it gets right up my nose that Wolf has any of our family!"

Galen nodded. "Agreed. The time has come."

Tighe felt a sudden chill at his brother's words. *Am I the hunted one, leading my family into the foretold danger and destruction?*

He was caught in a horrible snare. Either path he chose, there was danger.

And he had not forgotten that his chosen bride had a goody bag filled with incendiary party favors with Wolf's and his merry band's names on them. Tighe knew River well enough to suspect she'd throw quite the party on the way out. He closed his eyes. *I'm marrying a warrior. She scares the hell out of me—but I kind of like it, too.*

"Have any of you ever wondered why Callahan men choose to fall for such headstrong women?" he asked.

"I know exactly why," Dante said. "First of all, that's the way we like them. But I'll remind you that I spoke into the wind a blessing on all my brothers, that you would each have a long and arduous chase to get your woman tamed." He looked very satisfied with himself, and they all booed him. "As it's spoken, it shall be done," he reminded them. "All blessings can come to pass."

"Thank you, Oracle. Can you please go back to minding the well or the River Styx or whatever you do in your spare time? We have a rescue to plan." Tighe looked around at his family. "When do we leave?"

"Zero three hundred hours," Ash said. "Set your watches against the clock on the wall. And may I remind everyone that this is a secret mission? I think we can all agree that Grandfather would not be pleased. It's best if we keep this journey to ourselves."

At the word *journey,* Tighe felt that strange breeze of fate blow across his soul once more. He shivered, and set his watch.

At the exact appointed time, they piled into two vehicles, one a truck comfortable enough for all of them to ride in, and the jeep for backup. One of the vehicles would be used to block the road leading from the hideout, and the other would be used to carry Fiona and River away from danger.

Tighe was more nervous than he'd ever been. He wished he could get a message to River, but she might be right: they might have some kind of device that picked up cell signals. It wasn't worth risking it. Wolf was very experienced at this type of warfare. He was financed by people with deep pockets, and the equipment necessary to achieve their goals.

But Wolf would never achieve his goal as long as there were Callahans at Rancho Diablo. Tighe's temper boiled a bit, the same temper he'd been holding back ever since Fiona had been kidnapped, and which had overheated when River was taken. He couldn't wait to exact revenge on Wolf and his gang.

Tighe and his siblings had left foremen at the ranch on lookout, telling them that not one soul, not even a family friend, was to step foot on the property while they were gone.

Tighe hoped it was enough. The foremen were to keep plenty of activity happening on the grounds so that it looked as if the family was at home, the ranch fully staffed, the place bustling.

"What are we going to do about Storm's offer?" Ash asked. She rode beside him in the jeep, following the truck.

"I don't care. That's Running Bear's and Fiona's issue."

"They think we don't know that Storm bought the land. Remember? We're all supposed to be eager for it." Ash stared down into a bag she'd packed for the trip, pulled out a water bottle for each of them. "I think if we buy it, they'll be disappointed. It'll be like opening presents before Christmas Day."

"I can't think about land right now." Tighe was going over every single detail of the plan they'd elaborately and meticulously laid out last night. They'd gone through every scenario that could possibly occur, and then some that couldn't occur unless a meteor struck the earth. But he wanted nothing left to chance.

"Look!" Ash exclaimed.

He glanced over at her window. A shadow raced alongside them, a man on a mustang, his hair blowing wild and free behind him. "Holy crap," Tighe said.

"It's Grandfather," Ash said. "We should have known we couldn't get away with sneaking off on him."

The shadow disappeared. She glanced at Tighe.

Their gazes met, and neither one of them spoke about what they'd just seen. They looked back at the road in front of them, and tried to remain calm.

Running Bear was with them—in spirit.

Chapter 15

River knew the moment Tighe returned to the hideout. It wasn't obvious to anyone else, likely not even Fiona. But River heard a wolf howl long and loud, and she knew Tighe had come back for her.

Which was a good thing. She'd begun to feel some stray aches and pains that seemed unlike the previous ones, which came and went without a pattern. These seemed more rhythmic, and not as random.

"Hang on," she told her babies. "Daddy's here."

The babies settled at the sound of her voice, maybe her words. She didn't know. They seemed to shift a lot more now, probably searching for space. She'd be glad to get to a real doctor and learn what was happening with her beautiful children.

She looked in her backpack, made sure everything was ready. The cabin was cold enough that she worried the guns might need cleaning or oiling, but there was no way to address that without putting herself in a position to be caught.

She'd opened her backpack only twice since she'd been here, each time when she was tempted to plug in her cell phone and send Tighe a text. The nights had been long; sometimes fear had descended upon her.

She hadn't given in to it. But it pressed on her, as she was sure it had on Fiona. River tried to learn from the older woman's brave face, and wore her own consistently—but the nights grew long without Tighe's arms to hold her.

Once she returned, she was going to marry him, magic wedding dress or not.

Almost as if she conjured it, it appeared on her bed, beautiful and shimmering with love and magic. "Oh, my goodness," she murmured. "Oh, you are so beautiful!"

She couldn't fit into it now, of course. Even magic wedding dresses couldn't accommodate a belly the size of hers. The only clothes she wore these days were two pairs of sweatpants—men's—that Wolf's women had bought at a Walmart for her. In fact, the sweatpants and tennis shoes she had were hardly appropriate for making an escape through mounds of snow, but she'd manage somehow.

The dress twinkled encouragement at her. "May I touch you?" she said out loud, and the wedding gown threw off a few sparks of iridescence in response.

River ran her fingers over a cap sleeve, touching the delicate lace and diamante sparkles. Tears jumped into her eyes as she gazed at the beautiful dress she would one day wear. "Thank you," she murmured. "Thank you so much for letting me know that I will be a true Callahan bride one day."

The dress glowed with an evanescent quality, and River grabbed her cell phone. "May I take a picture? I want to remember everything about you until the day I finally get to put you on."

She didn't know if photos were allowed before the wedding day. But the garment didn't disappear, so River plugged in her phone and took two quick snaps, making sure she'd captured the image.

She smiled when she saw her dream dress photos. "Thank you," she said again. "I'm so happy to know that I'll have such a lovely dress to wear when the time comes."

The dress sparkled, emitting a few beams of light, then suddenly disappeared.

In its place was the black ensemble she'd seen in the magic wedding dress bag: a long-sleeved thermal shirt, plus black pants made of some kind of thick fabric suitable for braving the cold. The boots were black and lug-soled, reaching to the knee. A waterproof black coat completed what looked very much like weather-appropriate military gear.

River wiped her tears and tried the clothes on. They fit perfectly, the shirt not too small for her newly large breasts, the pants comfortable enough for her bigger belly.

Now she understood what she'd seen in the magic wedding dress bag.

"If this is the work of my fairy godmother," River said, "I want to thank you for being so flexible and considerate. This is perfect!"

She wished Fiona had warmer clothes. Montana was

much colder than they could have imagined, and the cabin was icy much of the time. She'd worried so much for Fiona.

It was high time to get the Callahan aunt home.

River checked her backpack one last time, ready for whatever was about to unfold.

The closer they got to Montana, the more Tighe worried. River, the babies and Fiona were the first worry, but the fact that he'd dragged his siblings into this mission, compromising their safety and their families—those brothers who had young children and wives—cramped his gut. Though they'd gone over and over the plan, anything and everything could go wrong with even the best attack and rescue operation.

He breathed deep, focused the way Grandfather had taught him. Tried to think about the power of the forces that had brought them to this moment. Some things were out of their control—and others were in their control. It was up to them to walk the proper path.

His hatred for Wolf kept him in a dangerous place. Sometimes he dreamed of killing his uncle—dark dreams of violence that shattered his sleep. Tighe always felt the evil knocking, just beyond the door of his subconscious.

"This is the town," Ash said. He felt his sister's gaze on him. "Our brothers are slowing down, so they must mean to turn off before entering, likely so no one will see us and warn Wolf." She studied Tighe. "Are you all right? You haven't said a word for the past hundred fifty miles."

He was fine—and not fine. "I'm just ready."

"Good." Ash rolled down the window, and frosty air

hit him in the face. It felt good circulating in the jeep, waking him to the bitter cold. "We made it here in record time, considering the weather."

Night was falling on the small town, the tree-lined mountains in the distance already shrouded in darkness. They'd driven straight through, with very few stops. Gas, occasional bathroom breaks, that was it. They were trained to focus on the mission and ignore weakness in their bodies. Well-schooled first by life in the tribe and their grandfather, and then excellently trained in the military, they would work as a team until the mission was accomplished.

Ash put the window up. "I'm going to pour some coffee from the thermos. Want some?"

"Sure." The coffee would be lukewarm or cold now, but that wouldn't matter.

Suddenly his mobile phone binged, alerting him that he had a message. He glanced at his cell, stunned to see that the message was from River.

Are you coming?

"It's River. She wants to know if I'm on the way." He looked at his sister. "What do you think?"

"It's a trap." Ash shook her head. "I wouldn't reply. What if Wolf found the phone on her and forced her to send the message?"

Exactly what he'd wondered.

"It won't do her any good to know, anyway," Ash said. "If she knows we're close to starting the operation, she'll be nervous. At least if she doesn't know, she might rest until we make our appearance."

He nodded. But it was hard. He wanted so badly to

tell her that he was on the way. To ask how she was doing, ask about the babies.

After tonight, it would be all over. The hell they'd endured for the past several months would be a nightmare past. They would be together for the holidays, as a family.

He closed his eyes and listened for any words he might hear in his mind, any directions for the journey he was about to undertake.

Silence.

Rhein came to get her, the scar on his face standing out against his dark skin. "Wolf wants you."

She looked at him, unafraid. She wore the jogging outfit and tennis shoes she'd always worn. When the time came, she would dress in her new clothes—her version of a fairy godmother's gift—and she would be ready to get Fiona and go home. "Fine."

She followed Rhein to the sparsely furnished den. A tiny fire burned in the fireplace, not enough to warm the room. Otherwise the space was totally dark. Even the shades were drawn. River stood in front of Wolf, not speaking.

"I've just talked to Fiona." Wolf's eyes glittered in the small, dark room. "Despite the fact that I question her every day, she refuses to give any information about Jeremiah's and Carlos's whereabouts."

A snake of fear jumped into River's veins. Fiona had never told her that she was being questioned often by Wolf. River glanced nervously at Rhein, and the big man stared her down.

"Well, we must work with what we've got." Wolf stood up, placed a hand on her stomach. Purely by reflex, River kicked him hard in the shin, stunning everyone, including herself.

He sank into the armchair by the fireplace, his eyes closed. Rhein snatched her arm in a viselike grip.

Wolf took a deep breath after he'd rubbed his shin. "As I was saying, we must work with what we've got. Rhein will show you to your new room."

River jerked against the thug's arm as he pulled her toward the front door. Horrified, she realized he was removing her from the house. "Where are you taking me?"

"To another location," Wolf said, following behind, prodding her forward when she dug in her heels.

She couldn't leave this house. Tighe would be here anytime to rescue her. "Don't make me leave. I need to be with Fiona."

"That's precisely your worth. I thought time away from her family would break the old woman, but she thinks she's running the show around here." Wolf stood back, watching, while Rhein guided her into the off-road vehicle with less than gentle hands. "The old lady is locked in her room now. No one will be happy for a while. They'll miss her cooking. But I'm not going to be happy until I have the information I'm seeking, so," Wolf said, his gaze on River, "she's going to get plenty of time to think about being more forthcoming with that information."

"Fiona will never say anything," River declared.

"She very well might, once she realizes you've been taken to that shack up there," Wolf said, pointing to a cabin high atop the mountain, surrounded by woods, barely visible from their location. "That's our lookout house, a guard shack, you might say. You'll be there for some time, I'm sure, so get used to it. There'll be a team to keep an eye on you, make sure you're being a good girl." He stepped back from the vehicle, and Rhein got behind the wheel. "It's very, very difficult to get to. People have gotten lost in those woods and never been found. In these conditions, you wouldn't last long."

River's blood chilled. Tighe wouldn't know she'd been taken from here. She looked up at the shack that was to be her new home. "Please let me stay here."

"No," Wolf said, "we've got to break the old lady down somehow. The best way to do it is for her to know that you and those little babies are suffering in the cold. No heat or electricity up there, by the way. For your sake, I hope Fiona breaks quickly."

"I hope she never breaks," River retorted. "I need my backpack. It's got my only change of clothes in it." Her magic wedding dress clothes were tucked in the back of the tiny closet. She hadn't wanted anyone to glance in the room and see them. Wolf's gang would know she hadn't come with them, and would instantly know Tighe was close by.

Wolf shook his head. "In a day or so, when the old lady realizes you're stuck with nothing, she may loosen her tongue a bit. Until then, Rhein will take good care of you. And I'll tell the girls to make certain your backpack is put away safely."

River glared at Wolf, hating him more than she'd ever hated anyone. "If anything happens to me, Tighe will make you regret it."

"Live by the sword, die by the sword, I always say," Wolf said. "Rhein, get her out of here."

It was cold on the mountaintop, colder than she'd ever been in her life. The sweats she wore weren't suited for snow and icy conditions, nor were the tennis shoes.

"It's going to be a bit chillier here than the hideout," Rhein said as he parked the vehicle behind the shack, where it couldn't be spied from the road or sky.

"Don't talk to me," River shot back.

"It's pretty lonely up here. You'll want to talk to someone soon enough. You and the old lady are quite the chatterboxes."

"Are you deaf?" River snapped. "I said don't talk to me."

"All that prissiness is going to get you nowhere." He walked her to the back door, opened it. "Welcome home."

She ignored him and went inside. The chill of the place practically smacked her in the face. It was dark and felt damp from lack of heat. Her breath made puffs in the cold air.

"If you're nice, I'll see you get a blanket. But all that attitude's going to make sure you just sleep with sheets."

She looked at Rhein, let him know with her gaze that she considered him reprehensible. "I'll be fine."

"There's your room, princess." He pointed down the hall.

She marched into it, closed the door, locked it. Curled up on the ratty cot with the nasty gray sheets and began to plan her escape.

Chapter 16

The Callahans crouched, well hidden by the woods, and gazed at the hideout. Tighe studied the opportunities for entrance and egress, and looked for signs of recent activity. He was ready to bust in there now and grab River and Fiona, so he had to force himself to think clearly, logically, rationally. Any mission had to proceed according to the best-laid plans, carefully crafted with painstaking detail.

But the wait was hard.

"Four lookouts," Jace said, staring through binoculars, "and a fresh set of tire tracks with chains leading to the west."

"And up that mountain, is my guess." Tighe squinted up at the thick pine woods where the fringed branches were heavy with snow. The air was crisp and clear, the silence around them complete from the shroud of snow wrapping everything in sight.

"There's something up there," Ash said, peering through her own binoculars. "But no road."

"Off-road vehicle, with no obvious sign of departing along the main road," Galen whispered. "No doubt a lookout is posted somewhere up there."

The Callahans had chosen this site for their base. Cloistered among the trees, they felt comfortable that they couldn't be spotted. The site was also situated downwind, so their voices wouldn't carry. It was an ideal location.

But those tire tracks bothered Tighe. Something about them kept nagging at him. The tracks were fresh, and there was just one set, so the route clearly wasn't driven often. "Maybe the lookout only changes once a week. It's possible new snow covered up older tracks."

"Possible," Dante said. Tighe's twin stood next to him, lending his support. Ever since they'd decided on the mission, Dante had stuck to him like a burr, as in the old days, when it was the two of them against the world. Tighe appreciated him being there.

For his part, Dante was no longer laughing and teasing about words he'd once spoken into the wind, wishing for his brothers to be set on torturous paths to win their women. He had been much more taciturn lately. "Possible, but I'm going to postulate that something's been moved into the mountains for safekeeping," he said suddenly.

Tighe squinted up into the snow-covered forest. "Whatever it is, it's frozen now."

"Maybe some equipment," Ash said.

"Something Wolf considers a valuable target, something he wouldn't want us to have in case we attack." Falcon looked through his rifle sight, checking for movement. "He's got more backup this time. And no doubt more weapons."

Tighe looked at the sky, seeing thick clouds obscuring the stars and moon. Perfect for what they had planned.

Ash wrapped her arm through his. "It's going to be all right."

He hoped so. It was a night fit for a Shakespearean play, maybe some witches howling out of the darkness and whatever other foul luck might stand in the way. Tighe tightened his hood. He prayed he hadn't brought his family here to meet their doom.

His phone buzzed once in his pocket, signaling a text. Tighe pulled it out to peer at it.

River taken to other location. Look for small shack in the woods. F

Holy smoke. Tighe's gut clenched. He blinked, read the text again.

"You know how we planned for every contingency?" he asked.

His family's attention riveted on him. "Text from Fiona. River's been taken to a satellite location."

They all stared at him, and he read in their eyes exactly what he knew—all the careful planning had just gone up in flames. "And I don't know if this is good or bad news, but River doesn't have her backpack." He held up his phone for emphasis. "Fiona used River's cell phone. I can see several scenarios where all of the above is bad news." He took a deep breath. "Wherever River is, she doesn't have a communication device to

392 *Callahan Cowboy Triplets*

reach us, nor weapons, either. Fiona, on the other hand, has River's backpack, and her mobile."

"That's the good news, then," Ash said. "We can communicate with *her* if we have to."

"It also means our spry and occasionally feisty aunt has a full bag of weapons, some of them incendiary. I don't think I have to spell out to any of you what the combination of Fiona and some really interesting fireworks could mean to our battle plan."

"Not to mention the side of this mountain," Jace said.

"We could be talking landslide," Ash said, her voice awed. "Like Christmas in July, complete with fireworks in the snow."

"Snowmageddon," Sloan said. "Snow, ice, tree limbs everywhere. Apocalyptic."

"Yeah," Falcon agreed. "Fiona's always liked to do things for folks to remember and talk about for years to come."

"She does like legacy-building, one-for-the-record-books stuff," Galen said, sounding very worried. "I can think of no worse combination than Fiona and a chance to take out years and years of frustration against Wolf."

"Pray she doesn't realize what she's holding in that bag," Jace said. "Her chance for revenge."

It was too terrible to contemplate. But first things first. "I'm going to follow those tracks," Tighe said. "I have a funny feeling I know what I'll find at the end of that yellow brick road."

"Wait," Galen said. "We must plan. There is no margin for error."

The family grouped together. But Tighe said, "I can't wait for a plan. Start without me." And he took off toward the mountain.

* * *

It was bitter cold in the shack, and even River's best attempts at mind control couldn't disguise the discomfort seeping into her limbs. Silence enveloped the shack after four or five hours of three men laughing raucously and, River suspected, drinking to keep off the chill. They took turns, by the sound of things, one going outside for watch detail, and the other two keeping warm. Yesterday someone had loudly plopped a tray on the rickety table just outside her room. She hadn't bothered to get up. There was no light to see by, anyway, and she wasn't going to touch whatever was on the plate.

Rhein wasn't running a very tight ship. She listened for the sounds of their activities, looking for a schedule. It seemed that every three hours the watch changed.

The only time the men paid her any attention was when she opened the door to go down the hall to the bathroom. She felt their eyes on her, watching to make certain she didn't make a dash for it. Her bedroom window was nailed shut—she'd already checked that opportunity for escape.

She was going to have to make her escape soon. Her stomach cramped and shifted, the babies uneasy in her stomach. The dull cramps had returned, and that more than anything worried River.

Something soft and delicate settled over her as she lay on the bed, like angel wings floating down on her. She sat up, peering through the darkness. It was white and shimmery, catching the tiny bit of moonlight slivering in the window. She must be dreaming, so cold she was beginning to hallucinate. River reached out to touch the magic wedding dress gratefully. "I knew you'd come," she said. "Thank you, thank you, for letting me know I'm a true Callahan."

A few twinkles sparked in the air, and she smiled, comforted.

But then the dress changed, and she realized she wasn't dreaming at all. Her black, cold-weather gear lay on the bed, the boots on the floor. She gasped and sat up.

There was only one reason her prayers had been answered. It was time to make her escape.

She went down the hall to the bathroom, making sure that her napping guard dogs woke up to take notice of her. Then she went back to her room and closed the door. She slipped the black gear on, and put the gray sweats under the ratty sheets, ruffling them so it looked as if a body was sleeping in the bed. The tennis shoes she put on the floor, as if she was snuggled up cozily. The men never came into the dark room, anyway. She smiled, pleased with the way the thick sweats bunched up the sheets. "That'll freak them out."

She listened for sounds of activity, but the shack was wrapped in a wintry silence. Her trip down the hall had revealed that Rhein was not on watch outside; he was tucked up at the small fire, a bottle of whiskey at his side. He'd looked distinctly groggy, and annoyed to be awakened by her jaunt to the washroom.

As long as Rhein wasn't on watch, she had a chance.

She waited a little while longer to give them time to be deeply into the whiskey. Then, before the sentry changed, she opened her door and crept down the hall, walking right out the back of the shack. It was dark outside, which would give her cover. She looked for the watch, figuring he'd probably be situated on the roof with binoculars. But to her surprise, he was sound asleep against a tree, sitting on an old crate of some kind, an AK-47 across his lap. River noted a flashlight lay on another crate nearby, which was used as a table. Cigarette butts were scattered about, and an empty bottle of something—probably whiskey—and a coffee mug.

There was no point in wasting good supplies. River dug down in the snow, packed a huge snowball and threw it into a tree ten feet away from the lookout. She hit the branch she'd aimed for dead-on, and ice and snow showered down. The lookout didn't even move.

She walked over, took the flashlight and melted into the woods. If she could get an hour's head start down the mountain—or maybe even more—perhaps she could make it. The sky was dark, with rolling clouds and only threads of moonlight coming through the trees. There'd be a storm by morning, and with any luck, her tracks would be obscured.

It would be as if she'd simply disappeared.

Tighe was making good time up the mountain. This terrain was no different than some of the other cold locations in which he'd been deployed, except that the pathway here was fairly smooth, less rocky under the thick snow.

He used no light, only night vision goggles. He didn't worry about footprints—the coming storm would take care of that.

This was the easiest assignment he'd ever had. Like any other mission, this one had a definite goal, a preferred outcome that he would achieve.

Suddenly he stopped, certain he'd heard something

other than wind gusting the trees, or icy limbs falling. Whatever it was stopped, too. Or maybe he'd imagined it.

No. He didn't imagine things, and that sense of danger that had saved him many a time was screaming, a banshee curdling his ears. He stayed still, barely breathing.

The sound resumed, a steady *squish* of footfalls sinking into the snow. He leaned up against a tree, quietly pulled a Sig Sauer 9 mm from his pack and waited, tense, listening.

Shuffle…step…careful sounds of boots marching forward with determination. The strides were long when possible, the crunches lighter than a man's boots. Tighe straightened, a crazy thought dawning in his brain.

The steps were a woman's.

The only woman on the mountain who would be on a mission to get off it would be—

He took a deep breath when he heard a female voice mutter something that sounded like a prayer, a chant, a quiet invoking of spirits to keep fear at bay.

Tighe put the gun away and moved behind a tree to wait and see if a miracle was possible on this frozen night.

Chapter 17

River hurried, determined to reach the bottom of the mountain, where Tighe or the other Callahans might spy her. She knew they were nearby; they had to be. The flashlight beam shone in front of her, leading the way over the snow-covered ground.

If she was wrong and the Callahans weren't here, she'd walk to the main road, try to flag down a car. It was miles away, but anything was better than being trapped in that filthy cabin with Rhein. If she could get help, maybe she could rescue Fiona.

A tall figure stepped from behind a tree, and River gasped with fear.

"River. It's Tighe."

She could hardly believe it. He reached out his arms, and she rushed into his warmth. "Tighe! How did you find me?"

"They left tire tracks. And Fiona sent us a message that you'd been moved. It wasn't hard to figure out. What are you doing here in the dark?" He hugged her close, and her knees sagged with relief.

"I got out. My guards and the lookout were asleep." She buried her face in his chest, realizing she'd held a secret fear inside her that she might not ever hold Tighe again. He kissed her, and River melted against him, relieved that he'd come to take her home. Finally, the long nightmare was over.

He broke away far too soon, but didn't let go of her hand. River craved his touch, the feel of him. "Come on. There's no time to waste, as much as I would love to hold you all night," he said.

"There'll be time enough for that when we get back to Rancho Diablo. I intend to spend plenty of time alone with you." She let him help her walk in the snow so they could make faster time. "Are you alone?"

"The whole gang is here. And Fiona's got your backpack. The others are going to get our aunt out of there, so we don't want to be late for the departure."

River put one foot in front of the other—she could only breathe, not talk. It seemed she'd been walking forever, and her stomach was cramping like mad.

"Are you all right?" Tighe asked, stopping to peer at her.

"Just a little tired." She tried to smile when he gazed into her face, pushed her hair back. "My stomach hurts a bit."

"Is it the babies?"

"I don't think so," River said, "I think it's that I haven't had a healthy meal in ages, and I've been living in dirty places." She realized she was about to cry, and wouldn't let herself. "I'm so afraid they'll discover I've left. They've got an off-road vehicle, so we have to hurry, Tighe."

She didn't want anything to happen to him, and if Rhein found out she'd left, he and his goons would come after them. He could also send word to Wolf to have the other men watch the bottom of the mountain. She wouldn't be much help to Tighe.

River tried to walk faster, telling herself that the sooner she got off the mountain, the sooner her babies and her man would be safe.

They got to the bottom without mishap, then Tighe texted Ash that he planned to have River rest until Operation Rescue Fiona began. He was seriously worried about River. She was putting on the bravest of faces, but it didn't escape him that occasionally she stopped, rubbed her belly and took long breaths.

Anyone would be winded walking down a mountain in heavy snow, but River was in excellent condition. He remembered when he and Dante had thought the nanny bodyguards walked like panthers, strong and graceful, with long, purposeful strides. Her steps had changed, and while that was to be expected, given the circumstances, Tighe felt certain she was in pain. She wasn't the kind of woman who would complain very much when there was nothing that could be done about it, when a mission was in play.

Rage against Wolf filled him, as it always did lately, a gnawing, burning sensation that focused him on what he had to do, and also sharpened his desire to kill his uncle. He'd been forbidden to do so by his grandfather, and Tighe only hoped he would remember Running

Bear's warning. The urge to end the curse that was Wolf burned strong in him.

"Sit," he told River, helping her to a fallen log well hidden from the snow-crusted path the off-road vehicle had taken up the mountain. "Someone will be here soon to help you get to the truck. Then if you need to go to a hospital, all you have to do is say the word." He knelt to look in her face. "I know this isn't the right time to tell you this, but you're beautiful, babe. The most beautiful, amazing woman I've ever known."

She smiled, her eyes glowing for just a moment. "It's a great time to hear those words. Thank you. I know it's not true—I haven't even washed my hair in three days—but you're a prince for trying to make me understand that the end is in sight."

"It's in sight, all right." He heard the sound of tires crunching through the snow behind him and turned. "Of course my sister has to spit in the eye of the tiger," he said, helping River to her feet. Ash pulled the jeep up, and he heard a door open. "Come on."

"How do you know it's Ash?"

He escorted her forward. "Because she's just a little closer to crazy than the rest of us. When I told her that I had you and was ready to go, I didn't mean for her to drive a vehicle right up where Wolf and his men could see it."

River giggled. "Ash is awesome."

"She is. And so are you."

Darkness enveloped the forest and the jeep, hopefully covering their movements. If the dirtbags on the mountain were still out like lights, then they wouldn't have notified Wolf that River had escaped and might not have a sentry posted at the front of the cabin. *Maybe, just maybe, we can get away with this.*

Ash appeared at his side, and took River's other arm to guide her over the snow. "Long time, no see," she told her. "Let's get you home."

They piled River into the jeep, and Tighe wrapped her in a blanket. Dante and Jace were posted in back, with long rifles aimed at Wolf's cabin.

Okay, so Ash hadn't completely thumbed her nose at the devil. For the first time, Tighe began to breathe a little easier.

"Here we go," his sister said, and without turning on the lights, slowly drove toward the stakeout location. "How are you doing, River?"

"Fine. Thanks for providing the rescue party."

Tighe held River to him, keeping the blanket tight around her. She was starting to shake, from either the aftereffects of stress or the severe cold, or both. "When we reach camp, I'll get you a cup of tea."

"Sounds like heaven," River said, and laid her head against his chest.

He met his sister's gaze in the mirror. Ash appeared worried, her brows raised, then she looked back at the road.

Tighe held River, stroking her hair.

They couldn't be back at Rancho Diablo soon enough.

Thirty minutes later, Tighe had River bundled up in the back of the truck, a cup of tea in her hand. "It's not as hot as it could be, but we're using the lighter plug instead of building a fire."

"It's perfect." She gave him a wan smile.

"I wish you'd lie down."

"I can't. I don't want to miss a thing."

Fiona's rescue would begin in a few minutes. His brothers and Ash were gearing up and checking their weapons. They'd texted Fiona one final time: Get ready. 0400.

Tighe figured they were all as ready as they could be.

"You love this, don't you?" River asked with a smile.

"I'm not going to say that my blood doesn't speed up a little bit at the thought of getting Fiona out of there, and everybody home safe."

"You're going, right?"

"I'm sitting here with you. We'll watch the proceedings together. I'll be driving the truck when we haul ass out of here. You'll be snug as a bug in a rug in the back, waving goodbye to Wolf." At least that's how he hoped it went.

"Don't stay here because of me. I don't want you to miss anything."

He laughed. "I'll be fine. Someone needs to cover the front, and someone with decent driving skills has to get us out of here. I feel plenty useful." He patted her leg. "Besides, I'm not letting you out of my sight yet."

She smiled, and he went back to helping his brothers and sister gear up. Checked the sky, and the time on his watch. Watched the road, front and back, where they would clear out of the woods.

"Remember Grandfather's words," he reminded them. "No killing unless absolutely necessary. I feel confident we have the skills to pull this off without a single shot fired."

They nodded in understanding. Tighe studied their faces, satisfied with what he saw. "It's time," he said softly, and for one final, brief moment, they came together as a team, as a family, and stood in a circle. Tighe felt no fear; they were too strong for that.

"Here we go," he said, and his sister and brothers disappeared into the thick woods. Galen would drive the jeep, so took watch at the top of the road, his eye to his weapon as he lay on the ground, ready to fire. Tighe sat in the back of the truck, his rifle pointed toward the hideout, checking for any snipers on the roof as his family approached.

"Stay down," he told River, and she obeyed—although he noticed she didn't really lie down so much as crouch, so she could peer up over the window frame to see what was happening. Satisfied that she intended to stay put, Tighe went back to staring through the rifle sight.

He tried not to think about what he was sending his family in to do. He hoped like hell that he hadn't jinxed the mission by insisting on moving up the target date.

He refused to doubt his gut instinct, and the knowledge that had come to his spirit, that danger lay in inaction just as much as in action.

Tighe squinted, watching, waiting. Grateful for every moment of silence, because that meant his siblings might make it in and out without discovery.

And then all hell broke loose.

Chapter 18

He picked up his ringing phone. "Yeah?"

"Fiona failed to mention she's had a fall," Ash said. "She's not as ambulatory as we'd thought."

He could hear the sounds of fighting in the background.

"How many operatives?"

"Two women and at least five men. I'm not saying we're pinned down, but we could use some help extracting the package."

He could hear Fiona in the background insisting that she was fine, that she could outrun all of them.

"Coming."

He handed River the rifle through the back window. "Aim for anything that comes through that door that isn't a Callahan."

She put down the window and aimed toward the hideout.

He took off through the woods, circling the open clearing in front of the cabin, his heart thundering. Loud noises seemed to shake the house; he could hear Wolf's men yelling to each other.

He didn't hear his sibling's voices, which was a good sign. When he slipped around back, the first person he came into contact with was Fiona. She was bent down behind a snow-covered barrel. "Fiona!"

"Hello, nephew!" She beamed. "I'm ready!"

She had River's backpack on her shoulders, and a grin on her face. Her rubber-soled boots were on her feet, and her hair was covered with a black hood.

"Where are you injured?" he asked her.

Her chin rose. "As I told my bossy niece, I'm fine. Don't you worry about your old aunt. I'm in better shape than all of you."

Okay. Feistiness still in place. The mission was still good. He took his aunt's arm as Ash appeared.

"Can she walk all the way to the truck?"

"Of course I can!" Fiona was indignant. "Do you think I need to be carried out of here by flying monkeys? For heaven's sake! It's a twisted ankle, that's all."

Tighe glanced at Ash. "We'll get as far as we can. See what happens."

Thick snow started falling, coming down fast, and a fierce wind sprang up.

"They're almost finished," Ash said, her finger pressed to her earpiece. "Let's move." She took Fiona's other arm.

"Just a moment," their aunt said.

"We can't wait," Ash insisted. "The team is departing and about to head out. We can't get left behind. Wolf and his men will return soon."

"That's all right. I've been here long enough. I'm in no hurry to leave just yet." She took off the backpack, rooted around inside, came up with Jace's just-in-case surprise.

Fiona looked at Ash and Tighe. "I'll be right back."

She disappeared inside.

"Great Spirit," Tighe said, and it was a prayer. "If our parents were like her, we've got some catching up to do."

"I think about that sometimes. Hurry, Aunt Fiona!" Ash yelled toward the house.

"You think she knows how to set that thing?" Tighe asked.

"I wasn't about to ask, and neither were you. Because I'm pretty sure the answer is yes."

He sighed. "It was a fairly simple device. Jace sent it along for River's use. I'm pretty sure she's baked cakes more involved than that."

Fiona reappeared with a big smile on her face. "Race you to the meet-up point."

Tighe looked at Ash over their determined aunt's head. She smiled, and they helped Fiona walk as fast as she could into the woods, Tighe covering their backs.

Once they made it deep into the woods, the snow wasn't as thick. Fiona stopped. "Just a minute."

She took out a device and pushed it.

An explosion rocked the house, and Tighe could feel the ground trembling below his feet. Fiona grinned.

"Nobody throws a party like I do," she said with satisfaction as they watched fire envelop the structure. "I'm sure Wolf will kidnap me again, because I'm the only one besides Running Bear who knows the information he wants. But I'll never be here, nor will any of the other Callahan women, ever again."

She started walking, then turned around to glance at Ash and Tighe, who were studying her handiwork. A fireball blew toward the sky when the gas stove exploded. Fiona looked pleased. "Running Bear will be so proud. Now let's go home. I can't wait to bake cookies in my own kitchen and drink my own coffee."

At the truck, Tighe handed his aunt over to Dante, and his siblings all grabbed their seats. Tighe didn't think he'd ever been so glad to leave a place. "Everybody good?" The question was generic, but his gaze went to River in the rearview mirror.

"Yes," she said. "What caused the explosion?"

"Fiona left a party favor. When we get home, take your backpack from her, will you?"

River smiled. "Some party favor, Fiona. Good thing the snow will keep that little campfire in check."

Sitting in the front seat, Fiona looked out at her destruction as they drove away. "Wolf, you ornery son of a gun, you'll never, ever beat this family. It will happen over my cold, dead body," she murmured.

Chills shot all through Tighe. His glance met River's in the mirror, and he knew she'd felt chills, too.

At Rancho Diablo the next day, Tighe felt as if he was in recovery mode, but River was just excited to be home. She ate anything he brought her, and said her stomach felt better—though he'd insisted on taking her straight to the hospital for a thorough checkup. They made an appointment in Santa Fe with a doctor who specialized in multiple births and high-risk pregnancies.

Tighe also bought the largest bottle of prenatal vitamins he could find, and several plump oranges for her to eat. "Every time I see you, I expect you to be in that rocker, with an orange and a glass of water in your hand."

River shook her head. "Will you quit worrying?"

"Absolutely not." He'd installed her in the main house, so everyone could keep an eye on her. She was next to a window, so she could sit and enjoy the warmth and the sunshine. River insisted she didn't need so much attention, that she felt like an old turtle sunning itself on a rock. The family responded by backing off a little, but making sure she was never without something to eat and drink.

River seemed thin to Tighe, but then she'd always been athletically built. He'd missed her body and he'd missed her smile like mad. It was so good to have her home.

"Fiona baked gingerbread," Tighe said.

"Oh, good." River looked expectant. "I'll get up and grab some when the timer dings."

"I'll bring you some, and a nice glass of milk."

"I'm not bed-bound yet, Tighe. Don't make me be still before it's my time."

"You've recently walked down a mountain. You've had plenty of exercise to last you for the next four months. Right now you're staying in this room with this nice fire."

"He's going to be insufferable until the babies are born," Fiona said, strolling into the room. She waved a calendar. "In view of our recent adventures, and our coming new additions," she said with a smile for River, "I am proposing moving the Christmas ball until after the babies are born."

"Don't change schedules on my behalf," River said. "I'm fine! Tighe is just being overprotective."

"It's not just that," Fiona said, "although your pregnancy is a big consideration. I'm a bit tired from all the travels, I must say. I wouldn't want to do a Christmas ball without my usual vigor." She gave them both a sly smile. "Besides, I'm thinking that a wedding might occur sooner than later? Perhaps around Christmas?"

She gave them a pointed look.

Tighe glanced at River, who slowly met his gaze. He grinned at her. "Aunt Fiona thinks we should get married."

River didn't say anything.

"Yes," Fiona said. "Since you were wearing the magic wedding dress yesterday, which I thought looked lovely on you—"

"What magic wedding dress?" Tighe demanded. He hadn't let River out of his sight, and he hadn't seen a sign of wedding white. He wished he had.

"I'll let River tell you," Fiona said, leaving the room with a flourish of her calendar.

River gave him a slight smile. "You didn't notice?"

"Notice what?" He was truly adrift. "As much as I'd love to see you wearing any wedding dress at all, I must have been asleep. We were on the road for so long after we left Montana, I must have conked out when Ash was driving."

"Yes," River said, "and I was wearing the magic wedding dress. Do you think it's a bad sign that you didn't notice? Isn't it supposed to be obvious to my one true love that I have it on?" she teased.

"All I was thinking of was you and the babies." He frowned.

She held out her hand, and he took it. When she pulled him closer to her, he knelt beside her.

"Tighe, I agree with your aunt Fiona."

He perked up. "About a Christmas wedding?"

"Not exactly." She kissed him on the lips. "I think a wedding as soon as you can find Running Bear. I'd like to do it while I can still stand."

Tighe felt shell-shocked. "Thank you."

"Thank you?"

He pressed her palm to his lips. "Thank you for marrying me. I'll be the best husband I can be." They'd been through a lot; she'd been through more than he ever thought a fiancée of his should have to endure. "I'll make everything up to you."

"There's nothing to make up." She frowned at him. "I wish you didn't feel that there was."

He didn't know what to say. "I'll see if I can hunt up Running Bear. In the meantime, I…" He looked at her. "Did you really have the magic wedding dress on yesterday, or is Fiona pulling my leg? Because I went looking for it one day, and I couldn't find the thing. I was beginning to think it had gone AWOL and wouldn't make an appearance to work its magic for me." He blew out a breath. "I don't feel very lucky these days."

"Did you feel lucky when you rode Firefreak?"

"I felt lucky—and then I felt broken. In pieces. But I've healed. And I'm not going down that road again. Firefreak will torture other cowboys, but not this one." Tighe knelt down beside her. "You marrying me? Now that's lucky."

"Oh, Tighe." She leaned forward to kiss him. "I would support you if you decided to ride Firefreak again. I really would. I shouldn't have plotted against you." She smiled. "I had a lot of time to think about that night while I was gone, and while I shouldn't have ganged up on you, I'm glad you spent the night with me. That was a lot of fun, being seduced by a wild-eyed daredevil cowboy."

He felt his chest puff out a little. "You think I'm a wild-eyed daredevil?"

"A sexy, wild-eyed daredevil."

"Well, then." This was looking up indeed. "I think being a dad will be adventurous enough for me. I've given up Firefreak for good."

"Adventurous *and* sexy," she said, and he decided River's smile was the best part of his day.

"So you'll tell me how I missed the magic wedding dress when I return?"

She nodded. "I will. I'll be glad to spin you the yarn, though you may not believe it. Even I'm not sure I believe it. But it happened."

"I'll believe anything around here these days," Tighe said, and departed with a grin.

"The thing is," Tighe told his grandfather, when he'd located him in the canyon, "I want to marry River because I'm crazy about her. I love her. And we're having children." He straightened, realizing she'd had several tests, one of which would have probably revealed the gender of the children, which she had not shared with him. He'd have to remedy that later. "We're having triplets, and so River needs to marry me so I can be a father and a husband. It's going to be awesome."

He sat on the ledge with his grandfather, gazing out at the painted canyons and listening to the soothing sound of an eagle's cry overhead. It was peaceful here, and he had no peace inside himself. Maybe that's why he loved the canyons so much.

"What worries me is Wolf. And all the craziness, the insanity. I get a pain in my chest when I think about him taking one of my children, or one of the other Callahan kids." Tighe wasn't sure how to express his worries better than he was, but his grandfather's eyes held no judgment, no condemnation, only the patient wisdom of seeing things as they should be seen, borne of long years of experiencing life. "I hated it when Wolf was holding River."

"She's strong," Running Bear said.

"Don't I know it. Stronger than me," Tighe freely admitted. "But that's just the thing. She shouldn't have to be."

"What should River be?" Running Bear looked at him, his gaze curious.

"River should be free to be a wife and a mother. She shouldn't have to live in fear. There may never be a day when she doesn't worry about the babies as they grow up—that's normal. But I don't want her to have the extra worry of knowing Wolf is out there, waiting for us to let our guard down. It's a lot to ask of a woman."

Running Bear nodded. "It is. But River was strong before she came to Rancho Diablo."

True, but what had been asked of her since she'd been here was more than an employee should have to bear. And most certainly more than a wife should have to worry about.

"You and your brothers and sister, and your cousins, all of you deserved the chance to grow up as children with no worries," the old chief said. "We protected you, we taught you the ways. Then we prepared you for the fight. What would you say to your own children?" Running Bear's dark eyes were patient. "Would you tell them to give up? Sell the land? Give it over to the cartel?"

Tighe hadn't thought of it that way. "Is there no other option, no place in between, where they can just be children, and my wife can just be a wife?"

"Were you just a child with no cares? Or did you embrace the fight once you understood what was at stake?" His grandfather looked out across the undulating canyons that had been carved from time. "Why did you go to Afghanistan?"

"Because I believed in the mission. I believed in a world where people could be free," Tighe said softly. "I believe everyone has a right to clean food, clean water and peace. I believe everyone on this planet has the right to raise their family, and love each other. And I fought for that."

"But the price was high."

"The price was high." Tighe nodded. "For me, it had to be paid."

"What would you tell your children? That they are above paying this price?"

"I don't want my children to be afraid. I want them to live without fear of danger."

"That is a fairy tale," Running Bear told him. "And you don't believe in fairy tales, or the supernatural life, or the ways that cannot be explained."

"I believe. Not in magic," Tighe said softly. "But I know it's important to put my faith and trust in that which I don't understand. But fairy tales for my children—is that wrong to want?"

"Even you do not believe in that," Running Bear

said, "so why do you want to give them a way of life you do not know?"

"Because they might get kidnapped," Tighe confessed. "I just lost my best friend for the past three months. She's come back with a big stomach, three of my children growing inside her, and she walked down a snowy, icy mountain to save herself. Frankly, I think that's too much to ask."

"Will you not ask it of her, then?" Running Bear asked.

"I have asked it of her. I'm just not sure it's the right question to ask."

The old chief turned to face him. "Your journey is not yet complete. It cannot be complete until you know the answers. The answers are only inside you."

They sat companionably for a while, giving Tighe a chance to chew on that bit of chief wisdom. He couldn't solve it all right now. He was too afraid for River and his unborn children. "So... I guess you heard about the parting gift Fiona left behind for Wolf?"

A slight shadow, which might have been a smile, passed over Running Bear's face. "Fiona's blood—and the blood of your parents—runs strong in your children. You must remember that. This is a family, an unbroken line, of warriors."

He rose and disappeared. Tighe stared after his grandfather for a moment, thinking about what he'd just been told.

Great. His children would follow in the family footsteps. It was a helluva combination: the past, the future and all the magic that lay between the two.

The thought of watching his children grow up, walking in the shadows of their forefathers and relatives, brought the biggest smile to Tighe's face. *Grandfather's right. I wouldn't want my children to live in a fairy tale. I want them to fight the good fight.*

It's going to be epic.

I'll hang on as hard as I can for that ride.

Chapter 19

The specialist in Santa Fe ran her tests on River, and concluded the same thing she'd been told before: the babies were healthy, and so far the pregnancy was progressing normally. River smiled at Tighe as they drove back to Rancho Diablo.

"I told you there was nothing to worry about."

He grunted. "Worry is my middle name these days."

"I told you I took good care of myself in Montana."

He winced. "I don't want to think about that anymore. Can we not mention Montana?"

"That's fine by me." River looked out the window. She didn't really want to talk about the time she'd spent away from Tighe, either. But it had happened, and sometimes she felt she had feelings she needed to express to someone.

She and Fiona sat and chatted about those months often. Tighe's aunt had said they had to keep a stiff upper lip about it, that the experience would ultimately make them stronger.

"Hey, if you smile, I might tell you the gender of the babies."

He pulled over at a roadside café and her stomach rumbled. Seemed as if she was hungry all the time now. River sighed with anticipation.

"Okay. I'm smiling," Tighe said.

"There's no smile on your face." She shook her head. "I'm waiting for the real thing."

"I smiled in Dr. Simone's office."

"When she told you we could still enjoy marital relations for at least another week."

He snapped his fingers. "That's right! I forgot!"

River laughed. "I'm pretty sure you didn't."

"Maybe not. You want some hot tea? Something to eat?" He checked his watch. "Pretty sure I need to keep you on a regular eating schedule."

She sighed. "Aren't you even curious about what the sexes of the babies are?"

"No. We're having boys." He picked up her hand, pressed a kiss to her fingertips. "Is that what you're just dying to tell me?"

"We're not having three boys."

"Three girls?" A smile spread across his face—finally. River kissed him. "Not exactly."

He held up his hands. "I don't want to know."

"You don't?"

"I'll know in two months—at the earliest. But I'm going to do everything I can to carry you around on a cushion and get you to relax so my children stay in that nice, soft tummy of yours as long as possible." He looked at River, his smile turning sexy. "Listen, if you're not hungry, if you can wait until we get to Rancho Diablo for some of Fiona's snacks, there's no reason to eat diner food."

"What's on your mind?" River asked suspiciously.

"It just occurred to me that if we only have another week to make love, there's no time to waste."

"Then I'll wait to eat at Fiona's."

"That's my girl. Let's see if I can break some sound barriers getting home. By the way," Tighe said casually, "Running Bear said that he'd be happy to bless our union today, if you want."

River blinked. "Today?"

"Sure. There's no reason to wait, is there? Especially if the babies arrive sooner than later. February is too soon, in my opinion, because you'll only be eight months along, but the babies may be eager to see the world. I want us to be married when they decide to check out of your beautiful body."

River swallowed. "All right."

"All right?" He glanced at her. "We don't have to get married today, if you don't want to."

"Of course I want to." She looked at Tighe, feeling a bit shy. "I was just hoping to have a wedding like the other Callahan women. You know, guests, cake, magic wedding dress. All that bridal stuff. I didn't think I wanted it before, but now I feel it would be nice."

"I don't think we should wait to plan a big wedding. That could take months, and to hear Dr. Simone tell it, you won't be moving around too much for a while."

"I know. All right. Tomorrow is our wedding day." She smiled at Tighe, and he kissed her hand and drove toward Rancho Diablo.

River looked out the window and wished she could wear the magic wedding dress just one more time. When she'd put it on to escape from Wolf, she hadn't seen her dream man, her one true love. There'd been no vision, no visitation of a princely variety.

Maybe the Callahan women played up the myth.

It would be just like them to work that story for all it was worth. Of course. That's what it was, nothing more than a fairy tale.

A marriage wasn't born of fairy tales.

Then again, maybe she should try the gown on just one more time. Fiona had taken it from her when she'd gotten home, saying that the black pants and top and boots needed to have some TLC to put the magic back to rights. River wasn't certain how one put a magical dress "back to rights," but nevertheless, Fiona had seemed confident.

And River wanted to be married in the dress.

I'll ask Fiona if I can borrow it one more time. I just have to know if the magic wedding dress will turn into black fatigues again—or if I was ever meant to wear a lovely gown.

Suddenly she realized why she hadn't seen Tighe when she'd put the gown on. Tighe was nervous. He was nervous about the babies, too—he didn't want to know the sex. Didn't want to let her out of his sight— because she might get kidnapped again. Didn't want to wait to get married, because she might go into labor sooner than later.

She eyed him as he drove. *Lover, you're going to have to get a grip.*

If I have to wear black fatigues in lieu of a wedding gown, you'll have to suck it up, too.

* * *

Running Bear came by the next day, his face reflecting its usual inscrutability. Tighe considered his grandfather. "This is your wedding face?"

"There are men in the canyons."

"Men?" Tighe glanced at the den to make sure River was far enough away that she couldn't hear Running Bear's warning. "Like, Wolf's men?"

"It seems so."

"I guess they have no place else to go, after Aunt Fiona's little party favor."

Running Bear nodded. "No doubt he is angry."

A lightbulb went on for Tighe. "You think Fiona may be in danger."

"I think we shouldn't overlook any possibility."

"All right." He took a deep breath. "Christmas is in three weeks. We'll send Fiona to Hell's Colony in Texas after Christmas."

"Tomorrow," Running Bear said.

Tighe had been reaching for a cup to offer his grandfather some tea, but now he hesitated. "You're really concerned."

"There is no need to trouble ourselves over this if we stay one step ahead."

"That is not going to go over well with the redoubtable aunt." He met the chief's gaze. "I'll tell her after you bless River's and my marriage today."

Running Bear nodded. "River must go, too."

Tighe blinked. "Oh, she's not going to like that."

"The risk is great."

He poured a cup of tea and put a couple of chocolate chip cookies on a plate, pushing it across the counter for his grandfather, who seated himself with an appreciative nod. "I see your point. It makes sense. But River believes she can take care of herself. She's always been strong, maybe stronger than most men. I don't think she'll go."

Running Bear nodded. "It will be hard to convince her."

Tighe went and looked out a kitchen window, staring at the snow and the icicles limning the roofs of the barns and bunkhouse. "I'll tell her after you bless us, Grandfather."

"I will take her and Fiona to Hell's Colony tomorrow. You stay here on post."

Tighe nodded. "Thank you." He wanted River and his babies to be safe. He didn't want her to leave, but at the same time, he couldn't bear the thought of her suffering another kidnapping or attack. He wanted her to relax and enjoy her pregnancy, which she hadn't been able to do yet.

He went to find River.

Two hours later, Tighe could barely believe his good fortune when River held his hand in front of their family and listened as Running Bear spoke the ceremonial words. Tears jumped into Tighe's eyes as he slipped a beautiful ring—three carats to represent their three babies—on his bride's finger.

"You're beautiful, wife."

She smiled. "You're a handsome groom, husband."

They fed each other blue cornmeal, and then it was over. Fiona rushed to hug River. "Congratulations! A new Callahan bride." She hugged her nephew. "I'm so happy for you!"

"Thank you, Aunt Fiona." He felt a tiny bit guilty. Neither River nor Fiona knew that tomorrow they'd be living in Hell's Colony in the Phillips' compound.

Still, he smiled, feeling over the moon that he was finally a husband.

He and River would spend a honeymoon night together, and then she would leave. He knew it was for the best, but that didn't make it any easier.

He went to kiss his bride. "I hope you're not too disappointed that you couldn't wear the magic wedding dress. But you're still beautiful."

She glanced down at the velvety, cream-colored chemise Ash had brought from the wedding shop. He thought River was gorgeous, but he knew she'd wanted to wear the fabled gown. It couldn't be helped; Fiona said the magic wedding dress was out of commission at the moment, whatever that meant. Maybe the thing had sputtered out of magic. He didn't care—he had his sexy bride in his arms.

"I'm slightly disappointed." She smiled up at him. "But I'm a very happy wife."

"That's the way I want my woman."

"You realize you sound terrible overbearing when you call me your woman."

He smiled down at her, touching her soft, whiskey-colored hair. "I am no-holds-barred overbearing."

"What if I called you my man?"

"I wouldn't think you were overbearing at all." He kissed her again, loving that he could do this as often as he wanted. "I'm the happiest man on the planet."

She put her head on his chest, then looked up at him again. "By the way, I heard you and Running Bear talking in the kitchen."

He perked up, recognizing trouble. "Oh?"

"Yes, I did. And I just think you should know that I have no intention of leaving this house. Or you. I'll be staying right here, with my man." She giggled, and Tighe shook his head.

I knew this was exactly how that conversation was going to go.

Truthfully, he was glad, even though he knew he should press River to leave.

He'd been without her too long to give her up now.

Tighe wasn't going to say fear hadn't become a part of his life, because it was now. He stewed every second he was away from River, and she gave him grief about it when he was with her. He wanted to set a guard on her.

She refused.

He suggested having Sawyer come back to watch her, saying that Isaiah and Carlos could be folded into the huge family gathered in Hell's Colony.

She pooh-poohed that and told Tighe not to dare.

There was no one left here except for Jace, Galen, Ash and himself. Everyone had taken their families to enjoy the Christmas holidays in Texas. Burke and Fiona had packed plenty of cookies and casseroles in the freezer for them and Fiona had left plenty of instructions for River to take care of herself.

There were plenty of hands around to help out, and some foremen to ride fence, but as for keeping an eye out for trouble, Tighe couldn't say he was entirely comfortable. It never really felt like the holidays to him. He was just glad to have his wife home, reclining in the occasional puddle of sunshine that shone through the window, illuminating her and the pretty Christmas tree Fiona had put up before she left.

But his grandfather's warning was never far from his mind.

Chapter 20

It seemed winter would never end. The holidays had been quiet events. Now it felt as if they were hibernating, stuck in a snow globe. Tighe felt restless, caged, and he knew River surely had to feel the same. She'd kept very still—doctor's orders—since early December. Actually, ever since their wedding night, which was the last time he'd been able to make love to her.

But he wasn't complaining. The sex wasn't the issue; that would come back into their lives. What was making him crazy was the ever-present feeling that they were being watched. River was so vulnerable now, though she seemed completely relaxed. She knitted things, she read books, she wrote letters. Her favorite activity was decorating the nursery in the foreman's cabin they'd decided to renovate. It hadn't been used in years, and River thought they could easily build onto it.

Of all the bunkhouses and other outbuildings that could be renovated, the foreman's cabin was closest to the house, so Tighe had agreed. It was built in a rugged style, and on days when the snow wasn't piled thick, workers banged away, creating extra bedrooms.

And River sneakily had brought in a decorator, who was helping her create a spacious nursery for the triplets. The two of them busily studied books and paint chips and fabric selections—and every once in a while a burst of laughter would erupt, making Tighe smile.

"You can't look," River told him once when he'd walked into the den to see what all the fun was about. "You don't want to know if we're having boys or girls, so go away."

He clapped his hands over his eyes in mock horror—but not before he'd seen lots of pink and blue. And white and teal.

Then it hit him: he was actually going to be a father to three little people. He sagged onto a sofa in the upstairs library and tried to take that in.

River was almost at her due date. They had a C-section scheduled just in case, for the end of the month. Dr. Simone really didn't see River being able to carry longer than that. She said the babies were growing fast, and that they were actually quite large for triplets. Tighe puffed up with pride at the time, thinking, *Of course they'll be big, they're Callahans.* Had the doctor expected runts?

All Callahan men were big.

But he'd seen pink just a moment ago, so there were going to be girls in the picture. He saw spots just thinking about three girls. Three River types. Three fearless, hell-raising rodeo sweethearts, with River, Fiona and Ash for role models.

He broke out into a cold sweat, knowing that he would stand little chance in a home where four women ruled the roost.

"They'll wrap me around their little fingers," he muttered to himself, just as Ash walked into the room.

"What, brother dear?" she asked. "Were you talking to yourself?"

"A little. It wasn't very productive, though."

"Your beautiful bride is snoring downstairs. It's attractive."

He grinned. "I know. I love it when she does that."

"It's so soft and peaceful, isn't it?" Ash gave him a teasing glance as she fixed them both a drink. "You know, I never thought I'd see you be so happy to hit the altar."

"Wild horses couldn't have stopped me from marrying River."

"And that turquoise squash blossom necklace you got her for Christmas is gorgeous. You're really coming along." She handed him his drink and sat next to him. "Now we just need to make some little tweaks, and you really will be Prince Charming."

He shook his head. "No tweaking. I'm already Prince Charming. Tweaking at this stage ruins the prince."

"Tweaking," Ash said. "I just want you to promise me that when the babies are born, you'll quit going around with that hangdog expression on your face, like the weight of the world is on your shoulders. You're scaring River. In fact, you're scaring all of us."

"I'll try. But I'm not making any promises. I'm pretty sure my face is just my face. It does its own thing." He brightened. "River hasn't mentioned that I'm scaring her. In fact, just this morning she said I was her handsome Studly-Do-Right."

"Oh, no," Ash groaned. "I'm pretty sure she's the best wife in the world. She's propping your ego up."

He deflated again. "You think?"

"Probably. Anyway, when the babies are born, I want you to remember to smile. You'll scare the poor things."

"Of course I'll smile at the babies!" He was indignant. "They're going to love me. And think I'm the best, most handsome dad ever."

"Good. Hold on to that positive mind-set," Ash told him, "because your bride asked me if you'd take her to see the doctor."

He blinked. "We don't have an appointment today."

"I know. She said she's having twinges. Then she dozed off."

It was as if electricity zipped through him. He jumped to his feet, slammed his glass on the end table. "Why didn't you say so?"

"Because you need to smile! You're going to scare River! She needs peace and calm around her, not the beast face that's been permanently puckering your puss."

He heard his sister's words, but he was shooting down the stairs so fast he nearly took a face-plant at the bottom. Dashing into the den, he rushed to River's side, waking her. "Are you all right? What's happening?"

"Everything is fine. I called the doctor and said I was having some twinges, and she said that we should make our way over. Do you think the roads are clear enough?" River looked out the window, obviously tense.

"The roads are fine. I'll get your bag. Jace! Galen!"

he bellowed, and his brothers came running. "Please help River to the jeep. Don't let her fall, or I'll hurt you." His chest was tight as he glanced around for his keys, his hat, River's bag.... Tighe looked at River. "Don't move. I'll carry you."

She shook her head. "Your sister will help me to the car, because you make me nervous and we'll both slip and go ass over applecart into the snow. Just calm down, and everything will be fine."

He hoped so.

The babies were born that evening and Tighe thought he'd never seen such an amazing sight. Two boys and a daddy's girl, for sure. Burkett, Liam and Chloe.

He grinned at his amazing wife. "Look at these children. They're Callahans, every last ounce of them."

He was proud as he could be. It came to Tighe that he had the same rush he'd gotten when he'd been on the back of Firefreak, that same sense of sliding-down-a-slide-and-can't-turn-back-now, but this was a good sensation. It was wonderful, a wild ride, something that would be his for the rest of his life. "Thank you," he told River, kissing her. "I know you need to rest now, but I can't thank you enough for agreeing to be my wife."

She smiled. "You're a lucky man, indeed."

"Exactly what I think." Tighe took her hand in his, kissed her fingertips and remembered to do exactly what his sister had recommended: he smiled.

He smiled big as the moon.

Chapter 21

The babies changed Tighe's life in ways he'd never imagined three little tiny bundles of joy could. He brought River and the babies home after a week in the hospital, and settled them into the new house and the cozy nursery, which before now he hadn't even peeked at. He'd had no idea what magic she was cooking up, and had been too focused on her to worry about baby cribs and drapery swatches.

"Every time I go into the nursery," he told River, who was trying to do a little walking from the bedroom to the nursery to help heal her body, "I'm amazed by how much you got done. That's quite a wonderland for babies." He grinned. "You realize that had I come to view your handiwork early, I would have known exactly what we were having." She had the babies' names painted on a plaque over each white crib.

River winked at him. "I knew you wouldn't look. You had too much on your mind."

That was certainly true. To him, the births had been a far-off dream, an amorphous event he knew was coming, but like everything else, couldn't exactly plan for.

"How did you do all that?"

"I had a lot of help." She eased onto the leather sofa she'd ordered for the den, and he sat next to her, determined to rub her legs. "For one, the Books'n'Bingo Society ladies turned me on to a great decorator. And they did all the shopping for baby gear and supplies. I can't thank your aunt's friends enough."

He grinned. "They're old hands at it."

"By the way, they've decided to put the ball off until June, the month of weddings." River situated the monitor next to her and allowed him to spread a soft blanket over her. He never let her out of his sight now. He had four people to protect, and he knew Wolf was out there somewhere; Running Bear had said so. "They're going to do a masquerade ball with some kind of scavenger hunt."

"Matters not to me. I've already been won." Tighe leaned over to kiss her, once again loving the fact that he could kiss her now whenever he wanted, for as long as he liked.

It was heaven, a great change in his life that agreed with him very much.

"Hey," he said, "I don't know if you know this, but June is the month for weddings."

River looked at him with a suspicious smile. "Didn't I just say that?"

"You know," he said, getting up next to her and wrapping his arms around her, "I think we should get married."

"We got married, Tighe. Remember?"

"Yeah. But I don't think you got married enough."

She laughed. "Enough?"

"I've waited an awfully long time to tie you down, darling. Maybe I need to double tie those knots. All the Callahan brides marry twice."

"Tighe." River sighed with pleasure as he kissed her neck, along her collarbone, and then pretended he was going to nose around in her sweater. "I feel pretty tied. Don't you?"

"Well, we have those three little ties in there," he said, pointing to the nursery. "But I think that one day they're going to want to see video of their mom taking their father off the market."

"Really?" She raised a brow. "Not the other way around?"

He stroked her hair and smelled it, and wished he could tell her how much he loved her without sounding as if he was crazy. Which he was—for her. "Maybe the other way around."

She kissed him. "They're going to love their daddy. All kids love their daddy, but they're going to know you're awesome."

"I am, aren't I? He brightened, thought about sneaking down in her shirt a little more, figured he'd better not push his luck and settled for holding her hand instead. "I want to be able to give my kids what I never had."

River looked up at him. "Being there for them?"

He nodded. "Lately I've realized how much of a sacrifice my parents made. When I hold those babies, or I watch you holding them, I think about how terrible and wrenching it would be if we had to leave them behind."

"You're scaring me, Tighe." River curled up against his chest, and he held her tight.

"I'm not scared. I've got my own personal body-guard. I'm feeling very safe these days." He wondered if he could make the same decision his parents had had to make. It was a high price they'd paid—all of them had paid. The alternative was to be hunted by the cartel, and worse. His parents—and the Callahan cousins' parents—wouldn't have wanted that to happen to their children. They'd chosen a life in hiding rather than risking their family.

He saw goose pimples had risen on River's skin and kissed them away, comforting her. "We've got Wolf on the run. He knows what kind of women we have here at Rancho Diablo now. You're tough, babe."

"I know. I knew what I was getting myself into when I seduced you."

"Ah, one of my favorite words." He kissed her lips, and then her forehead. "How long until the doctor says I can return the favor and seduce you?"

"Easy, cowboy," River teased, and Tighe held her close, stroking her hair as she lay on his chest. "It may be a few months."

"We'll see if you can hold out that long," he said, and she laughed, and then they napped together for a whole twenty minutes until they heard sweet baby noises on the monitor.

Tighe grinned. It was music to his ears.

The babies grew fast over the next several months, and it seemed to River that her husband tried to capture every minute and every action of his babies' young lives, taking constant videos and pictures. River thought her husband was pretty sexy, given how enamored he was with his children.

He barely ever left the babies—or her—alone. When he had his post assignments, he did his job and then hurried back home.

It had been like this for the past four months.

At first he'd said that she needed his help with the babies while she healed. He waved off all offers of assistance from the Books'n'Bingo Society ladies, and everyone else who wanted to help.

Fiona and the rest of the family had returned, and while he allowed them to help River while he was gone, he stuck close to home and insisted on being in the thick of things.

River tried to shoo him back to work, telling him that he'd had his eight weeks of maternity leave. Tighe's response was that in some countries around the world, he'd get a year.

"I'm never going to get rid of him, Fiona," she said, when his aunt came to visit and bring cookies. "I used to be a nanny bodyguard, but now I have my own personal bodyguard. He won't go anywhere unless I have four cell phones, three armed guards, two babysitters and a bat signal in a pear tree."

"It will wear off." Fiona gazed at the new babies with a smile. "He'll calm down. His twin did. Of course, Ana wasn't kidnapped for several months." The older woman looked up. "Then again, maybe he won't get over it anytime soon."

"It could get worse over time." The thought bloomed,

large and worrisome. "Can you imagine how he'll be when Chloe wants to date?"

"Well, she just won't," Fiona said, laughing. "At least not without her father in the backseat."

They giggled together. River smiled at Tighe's aunt. "Did I ever tell you how much I appreciated you keeping my spirits up in Montana?"

"The spirit is important. That's what Running Bear always says." Fiona sat down with a cup of tea and rocked in one of the new white rockers, complete with ruffled teal cushions. "Speaking of spirits, did you know Storm Cash offered to sell us the land across the canyons? He was dead set on getting that parcel, all twenty thousand acres, and now he's told me he'd like to sell. He's giving us first right of refusal. But he didn't have the land long enough to make a profit or clear his commission. I'm not sure what's up with that old goat."

River shook her head. "Tighe has never mentioned it, so I don't think he has any better idea."

Fiona sipped her tea. "I'm suspicious that Storm planted his niece over here, too. I'm not certain, but I believe Sawyer's got a target drawn on Jace."

"I'm not sure how I can help, Fiona. I don't know anything about all that."

"Here's the thing," she said, setting down her cup and reaching for Burkett when he started up a tiny squall. "I feel a cold chill coming from that side of the property."

"You mean from Storm?"

Fiona nodded. "Yes."

"Talk to Tighe. Maybe he can find something out."

"I was wondering if you'd talk to Sawyer."

River hesitated. "Me? And ask what?"

"Just see where her interests lie. What's on her mind. She just might let something slip."

"I can talk to her," River said. "But Kendall might know more, since she's Sawyer's employer."

Fiona made faces at Burkett to get him to smile, which he was too young to do. "You know that you and Tighe would be up for ownership of those twenty thousand acres, if Rancho Diablo takes them on. You'd have your own real house."

River blinked. "That would be up to Tighe, Fiona. I have a feeling he won't want to be farther from the main house than necessary." She could pretty well bank on Tighe not wanting her and the children to be across the canyons.

"Imagine having your own place, though. Your very own. Not part of a conglomerate, where everybody has a piece of everything. Stake your own claim, as it were."

"Fiona, are you asking me to spy on Sawyer in lieu of a favorable outcome to the ranch raffle you've been trying to set up for the Chacon Callahans all along?"

"Yes, I am," Fiona said. "Just something to consider."

River took that in. "I don't see how this helps Jace."

"It helps all of us to know whether the Cashs are friend or foe," Fiona said. "It's important to know who's on your side."

River closed her eyes, then opened them. "Fiona, I spent many months with you in Montana. We spent a lot of time talking to each other, and I believe I've gotten to know how you think. You want to keep Sawyer and Jace apart."

"Well," the older woman said slowly, "now that you mention it, yes. I don't want my nephew falling for a woman who is out to get to us through him."

"Isn't that Jace's business? Who he falls for?"

"Jace is a smart man, but he's not going to be able to withstand the amount of feminine firepower Sawyer's aiming at him. I saw her the other day taking a basket lunch out to him in the barn." Fiona looked outraged. "Every woman knows the fastest way to a man's heart is through his stomach, and my nephews are all very susceptible to that type of lure."

"I never cooked for Tighe."

"That's right. You caught my nephew fair and square, without lures." Fiona nodded. "Believe me, I recognize a trap being carefully set when I see it."

River laughed. "Fiona, you're a treat. Don't ask me to help you with keeping Jace and Sawyer apart. I can't do that, not even for a house of my own on a few acres of land, tempting though it is. Ask Ashlyn. She's always up for a plot."

Fiona sighed. "I think you should accept the challenge. You're a new Callahan, and a new mother. No one will suspect you."

"I'm so sorry, but no." River shook her head with a huge smile. "I don't even know if Tighe wants any of that land over there. But even if he did, he'd want to win the raffle fair and square."

"Honorable of him," Fiona grumbled. "What if Sawyer's up to no good? And she snags Jace?"

"Then you'll welcome her to the family, just as you have welcomed me." River patted her hand.

Fiona sniffed. "Yes, we have. I guess we could welcome Sawyer. Although perhaps not."

"Anyway, I've given up subterfuge. Didn't you know?" River smiled. "I gave up on plotting over Callahans when I tried to keep Tighe off his dream bull.

You see how that turned out for me. He still rode that animal, nearly got himself squashed, and now I'm married to him."

The two of them shared a laugh. "And in that regard, what's this I hear about another wedding?" Fiona asked.

River smiled. "Tighe wants to do it again. He thinks we need our marriage vows on video, and pictures of it for the children when they grow up."

"A fine idea, indeed," Fiona said. Her expression turned cagey. "I imagine you'll want to borrow the family fairy-tale frock?"

"I've already borrowed it once," River said with a fond smile. "Although it was all-weather gear and black, I certainly appreciated the chance to wear it."

"Clearly, it's meant to be," Fiona said, "or the gown wouldn't have transformed itself for you. If anything, I believe you should try it on sooner than later, my girl. There's no time to waste."

"No time to waste?" River blinked. "Certainly there's no rush. We're already married, so it's not like I need the fairy dust and the vision of my one true prince, right?"

Fiona sucked in a breath. "Oh, my dear, there can never be enough magic in one's life. You just remember I told you that. Magic is the stuff of dreams. It's the air we breathe, and the hope that keeps our hearts beating. Now," she said, her expression hopeful, "can I help you plan this wedding?"

River smiled. "I can't imagine anyone else I'd rather have helping me plan the perfect wedding." She hugged the woman she'd come to know so well over the long months in Montana. "Thank you, Fiona, for everything."

"Thank *you*," she replied crisply, "for wrangling my nephew to the altar, and for bringing these three adorable Callahans to our family."

Tighe strode in, a little sunburned from working outside, a bit rumpled in his nicely fitting blue jeans, straw Resistol and blue work shirt. He was the sexiest man River had ever seen, and when he mouthed *I love you* to her over Fiona's head as he hugged his aunt, River felt like the luckiest woman in the world.

She smiled at Fiona, then at her babies. From plot to stop Tighe from riding, to happily married wife, her life as a Callahan was magical indeed.

Epilogue

The day of their wedding—second wedding—River hadn't yet tried the magic wedding gown on again. Fiona had told her to but there was no need. Hadn't she already worn it?

It would be perfect.

Any bride would be anxious not trying on her wedding dress until the big day, but River trusted the gown.

Now was her moment. Outside, white tables basked in sunshine for guests, who'd arrived on this beautiful balmy day to celebrate another Callahan wedding. The cousins had arrived from Hell's Colony, and Rancho Diablo literally crawled, hopped, jumped and squealed with children.

River's babies were being passed around by delighted guests eager to get their hands on them. There were lovely cakes and enough food to feed all of Diablo.

It was a perfect day—if the dress worked out.

She had the pictures she'd taken on her cell phone in Montana to dream by. So now she was in the attic, ready to step into the magical Callahan world of enchantment.

She pulled the zipper on the bag down, and gasped when she saw twinkles inside. Soft music played somewhere, enticing her to lift the gown out. She did, gasping with joy when she realized the dress looked exactly as it did in the photos—and the way it looked in her most fervent dreams. Elegant, white, long, gorgeous, the gown beckoned her to step into it.

River did, easing the garment slowly up her body, breathing in the fairy tale. No black fatigues this— this dress was meant to be worn by her, casting her in softness and beauty. Even her dreams of this had never been so beautiful.

She went to the cheval mirror, her eyes widening at the splendor reflected there. It seemed that light and sparkles bounced off the fabric, scattering twinkles of magic across the floor.

Tighe walked into the attic, and she whirled to face him. "I'm so glad you're here!"

He smiled, her handsome, wild-man husband, who would forever be hers. "If I never told you that I love you," River said, "I do love you, Tighe. When you came to rescue me, I knew you were a prince among men, but I fell in love with you when you were tossed off that stupid bull. Actually, I've been in love with you for a very long time."

She drank him in with hungry eyes, her tall, handsome husband who looked fiercely sexy in his tux. But she thought he was sexy all the time—and never so much as when he was holding their babies.

"I just wanted you to know," River said. "I couldn't wait another moment to tell you." She went to kiss him, show him that he was the man of her dreams—but then he was gone.

River smiled. She'd had her vision of her dream man. She was finally a real Callahan bride—and she would be, forever.

Tighe loved it when River said *I do* at the altar. It was a moment that would forever be burned into his memory. He'd waited so long to win her—and when she said her vows in front of all their friends and family and their three tiny babies, he laughed out loud from joy.

He'd hired two videographers to capture that moment from every angle. He didn't want to miss a single word of her becoming his.

"I have a gift for you," River told him as they walked toward the canyons so they could be alone for a moment.

"I know you do," Tighe said, "and believe me, I can't wait to collect on our honeymoon."

She laughed and shook her head. "No, I really have a gift for you. I hope you like it."

He let her lead him to the getaway truck they'd parked near the bunkhouse, hoping his brothers and sister wouldn't find it. They had, decorating it with streamers and Just Married signs. "They found our getaway vehicle, after all."

"We didn't really think we'd get away with a clean ride for our honeymoon."

"No." He studied his beautiful bride. "So that's the magic wedding dress."

"Yes, it is." River smiled at him, her gaze full of sexy secrets.

"So…is it true?"

"Is what true?" River asked, and he knew she was tormenting him.

"Is the legend true? Did you see your one true love?"

She laughed. "Not telling."

"It doesn't matter," he said, drawing her into his arms for a sweet kiss. "I always knew I was your one true love, even if it took you a really long time to figure it out."

"Oh, I knew," River said. "I just wanted you to finish your journey thing."

"I have. I found what I was looking for." He kissed her, wanting to hold her forever. "I love you so much. Have I told you?"

"Yes," River said, laughing. She pulled away from him. "Let me give you your gift."

"You're supposed to stay in my arms and give me a gift," he groused, but he let her go. She reached into the back of the truck and pulled a large, brown-paper-wrapped frame from the truck bed. "What's this?"

"The gift. Open it and see."

He unwrapped the paper, and grinned.

It was a very large black-and-white photo of him on Firefreak, at the very moment the bull had burst from the chute. Tighe's hat was on, his arm was up, and Firefreak was in full kick.

"The beginning of my journey." Tighe smiled. "I can't believe you took this. Thank you for capturing my moment of glory."

"Believe me, I had to act fast. I only had three seconds," River said with a smile, "but it was quick enough to catch you."

"Don't I know it," Tighe said. "Don't I know it. And I do love being caught."

He put the picture back in the truck and pulled his wife close. In the distance he saw a shimmering of color, a scattering of stardust or something that looked suspiciously like fairy dust on the wind. He heard the black Diablos thundering in the canyons, and then he saw Running Bear and his parents, smiling at him in congratulations.

They waved and disappeared, but the sound of hooves thundered on as he held River, etching the memory of what he'd seen into his soul. It was magic, and he believed again, every word and every way that he'd always known in his heart.

"Let's go back and find our children, gorgeous," he said, and they walked back home, eager to hold the next generation of Callahans close.

It was just the way he'd always known magic should be.

Enchanting.

* * * * *